Death Roll

Death Roll

Marilyn Victor

Michael Allan Mallory

FIVE STAR

An imprint of Thomson Gale, a part of The Thomson Corporation

Detroit • New York • San Francisco • New Haven, Conn. • Waterville, Maine • London

Set in 11 pt. Plantin.

LIBRARY OF CONGRESS CATALOGING-IN-PUBLICATION DATA

Victor, Marilyn.
Death roll / Marilyn Victor and Michael Allan Mallory. — 1st ed.
p. cm.
ISBN-13: 978-1-59414-544-5 (alk. paper)
ISBN-10: 1-59414-544-X (alk. paper)
1. Zoos—Employees—Crimes against—Fiction. 2. Zoo keepers—Fiction. I. Mallory, Michael Allan. II. Title.
PS3622.I286D43 2007
813'.6—dc22 2006038261

Published in 2007 in conjunction with Tekno Books and Ed Gorman.

Printed in the United States of America on permanent paper
10 9 8 7 6 5 4 3 2

It took as long to write this book as it does to make an elephant. Thanks to our Monday Night Writer's Group and the Twin Cities Racket Squad for making it almost painless, for all of their input and prodding and not letting us give up. And a special thank you to Susan Sizemore for her unbridled enthusiasm for Snake Jones and for generously sharing Ethan. And, of course, Ethan Ellenberg—thank you!!

CHAPTER 1

Call me Snake.

Everyone does.

I picked the nickname up in grade school because of Arnie, a pet garter snake I emancipated from my grandma's basement. The name stuck. So did my love for creepy crawly things. Much to Mother's horror.

My real name is Lavender. Lavender Clark Jones. I don't know what Mom was thinking, giving me a name like that. Maybe she had visions of me decked out in billows of lace and crinoline, floating down the aisle on the arm of Lance Millionaire, Industrial Tycoon. Sorry, Mom.

My husband, Jeff Jones, is a Top Ender, growing up in the Northern Territory of Australia. His idea of formal wear is to tuck in his shirttails. He's a dear, though. And a tad bit crazy. What else do you call a guy who willingly jumps into the mangroves to rescue a giant saltwater crocodile who doesn't want to be saved? And what do you call a woman who thinks that's an acceptable way to spend a honeymoon? Guess that makes me a little nuts, too.

Don't get me wrong. I'm told I clean up pretty well. Still, I'm a lot more comfortable waiting out a downpour in the Venezuelan rainforest while tracking jaguars than I was dressed in the floor-length sequined gown I was forced to wear for the evening's Beastly Ball, the black-tie fundraiser at the Minnesota Valley Zoo. Both scenarios are part of my job description as zookeeper and co-host of *Zoofari,* the zoo's very own cable program. The trouble is, when I'm introduced as Lavender Jones, some people think I'm an exotic dancer. No, the name is Snake, just Snake.

"Snake!"

Gary Olson popped his mop of dirty dreadlocks through the doorway of the cramped office I shared with an assortment of frogs, geckos, an arthritic fruit bat named Buster and the other zookeepers who worked on the Tropics Trail.

I looked up from the computer where I was logging in Buster's feeding schedule. Gary's face was flushed, eyes snapping with excitement behind rimless glasses. His style screamed hippie, an era of rebellion that seemed out of fashion these days. But what did I know? My last act of adolescent mutiny was lying about my age and having my ears pierced.

A sophomore at the University of Minnesota, Gary was earning college credits as *Zoofari*'s first intern. Though he was an earnest young man, I wasn't convinced he had been the best choice of the candidates that had applied, but his eagerness to play gofer for the summer had made him an instant hit with our crew.

"Didn't you hear?" He held up his *Zoofari* crew radio in lieu of an explanation, his oversized watchband slipping on his wrist.

I nodded down at the tight lines of my black sequined dress. "Not a lot of room to carry a radio in this get-up."

"Jeff—" Gary gulped in a breath, trying to contain his excitement. "Jeff fell in the water with the crocodiles."

Shit.

I sprang up from my chair, elbowed past Gary and made a mad dash through the exit and into the service tunnel that comprised the inner circle of the Tropics building, part of an elaborate system of access corridors that threaded its way behind the zoo exhibits.

As I picked up speed, the sequined prom dress and hooker heels proved problematic. I managed a fancy toe dance and shuffle past the tapirs' holding area, nearly colliding with a trashcan before pausing long enough to kick off the shoes and hike up the skirt. Then I went into high gear.

"Wait up!" Gary labored after me, his five-foot-ten, two-hundred-pound frame not designed for quick sprints. "He's the Crocodile Wrangler. He knows what he's doing."

I stifled the urge to stop and cuff him across the ears. Jeff Jones had been wrangling crocodiles since he was twelve, but that didn't make him impervious to sixty stabbing teeth and a jaw that could snap shut with a pressure of two thousand pounds per square inch. Yesterday *Zoofari* lost a camera to Sebastian, our fifteen-foot male. The camera, mounted on a crane for an overhead shot, had come in too close and the croc exploded out of the water and demolished it in one chomp.

I darted forward, taking a shortcut through the building's kitchen. At the stainless-steel counter, a keeper chopping a pail of frozen fish looked up and whistled admiringly as I padded by. Seeing me running through the kitchen wasn't an unusual sight, but me decked out in a formal gown was.

The kitchen was the nucleus of the service tunnel encircling it, like the hub of a wheel. Crossing through and exiting the opposite door left me at the end of the Tropics Trail. I bolted to the left, toward the main plaza that connected the building with the recently added Australian building and its manufactured billabong that was home to two of the most cantankerous saltwater crocodiles on this planet. I needed to get there before the little beasties ended up adding something besides chicken to their diet.

News reporters had already arrived to cover tonight's events at the Beastly Ball and I found a media crew from WCCO heading in the same direction I was. Bad news travels fast.

"Mrs. Jones!" An eager young reporter thrust a microphone in my direction. "Do you think your husband is—"

I didn't slow down.

I barreled into the main plaza, a labyrinth of round tables decked out in white linen tablecloths and china place settings for this evening's dinner. Beyond the plaza rose a barrier of artificial eucalyptus trees that simulated the declining forests of Australia. A bird's cry—almost a scream—rose from the free-flight aviary on the other side.

Ignoring the black-and-yellow-striped sawhorse barricade and "keep out" signs, I took a sharp left beneath the stone arch with its aboriginal designs that marked the beginning of the Walkabout Trail. The news crew was right behind me. My lungs sucked in the humid air as the sights and smells of lush tropical vegetation rushed past me. The animal exhibits flew by. Tiger cats. Tree kangaroos. Tasmanian devils.

The path curved and followed the re-creation of an Australian stream flowing into the crocodile's estuary. Yellow-crested cockatoos angled their plumed heads at me as I ran through the free-flight aviary and the mocking laugh of a kookaburra nipped at my heels. Artifice and nature collaborated to produce a realistic slice of the southern hemisphere, all of which resided under a looming roof of metal and glass that protected its inhabitants in an enclosed, climate-controlled environment.

The path softened beneath my feet, mimicking the feel of swampy terrain. A yellow and black sign warned me I was approaching Crocodile Island, home to the largest reptile in the world, *Crocodylus porosus,* the saltwater crocodile. The path led into a tunnel, which descended into an underwater viewing area that treated me to a fish-eyed view of Jeff's muscular bare legs dog paddling just beneath the surface of the billabong.

Alive!

At least for the moment. The water turned murky as his

thrashing legs churned up the sediment at the bottom. Good camouflage for a marauding croc.

I flew along the last few feet of tunnel as it climbed and turned, stepping out onto the six-foot-wide bridge that crossed over the edge of the pool. Jeff clutched the ledge where a section of the clear thermoplastic barrier, which served as the wall of the bridge, had been removed, his other hand struggling beneath the water. Inside the exhibit at the water's edge, our croc man, JR Erling, stood vigilant, smacking the water with a long bamboo pole, raising a ruckus in order to distract the agitated saltie who snarled and hissed at yet another intruder into his territory.

Two *Zoofari* cameras followed Jeff's actions from separate viewpoints, one at the bridge's entrance, the other on the trail just behind and above the patch of white sand beach where our other crocodile, Babe, glared at JR, displaying a full rack of pointed teeth and emitting a low guttural hiss to warn him away.

At the head of the exhibit, early comers to the evening's fundraiser had gathered, flashing pictures with disposable cameras that were gifts for the Beastly Ball's guests. I could imagine them showing their grandchildren the photos. "And here's the one where that old croc Sebastian ripped the arm right off Jeff Jones!" A stab of annoyance flashed through me. I'm sure it never occurred to these people to drop their damned cameras and help the man out of the water.

The old croc had clearly had enough. Having killed JR's bamboo pole several times, he dived under the water and torpedoed straight toward my husband.

"Three o'clock!" I rushed up to the gaping space in the bridge's fencing, my heart pounding at the looming shadow beneath the water's surface.

Without turning, Jeff grabbed my offered hand as I bent low.

Partly out of the water on the bridge support struts, he swung himself onto the deck planking just as Sebastian surged out of the water and his powerful jaws snapped shut at Jeff's feet. A dangling piece of bootlace caught briefly in the croc's teeth before it sliced neatly off at the eyelet.

Jeff was speechless. We all were. He stood next to me, waterlogged shirt and shorts pasted to his muscular form, rivulets of water dripping from his sandy-colored hair and into the craggy lines of his weathered face. Quickly checking that his foot was still attached, triumph visibly radiated throughout his whole body.

"Whoo-hoo!" He punched the air above his head, eyes glued to the retreating carnivore with admiration.

"Crikey! That was a shocker. He almost got me foot." His clear blue eyes were as wide as clamshells. "You're one gutsy sheila, sweetheart!"

My arms flew around his neck as he gave me a water-soaked bear hug and an exultant kiss. I should have reamed him up one side and down the other for taking such a risk, but instead all I could do was hold on, grateful he was alive and in one piece. Jeff's enthusiasm for life and the world around him was what had attracted me to him in the first place. It was like hugging an ocean wave, but I held on. I kissed him long and hard while cameras flashed around us. Everyone, it seemed, had a camera trained on us, from *Zoofari*'s two camera operators to the local television network that had followed my sprint down the trail.

"That was too close," JR called from the enclosure, visibly shaken. He exited through a gate in the eight-foot-tall chain-link fence, scant yards off the bridge path. He still clutched the thick bamboo pole, one end chewed to splinters.

"Did you see Snake?" Jeff beamed. "Leaned over to yank me out without a second thought, right in the line of fire, too!"

"Yeah," agreed the other with bemusement, "and decked out to the nines as well."

A ripple of laughter followed. My knock-off designer gown was in shambles, wet, wrinkled, and missing sequins. I let out a sigh of disappointment as I saw the damage. I'd put a lot of work into gussying up for the ball.

JR smiled at me. As tall as Jeff, with a slender, agile build and just a touch of gray in his dark hair, you'd never guess he was looking at the big five-oh next birthday. "Good thing you got here when you did," he said. "Otherwise, I would have had to jump in and save him."

It was easy to make light of the narrow escape because nothing serious had happened. Despite my race across the zoo, I knew Jeff could have gotten himself out of this scrape if he'd had to. Yet accidents happen, and I couldn't help but worry about my husband. Still, I felt some satisfaction as a helpmate, snatching my man literally from the jaws of death.

"Wow! You guys okay?" Gary Olson wheezed, one hand on his chest as he lumbered up to join us. Incredulous eyes shone behind his glasses. "Man, that was something! You came awfully close to being that croc's dinner." Gary edged back from the exposed opening in the bridge's safety barrier, eyeing the water below. "Those things can't jump, can they?"

Submerged yet watchful, Sebastian and his mate, Babe, were at the far end of the pool.

Jeff reassured him. "Not as high as this, not enough to smash through the fence and onto the bridge. Now I did capture a croc once that almost jumped straight out of the water into me boat! Nasty ripper he was too."

Gary turned a shade paler. "Probably good I wasn't here, then. I've never been that good with large animals." He gave a hapless gesture, swinging my black leather pumps, which he had been nice enough to snag while in hot pursuit of me, by the straps.

JR, who had knelt down to examine the half-hidden plumbing fixture beneath the footbridge, looked over and laughed. "With those shoes, I don't wonder."

Embarrassed, Gary handed the shoes to me as though they were contraband. Without anything in his hands, he looped a finger under the metal band of his watch and twisted it around until I thought it would snap.

Gary liked to think of himself as a naturalist, but he was at best a couch adventurer. He idolized Jeff and loved working with the *Zoofari* crew, but I could never imagine him steering a small boat up a backwater river in the middle of the night to capture crocodiles and relocate them. That's what Jeff had been doing at Gary's age. Decidedly unathletic, built on the order of a Teddy bear with gangly arms, the young intern was much more suited to the journalistic path he had set for himself.

Having finished his inspection of Jeff's work, JR joined us in the middle of the bridge. A thoughtful man of few words, he didn't often say much unless he had reason to, giving you the sense he was more at home with animals than people. The three of us had become great friends since meeting on a *Zoofari* location shoot in Cabo San Lucas, Mexico, last fall. A first-class reptile man in his own right, John Ray Erling was just the man Jeff was looking for. As curator of the Australia Walkabout Trail, Jeff had asked him to sign on as our crocodile keeper. He knew the passion JR had for his animals and, more importantly, Jeff knew he could trust this man with his life. That was critical when handling creatures the size and ferocity of Sebastian.

Zookeeping could be a dangerous business. Wild animals had a nasty trick of doing the unexpected, no matter how well versed in their habits you thought you were. Even Gary knew this. His mother had confided to me how his stepfather, a zookeeper, had been killed some years back by a usually docile panther in his care. The lesson was clear: — as a keeper, you never took the behavior of your animals for granted.

"The valve cover looks good, Jeff," JR said. "We shouldn't have any more trouble with it."

"Only had one chance to get it right."

Gary Olson stirred. "What happened? Did something else go wrong?"

"Just the plumbing, mate." Jeff exchanged a meaningful look with JR. "The water in this tank is supposed to filter every sixty minutes. One of the crocs has been chewing on an exposed PVC pipe, took a nasty bite out of the elbow joint."

"The pipes were exposed?" That surprised me. Leaving exposed pipes in a carnivore's exhibit was only asking for trouble. "How—"

"Far as I can tell, the faux rock shielding wasn't secured properly and broke off. We thought it would be a good idea to install a wire cage over the exposed pipe valve, as a little prevention." Jeff nodded toward the panel that had been removed from the bridge wall, which had allowed access to the plumbing. "At least until we can move the crocs out again and repair it properly. I thought I could fix the problem from the path, but I reached in a bit too far."

"You fell in?" I feigned surprise, giving him a wide-eyed stare. "I thought you'd had a heart attack or something."

For the first time Jeff looked embarrassed. Even so, he was still unable to wipe the broad smile off his face. Jeff prided himself on his agility. I'd seen him scarper up steep cliff faces freehanded and climb trees like the goanna lizards he loved to chase up them. I was never going to let him live this one down.

"Yeah, I fell in," Jeff admitted, then moved on to business. "But I got a crackerjack view and was able to get the cover attached."

I shook my head. "Leave it to you to turn a negative into a positive."

Voices from the top of the exhibit drew my attention. Across the billabong, some fifty feet away, a small audience of onlookers had assembled at the stone wall that served as the outer barrier at the top of the exhibit. In animated conversation, they marveled at Jeff's moment of peril. Now that he was safe and in one piece, they could openly enjoy that instant of horror.

I knew two of the amateur photographers. One was Butler Thomas, the zoo's assistant director. Leaning an elbow on the waist-high retaining wall, he looked like an ad for Calvin Klein aftershave. Mister Public Relations, Butler was the zoo's second-in-command and its most ardent supporter.

With him was Senator Ted McNealey, a man I disliked by reputation only, being too far down on the food chain to have met him personally. At least two decades older than Butler Thomas, he was a state senator and a key member of the budget committee. His favor could easily make or break the zoo, as a huge chunk of the operating budget was approved by the legislature. This explained why Butler was acting as his personal escort, no doubt giving McNealey a private sneak preview of the exhibits before the official opening that evening.

In their tuxedos, they looked like twin poster boys for high living and partying—

The Beastly Ball!

I'd forgotten that nearly two hundred people were even now arriving at the zoo for a posh dinner and tour of the new Australian Walkabout Exhibit.

I reached over and grabbed Gary's wrist. His scuffed up Timex said we still had thirty minutes before the official ceremonies were to start. Enough time for me to clean up a bit and slip Jeff of the Jungle into the tuxedo I had secreted in his office behind the croc exhibit.

My hopes for some badly needed quiet time were dashed when a voice thundered behind Butler Thomas and the senator at the head of the exhibit. The two parted like the Red Sea as a stern, white-haired man, also decked out in evening clothes, brushed past them and thundered down the footbridge, the soles of his patent leathers reverberating against the deck planking.

It was Anthony Wright, the director of the zoo. And he was in a foul mood.

"What the hell is going on here? Somebody said a man was being eaten alive!"

Chapter 2

With wide shoulders and a broad chest, Anthony Wright looked like a man who would be more comfortable on an wildcat oil rig—smudged in crude oil and barking orders to laborers on the platform below—than wearing a tux and pandering to the masses for funding.

"What is it now? Another delay? That's all I've heard since this project started." Wright's deep voice rattled in my chest like the bass of a blaring boom box.

He wheeled round, surveying the enclosure, his gaze raking over a sodden Jeff without sympathy, obviously laying all responsibility for any delays at my husband's feet.

Crocodile Island was the feature exhibit of the new Australia Walkabout Trail and should have been completed a month ago. At the start, there had been a push to complete the trail by this year's Beastly Ball. It was a huge project to complete in two years and Wright accepted no excuses for delays. He had advertised the grand opening heavily, was counting on great media coverage and lots of public interest. He had been especially protective of the trail's construction, never failing to remind us it was being paid for in large part by the considerable wealth of his in-laws.

"Look at this mess. Tools and plumbing parts scattered all over. And what's this?" He stabbed a finger toward the mangled thermoplastic panel lying on the grass below.

"We had to remove the panel to get at the plumbing," Jeff

said. "It fell in the water and Sebastian attacked it. Bent the frame."

Wright's hair, stark white and flowing, wavered as he whirled round. The color rose to his cheeks. "And why the hell were you messing with the plumbing, Jones?"

Gary Olson shifted uneasily and withdrew behind JR, who didn't appear comfortable in the eye of the storm himself. Earlier, Gary had been excited about the prospect of interviewing Jeff and Wright for his wildlife website, a chance to get real zoo people to talk about their concerns and issues. In order to do that, however, the young student needed the fortitude to face two distinctly strong personalities.

I was grateful when JR took him by the elbow and tactfully steered him quietly off the footbridge and out of sight. I didn't need Gary writing up this incident on his website for the whole world to see.

Unintimidated, Jeff met Wright's glare and explained the problem. With the rest of the trail's zookeepers busy with preparations for the Beastly Ball, there were no extra bodies to help move the reptiles to their holding area so he could repair the pipes the usual way. So JR and Jeff worked while keeping a close watch on two sets of murderous reptilian eyes.

Anthony Wright folded his arms across his burly chest, and I imagined the fabric of his tuxedo jacket straining tightly at his back. A man who could find fault with even the most beautiful sunset, Wright surveyed the area with a critical eye. "Better planning would have prevented this incident in the first place."

It was to Jeff's credit that he didn't make excuses or point out to Wright that he was only a consultant on the design of the project. The architects had conceptualized his ideas. The schedules, supplies and materials were the responsibility of the general contractor that had been awarded the project. As curator for the Australia Walkabout, it was Jeff's job to oversee the management of the trail's animal collection and its staff. He didn't have time to add babysitting construction workers to his job description.

Wright indicated the gap in the bridge's barrier with displeasure. "This is a safety hazard. How're we going to lead our guests down the path and across this bridge now? The place is a shambles. Look over there. The landscaping's not done, there are still plantings not in the ground. And now there's a plumbing issue? Not acceptable, Jones. I want it fixed—now."

"Be reasonable, Anthony. We don't have the manpower. We've more pressing things to look after in other exhibits."

There was the Tasmanian devil, who wouldn't come out of the hollow log in his exhibit, the cassowary that had attacked one of our keepers and left her with a broken arm, and the sugar gliders that hadn't yet left the Montreal Zoo due to a barrel of red tape.

"I don't care," said Wright. "We've got nearly two hundred people coming down this bridge in less than two hours. Get this place in shape."

"Working conditions are a bit dodgy down there at the moment. It's a bit of a challenge fixing the exhibit when the exhibit wants to kill you," Jeff said with good humor. "And Sebastian hates me."

Old Sebastian submerged into minimal exposure mode, only his eyes breaking the surface. He was angled toward the bridge, Jeff still in his sights. He could sit that way for hours, just waiting for Jeff to make another mistake and enter his domain.

"He doesn't understand I rescued him from hunters," Jeff went on. "That was ten years ago. Every time he sees me, he wants to kill me. That's his territory down there, mate. His job is to protect it and his girl. Anything or anybody that touches that water he'll attack." Jeff clapped his hands together in simulation of the crocodile's jaws. "He's strong enough to pull a water buffalo right off its feet. He'd rip me arm off given half a chance."

A look of discomfort spread across the zoo director's face. It was rare to see Anthony Wright at a loss for words. Smiling broadly, Jeff placed a hand on the other's shoulder. "We can always use another spotter down there with us. That'll get the job done sooner." He winked.

It was an invitation too easy to refuse. Wright stepped away, removing Jeff's hand with a shake of his broad shoulders.

"This hole in the barrier can be repaired, can't it? Can you put that panel back in place?"

" 'Fraid not, boss. Sebastian did a job on it. We'll have to order another."

Wright swore to himself. "Dammit, we can't leave it like this. Put up some temporary barricades for tonight. We can't have people falling in the water."

"Not to worry; we'll put a couple of planks across the opening. That should be fit for a day or two. We'll assign a volunteer to keep people away from the gap."

By now, Senator McNealey and Butler Thomas had joined us on the bridge. McNealey was taken by Jeff's offer. "You sure you can't lend a hand, Tony? That old croc might not be so quick to take a bite out of you. You're too ornery." A huge smirk spread across his pasty, well-lined face.

Nobody called Anthony Wright Tony, not even his wife. It was difficult to tell if this was a harmless jibe or if the senator had meant to hit a sore spot. The politician and the zoo director had worked closely together over the past two years, Wright trying to impress upon McNealey the importance of getting the zoo's budget approved by the state legislature. The senator should have known better than to call him Tony.

I waited for the bomb to explode.

When it didn't I was surprised.

Wright regarded McNealey circumspectly, his face reddening slightly, as if he wanted dearly to say something but struggled to keep a lid on it. Perhaps this was too public a venue, too many people around, including a couple of television crews still filming, eager for anything to spice up the evening news.

For whatever reason, the flinty exterior cracked. Wright's shoulders sagged slightly beneath the tuxedo jacket as he capitulated, turning to Jeff. "You're right. Do what you think best. The rest doesn't matter. Just make sure the bridge is safe." He surveyed the exhibit one more time, clearly disappointed it hadn't met his expectations. "Be sure you get to the dinner on time, too. You're the big media draw."

He swung round and left, briskly walking up the trail and out of sight, pausing briefly next to the red kangaroo exhibit to check his watch before vanishing around a dense clump of mallee and a display of the strangely shaped red and green flowers of the kangaroo paw.

Once the zoo dircctor was out of earshot, Butler surveyed the exhibit approvingly and spoke. "We're fine, guys. Don't let him get to you. Wright's so focused on the big picture he can't appreciate the view. If the old man gets his back up again, I'll talk to him."

Butler often served as a buffer between our demanding boss and the zoo staff. A lot of us felt he had been cheated when the board of directors overlooked him as the next director in favor of Anthony Wright. No one was better at soothing injured nerves than Butler, whose easy manner was reflected in ruggedly well-drawn features and a breezy smile, the sort you expected to find in a glossy magazine ad holding a whiskey glass. Style and class. The man was born to wear a tux. All of which made me acutely aware of the damp and rumpled mess that was my gown.

Curiously, McNealey continued to gaze in the direction Wright had gone, as if something were on his mind. Maybe it was just me, but McNealey often seemed too much like the eager-beaver used-car salesman who has the perfect deal for you. Something was always cooking just below the surface with him. He had that look now, gazing in the aftermath of Anthony Wright, brow furrowed, his mouth set in a thin line—the look that something needed to be done.

Finally, the senator roused himself and without explanation said a quick farewell then took off after the zoo director, waving aside a TV crew that wanted a statement.

Butler shoved a hand into his trouser pocket and jangled a set of keys. "I should get back, too, make sure the senator doesn't get lost," he said in his smooth baritone, before moving off in pursuit of Ted McNealey.

I had to wonder if Wright had given him orders to keep the senator out of his way. Which would mean Wright was confident of getting the funds he had asked for. On his way past the local news team, Butler stopped for a moment. Whatever he said to them, it did the trick. The press followed him down the trail like rats after the pied piper. Even our two *Zoofari* camera operators fell in step.

Alone, at last. I turned to Jeff, who was still dripping and standing in a puddle of water. "So what about the plumbing? Is there anything I can do to help?"

He burst into a grin. "No worries, luv. It's all fixed. We'll clean up the litter, set up some barriers and still have enough time to get ready for the big event."

The reception had been set up in the zoo's Biodiversity Center, a mammoth, greenhouse-like room that housed a family of ring-tailed lemurs and a troop of Japanese macaques. From here, you could connect to our Northern Trail, African Trail, Tropics Trail, Minnesota Trail and the reason we were all here, the new Australia Walkabout Trail.

Tables were set up throughout the large area, filled with a Hollywood mogul's ransom of donated items for tonight's silent auction. *Zoofari* had been generous in offering some lucky bidder a chance to join us on a trip to the Pacific Northwest to visit the Seattle Zoo and do some sea kayaking among a pod of orcas. Personally, I was hoping to be high bidder on a romantic getaway to the North Shore. A second honeymoon. One that didn't involve crocodiles.

Senior bird keeper Mitch Flanagan adroitly moved through the black-tie gathering, displaying a glorious bald eagle clinging to his gloved hand. A stoop-shouldered man of middle years with a graying handlebar moustache, his face was ordinarily that of a stoic Norwegian plainsman. Yet with his arm held away from his body, the eagle's talons perched on the leather gauntlet, Mitch attained a certain austere dignity as he strode through the gathering, like that of a medieval nobleman.

"Mitch. How do." His feathered companion flapped at my approach. "What a fabulous bird."

"Snake, meet Icarus. He's still in training, but seems to enjoy the attention."

The Raptor Center at the University of Minnesota had loaned us the bald eagles we keep on display. Because of injuries, these animals can no longer be returned to the wild, so they become ambassadors for their species and part of the zoo's bird show. Rehabilitating and training birds was Mitch's passion.

"You've done a great job with him. Bet you can't wait to break ground on the new raptor center so hc has more room to spread those wings."

In response, I got a grunt and glare.

Knowing Mitch's penchant for complaining, I wasn't sure I should ask, but I did. "What's up?"

"Ain't gonna happen, kiddo. Budget got slashed again. Damned penny pinchers." The color rose in Mitch's cheeks.

"Wright's so damned shortsighted. The only time the public sees these birds is in the bird show. We need an exhibit to display these guys." He stopped to soothe the feathers on the eagle's head. "After all that planning—all those meetings—the project gets put on hold. God, he pisses me off. Don't get me started, Snake."

All righty then. Guess I hit a hot button. I should have known better.

"Sorry to hear that," I said. And I was, but budget cuts were nothing new to zoo personnel. I hoped he wasn't going to spoil the evening with an outburst like that to a guest. "You know, Mitch," I tried, suggesting a strategy, "there are a lot of influential people here tonight. I know you're upset about your raptor center, but try to be on your best. Show them what you did for Icarus. Be positive. These are the folks who raise money for the zoo."

Mitch Flanagan gave me a cool look. I couldn't tell if he thought I was some kind of moron or if I had given him a good idea. He grumbled back something and went back to work.

So did I. Time to get back to mingling with the patrons.

Despite my initial dismay, I had managed to clean up fairly well. My gown, while no longer as crisp as before the crisis, looked presentable. While jeans, khaki shirt, hiking boots, and ponytail comprised my typical day-to-day wardrobe, this evening I needed to blend in with the well-to-do and help raise money. The rich-folk camouflage allowed me to get close to the well dressed and manicured without spooking them.

However, not everyone chose this tactic.

I stood in a small gathering of men and women, watching as a TV photojournalist and his bright lights maneuvered into our circle. His lens wasn't trained on me, or on the major food-chain owner among us. Nope. The camera zeroed in on the blond guy in the khaki short-sleeved shirt, matching shorts and beat-up hiking boots whose animated story held the throng in rapt attention.

My husband.

Persuading him to don the monkey suit had been unsuccessful. I'd brought him a change of clothes and learned so had he. Only his new wardrobe looked identical to the first. Silk ties and cummerbunds weren't his style. I didn't make an issue of it. Surrounded by a sea of formalwear, Jeff looked the odd duck. But he had their attention. He had roped them as easily as a lame wallaby. Any stories about European vacations or the latest corporate takeover simply could not compete with his party chitchat.

"—The fangs on that snake were *huge.*" Jeff used the fingers of his free hand to mimic the action of the reptile. "It lashed out and missed me arm by a whisker! I knew a bloke once who got just a scratch from the fierce snake—not a clean bite, y'hear—just a little bit of a scratch, and he was knocked flat on his back for a month. The bloke was lucky to pull through."

Jeff enthralled the audience. This was better than TV. The stories of his wildlife encounters never failed to entertain.

The eagle let out another cry as the aboriginal band began to play their native didgeridoos on a stage set near a large wall with a painted wildlife mural. The unearthly low whirling phrases of the long wooden pipes, along with the primitive beat of the drums, added a touch of surrealism to the evening.

"Snake," came a familiar voice, registering through the din.

"JR. Look at you!" I stepped back to appraise his tuxedo. He was tall, trim and handsome. "My God, you're gorgeous."

He smiled crookedly back, embarrassed.

"Seriously. You look great. See? It's not so hard to get a croc man all duded up. Go tell Jeff boy over there."

"That outfit is his trademark, Snake. Your cable show is popular and Jeff is getting recognized. People see him in those clothes and they know immediately who he is. That's good publicity."

"I suppose," I said sourly, still hopeful to see my beloved in long pants some day. Then a new thought struck me. "Say, where's Shari?"

"I slipped away for a minute," he confessed with a guilty half smile.

Shari Jensen was JR's girlfriend, the neediest woman I'd ever met. She clung to JR like a bad rash. I didn't blame him for wanting to give her the slip.

JR indicated my husband. "Would you tell Jeff I'm headed back to the croc enclosure? He looks busy. I've got to change into my work clothes for later."

"You're not going to the banquet?"

He smiled at my disappointment, explaining, "Too much work to do." Then he waved goodbye before I could protest further, melting into the crowd.

For a moment I stood there, deciding what to do next before navigating my way between one group and around another in search of familiar faces. Then I saw them. The entourage. Near the cash bar stood Butler Thomas and his own all-female fan club, comprised of young staffers and well-heeled patrons. Charming the pants off them was the phrase that came to mind.

"Movie star."

The voice came from behind. I turned to face Melanie Wright, wife of our director. Here was another woman out of uniform. Tonight she had dumped her khaki zoo outfit for a long white gown encircled by a beaded tiger, one paw slung over her shoulder, its body draped over a slender hip, finishing the dress's hem with its tail. Tall and slender, you'd never guess she was in her early fifties.

Melanie was senior keeper on the African Trail. As wife of the director and with boatloads of money of her own from a family that owned a chain of successful department stores, Melanie could have taken the easy route and gone society matron on us. Instead, she preferred the day-to-day experience of working with animals and regular people, which won her kudos from the rest of us. At events like this, however, her upbringing shined through.

Her attractive, expressive face considered the tableau before us with amusement. She gestured toward the handsome assistant director with a glass of champagne, moving closer to my ear to be heard over the band. "God, he looks good, doesn't he?" She laughed. "He belongs in Hollywood, ushering some over-sexed young starlet down the red carpet."

"Easy on the eyes," I agreed.

Melanie nodded. "The man knows what he's doing. Anthony may be the visionary and financial golden boy around here, but Butler is the detail man, the guy who gets things done. It won't be long before another zoo snaps him up."

And what a loss for us when that happens. Butler was too good to stay in the number-two spot forever.

"You're no slouch yourself tonight." She gave me the once over and nodded her approval.

"You should have seen me before the crocodile rescue. You haven't heard?"

I related a toned-down version of the incident at Crocodile Island, leaving out her husband's appearance and his tantrum over the trail not being completely finished for tonight's grand opening.

Rhinestone tigers danced on her ears as Melanie shook her head. "You need to put a leash on that man of yours, Snake. I can't imagine—"

Without finishing her sentence, she frowned, lines of tension forming around her mouth. She arched her brows in the direction of her husband who was waving her over from across the room with a cocktail glass in his hand.

"I'm surprised he doesn't just whistle." Knocking back a deep swallow of champagne, Melanie departed in a glimmer of opalescent beads. Her slender form slipped through the crowd with the easy grace of a jaguar merging into the rain forest.

Chapter 3

We sat down to dinner forty minutes later. By the time dessert was served, two rumors were circulating the main plaza. One rumor had it that Minnesota actress Jessica Lange and her companion, Sam Shepard, were attending this evening's festivities. The other was that Anthony Wright was missing.

Over two dozen round tables, each sitting eight people, had been set up in the plaza near the entrance of the Australia Walkabout Trail. Zoo officials and local celebrities had been scattered among the guests to answer questions and hopefully encourage the giving of generous donations.

Billie Bradshaw, our producer and director, and Arthur "Shaggy" Lutz, our inestimable lead cameraman, shared our table. A large-boned woman, Billie was at least a head taller than me, more so when she wore those damned heels. Pushing sixty, she had the stamina and voice of an Army drill sergeant and a pair of caustic hazel eyes that could land on you like a sack of bricks.

"It's good they saved money on the catering," she intoned in a way that was both complimentary and critical at the same time. "It shows our donors the zoo isn't frivolous with its money. On the other hand, too bad we can't get rubber chickens declared an endangered species." She pushed away her plate.

"The food's fine, Billie," Jeff jibed back, the last forkful of a strawberry cheesecake lifting to his mouth. "You've been around the crocs too often at feeding time. The smell of raw chicken carcasses has gotten to you."

Under her silver bangs, an eyebrow drawn in brown pencil arched. "I can see it hasn't affected your appetite, Jeff."

"Never does." He licked the fork clean. "The animals enjoy their feed and I enjoy mine."

Shaggy, the cameraman, leaned back in his chair and patted his stomach. "Life's simple pleasures, man. That's what it's all about."

The Shagster nodded to us with satisfaction, as though he had just imparted some lost pearl of wisdom. Tall, spindly, with mousy brown hair pulled back into a ponytail longer than mine, he had a sorrowful goatee sprouting from his chin and upper lip, which lent him a certain counter-culture hipness. Although in his mid-thirties, he looked like a refugee from the early seventies, replete with a laid-back view of the cosmos that was unfazed by little things like reality.

"Got some great shots of you in the water with the Old Man," Shaggy continued, referring to the big male crocodile, Sebastian. "Classic man-against-beast stuff. Can't wait to see it in the editing room."

"You may get more of that in a few days. We still have some work to do in the croc exhibit."

"Sweet."

Billie wasn't any more pleased to hear this than I was. She leaned forward with a stern expression. "That was dangerous, Jeff. Getting in the water with that reptile. You could have been injured—or worse."

"JR was there," Jeff replied matter-of-factly.

"Even so, Sebastian almost got you."

"But he didn't."

Billie made a growling sound in her throat, but said no more. She knew there were limits as to how much she could scold him. Jeff, after all, was the boss. He was creator and executive producer of the show. And even if he did stretch the limit of what she considered an acceptable risk, her director's eye also knew it made great filmmaking. Still, I suspected Billie felt she had a license to kvetch.

"On the flip side," Jeff added in a playful voice, squaring off to face our cameraman. "I didn't see anyone stop filming and come rushing over to help."

"Whoa, dude." Shaggy clutched his chest. "Cut me to the quick. If that gnarly old croc was, like, hanging on to your leg, I would've been there in a sec." He made karate chop movements with his hands.

The speeches were mainly a blur to me, Anthony Wright's absence becoming painfully obvious. Seamlessly filling in for him, Butler Thomas spoke at length on the history of the Australia Walkabout Trail. No one was the wiser that he was a replacement speaker; he was that good. Moreover, you could tell Butler enjoyed the moment, a chance to promote not only the zoo, but, to a lesser degree, himself. It wasn't until he thanked the sponsors that I noticed Melanie Wright slip into her seat at the next table. She seemed a bit flushed, no doubt embarrassed that she had missed the dinner or peeved that her husband had chosen this moment to disappear. It was his night. He had made this all possible, and it wasn't like him to miss an opportunity to take credit for his accomplishments.

Senator McNealey was next at the lectern, taking several long breaths before he started. Normally, he was a polished and witty speaker. Instead, he looked preoccupied, losing his train of thought as he spoke about the Minnesota Valley Zoo's sixty-million-dollar impact on the state's economy, as one of the top five tourist's attractions. His hands gripped the edge of the lectern as though to steady himself or, I wondered later, to hold himself back. His face looked drawn, his words sounded hollow, his voice speaking with forced conviction. The man could barely contain himself.

Thank God, he finished quickly, and Jeff bounced up to the lectern, full of enthusiasm.

"G'day!"

"G'day!" The audience shouted back with good humor. It was Jeff Jones they'd come to see and Jeff Jones they got.

"I'm a little nervous," Jeff confided at the podium. "I'm not used to talking in front of a big crowd. I haven't been this anxious since I nearly sat on a diamondback rattler! Grumpy little cuss he was, too. Nearly bit me in my privates." Jeff laughed and with large, sweeping gestures, he launched into another wildlife encounter story, stalling in hopes that Anthony Wright would show up to take his place and lead our patrons along the new trail.

While the audience was being entertained by Jeff's stories, I looked around and saw a stunning beauty in a cream-colored gown talking to a security guard. Suzanne Terak was Wright's executive assistant. A petite, shapely woman, her long, lustrous, straight hair hung down the length of her back like black satin. How she got it to shine like that was beyond me. Genetics? Killer shampoo? Or maybe she didn't have to wash straw dust and camel drool out of her hair like some people. Were she taller, she would have made a great cover girl, in which case she would've been the only supermodel with a cosmetic bag kept in alphabetical order. No one I knew was more organized than Suzanne.

What she was saying to the security guard I couldn't tell, except I was sure it had something to do with our missing zoo director. She looked at her watch then gestured toward the empty chair next to Melanie. The guard got on his radio. After it squawked a few times, he gave a half-hearted shrug. A look of annoyance barely settled on her face before she carefully schooled her features into the mask of cool professionalism she was known for. Disorder had no place in her world—especially in the carefully prepared schedules she set up for her boss. She kept tabs on him like most women kept tabs on their husbands, but it wouldn't do to let the public suspect anything was wrong.

"She's smart, that one. You can tell why Wright relies on her so much." Pouring wine from the carafe into her empty glass, Billie gave me her unsolicited evaluation of Suzanne Terak. "Not bad eye-candy, either. Our young intern is definitely smitten." She chuckled and took a long drink.

Gary Olson was young and certainly excitable. I'd seen the way his eyes sparkled whenever Suzanne entered a room, as though she had descended from Mt. Olympus. In the natural world, Ms. Terak would definitely have been battled over by the young bulls of the herd. Poor Gary didn't stand a chance; he just wasn't in her league and he knew it, too. Better for him he'd skipped dinner to pursue one of our volunteers, a young lady much more attainable than the exacting Suzanne.

My eyes came up in time to see her approach our table, a solemn expression clouding her lovely face.

"Have you seen Mr. Wright?" As long as I had known Suzanne, it had always been Mr. Wright. Never Anthony. You'd think that after four years of working with the man, she could lighten up a bit.

I frowned, trying to remember when I had last seen him. "It was about an hour ago. He was showing Senator McNealey and the governor around."

Suzanne nodded back with a magisterial ease, pursing her rose-colored lips together. "I saw him with the senator shortly afterward. No one has seen him since." She drew in a heavy breath. "I can't imagine where he's gone off to . . ." She was at a loss. She was not pleased by Wright's impromptu disappearance.

"Maybe something's happened—" I started to get up, but she

stopped me with a hand on my shoulder.

"I've checked his office and had one of the guards check the men's rooms. He hasn't had a heart attack if that's what you were thinking." She looked down her elegant nose at me. "This is the most important night in his career at the zoo. It's unlikely he'd leave under any circumstances."

There came loud, enthusiastic applause. Jeff had finished his presentation. Now it was time for action. He was the final speaker of the evening and had signaled for everyone to get out of their seats and start down the trail for the premiere tour of our new exhibit. Billie got up and joined Shaggy at the trail's entrance. He had his camera balanced on his shoulder, ready to walk backwards into the exhibit.

I reluctantly excused myself from Suzanne and joined Jeff, who bounded from behind the podium and hurried down to the trailhead, his footing ensured by the ubiquitous hiking boots. Without Wright available, Butler Thomas stepped up and cut the red ribbon with a round of cheers from our guests. We were now officially open, and this group would be the first to see the magnificent Australia Walkabout, journeying under the warm simulated sun of the lights above.

Jeff took the lead, putting a dozen or so people between us. We took the opposite path from the one I had run earlier in the day. This trail took us through the eucalyptus forests, home to Australia's most beloved marsupial.

"The first animal you'll see is the koala," Jeff told his followers. "The average koala eats two-and-a-half pounds of eucalyptus leaves each day. There's our girl." Jeff beamed, ducking under the perimeter fencing of the enclosure. "Contrary to what you may have heard, these leaves do not drug these little guys. Eucalyptus is not the most nutritious food, and as koalas eat it almost exclusively, they need to sleep a lot to conserve their energy."

A dozen fabricated eucalyptus trees stood beneath a roof of vines. Four Teddy bear–like creatures clung to the trees and blinked sleepily toward the crowd. Near the front of the group, one cuddly animal leaned from a branch to sniff at the newcomers, revealing a small koala peeking from her pouch.

"This is Lydia, our star." Jeff's face shone with pride and great affection. "Isn't she a cutie? And look at her joey. You're a good mother, aren't you?"

Koalas were always a crowd-pleaser.

We left the forest for Australia's scrublands, the territory of the red kangaroo, largest of the macropods, a nocturnal animal that stood as tall as six feet and could jump as high. They were a mob of three. The tallest, Boomer, was a rescue from an illegal sporting event. He sat upright, his wizened face looking almost human as he assessed the crowd. A ten-foot-wide trench surrounded the kangaroo exhibit, which was fronted at our end by a four-foot-high rock wall. A woman near me whispered to her husband, "That big one looks like he could work up enough steam and jump right over that."

I turned to reassure her. "Every zoo has its escape stories, but we've done everything possible to be sure that doesn't happen. For your safety and theirs."

Our next stop was Jeff's pride and joy, Crocodile Island. Here Sebastian and Babe resided and, with any luck, would reproduce. The large enclosure was sunk at least six feet below the walkway, edged by an eight-foot chain-link fence that was invisible from this part of the path.

"The saltwater, or estuarine, crocodile is the largest reptile in the world," Jeff said as we paused for a moment to take in the exhibit. "As you can see, their eyes, ears and nostrils are high on their heads, which allows them to sense their prey while partially submerged in the water."

Sebastian and Babe looked like a pair of floating logs, barely rippling the water as they shifted position and aimed their noses toward us. "When an animal comes down to the water for a drink, the crocs will inch silently forward. Before the poor bloke on shore knows what's happened, the old croc will launch himself out of the water. Once he has a bone-crushing grip, he drags his hapless victim into the water, rolling over and over until he drowns him. And if he's got a large animal, he'll stuff the carcass under a log or rock to rot and eat at his leisure."

Jeff led the group across the footbridge, cautioning them to watch their step as they passed the area where the panel had been removed late that afternoon and three one-by-eight boards had been put up as a temporary barricade. Except the top board was now broken in two. It looked like one of the crocs had taken a bite out of it. Jeff and I exchanged a puzzled look before Jeff waved a staff member over and instructed him to stay there.

Continuing down the ramp, an uneasy feeling tickled the back of my neck as the group followed Jeff into the underwater viewing area for a unique view of these fascinating animals. I lagged behind a few steps to make sure the group navigated the descent into the tunnel. I was facing away from the passageway when I heard the woman next to me gasp. Then another woman screamed and I turned.

Anthony Wright's body bobbed in the viewing window before us, his silver hair undulating around a pasty white face like the tentacles of a jellyfish. His lifeless eyes stared vacantly, bubbles from the water circulator rising around him. Caught in the roots of the artificial mangroves, his body was wedged between the edge of the pond and a support pylon for the bridge. His limp form swayed at the water's urging, while a handless stump of an arm wavered beneath his evening jacket.

CHAPTER 4

Emergency procedures were followed to the letter. Our on-site medical team was called to the scene. Security was notified and they in turn alerted the authorities. The rest of the staff along the trail struggled to turn people away and back down the path.

It was hard to stop the forward crush of people, many blissfully unaware of the grisly sight ahead of them, others—the macabre or curious, mainly—edged forward against the tide for a better look. Thankfully, most wanted no part of it.

Next to me, an elderly lady lost her dinner. A pregnant woman in a white silk dress slumped to the floor, the young man with her lunging forward to break her fall. Overhead the lorikeets screeched a painful chorus of complaint. Other animals stirred as they sensed the tension and panic, adding their voices to the cacophony of horror.

I tried to guide people away from the exhibit, barely holding back the nausea that gurgled at the base of my throat. Jeff's voice echoed in the tunnel, warning guests now entering to turn back. There were more screams as another unsuspecting group of people were brought eye to eye with Anthony Wright's body.

It was a disaster, a surreal snapshot reeling into slow motion. Reporters and photojournalists fought upstream against the surge of people, microphones and cameras in hand to record the ghastly shock of the event. Flashbulbs and arc lights glared against the thick window that separated the pool from the path. This was front-page news, not the staged press release hokum they usually covered on the social scene. This was the real deal.

At the top of the exhibit with most of the patrons, I stood at the waist-high wall looking down onto Crocodile Island. A female security guard ordered people to clear the area while another guard squawked into his radio to central command that someone had fallen into the crocodile exhibit.

Jeff and JR stood on the bridge, looking through the open section in the barrier that had been removed to repair the plumbing. Of the three wide boards temporarily fastened in place, the uppermost was broken, both halves leaning ominously into the enclosure.

There were more cries of alarm as two armed security guards broke through the throng, one positioning himself next to the wall, raising his rifle to his shoulder and taking aim at the dark shape in the water below. Shocked, I lunged in front of the man, knocking the barrel of the gun to the side.

"What the hell do you think you're doing?" I demanded.

The would-be shooter, a thick-necked man with a buzz cut and severe brown eyes, immediately brought the gun back up.

"Back off, lady. We've got to get that man out of there. He might still be alive for all we know. And those crocs sure aren't going to let us just walk in and help ourselves. We've got to put them down."

The rifleman drew a bead on Sebastian.

This time I grabbed the barrel with both hands and refused to let go, looking deep into the other man's face. "Wright's dead. There's no point in shooting the crocs. We can get him out of there without hurting them."

"I've got a job to do. Get out of my way. Lou." The guard motioned to the other man with a rifle. "Move over there. One of us should have a good angle to take a shot."

End of discussion.

I looked back toward the bridge where Jeff watched with narrowed eyes. Springing into action, he rushed over to a makeshift staging area just off the trail and took up a length of coiled rope. Ripping off his shirt and tossing it to JR with the word, "Blindfold," he vaulted over the railing, skidded down the curving slope to the parameter fence, scaled it in a blink of an eye and made an Olympian jump into the billabong. A second later JR plunged in after him. The armed guards lowered their weapons, staring gaped-mouth at the water below.

My heart caught in my throat and I rushed down the path and onto the bridge, leaning over the barrier to keep Jeff in my sights. A crush of people behind me craned their necks like a mob of prairie dogs trying to see the action below. Billie Bradshaw shoved her way up next to me, motioning *Zoofari*'s cameras to start filming. If Jeff survived, this would make a hell of an episode. But even as she gave the order to roll film the color had left her face.

The invasion into his territory stirred Sebastian to action. He swam with deadly purpose toward Jeff, who had dived under the water and was making for the shallow end of the pool. Jeff surged up and broke the surface, standing chest deep in the water, hastily scanning for the deadly crocodile. Sebastian was nearly upon him, whipping his powerful tail and changing direction. Jeff had expected this, shifted his hips, and stepped aside at the last second, the razor teeth slicing down in front of him, catching only air and water. Without hesitation, Jeff jumped on the back of the old croc, clamping his legs around him while tightening his grip round his head, to which the other answered with an angry whip of his massive tail. It put a large dent in the water and sent up a violent spray.

Under better circumstances the procedure would have been to lasso the rope over Sebastian's top jaw, then secure the snout. There had been no time for that. Jeff had to do it the hard way, using brute force in order to save the crocodile's life.

"Where the hell—" Billie grabbed for me, but swung at empty air as I sprinted past her.

Once more kicking off my shoes and hiking up my dress, I stormed down the path and into the tunnel. I flew through the emergency exit, along the service tunnel and out the keeper's door into the sandy beach of the crocodile exhibit, armed with the six-foot bamboo pole I had grabbed along the way. I was determined that Sebastian's mate, Babe, was not going to join the melee.

Babe was smaller and not as aggressive as Sebastian, but she was still a formidable opponent. My bare feet sank deep into the wet sand as I smacked her on the nose with the end of the pole. She turned away from the water with a hiss, her mouth now wide open, a guttural growl emitting from her throat. I backed up toward the holding pen. Wise to the deception, she swung back around toward the water again. I heard the fabric of my dress rip as I sprinted after her. Another rap on the nose forced her to attend to me and the pitiful protection of my bamboo pole.

Behind her, Sebastian thrashed in the billabong, sinking and trying to drown Jeff. They disappeared beneath the water, only to violently break the surface a second later, Jeff gasping in a lungful of air. He had managed to work the loop of rope into the croc's open mouth. Sebastian obliged and attacked the rope with a mighty crush. With the rope wedged in, Jeff quickly coiled the loose end around the snout twice and pulled it snug. They weren't secure, but they were precariously contained. Jeff shook the water from his eyes, clutching the reptile with all he had.

The rope cinched close around the croc's jaw, and he flung himself into a death roll. Great splashes of water took to the air as he rotated and thrashed, Jeff holding on for dear life to a fifteen-foot killing machine.

The crocodile surged and tumbled, smashing Jeff's body into

the concrete side of the billabong. Somehow, Jeff summoned the strength to right himself and pull back on Sebastian's head, which made the croc stop for a second. In that instant JR lunged toward them and wrapped Jeff's shirt over the croc's head, covering his eyes, quieting him for the moment. JR scrambled up the bank onto land, pulling the great crocodile's covered head as Jeff tried to lift the massive body onto the land. With a great effort, they landed Sebastian and immediately fell upon him.

"Could use a few more blokes!" Jeff called, out of breath, his face pressed against rough crocodile flesh.

I desperately wanted to help, but had my hands full with Babe, keeping her attention focused on the pole and away from the hidden door that allowed passage into the exhibit so the other keepers could safely enter and help contain Sebastian. Two of them, who had been trained by Jeff and JR, hurried over to add their body weight to keep the old dinosaur from moving.

Gary Olson chose that moment to play hero. With everyone's attention focused on the crocs, he had managed to climb down into the enclosure, where he fell into the billabong and fully submerged himself under the murky water.

Up on the bridge, Billie was livid. "What the hell do you think you're doing?" Leaning over the railing, she ordered him out of the water.

"Just wanted to help," he gulped back, going down again.

"If you want to work for me, kid, you'll get out of there now!" Hands on hips, she glared down at him. I wasn't sure if she felt responsible for him or was angry he was ruining her shot.

Annoyed, Gary cast a furtive gaze around from behind his skewed glasses then stood up, his soaking clothes dragging at his attempt to lumber up the billabong shore.

"Snake!" Billie shook a finger at me. "We are not taking that boy on location next month. I'm not going to be the one to tell his mother he's been eaten by a mountain lion."

Amen.

Shaggy moved up beside her, still filming. Intent on his art, the lens of his camera separating him from the drama, he mumbled encouragement to his subjects as if he were directing a movie and this was all scripted. I wished.

Minutes later the crew bodily moved Sebastian off the exhibit and into a restricted holding area. It was a much easier effort to persuade Babe to follow her mate, enticing her into holding with a chicken carcass dangled in front of her long nose.

A handful of people, mostly zoo staff, still lined the Walkabout Trail, looking numbed by the real-life drama they had just witnessed. The men with the rifles looked deflated, even annoyed. Quiet had once again fallen upon the gathering, broken only by the faint sound of nearby moving water and the rustle of leaves in the treetops. Somewhere in the distance, an approaching siren keened.

I was horrified to see Melanie Wright standing at the fence, staring into the russet waters below. In all the excitement, I had forgotten her, as had everyone else, it seemed. Obviously no one had considered sparing her the awful sight of her dead husband.

She seemed oddly detached—not holding back her grief or in shock, not even indifferent. It was as if all emotion had been shut off and she was trying to figure out what she was supposed to be feeling. The lines in her face tightened marginally as her hands clutched the railing. A split second later she carefully schooled her features into an expression of neutrality.

I took a step toward her but stopped when Suzanne Terak beat me to it. The petite woman with the dark hair moved quickly and stood by her late employer's wife, resting her hand on top of the latter's in a protective gesture. Suzanne scanned the pool for a moment, as if she could see her boss's lifeless body wedged under the dark water, then gently turned Melanie away, her own emotions in check.

"What the hell do you think you're doing!" demanded a new voice, full of dread and authority. Stepping onto the bridge, Butler Thomas made his way up to the lead rifleman. Butler had been positioned at the end of our ill-fated tour and had been caught up in trying to move our guests back toward the main plaza.

He looked a shade paler as he surveyed the restive onlookers, and I imagined he was already calculating what impact this tragedy was going to have on the zoo. Needless worry in my humble opinion. The publicity was priceless; it alone would guarantee the turnstiles would be jammed with thrill seekers and the morbidly curious who wanted a glimpse of the killer crocodile.

The rifleman gestured haphazardly. "You said—"

"I told you not to shoot unless someone's life was in danger." His eyes took in the gloomy water below and the now empty beach. "Make yourself useful. Escort this crowd to the plaza. I'm sure the police will want to talk to everyone."

Jeff came up the bridge from the lower regions of the exhibit, putting on his wet shirt and wincing as he slipped his right arm into the sleeve. "Almost broke my ribs," Jeff said with a shake of his head as he joined us. "Sebastian slammed me against the concrete pretty hard."

Butler surveyed the welts and cuts on Jeff's bare arms and legs. "God, Jeff! You could've been killed!"

Jeff's face was drawn and unequivocal. "I won't let anyone kill those crocodiles without good reason."

"Neither will I," Butler assured us, putting his hand on Jeff's wet shoulder.

Not everyone who works in a zoo is passionate about animals, but Butler's one of the most zealous believers in good animal care and exciting exhibits I'd ever known. What won him over to the zoo staff was his attitude that as far as the exhibits were concerned, the needs of the animals came first.

"The police are on their way," he added as an afterthought, looking around with a worn expression. "They didn't want us touching the body or anything in the area. Too late for that. I don't think they'll mind that you moved Sebastian to his holding area so they can get access to the body—or what's left of it. Oh, God." This last under his breath.

The noise level along the Australia Walkabout increased as the police began to arrive. Anxious guests and newscasters were led away, and the area was roped off so they could begin their investigation of the death.

I pitched in by grabbing a radio and helping to coordinate getting the rest of the animals into holding. Food was the main motivator. Breakfast was usually served in the exhibit each morning, an incentive for the animals to leave their holding areas. To coax them back in the evening, dinner was served in the holding area. Most animals knew when it was getting close to dinnertime, and at the end of the day you could often see them pacing in front of the hidden doors of their enclosures, waiting for their keepers to let them in.

Keeping busy with the animals kept my mind from other things. The adrenaline rush from keeping Babe at bay and watching Jeff wrestle Sebastian was slowly wearing off, and I found myself trembling. It wasn't from cold. The Australia Walkabout was kept a constant seventy-eight degrees. I tried not to think about what had happened, about Wright's lifeless body, a victim of a crocodile's deadly instinct.

"Lavender."

I swung around toward the voice and was surprised to see a

familiar face. I hadn't seen Ole Sorenson since our five-year high-school reunion some years back. He had always refused to date a girl named Snake, so had insisted on being the only classmate to call me by my given name. In return, I had dubbed him Bubba.

Ole was leaning up against the railing a short distance from me, the Aboriginal arch marking the head of the Australia Walkabout Trail behind him. He looked older than his thirty-five years, having aged into the old-fashioned family name his parents had saddled him with. His once thick, dark red hair had deteriorated into a thinning comb-over, the once-chiseled features now sagged into a thick jowl and added pounds lapped over his belt. He had been Roosevelt High School's football hero, buff and gorgeous, the love of my teenage life. Separate colleges and Buffy Randolph had ended that.

As he approached, I could smell the Juicy Fruit and Old Spice. Some things never change.

"You haven't changed much," I lied, self-consciously looping a fallen lock of hair behind my ear. My upswept hairdo was mostly hanging down around my face, still damp and muddy from the ruckus Babe had kicked up on shore, and my dress now sported more sand than sequins and had ripped up a side seam. So much for glitz and glamour.

He chuckled and patted his gut. " 'Fraid the guy I see in the mirror each morning don't quite jive with the picture of him in my head."

"That's true of most of us these days." The laugh lines seemed more apparent, the bathroom scale a lot less forgiving, but it never bothered me. Having always been more obsessed with animals than my appearance, the signs of age weren't as devastating to me as to some of the makeup queens I'd known in my school days.

Ole and I shared the usual banalities awkward meetings

require. He was now a detective for the Apple Valley Police Department. Buffy had divorced him and moved back to Atlanta with their two boys.

"You've done all right," he said with approval. "I've seen that show you got. You're getting to be famous. And that's some guy you hitched up with." He looked over with amusement at Jeff, who was sitting on the path twenty yards from us, drenched, dirty, scratched, and exhausted, talking to a uniformed cop.

"My kids love your show," he added with peculiar emphasis.

Meaning he probably didn't. My outlook on wildlife and the environment had been a huge note of contention between us as teenagers. I was passionate about it; he preferred the word "possessed." In fairness, I had felt the same about his obsession with any game involving a ball.

"I've done all right," I agreed, as I regarded Ole in my most businesslike manner, gathering my poise.

He took my cue and straightened. "Did you know the victim?" he asked after a thoughtful silence.

"I respected him. I couldn't say I really knew him." Anthony Wright had been a hard man to know; guarded about his feelings and personal life, never sharing any stories about himself. It was as if his mind was focused on one track. I'm not sure if many people knew him that well. He had a different face for each person he met, one for each role he played: PR man, zoo director, husband.

"Any theories on how this could have happened?"

Good question. Wright wasn't a pencil pusher. He'd worked in zoological parks before and knew the dangers of being around wild animals. What had he been doing here? Checking up on the repairs? Looking for someone? "It was Wright who insisted the bridge be made safe for the tour. He knew about the broken panel and the temporary boards we put up. He would have been careful." I shook my head. "The crocs would have to have been pretty riled to make a jump like that and destroy that barricade."

"When was the last time you saw Wright?"

"Well, I didn't see him at dinner. He missed giving his presentation. And that wasn't like him." I smiled wanly. "Anthony Wright was not a humble man. This whole exhibit was his baby and he'd want to be there to take due credit. But he disappeared. No one knew where he was."

"Who went looking for him when he didn't show up?"

I thought for a moment. "Suzanne Terak. She's his assistant. And I assumed Melanie had been looking for him as she missed dinner."

He noted this in a small spiral-bound pad. "What about John Erling?"

"JR? He's been in the pool with Jeff." I looked over toward my husband. JR wasn't among the group standing around him. He was probably tending the crocs in their holding area or changing into dry clothes. Confused, I narrowed my gaze. "Why all the questions?"

"Just trying to establish everyone's movements. One of the other keepers said JR wasn't at dinner because he was taking care of them oversized lizards. Well, if he was there, then he should have seen Wright. Maybe he did," Detective Ole Sorenson added with meaning.

He led me to the top of the trail and jerked his head toward the bridge below. "See them boards?" He cracked the wad of Juicy Fruit he'd been building. Ole never spat out the old gum, he just kept adding fresh sticks to the collection. "They're good lumber. Strong. You could trip, stumble into them and you'd only bounce off. See how that top board is broken? You can't see from way up here but up close the break tears through the wood in a certain direction. The crime scene guys'll confirm it but, it looks to me like that board was pushed out with a hell of a lot of energy. The only way it could have broken like that is if something was hurled against it with full force."

He seemed to find some amusement in the look of puzzlement I sported. It was a smirk I recalled all too well from our high-school days. Confident. Cocky. The cat with the canary.

He fixed a steely-eyed gaze at me. "I don't think the crocs killed him. If they had broken that fence, the boards would have been pushed inward, not out. We'll have to wait for the medical examiner's report, but I think Wright was dead before your big boy got him. Wright didn't just fall in, Lavender. He was pushed."

Chapter 5

I heard Bagger barking before I heard the pounding on the door. The sun was breaking through the bedroom curtains and the warm, cozy quilts I had cocooned myself in were not announcing my departure anytime soon.

Jeff's spot on the bed was already cold and long vacated. He had given up trying to sleep and left to check on Sebastian and Babe some time in the middle of the night. With that thought, the reality of the previous evening came rushing at me like a Mack truck. It would be a difficult day. The zoo was closed so the police could continue their investigation, and Butler Thomas was scheduling professional grief counselors to speak with employees who wanted to talk. All I wanted to do was stay under the covers and shut out the world a while longer.

An oversized hundred-pound golden retriever flattening my toasty pocket, and a wet tongue, encouraged me to rouse myself. Bagger nuzzled my ear with his cold, wet nose, forcing me farther under the covers. Kow Tow, our black-and-white tabby cat, joined me in retreat. The once-feral cat had been peacefully curled up next to me and was no happier at being disturbed than I was.

The incessant knocking continued. Bagger, now charged with a mission to defend his home, scrambled across the bare wood floors to bark at the back door. Struggling to an upright position, I clapped the light on and groped for the blue terrycloth robe I had dropped on the floor the night before. I gave up locating my slippers and figured the cold floor would help keep my eyes open.

It was difficult to believe Anthony Wright was dead, let alone murdered. At some point today, I would have to visit Melanie, give her my condolences, and offer any help she might need. I was worried about the way she had reacted at the exhibit; something about it was troubling, perhaps a sign that she was close to the edge. Rage, grief, anger. Anything would have been better than her lack of any reaction.

Truth be told, I'd never been overly fond of Wright. He'd been overbearing and an annoying micromanager on the Australia project, too used to having his own way. And yet he wasn't a bad man. He was a tremendous organizer, due in part to the very efficient Suzanne Terak, and could instill a sense of empowerment in those who worked under him. He had been the first person to give his unrestrained approval of *Zoofari*, and was one of its biggest supporters, understanding its educational value and the goodwill the program would promote for the zoo. Over the past five years, despite budget woes, he'd pushed the zoo into the twenty-first century, leading with a master plan that would make the Minnesota Valley Zoo a state-of-the-art zoological garden and a leader in wildlife conservation efforts around the world. He had the ear of rich and influential friends, none of whom escaped his prodding to give generously to our worthy cause.

Bagger's toenails clicked against the floor as he galloped into the hallway and barked at me from the bedroom's doorway. Shouting now accompanied the pounding on the door. I recognized the nasal whine immediately and groaned.

Shari Jensen. With even more reluctance, I cinched my robe, shuffled my leaden feet across the kitchen's worn parquet floor and went to the door. Shari already had the screen door open and burst into our old farmhouse with a gust of predawn chill.

A plumpish dishwater blonde, her round, uneven face was wet with tears, her eyes puffy and red, evidence of a night of crying.

"He's gone," she wailed, the syrupy magnolia-blossom accent thicker than usual.

I didn't have to ask who was gone. It had to be JR. Nothing else could get Shari so upset. She had driven to our hobby farm in Lakeville dressed in a pink chenille robe that would have modestly covered hot-pink ruffled baby-doll pajamas—had she opted to use the buttons. On her feet pink poodles pranced across the toes of her slippers. I wouldn't have been caught dead going to bed in a get-up like that, let alone driving across town. But then, remembering the daring plunge of the neckline on the bright red dress she had worn to last night's Beastly Ball, I knew good taste wasn't always part of her wardrobe.

I turned away toward the coffee pot. Thankfully, Jeff had left the coffee maker on. One needed immediate and heavy stimulants to deal with this woman.

"What makes you think he's gone?" I asked, getting out Grandma's old china and setting the cups and saucers out on the table.

"He didn't come home last night." Shari sniffed, then wiped her nose on a balled-up tissue. "He's just gone up and disappeared."

About time, I thought, turning my back on her and covertly picking up the telephone. Shari continued to cry behind me as I flipped through the caller IDs. There was an assortment of newspapers and television networks looking for a scoop on Wright's alleged murder, which is why we had turned the phone off when we got home late last night. Mom's number was sandwiched among them. She no doubt wanted to use this tragedy to convince me to get a real job. Maybe my brother had a receptionist job available at his law office. Right.

There was also a call from Betsy Olson, Gary's overprotective mother. I perked up a bit. Maybe she was worried about Gary's safety and wanted him to quit his internship. I should be so lucky.

The sniffling behind me had stopped, so I quietly replaced the phone, poured the coffee and joined her at the table. For the moment she was reflective, as though the comfort of being with someone let her find her bearings. The bright sun coming through the window made the angles on her misshapen cheekbone more pronounced.

Smoothing out my hair, I gathered it into a ponytail and caught my reflection in the toaster on the counter. Green eyes looked back at me still half comatose, not yet betraying my annoyance at being roused before I was ready.

"JR is probably at the zoo with Jeff." I yawned, adding sugar and cream to my brew.

"He would have called me or something. He hasn't answered his cell phone."

"When did you see him last?"

She screwed up her face to think, a difficult task at the best of times. Bagger sat next to her, prodding her hand with his nose, impatient for attention. Shari was my age and at least fifteen years younger than JR. She was a high-maintenance woman, JR low-key and easygoing. I could never grasp the connection between those two, but I'd seen stranger pairings.

"I reckon it was when he jumped in with them crocodiles to help Jeff."

"So you didn't see JR after the police showed up?" I ventured with surprise.

Shari dumped three teaspoons of sugar into her coffee, stirred it and dropped the wet spoon back in the sugar bowl. "They've been looking for him."

After the discovery of the body, the police had gathered all visitors and staff into the plaza for questioning. With all the commotion, I hadn't realized JR wasn't present. I just assumed he was helping with the animals along with Jeff and the rest of the staff. Now I understood the reason behind her distress, although it didn't make me any more sympathetic.

"Why would the police be looking for JR?" I couldn't think of anyone more unlikely than JR to have problems with the law.

"There's no reason," she said quickly, with a shake of her head. "Why wouldn't he come home? Why didn't he call?"

Her mouth grew tight, the scar on her lip darkening. Fresh tears spilled onto her cheeks, one more angular than the other, as if she'd broken a cheekbone at one time. I had no answer for her and stalled for time, rubbing at a spot on the old oak table. The table had been my grandmother's. I'd rescued it from my parents' basement, stripped off the layers of wear and given it a new home in our large country kitchen. It listed a bit, but I wouldn't have parted with it for the world.

Her troubled eyes fixed on the table, Shari said in a barely audible voice, "What if something happened to him . . . ?"

Oh. That thought hadn't occurred to me. Spats had been common between Shari and JR lately. Because of this, I had initially viewed her mewing as yet another call for understanding in relationship discord. Whereas the real crux of the matter was that she was worried that something had physically happened to him. The idea seemed foreign; the man was so robust, so physical, an experienced wildlife handler. It didn't seem as though anything could hurt him. Yet, last night a man had been murdered. What if JR had witnessed something he shouldn't have and had run? But that didn't make any sense. He had been there after Wright's body had been found. If he had felt threatened, wouldn't he have taken off before that? Or maybe the murderer had struck again. Maybe there was another body to be found—

Early. It was too early for me to think clearly about anything this important. My mind was bouncing all over the place. I needed to slow down.

"Nothing's happened to JR," I said with false conviction, giving myself a mental shake. Shari's hysteria was becoming contagious.

"You really think not?" She clutched the wadded tissue in her hand, her eyes hopeful.

"It doesn't do any good to think the worst if there's no reason to."

She nodded, finding consolation in that. Bagger, Godzilla-dog, put his head on her lap, insistent on attention. Her small, delicate fingers absently stroked his neck, which sent his tail thumping against the parquet floor.

After a few moments, Shari gave me a sly look through the sleepless tangle of hair framing her round face. "Snake, you don't think there's another woman, do you?"

I sat up and blinked. Where did she dig up this stuff? No wonder she was so often a basket case. "What would make you think that?"

"It's stupid. I shouldn't have said anything." She looked into her now empty cup and I refilled it. "It's just that, well, Johnny Ray has acted kinda funny ever since we moved up here."

"Funny, how?"

She bit her lower lip, and for the first time held my gaze as she spoke. "He just started behavin' different once we got to Minnesota, sort of more reserved. Not real different but . . . well, like he wasn't telling me everything. That's when we started fighting more." She exhaled, then took a long sip of coffee, her eyes still locked with mine.

What could I possibly say to that? Kow, the cat, having left the comfort of the bedroom, brushed up against my leg to squeak up at me. Somewhere in her feral life, she had lost the ability to meow and sounded like a child's squeaky toy. I was glad for the distraction. I reached over and picked her up. She curled up in my lap and began to lick my forearm with a tongue like wet sandpaper.

"There's something you're not telling me, isn't there?" Shari looked at me expectantly, her eyes brimming.

"Shari," I said with some exasperation, "I've never seen JR with anyone but you." I shook my head. "I don't get it. First, you're worried about his safety, now you think he's cheating. You're dwelling too much on the negative."

And who died and elected me Pollyanna? Like I was known as the voice of optimism. But the woman was bringing me down. I was feeling decidedly uncomfortable in this role and wished I had left for the zoo with Jeff.

Shari nodded in agreement. "That's what JR's always telling me." She managed a fatalistic smile over her coffee cup. "He says I'm always looking at the bad side of things. Y'all 're lucky to have a man like Jeff. He's so steady and faithful."

Again, where was this coming from? Was Shari just fishing for sympathy? Well, there was only so much of it she was going to get, particularly after she'd dragged me out of bed after a sleepless night. I poured some cream into a saucer and set it on the floor for Kow, compensation for having been tossed out of bed so early.

With what seemed a little like envy, Shari added, "Jeff's one of a kind."

Didn't I know it? It had been love at first sight when we were introduced at the zoo two years ago. It was January in Minnesota, land of ice and severe wind chills, and there he was, dressed for the Sydney summer: bush shorts and a khaki short-sleeved shirt. I took him in hand, dragged him to the Mall of America and suited him up properly for the sub-zero winter. We both hated shopping, loved animals and—to the astonishment of all my friends—were married four months later.

It was the most impulsive thing I'd ever done in my life. And the best.

And I should have been hauling my ass to the zoo to help him clear up the mess from the night before, not sitting here listening to Shari's whining. I grabbed Bagger by the collar as he made a move to share Kow's cream. Bad idea. Even though I called Kow the Audrey Hepburn of cats because of her delicate build and sleek manner, she wouldn't take the intrusion lightly. A rash of claws across the nose was all he was likely to get if he messed with her when she was eating.

While holding Bagger at bay, I looked at Shari. "Any ideas where JR might have gone?"

"We don't have that many friends here yet, no family. Back to Mexico, maybe?"

"Mexico? Why would he suddenly pack up and go there?"

"He didn't."

"You just said—"

"Pack up. He didn't take anything with him."

"I thought you'd said he left."

"He didn't come home, Snake."

"But you don't know he's actually left town, then." With Shari, there was never a direct route to any answer you were looking for; it was usually a tortuous path. I filled my cup to the brim with the brown magic juice again, leaving out the sugar and cream this time.

"He did," Shari insisted.

"But he didn't take any clothes or luggage?"

"No, ma'am."

"Shari, listen to me. That doesn't mean JR's left town. Just a moment ago you suspected him of being with another woman. I'm confused." I didn't know whether to knock my head against the table or hers. As though he too had had enough, Bagger snorted and went to sit by the refrigerator.

Shari grew indignant. "A woman just knows these things."

Things? What things? Excuse me? I'm a woman. I don't always know these things. Did someone forget to pass out the "How to Be a Woman" manual to me? I certainly didn't have a clue what she was talking about. This was getting me nowhere.

"Shari, I'm going to go over to the zoo and talk to Jeff. He probably knows exactly where JR is. Okay?"

She immediately brightened at that ray of hope, though it dimmed rapidly a second later. "You won't tell him it's me that's looking for JR, will you? Johnny Ray'd be awful mad if he thought I was bothering you about this."

I looked at the clock. It was much too early to put something stronger than cream and sugar in my coffee. "I promise not to tell."

Shari beamed with a triumphant smile that faded into a yawn. I jumped on it, convincing her to go lie down, promising to call her as soon as I found out something. It was probably nothing, I reassured her. I was certain JR was with Jeff. I bundled her off to our guestroom, fed the animals, and was about to pour myself another cup of coffee when there was another knock at the door, sending Bagger into a barking frenzy.

Now what? Jeff and I had bought the hobby farm as a buffer from the rest of the world, as our own little piece of wilderness to recharge our spirits and provide peace from the madding crowd. It wasn't working today. The crowd was finding me.

I pulled the curtain aside and saw Detective Ole Sorenson standing on my doorstep. Holding onto Bagger's collar, I opened the door and Ole displayed his badge.

"Bubba, I already know who you are." I managed a humorless smile.

Ole's demeanor was solemn, officious.

"Lavender, this isn't a social call," he said in a voice that got my attention. We stood in the doorway. I hadn't moved. "Are you gonna ask me in?" he said after a moment.

"I'm not sure I should. This is an ungodly hour for a lawman to show up at my door."

"It's seven o'clock."

"Exactly. And it's my day to sleep in." And I was still in my robe and barefoot, feeling none too comfortable standing with the door open.

Ole accepted this and went on. "I'd like to talk with you if I could."

Behind him the sky was baby-blue and cloudless, promising a warm summer day. With little grace, I moved aside and offered him a chair.

Ole sat down at the kitchen table, eyeing the two cups of coffee. I didn't offer him any. His gaze moved around the country-sized kitchen, taking in the bright yellow walls, gingham curtains and painted white cupboards. I leaned back against the kitchen counter and cleared my throat.

Taking the hint, he turned his attention back to me. "Have you seen John Ray Erling since last evening?"

JR again. A feeling of deep dread began to set in. "Has something happened to him?"

"Do you know where he went after he left the zoo last night?"

"Bubba—"

"Have you received any messages from him?"

"What's all this about?" I lowered my voice, not wanting to wake Shari. "If something has happened to him, I want to know."

Ole's eyes went to the table and the second cup. "Is someone here besides you? There's a car outside with a warm hood."

I wrapped myself more tightly in my robe. "JR's girlfriend," I answered.

"I'd like to talk to her, if I could."

"Why? She doesn't have a clue where he is. If she did, she

wouldn't have come pounding on my door before sunrise." I pointed a finger at him. "Now, I just managed to calm her down. I'm sure as hell not going to let you go upsetting her again."

Ole gave me a hard, thoughtful look. "All right," he reconsidered. "I'll talk to her later. But if Erling shows up I expect you to contact me." He threw his business card down on the table. "Harboring a fugitive is against the law."

I moved away from the counter. "Fugitive? JR?"

In measured tones Ole Sorenson replied, "No one has seen Erling since he crawled out of the crocodile pool last night. He's wanted for questioning for the murder of Anthony Wright." Ole pulled a stick of gum from his pocket and began to unwrap it. "His background doesn't quite check out. In fact, we're not even sure John Ray Erling is his real name."

Chapter 6

"He's a big guy, all right," I said admiring the big red kangaroo inside his exhibit, some thirty feet from me.

Boomer angled his head to the side, regarding me with keen interest. Standing on his powerful hind legs, he was an impressive six feet in height, taller than my husband.

The kangaroo enclosure along the Australia Walkabout Trail was a one-acre parcel of grassland that sloped downward toward a four-foot-deep ditch. From there a stone retaining wall extended a solid eight feet above the ground where it became a waist-high barrier for visitors to prevent them from falling into the exhibit.

Three kangaroos lounged in the mid-afternoon sun that streamed through the panels of the glass dome. One female snoozed under the shade of a lone little tree on the island, while the other leisurely hopped near the perimeter moat, occasionally stopping to scratch her stomach and raise her head to sniff the air. In the plains and woodlands of Central Australia where they live, red kangaroos are primarily nocturnal, preferring to rest during the day when temperatures can reach over one hundred degrees Fahrenheit by early morning. The Walkabout was kept a constant seventy-eight degrees, cool by comparison.

Boomer, the large male, was the only one among them interested in my presence, contemplating me with intelligent brown eyes.

I knew why, too. He was waiting for his treat.

"Want something to eat, Boomer? Are you hungry?"

His velvet, donkey-like ears perked up. Inside my pocket was a homemade zoo concoction of ground oats, de-hulled soybean meal, wheat germ, molasses and a few vitamins and natural additives pressed into what resembled a granola bar. I fished the "roo" bar out and showed it to him. Boomer stood even taller now, alert. His long powerful tail thumped in the rye grass.

"You want this?" I called to him, displaying the treat more prominently. "Is this what you're looking for?"

He gave a short bark and I tossed him the granola treat. With little effort, he hopped ten feet in one stride to where it had landed, then gnawed at it with unabashed enthusiasm.

I turned with a broad smile to the woman standing next to me.

"You spoil him," Diane said with a playful shake of her finger. She sat down on the edge of the retaining wall, dressed in the brown-and-khaki uniform of the zoo. She had a round, comely face and pleasant manner that instantly put a person at ease.

"Busted." I held my hands up. "But, I logged it in this time, I swear."

Technically, I shouldn't have been feeding him. I wasn't his assigned keeper, Diane was. In order to maintain their optimum health, the animals have a strictly controlled diet. A daily log is kept to record what each animal eats. So, before grabbing a couple of snacks from the kitchen for Boomer, I had logged in the time and amount and signed my name. It's a critical routine. A lack of appetite is often a keeper's first indication an animal isn't feeling well. It also keeps us from having an overweight kangaroo on our hands, should some other well-meaning keepers decide to spoil him.

But I had some history with Boomer. Jeff and I had rescued him from an animal show in South Dakota that had been holding fights between Boomer and any man or woman who thought they could hold their own against a two-hundred-pound kangaroo. Thankfully, the roadside menagerie had been shut down before anyone was seriously hurt. An adult male kangaroo could easily cause internal injuries with one well-placed kick.

Boomer had been undernourished and distrustful of humans when we found him. Our barn was set up as a temporary quarantine pen until a place could be made ready for him at the zoo. Normally, the zoo doesn't take in animals they haven't purchased or gotten on loan from another accredited zoological garden, but Jeff was willing to bend the rules to keep this beautiful macropod from becoming some misguided animal lover's unmanageable pet. But because his lineage was unknown, he wouldn't be allowed to mate with our females.

"He's doing very well," Diane said. "The three of them have been getting along great. I think he's happy for the company of his own kind."

I turned away from Boomer and gave Diane my full attention. She looked tired.

"How about you? You holding up?" I asked.

"I'm managing," she said after a pause, her young face clouding slightly. "It's just all so hard to believe."

It was. Anthony Wright may not have been my favorite person, but it was hard to imagine I wouldn't see him barreling around the corner, calling out my name, demanding to know why both sun bears weren't on display together. But that's not how I would remember him. I had been one of the first to come upon his body. I would forever see him bobbing under the surface of the water, his body entangled in the roots of the mangrove plants where Sebastian had tucked him away to snack on at his leisure. I couldn't shut out that macabre image.

Diane picked at a spot on the leg of her pants. "The police asked a lot of questions last night. There's a rumor going around that it wasn't an accident. That Wright was murdered."

I wished I could tell her differently. "As far as I know, the police are still waiting for the medical examiner's report. But that seems to be the prevailing theory."

"And the police closed the zoo. How long is that for?"

"I don't know. It may be only for today. We probably would have been closed, anyway, out of respect."

"You don't think they'll shut us down for good, do you?"

I shook my head. "Nobody is going to let that happen."

"I hope you're right, Snake. Budgets are so tight right now. We can't afford to lose another day of revenue."

With no lines of children and their parents parading along the paths, there was an unearthly stillness about the building. This was supposed to have been the grand opening of the Australian building and its Walkabout Trail, an event sure to raise extra revenue and publicity, as last night's fundraiser had been meant to do. Now the police had closed the zoo until they were done gathering whatever information they needed to pursue their investigation. Who knew how long that would take?

A news helicopter from a local TV station flew over the glass roof and passed out of sight. Boomer and the other kangaroos raised their heads skyward. In the next enclosure, a dingo whined. Getting past the growing herd of news reporters and thrill seekers camped outside the zoo entrance this morning had been a challenge. I hoped the appearance of a chopper didn't mean I'd be followed down the highway like OJ when I left.

Diane shuddered. "I know it sounds dumb, but I'm almost afraid to be here. I'm as jittery as an old lady. It's like I expect the murderer to jump out from the bushes and bludgeon me to death—"

"It's not dumb, Diane." I rested a hand on her knee. "This kind of thing happens to other people. The people you see on the ten-o'clock news. I never expected someone I knew would be murdered."

"I feel violated." She brushed her hair back with fingers toughened by regular physical work. "That safe little world I lived in has been totally shattered."

I slid over and put my arm around her shoulders, for my own comfort as much as hers. The working hours of a zookeeper weren't always regular. Regardless of life's tragedies, the animals still needed to be fed and cared for, pens had to be cleaned, medications given. The animals were used to a certain routine in their lives; they relied upon it and it kept stress levels down. Come rain or shine, record blizzards or the disruption of a murder investigation, people like Diane had to get to the zoo. That took dedication and a love for animals. And Diane was dedicated.

I remembered her first month at the zoo. Assigned to the Minnesota Trail, she was helping move a pair of North American otters from their pen into a new enclosure. A carrier fell and sprang open, releasing the otters. One startled otter was easily captured. The other made a mad dash for freedom by scrambling up a startled Diane, over a fence and down the path toward the zoo's marsh. Diane had bolted after it, plunging headlong into the swamp and mud, grabbing and losing him at least five times before getting a firm grip on the champion squirmer. Covered in mire, she delivered the indignant animal to its new home without injury. Diane, however, needed six stitches from a bite on her hand. She had proven herself that day with one of our wiliest critters.

She sat back, pulling a tissue from her pocket to blow her nose. "And then there's the whole thing with JR not showing up. . . ."

I sat up straighter. "He hasn't come in yet?"

"No. And he usually stops to see how Boomer's getting along by now."

"And you haven't heard from him? He didn't call or leave a message?"

"No. No one has heard from him as far as I know."

Boomer barked at me and I absently tossed him the other roo bar. I had come to the zoo to track down my husband, fully expecting to find JR mucking out the crocodile enclosure. I had hoped his failure to come home last night had been a way of not dealing with a highly volatile girlfriend and that he would show up at work as usual. I hated to admit it, but maybe Shari's fear wasn't all that unfounded.

I told Diane about Detective Ole Sorenson's visit to the farm earlier this morning looking for JR. It didn't make sense. JR was too responsible, cared too much for the well-being of the animals and his co-workers to shirk his responsibility like this. Without JR, the onus of keeping the crocodiles' care and feeding schedule fell on my husband and other keepers like Diane. That meant extra hours and rotating shifts.

Behind me, I heard Boomer demolishing the last of his granola treat. I turned to Diane, shielding my eyes from the sun that pierced the exhibit's glass ceiling high above.

"Where were you during the dinner last night?"

"Feeding the wombat and cleaning up after the dingoes. Exciting, huh? The glamorous life of a zookeeper."

"And afterward?"

"I took my post by the information kiosk. Why?"

"And you can't see any of the crocodile exhibit from either of those places?"

She shook her head. "No."

"You didn't see or hear anything unusual last night? Before we brought the guests down, I mean."

"Snake, the police asked me all this last night. And this morning."

I let my shoulders slump. "I know. I just can't imagine that

JR has anything to do with this."

"Maybe the police just want to ask him some routine questions. I don't think they got to talk to him last night."

And that was what had me worried. JR would have to be deliberately ducking the police to have missed being questioned by them. Why?

Punctuating the silence that fell between us, the rolling, machine-gun laugh of a kookaburra came from the aviary. The crazy, almost human laughter, one of the most recognized bird calls in the world, made us both smirk.

"Jacko," I murmured.

Diane stood up, giving me a sad smile. "That reminds me, I promised Mitch I'd help him spread a load of gravel around the aviary and feed the gang later. Then I need to inventory that delivery of prey mix and DBC that came yesterday."

DBC: dead baby chicks. Partial to the young of other birds, snakes and other small reptiles, kookaburras in captivity were fed a commercial bird of prey mix and dead baby chicks.

"Happy feeding." I turned toward the grassy enclosure behind us. "And I'll see you later, Boomer."

The roo hopped a few short steps, sniffed the air and looked at me expectantly. Time to find Jeff. I'm sure he was up to his eyeballs in work, given the no-show by JR. Certainly he wouldn't refuse a helping hand. I turned in the direction of the crocodile exhibit, behind which was Jeff's office.

Diane stopped me. "If you're looking for Jeff, I saw him head outside with Dr. Steve just before you showed up."

I waved thanks and started back up the path as Jacko's laugh rippled through the air once more. "Laugh, kookaburra, laugh," went the old song as I started to hum it.

Once outside the enclosed habitat of the Walkabout Trail and into the real outdoors, I felt a rush of energy. The late morning sun was bright, the day warm and cloudless. For the next three months, people here would forget about snowdrifts, ice-slicked roads and below-zero wind chills. The only thing natives of the upper Midwest had to worry about now was how to avoid the overabundance of road construction, whether it was going to rain on the weekend barbeque, and keeping an ample supply of mosquito repellant on hand.

I followed the left loop of the Northern Trail where animals from the northern hemisphere were exhibited. These animals thrived in a Minnesota winter and were comfortable being outdoors throughout most of the year. I stopped for a moment to watch a pair of our Amur tigers batting a large ball around the pool that fronted a portion of the exhibit. Unlike domestic cats, tigers enjoyed the water. It was a great way to cool off on a hot summer day. Later they would sprawl out in the grass near the back of the exhibit where the trees were thick and the shade cool.

I found Jeff farther along the path, leaning against a reinforced split-rail fence, sipping at a can of pop, and engaged in conversation with one of the zoo's veterinarians. Not far behind them, a bull moose stood neck deep in the pond that took up a fourth of his enclosure.

As I approached, the monorail passed overhead. It was virtually empty, underscoring the fact the zoo was closed. I spied three figures inside one of the coaches. Police, most likely, trying to get a bird's-eye view of the terrain.

The veterinarian conversing with Jeff was Steve Coen: Dr. Steve, as he was called by most of the staff, in order to distinguish him from Intern Steve, Zookeeper Steve, and Security Officer Steve. Indeed, the Minnesota Valley Zoo was well on its way to completing the entire Steve collectible set. One might eventually hope to see Curator Steve and Gift Shop Steve.

Jeff raised his beverage in greeting, looking worn-out.

Dr. Steve gave me a toothy grin. "Snake. It's been a while," he greeted, then continued to Jeff, "Stop by sometime if you get any ideas. I have to attend a pregnant giraffe. Good to see you, Snake." He shot me another, broader smile and ambled off.

"What's up?" I asked.

Jeff guzzled from his pop can then wiped his mouth. "The Komodo dragon has been off his feed the past two days but seems okay otherwise. The doc was wondering if I wanted to take a gander at him."

Jeff was a leading herpetologist and had worked with Komodo dragons before. To consult an expert in his own backyard would have been a blessing for Dr. Steve.

I nodded and said nothing, enjoying the quiet of the moment. A gentle wind moved through the treetops and the warm breeze felt soothing on my face. I let Jeff enjoy this brief reprieve in what must have already been a very long day. There were so many things needing our attention—*Zoofari* for one. I was already two days behind on the scripts and needed to get into the studio to do a voiceover. I was grateful we had five shows in the can, but we needed to meet with our production staff soon, and start making some concrete plans for our trip out west.

For a few minutes we just stood there soaking up the sunlight and admiring the moose as he dipped his head below the water and came up with a green moustache and weedy tendrils decorating his massive antlers. He must have been almost six feet high at the shoulder and weighed nearly 1,400 pounds.

Finally, I said, "I heard JR didn't show up."

"No message. Nothing. Good thing I left the house early this morning to come in."

"Ah, yes, you missed the excitement." I filled him in on Shari's visit and, more importantly, what Detective Sorenson had said about JR.

Jeff shook his head, his disappointment apparent. "Perhaps it's just as well the police closed the zoo today," he went on fatalistically, always ready to look at what he could do, not what he couldn't. "Gives us a chance to catch up on a few projects. The police won't let us touch the croc exhibit until they're done, so we can't mend the bridge. Not that we have time for that today, anyway."

"You look tired. My afternoon is open. Need some help?" *Zoofari* would have to wait; the animals took priority.

"Yeah," he answered with a grateful sigh. Once again, he leaned his back against the rustic fence as though in need of something to prop himself up. "There's plenty to do before feeding time. I had a meeting with the staff a few hours ago. Don't know how long this thing with JR'll last, but we've rejiggered the schedule. As such, it'll be the dawn patrol for me the next few days. Have you been to see Melanie yet?"

"No. That's next on my list, just as soon as you can spare me."

"I won't need you long. We've things under control now. But it's tough, sweetheart. This thing's hitting all of us pretty hard. The staff is feeling vulnerable. You can see it in their faces, the uncertainty. Can't say as I blame 'em. The zoo bigwigs are meeting behind closed doors right now, working out some kind of strategy."

"Someone will have to fill Wright's shoes, at least temporarily."

"Butler has my vote. He's a good bloke who knows the politics of the job and how to handle the media."

Jeff stood away from the fence, his old energy rushing back. Whether real or feigned to mitigate my worry, his face glowed with renewed confidence. "It's an awful thing to have happened, but she'll be apples. You can bet your khakis on that!"

Khakis. Except his Aussie accent pronounced it "kah-keys,"

like a mangled attempt to explain what a Bostonian would use to start his car.

It made me smile in spite of myself.

Chapter 7

The Wrights lived on the edge of downtown Minneapolis, in the area known as Kenwood. They were just up the hill and down the road from the Walker Art Center. It was a wealthy, cultured neighborhood of great old houses, tall, dense trees and a sense of unaffected worldliness where students and starving artists brushed elbows with department store magnates and a resident movie star. While not as ostentatious as the mansions encamped around Lake Minnetonka, the homes of Kenwood displayed their well-to-do ambience with a graceful, old-world charm, where stylish houses mingled with old brownstones.

An eight-foot stucco wall shielded the Wright mansion, a three-story, Tudor-style English home teeming with pink and white climbing roses edging its foundation, from the street. My beat-up old Jeep seemed especially worn and battered as I pulled through the open gates and parked next to a brand-spanking-new silver BMW. At least the place wasn't swarming with visitors. There were no other cars in the circular driveway.

An unknown middle-aged woman dressed in black answered the door before I could lift the lion's-head door-knocker and stepped aside to let me in. Without a smile, she led me across the white marble floor toward the back of the house to wait in the solarium among the bronze fairies and dragons that peeked out behind green palm fronds and sunflowers. Telling me she would inform Mrs. Wright of my presence, she left me alone.

This was the house Anthony Wright had considered worthy

of a man in his position: a man with a good job, a rich wife and a bright future. Nothing the affluent suburbs spat out could match the art and craftsmanship of the polished hardwood floors, embossed ceilings and stained-glass sidelights of this house. Melanie referred to it disdainfully as "the castle."

The glassed-in room where I had been left to wait overflowed with tropical plants and sunshine. Sitting in the middle was a small mosaic fountain, bubbling water issuing forth from the hands of a sprite kneeling on a lily pad in its center. A white wicker love seat and two matching chairs were positioned in front of it. You could scarcely imagine a cozier, calmer spot in which to find relief from the outside world. I lowered myself into a chair to soak up its tranquility in the brilliant, late-afternoon sun.

Waiting gave me extra time to practice what I was going to say to Melanie. There were no right words. My condolences sounded so banal and pointless, even more so now that I knew Wright's death might have been a homicide. What could I possibly say to her? Last night she looked devoid of emotion, like a blank, white canvas waiting for the life of an artist's brush.

The unknown woman in black returned, carrying a tray laden with hand-painted china cups, a carafe of coffee and ceramic teapot. With solemn efficiency, she set the tray down on the glass coffee table in front of me. Mrs. Wright had company, she explained, and would be along presently. She offered a faint smile and took her leave. I half expected a curtsy.

Footsteps echoed across the flagstones in the foyer. Between the draping palm fronds that separated the solarium from the rest of the house, I could see Melanie and Senator McNealey come into view. Melanie was not dressed in widow's black, but in an off-white pantsuit accented by a bright pink blouse. In her arms she cuddled her small white dog, a bichon frise named Lacey. McNealey, his demeanor as iron-gray as his attire, spoke in comforting, low tones. I couldn't make out what they were saying, though I could see McNealey's hand squeeze her shoulder in a way that seemed a bit too familiar.

As he said his goodbyes, he looked past Melanie and saw me watching them. I bowed my head slightly and offered what I hoped was an appropriately solemn smile. We were, after all, both here for the same purpose. He inclined his head, his brows dragging into a frown, then abruptly dropped his hand.

Melanie smoothed Lacey's head as she watched him depart, a pensive look on her face. She was an attractive woman, tall and slender, looking much younger than her fifty-three years. I had never felt the age difference between us and had counted her as my friend almost from the moment we met. I didn't have many female friends. The added responsibility of the cable show gave me little time for socializing, and having someone like Melanie to talk to was a blessing I didn't take lightly. She understood my commitment to wildlife.

After the front door closed behind the senator, Melanie turned toward me and approached with a half-smile of greeting. Oddly enough, she seemed more like her old self; poised and relaxed, the blankness of last night having disappeared.

"Snake, how nice of you to come." Her voice was warm, and she seemed genuinely glad I had stopped by. I rose to greet her with a comforting embrace. Lacey tried to lick my chin as I pulled away.

"I'm sorry to keep you waiting. You know what the senator is like." She glanced in the direction of the front door and let out a heavy sigh, looking put out. "I suppose all of Anthony's political cronies will be calling on me soon. They'll probably want to make sure I live up to all his empty promises."

"McNealey was asking for political favors at a time like this?" I was appalled.

"Oh, no, dear." Her laughter was a gentle ripple. "Not in so many words. He offered his condolences and assured me that he would help me if I needed it either personally or in the continuation of Anthony's good works, some of which will no doubt benefit him greatly."

Sleaze ball.

I didn't say it aloud, on the off chance she actually liked Ted McNealey. I hadn't come to criticize her guests. But, as if reading my thoughts, Melanie shrugged indifferently and gave a weary exhale.

She was either a very brave woman putting on a good front, or the reality of last night hadn't set in yet. I don't know exactly what I had expected, but it wasn't this cool, composed woman. I would have been less taken aback if she had ranted and cried the way Shari had this morning. Melanie, at least, had earned that right. Who'd blame her? The horror of last night washed over me again; the memory of seeing Wright's body floating by the view port played in my head like a stuck video. I gave her another hug, in part to hide my own watery eyes.

She guided me back to the wicker chairs, refreshed my coffee cup and poured herself some tea with a steady hand, sharing a sugar cube with Lacey who curled up next to her. Self-possessed, she looked almost serene in an odd sort of way, which was just a façade I was certain. Losing someone you cared about was difficult enough, let alone having them viciously murdered. It was hard for me to imagine what she was going through, but she was handling her situation far better than I would have. At least on the outside.

The woman who had answered the door came in again to see if we needed anything. Melanie showed a spark of irritation, assured the woman we were quite fine, and sent her away.

"Who is that?" I asked, leaning toward Melanie and speaking in a whisper.

"A gift from Anthony's sister."

She smiled at my look of surprise. "She won't be able to make it to her brother's funeral—if the police ever release the body and we're allowed to have one—so she hired someone to take her place and help out."

"You're kidding me."

Melanie shook her head, blowing on the steam that rose from her teacup. "Families are wonderful, aren't they?"

I didn't know what to say. When my father passed away, our house was full of relatives and neighbors for days. My mother was never left alone. And here was Melanie in this big old house with no one but a stranger her callous sister-in-law had hired.

"Are you doing all right, Mel?" I asked, wishing I had come sooner.

Unlike Shari Jensen, there were no puffy red eyes, no indication of a sleepless night. She sat back in her chair, letting her head loll back against the cushion, looking up at the pale-blue sky through the glass ceiling of the solarium. "I feel free."

Melanie could be remarkably candid when she wanted to be, but I wasn't sure if I had heard right. She turned her head to the side and leveled her unblinking gaze at me. "I feel relief, Snake. Is that so awful?"

She sat up straight and set her teacup down on the table, resting her elbows on her knees. "You know more than most, Snake. There wasn't a lot of love left in my marriage. I still cared for Anthony, though at best we were friends. Sometimes not even that."

I had known for a long time that Melanie hadn't been completely happy in her marriage, but we had never talked about it at any great length. She had always changed the subject. "Was it that bad?"

"Sometimes," she answered after moment's reflection.

"Why didn't you just leave him?"

I immediately wanted to bite my tongue. That wasn't the

most appropriate thing to say under the circumstances. Maybe because Jeff and I got on so well together, I couldn't imagine a marriage without love and friendship. But I had enough life experience to know nothing is ever that easy. And leaving didn't always make things better. Still, she was smart, independent, and there were no children to consider. She didn't need him to lean on.

Melanie managed a furtive smile. "It was a comfortable enough relationship after all these years. We had our separate lives, our own interests, and there were times we spent together which were really nice. But keeping up that public image was getting harder all the time. And now, I don't have to do that anymore."

And she smiled without reservation, her amber brown eyes, slightly careworn from experience, radiated charm and life again. She looped her hair behind her ears. Her slender hands, so small, hardly seemed those of a zookeeper; but I had seen her deal with animals bigger than she was and knew they could be tough when they had to be.

She got up and walked to the windows that overlooked the backyard, Lacey moving into the warm spot she had vacated. "Anthony used to be a man I admired," she said. "He was outspoken, always there to right an injustice. When we first met, he was a committed environmentalist and animal activist. We were young and full of dreams." She gave a little laugh. "He was a forceful young man. But not forceful enough to stand up to my parents, who just wouldn't let us be. Eventually they made him an offer he couldn't refuse."

She had told me about her parents before, not the most supportive people a child could have. And she had no brothers or sisters to deflect their attention. They had made Hanley-Holm Department Stores a household name across the country, buying up a couple of bankrupt discount stores and turning them into multimillion-dollar companies.

The corners of her symmetrical mouth turned down as she pondered the memory, maybe hurting over what had been lost. "They naturally wanted their daughter to reinforce their status by marrying someone of the proper rank and social standing." Melanie snorted derisively, her mouth twisting in bemusement. "Anthony was a nice fit—not rich, but an up-and-coming young lawyer, confident, photogenic. Like my father, he was a self-made man."

Her eyes returned to me with a sparkle. Whatever her relationship with her husband had evolved into, clearly she had fond memories of him. But what she had said surprised me.

I leaned closer. "I always thought Anthony was 'to the manner born,' as they say. He seemed like such a natural."

"Goodness, no. His parents owned a broken-down old zoo in Texas. That's why I married him." She broke into another smile, as the ghost of happier times swept over her. "I wanted to work with animals and he supported that. My parents didn't. And for some reason, I thought his struggle to overcome his financial hardships made him noble, more honest. I thought his upbringing would protect us from my parents' influence."

I set my empty coffee cup on the tray and looked up at her as she moved back toward me. "Why haven't you ever told me this before?"

A shade of regret touched her eyes as she sat down again. "It wasn't horrible. I really shouldn't complain; it's just that . . . well, part of the reason for my wanting to become a zookeeper was so we could take over his dad's zoo and turn it around. And we did. But before long, Anthony was helping my father with this deal and that deal. He was a very bright lawyer with good business smarts, which, in my father's opinion, 'shouldn't be wasted on some two-bit petting zoo.' "

Melanie shook her head with quiet resignation. That little zoo had represented something to her and it had been taken away. The delicate features of her face darkened in some private reverie. "Before I knew it, he was offered a partnership in a law firm and off we went. I'm sure my father had a part in that. We still owned the zoo, but we moved to Miami and Anthony got caught up in corporate deals and take-overs." She gave a shrug.

I began to understand that compromise had played a large part of Melanie Wright's marriage. This in itself wasn't a bad thing, but a person can compromise herself out of a loving relationship if the compromising is all done on one side.

My gaze turned from the greenery around us to the yard outside. An overgrown cottage garden filled the backyard. Drifts of pink, yellow and white flowers undulated across the lawn. Red and pink roses climbed the fence that separated the backyard from the neighbors. I wasn't much of a gardener, but I recognized peonies and hydrangeas, flowers my grandma had always had lots of in her gardens.

Melanie artfully changed the subject. "I understand this police detective is a friend of yours," she said, looking interested.

It was my turn to shrug. "We dated in high school."

She regarded me with mild surprise and almost giggled. "He hardly seems your type."

"He wasn't. And I thank God for that." Naturally, I hadn't thought so at the time, but think of what I would have missed with Jeff if I'd stayed with Ole Sorenson. I sat up abruptly, my ponytail brushing against the back of the wicker chair. It was time to change the subject. "Have the police told you anything?"

"I know Anthony's death is being considered a homicide. They fully expect the coroner's report to substantiate their theory. I just can't imagine it."

I wasn't sure if I should volunteer this information but I saw no reason not to. "The police seem to be honing in on one of Jeff's keepers, JR Erling."

She almost spilled her tea at the news. "They've arrested him?"

"They have to find him first. He disappeared last night."

Her gaze locked onto mine, her pale brows drawn into a V. "They don't honestly think he killed Anthony, do they?"

I didn't miss a beat. "No way. I haven't known JR that long but I can't imagine him hurting a soul."

Melanie found some comfort in that. Her body visibly relaxed, as though she was relieved. "I can't imagine anyone at the zoo being involved in this."

"Did Anthony ever mention JR? Is it possible they knew each other?" I asked.

JR certainly hadn't let on if he had. Sure, Wright had been head of the zoo, but most of the keepers dealt with the curator of their animal collection, and the curators dealt with the zoo director. JR's interaction with Anthony Wright would have been extremely limited.

For the first time a trace of bitterness edged Melanie's voice. "I'm afraid I'm not the person to ask about something like that. Anthony rarely confided in me. If you want to know if he knew your friend JR, you'll have to ask Suzanne Terak." She set her cup down with an ungentle clatter. "She did everything but bathe that man. I'm not complaining; she certainly made my life easier. I should show you the beautiful cashmere sweater she picked out for him to give me on our anniversary. The woman really does have exquisite taste."

But maybe not so much sense? And that surprised me. Were the rumors about Suzanne and her boss true? Had there been more than a working relationship there?

"Was she sleeping with him?" Melanie echoed my thoughts, once again looking relaxed. Or was it relief? "I don't really know," she went on. "And frankly, I don't care."

CHAPTER 8

The sun was just dipping below a rose-and-lilac horizon when I arrived home to find Jeff and Gary Olson sitting at the kitchen table discussing crocodile poo.

Gary looked startled as I burst through the door, my arms full of groceries. Chewing the end of his pencil, he slouched down in the chair, offering me a small, self-conscious smile. If he only knew how often the subject of animal scat was discussed at our dinner table. Sieving through animal excrement was a good indication of the size and health of an animal and gave researchers important information on dietary habits. I said as much, trying to put him at ease.

"So you're saying crocodiles aren't like sharks?" Gary took up the line of conversation I had interrupted.

Jeff, good husband that he was, jumped up to help his wife with her heavy load.

" 'Bout time, woman. We're fair starving here," Jeff teased, setting the bags on the counter and giving me a kiss before facing Gary again. "Aren't like sharks, how? I don't follow you, mate."

"I mean, with their scat . . ." Gary struggled as though stepping around something delicate. "Like, if a crocodile were to eat a tin can, say, would it pass through his bowels intact, or get pulverized to bits?"

"A bit of both, I think, unless he swallowed it whole. Crocodiles can't chew their food. Their teeth are designed for grabbing and tearing." Jeff clawed his fingers, bringing both hands together like a crocodile's jaws to demonstrate. "And they swallow stones to help mash up the food that they've eaten. So anything that's not digested would be a bit roughed up before coming out."

"Ahhh, okay." Gary sat back, a thoughtful frown on his face as he pondered this last.

"Is this the interview for your website?" I asked as I distributed the groceries between the cupboards and refrigerator.

Weeks ago, Gary had asked to interview Jeff and Anthony Wright for his student website, "Wildlife Times." An aspiring writer and journalist, Gary tended to dip too much into editorializing. The last article he wrote was a flaming opinion piece on the use of All Terrain Vehicles in the wilderness areas of northern Minnesota. It was, he said, clearly reckless and irresponsible, an environmental disaster in the making. He had done his research; I had to give him that—with photographs of torn-up marshes and heavily rutted tracks in once pristine grasslands—but he was definitely on the extreme side of the debate. To be honest, I wasn't quite sure how I felt about him inserting a piece about us on the same site. Under Jeff's influence, though, our young firebrand seemed to be finding more of a middle ground. Jeff was always more than happy to nurture along a budding environmentalist.

Gary, who seemed momentarily preoccupied, shook away the mental cobwebs. He tapped his yellow legal pad proudly, as though somewhere in the crammed notes lurked the seeds of a Pulitzer Prize. "Yeah, it's awesome. Jeff's given me so much material, enough for four articles."

"No surprise, Gary wants to be a journalist after he graduates," said Mr. Jones with an air of seriousness, as he raided the groceries left on the counter. "But I think he has the makings of a good croc man. He certainly has the interest, been asking me all sorts of questions about 'em, like how they attack, how they eat, even what's in their poo." Jeff chortled with amusement. Few things endeared people to him more than a genuine interest in his favorite animals.

Shrugging off the compliment, Gary rubbed a hand up and down his wrist in a self-conscious gesture. "I think I'll stick to writing for now. I'm not all that good with animals, though I wish I were."

"But you write passionately about animals and habitat all the time. That counts for something," I told him, hoping he wouldn't ask me for specifics.

I turned to Jeff and changed the subject. "Is Shari still here? I saw her car."

"She took Bagger for a walk about twenty minutes ago. She needed it, too."

"Still crying?"

"She had run out of juice by the time I'd gotten home. She's pulled herself together, I think—worried sick over JR. Can't say as I blame her."

"Have you heard from him at all today?" I asked, knowing the answer.

Jeff shook his head, his brow darkening. "A bit wonky, this. Not a blessed peep. That's not like him. The police say he didn't go home last night. They think he might've pulled up stumps for good."

"Run away?" The thought had never occurred to me, particularly with the implications behind it. I slumped back against the sink and exhaled heavily, trying to make sense of it.

An awkward silence fell onto the room.

Then Gary stirred. "Um," he began with difficulty, tentative eyes looking between Jeff and me. "Do the police think JR killed Mr. Wright?"

"I'm afraid so," I heard myself saying, feeling sick at the very thought of it.

"Not bloody possible," Jeff protested, almost defiantly, looking ready to take on the world. "He's a good bloke, saved my arse once or twice from them crocs. No, mate, I can't believe he did it."

But that wasn't the question. "I can't believe it either, Jeff," I soothed, "but I'm afraid the vibes I got from Ole this morning weren't good. JR looks as guilty as hell, running off like that." A knock on the door made us all jump. Speak of the devil. Detective Ole Sorenson stood on our doorstep.

"Lavender," he said curtly, without preamble, stepping just inside the door. He removed his Minnesota Twins baseball hat, thin wisps of hair refusing to join the comb-over. His partner, a large black woman with the blank expression of a sumo wrestler, stood on the bottom step and surveyed the assortment of bird feeders in our yard. It was getting dark and I began to wonder where Shari and Bagger had gone.

"One of your neighbors just reported seeing a suspicious-looking man lurking around your yard, then running back into the woods."

My gaze went across the road to the neighbor's house on the hill above our property. Old Mrs. Anderson, an elderly woman on her own with an inordinate amount of curiosity, particularly about the goings on at our place. The lights in her house were ablaze, and I pictured her stooped figure peering out from behind the curtains, satisfied that the police were doing their job.

"I appreciate the special attention, Detective, but aren't you a little out of your jurisdiction? Last I heard Lakeville had its own police force." Something told me I wasn't going to like what he said next.

He leveled a steely gaze on me while chomping on a wad of

gum. "We have reason to believe it may be John Erling."

"Well, that'd be dumb, wouldn't it? This is the last place he'd be. If he were running from the law, he'd be long gone by now."

Ole didn't answer, his eyes looking at me the way he used to when he thought I was being unreasonable.

At the table, Gary scraped his chair back. "It could have been me. The dreadlocks freak out some of the old-timers." He gave a tired shrug, as though this was the bane of his life.

Ole looked skeptical. "It's a possibility. When did you get here, son?"

"About an hour or so ago."

"Did you go into them woods?"

Gary pushed his glasses back up to the bridge of his nose. "No, I've been in here talking with Jeff since I got here . . ."

Ole wasn't convinced. "The call came in earlier. Sounds like someone else has been creeping around here. It could still be Erling. Is he here, Lavender?"

Jeff appeared next to me and I felt the comfort of his arm encircle my waist.

"You think JR is hiding here?" he challenged softly.

"Maybe."

"Then come in. Have a look."

Maybe it was Jeff's openness or maybe he didn't want to look foolish in front of an old flame, but Ole Sorenson hesitated. His gaze swept the kitchen, then took a quick tally of the number of coffee cups on the table versus the number of people in front of him. For a moment he appraised Gary with a penetrating look, as if he could make the younger man confess to JR's whereabouts. Finally, Ole looked from Jeff to me.

"Won't be necessary," he said with forced professionalism. "Leastways, not the house—"

"Did it ever occur to you that whoever killed Anthony Wright could very well have done something to JR?"

"It has." He shifted his eyes toward Jeff again, dismissing me. "We'd like to check out the yard and the barn, if you don't mind."

" 'Ave a go, mate."

Ole grunted back and took off with his partner. After all these years, he could still push my buttons. I checked my anger and watched for several minutes as the detectives went to the barn with drawn flashlights, splinters of light flashing between the wallboards marking their progress.

"Do you really think that could have been JR someone saw in our yard?" I asked Jeff.

"I hope not," Jeff replied in a hushed tone.

Twin beacons flashed toward us as Ole and his partner emerged from the barn. After another five minutes in the yard, they finally returned to their vehicle and drove off. Their taillights faded from sight as a thought occurred to me.

"Jeff, when did you say Shari left with Bagger?"

"About twenty minutes before you came home. She offered to take some trash out back and walk the dog."

"She took out the trash?"

We looked at each other for a moment. Something had struck us both as wrong. Before I could say something, the back door flew open and Bagger bounded in, making a beeline for his lord and master. Jeff sank to his knees and unhooked the leash while dodging some of the slobbering affection directed at him. Shari glided in a second later, looking refreshed and composed, attired in a pair of my shorts and Australia Zoo T-shirt.

"Snake, honey, I'm so glad you're home. Thanks for letting me stay this morning."

"You're looking better than when I left you."

"I feel better, too." She gave a nervous laugh, which grated on my already taut nerves. "What did the police tell you? Did they find anything?" She looked at us with questioning eyes, not nearly as fearful as she had been that morning.

"Should they have?" I came back with an uneasiness rising in my gut.

"No," Shari answered a little too innocently. "It's just that detective man makes me nervous. I don't think he likes me at all. He was just telling me to be careful."

"You spoke to Ole?"

"Not but a few minutes ago when I was walking back to the house from behind the barn." Shari's eyes darted among the three of us. "What did he say? They're gone aren't they? I saw them drive away just now."

Something fell in the basement, clattering as it bounced across the concrete floor. The sound startled all of us, freezing us in place as we listened, trying to decipher what we had just heard. Bagger began to bark, jumping at the basement door.

Shari grabbed my arm as I made a move toward the basement door. "It's just that old cat . . ."

But it wasn't the cat. Kow Tow was lapping water out of Bagger's bowl, oblivious to anyone else in the room.

As I restrained our protective golden retriever, Jeff threw the basement door open.

"Get up here!" He called down in a voice not to be messed with.

Silence. Then heavy footsteps mounted the treads and a stooped, dejected figure stepped into the kitchen. John Ray Erling looked tired, dirty, and at the end of his rope.

Bagger stopped barking as soon as he recognized his friend, straining against the hold I had on his collar. Shari flew past me into the arms of a very ill-at-ease JR. It now became clear why Shari had volunteered to take out the trash. It was camouflage for the food she had gathered for JR. And it had to have been JR the neighbor had seen. He must have come to the house earlier, before Jeff had come home, and been lurking around ever since.

"I told you to stay in the woods," Shari Jensen cried. "I said I'd take care of you, Johnny Ray."

Quietly I pulled down the kitchen shades and turned off the yard light. Then I thought again and closed the windows, locking out the serenade of frogs and crickets that performed nightly during the summer. JR set Shari aside and plopped himself down in one of our chairs, his shoulders slumped with the weight of the world, and regarded us with mute despair.

"Are you nuts?" I couldn't help myself, I was furious at him for running and for putting us in this position. "The cops just left and they already think we're hiding you."

JR lowered his gaze and capitulated. "I'm sorry . . . I had no place else to go. I'll clear out of here." He started to rise.

"Don't." I softened, feeling guilty for berating him. "Stay. Did you get enough to eat?"

He fell back into his seat again. "Yeah, Shari fed me earlier and just brought me something a while ago."

Jeff straddled the nearest chair and turned it toward the fugitive. "You've got some explaining to do, mate."

JR hung his head and Shari knelt at his feet, draping her arms across his lap.

"Why'd you bolt, mate?" Jeff asked, his voice stern. "It doesn't look good."

JR didn't look up. "I got here a couple hours ago. I needed to talk to you." He looked up at Jeff for an instant then back down at his clenched hands. "Shari was here. I hid in the basement until you got home."

"Oh, honey—" Tears threatened to spill over in Shari's eyes.

"That's when I had second thoughts about dragging the two of you into this. I went out into the woods instead, but didn't know where to go." He searched our faces for understanding.

"What about Anthony Wright?" I asked.

"I didn't kill him. You've got to believe me."

"Then why'd you bugger off?" Jeff wanted to know.

Gary had been unusually quiet since the police had shown up at our door. Now he looked at JR with a worried expression. "Did you see who murdered Mr. Wright? Is that why you took off?"

There was a heavy silence, broken only by the sound of Bagger's tail sweeping back and forth across the floor. JR seemed to struggle for the right words.

"You don't have to say a thing, Johnny Ray," Shari said, looking up at him with bright, tear-filled eyes, shaking her head from side to side. "Please don't say anything, honey."

"Yes, I do. I owe them that." He drew in a lengthy breath. "There was some trouble a few years ago."

"What kind of trouble?"

JR looked at each of us in turn then locked eyes with Shari. "I used to own and run a wildlife rehabilitation center in Sweetwater Creek, Florida. A beautiful place, not far from the Everglades. There was some trouble at the park and I was blamed for it."

"What kind of trouble?" Jeff repeated.

"We had some panthers. Florida panthers. We were doing everything we could to get their numbers up." His eyes shone with the passion of an animal lover. "There's only about seventy left in the wild. When one of our rescues had cubs, we were ecstatic. Not all of them survived—or so we thought."

"Someone sold them illegally, didn't they?" Gary jumped in, his eyes wide, eager. He looked to each of us in turn. "I researched some of that stuff months ago. You wouldn't believe how endangered animals are sold to private owners for pets and canned hunts. It's almost as lucrative as drug dealing. Even zoos get in on the action."

Jeff turned on him. "Not true. No zoo is going to risk their accreditation doing something that stupid. For some species, we're the last hope for survival. They don't even exist in the wild."

Gary quickly deflated at being upbraided by his hero. He slumped back in his chair.

"He's not far off base, I'm afraid." JR's eyes were filled with a strange mixture of anger and acceptance. "There's always some unscrupulous bastard willing to do anything for a few extra bucks. Somebody set me up and I was too busy trying to keep the place going to notice."

JR clasped his hands together and his face hardened. It was easy to see how difficult this was for him as the memories flooded back. He waited a moment before continuing. "Before I knew what was happening, it was all dumped on me. The books were altered so it appeared I'd made the illegal sales. My reputation was ruined."

"Someone framed you?" Isn't that what all the crooks on TV claim? That they were taking the fall for the real villain? It was always easier to blame the other guy when something went wrong. But I had seen JR work with animals in Mexico, where we met him, and at the Minnesota Valley Zoo. That concern for wildlife wasn't a smoke screen. I couldn't believe I was that bad a judge of character. Still, enough skepticism crept into my voice to sting.

Averting his gaze, JR sat back in his chair, his energy rushing out of him like a punctured tire. You could feel the tension in the room as we waited for his answer. Swiftly, Shari jumped up and wrapped her arms round his neck, her face etched with pathos. "Don't say any more, honey. It'll only upset you. Don't."

After a moment, JR gently removed her hands, kissed them lightly, and then sat her down in a nearby chair.

Jeff leaned back stiffly, eyeing his friend with circumspection.

"Who framed you?"

The quiet anguish of the past came out as JR whispered, "I don't know . . ."

Gary Olson swallowed hard, clearly moved. I knew how he felt. None of us said a word, waiting patiently for JR to resume. When he did, it was with a sense of detachment.

"I lost the animal park," he continued, hesitant, staring at the floor. "My life fell apart. I knew no one would hire me, not in this country. I had to clear my name but I could barely support myself. Finally, I went to Mexico, and tried to start over. That's when I met you guys—"

A fist pounding on the back door made us all jump. Bagger threw himself at the door, barking until Jeff grabbed him by the collar. My heart sank at the sight of Detective Ole Sorenson and two uniformed police officers standing on our stoop. For one insane moment, I thought of keeping the door shut until JR could make a run for it. But we were already in enough trouble just having him here.

"I thought so." Ole grunted with satisfaction as he pushed into the kitchen, flanked by the two officers. He shot me an accusatory look mixed with disappointment. The last time I'd seen that look was the summer of my seventeenth year. Ole had taken me to a party and I'd had a couple of beers. I was no wild thing, but from the disapproval on Ole's face you'd have thought I was dancing naked on a tabletop. I had fallen off the pedestal he had put me on. He couldn't accept me for who I was, only for what he expected me to be. That look hadn't changed. This time I felt a genuine pang of guilt because we actually had been harboring a fugitive—without our knowledge, yes, but Ole would never believe that.

For his part, JR looked almost relieved to see the police. The tension eased out of his face, as if Fate had taken the anxiety of his next step out of his hands. He looked resigned to whatever happened next.

Ole stepped over to him, his manner brusque. "We ran a check on you, Erling. And you know what we found? Nothing. Then this morning we got a warrant to search your apartment." Ole spoke directly to JR as if the rest of us were of no consequence. "We found a copy of your birth certificate and checked it out again. And guess what?" Ole's voice rose in mock surprise. "There was only one John Ray Erling born on August fifteenth, 1945, in Ashland, Wisconsin, and he died at the age of three with his parents in a car accident."

JR hung his head. His voice was barely audible. "My name is James Robert O'Malley."

Shari clung to him. "Don't say another word, hon! We'll get you a real good lawyer. But don't say nothing."

With an air of defeat, he waved her off.

Ole stepped closer as one of the officers came forward with ready handcuffs. "Thanks for making it easy for us. But it didn't take us long to find out your real name—and your past. Better take your girlfriend's advice, O'Malley. You'll need a good lawyer."

Too dazed to speak, the rest of us watched silently as JR slowly hauled himself up, turned around and let his hands be cuffed behind his back.

Ole's voice tolled like a bell. "James Robert O'Malley, you're under arrest for the murder of Alexander Beatty in the state of Florida. You have the right to remain silent . . ."

Chapter 9

It was a struggle getting JR out the door, not through any resistance on his part. Quite the contrary. The spirit had left him, his face and body an empty shell of dejection. It was Shari who impeded his progress. She hung around his neck like the albatross of the Ancient Mariner, weighing him down, dragging like an anchor. As the police attempted to separate the two, she let out a mournful howl a trumpeting camel would have been proud of. I was ready to dig out the tranquilizer gun and shoot her, except that we'd still have to listen to her wail on for a good ten to fifteen minutes as the drug took effect. A clunk on the head would be more effective.

I should have been more sympathetic, I suppose, but this show of despair was over the top. She was a *Jerry Springer* episode waiting to happen. She refused to let go and allow JR what little dignity he had left.

Ole pushed open the door for the two officers, letting a much-needed breeze swirl through the airless kitchen. With his hands cuffed behind him, JR struggled to remain upright as the two uniformed officers each hooked an arm and escorted him and the adhering girlfriend outside as one conjoined unit. He lost his footing on the steps, nearly toppling Ole and the entire crew over the wrought-iron railing, and still Shari would not let go. For a moment, I thought they might toss her into the back of the police car along with JR; but they thought better of it, making another attempt to pry her loose.

Jeff finally joined the scuffle, adding his strength to wrestle her off JR, so the police could lock him into the back seat of the squad car. I swear, it was almost as much work as mud wrestling a crocodile. Eventually, the squad left with its prisoner, and Jeff and Ole dragged the inconsolable woman back into the house.

Stumbling across the threshold, she slumped onto the floor, back pressed against the wall. Overhead, a bull elephant charged at us from the page of a wildlife calendar. In a gush of silent tears, her knees came up to her chest and she buried her face into her folded arms, her body trembling between muted sobs.

Gary sat transfixed, like a deer caught in the headlights of an oncoming car. His face reflected the pain and betrayal I felt, the same raw wound I read in Jeff's face as he slouched at the kitchen table.

"I liked JR," Gary said, his voice barely a whisper, his eyes downcast. "He never got tired of answering my questions. He even let me touch Sebastian's tail once. This really sucks."

"Let's not talk about him in the past tense, shall we," Jeff said tersely, absently rubbing Bagger's head. He regarded Ole with a frosty stare. "JR was just telling us he was framed. Accused of selling endangered animals."

"That's his story," Ole said pointedly, still standing near the kitchen door, baseball cap in hand.

"And you say he's wanted for murder." It was a statement, not a question, the shock of what had happened written in the tense lines around Jeff's eyes.

Shari began to sob openly again, rocking back and forth, her muffled wet gurgles painful to listen to. It was as if her very soul had been ripped away.

Feeling as awkward as the rest of us, Gary rose slowly, as if under a heavy burden, and gestured haplessly toward the kitchen door. "Mom's going to wonder what happened to me," he said, backing toward the door, slipping past Ole, his eyes downcast.

We half mumbled a farewell, Jeff telling him to drive safely, and we were alone again with Ole. I wished I could have gone with Gary, but it was my house, so I did the next best thing and went to the pantry and came back with a box of tissues, placing it on the floor beside Shari. Part of me wanted to do more for her, but it wasn't in me. She was like a wild prairie fire that needed to burn out on its own.

"He didn't kill anyone!" Shari cried into her knees, her voice trembling.

"How do you know that?" Ole asked with gentle skepticism.

I was standing next to Shari as she gathered herself together. She lifted her head, scrubbing at her dripping nose with a shaking hand and the sleeve of my T-shirt. "I just know Johnny Ray," she said staring at the toes of her shoes. "He's not a killer."

"Really?" Ole shook his head and spoke to us as if he was addressing a kindergarten class. "Five years ago Alexander Beatty was murdered in Florida. Last night another man died. Both bodies were made to look like a wild animal had attacked them. Your friend was in the vicinity at the time of both murders. He ran away from both crimes. And he's been using an assumed name. Exactly what part of his behavior makes you think he's innocent?"

My confidence wavered. I felt the tension that had been building in my neck and chest let go as I realized I really had no absolute reason to think JR was innocent. For Jeff, who had grown up in the outdoors and was used to the simplicity of reading the measure of a person or an animal as though it were a well-marked trail, this was hard. Too many nuances to take in at once. His weathered face darkened with mixed emotions as he ran his hand through his sandy-colored hair.

We had trusted JR—or James O'Malley—or whatever his

name was. We had called him friend, and now we were in the middle of this mess. The two of us had taken an instant liking to JR when we had met him at the Croco Cun Zoological Gardens south of Cancun, Mexico. His hospitality had put us at ease, and to a seasoned croc man like Jeff, there was no finer testament to the man's character than seeing his dedication to crocodilian research and care. JR had taken it upon himself to drive us down to the beautiful Sian Ka'an Biosphere Reserve, where we observed American crocodiles and morelettis in their wild habitat. He had never worked with saltwater crocs before and pumped Jeff for every bit of knowledge he had.

It was Jeff who finally asked him to come to work for him at the zoo. JR had hesitated at first, but when we told him about the sizeable donation Hanley-Holm Department Stores was sinking into the new Australian exhibit and our plans to transport salties to Minnesota, he started to come around. It was Shari who had continued to oppose the idea. And we would have happily left her in Mexico.

"Did you know O'Malley back then, in Florida?" Ole asked, squatting down in front of Shari.

"No." She spat the answer at him, then sniffed. "No, I didn't. I told you before, I met him in Mexico. I've never been to Florida." Her eyes filled with tears again and the old scar on her lip turned a shade darker.

She was lying.

And I wondered why she hadn't lied in the first place in order to give JR an iron-clad alibi at the zoo. If she had vouched for him, the police might have turned their radar toward someone else. She hadn't been with him the entire evening, but had left the dinner to get a plate of food so JR could concentrate on Sebastian and Babe. Or so she had said. I hadn't seen her at dinner. Or during the confusion following the discovery of Wright's body.

Coolly, Ole said to Shari, "It's not hard to check that out, y'know."

Shari Jensen gripped her legs tightly and her body shook as she choked back a sob. Jeff and I exchanged looks. We were getting the same vibes. After you've dealt with animal behavior as long as we had, you realize humans react much the same as our four-legged kinsmen. Shari looked like a cornered animal, curled into a defensive posture, as if protecting her vulnerable parts from a predator. If I hadn't known better I'd have thought she was scared—not for JR, but for herself.

Ole seemed to take pity on her. He scratched at his thinning hair before setting his cap in place. He fished a business card out of his jacket and laid it on the table next to Jeff. "When she gets control of herself, have her call me. I still have questions for her. There's no point in subjecting her to this now."

With measured steps, Ole Sorenson moved closer to the door. The world-weary face under the baseball cap took us all in carefully. When he spoke, he sounded almost defensive. "I know this is tough for you. You thought he was your friend. But right now we don't have any reason to look any further for another suspect in Wright's killing. The facts are simple: O'Malley was supposed to be at the croc exhibit last evening. If he was there, then he would have seen or heard what happened to Wright and could explain it—except he can't explain it because it would implicate him. So he ran. He ran because he knows who killed Wright: he did. The proof will be found, and if it's not, he'll be extradited to Florida. Either way, he's dead meat." Ole opened the back door to leave, clearly uncomfortable. "I'm sorry about all this, but it's my job. People are taken in by con men like O'Malley all the time. I'm just sorry it had to be you."

The door shut, and for a moment the only sound in the country kitchen was Bagger whining because Jeff had stopped stroking his head. Jeff rested his elbows on his knees, leaning closer to Shari. His complexion reddened but he did a good job of keeping the anger out of his voice. He was a man who was dead loyal to his friends, and he had been let down, first by JR and now Shari.

"You're not telling us everything," he said, the weariness heavy in his voice. "If you know something that will help, you need to tell the coppers. They reckon they've got their man and they aren't going to look further. You heard the detective say as much. Shari, look at me. . . ."

Slowly she lifted her head, but she did not meet Jeff's eyes. We could see the wheels turning behind those troubled eyes as she blew her nose and wadded up the tissue. With a hard swallow, she spoke in a voice barely audible, "You have to help him. He was framed for that killing in Florida. He told you he was framed. Why can't you believe him?"

"I'd like to believe him, Shari, but he lied to me about his past, about who he was—how do I know he isn't lying to me about this, too?"

"He only lied because the police were after him. Would you have hired him if he'd told you he was a wanted man?"

"No."

"See?"

There was a pause.

I rolled my eyes. "Why didn't you just stay in Mexico where he was safe?"

"Because he had to come up here to work with them damned lizards of yours."

"It seems a hell of a risk to take."

"Well, and there was—" She cut herself off.

"Yes?" Jeff prompted. "You were going to say?"

"Nothin'."

"Sounded like you had something to say."

Shari slowly twirled a lock of her curly hair around her finger.

"It's just . . . well, he was desperate to work in the States again and to try to prove he didn't kill that man."

Jeff moved his chair closer. "How about telling us what happened in Florida? JR left that murder part out when he was speaking to us. What d'you know about it?"

"Johnny Ray told me what happened." Shari popped a tissue out of the box and dabbed at her eyes, her voice growing stronger, filled with purpose. "He told me the whole thing."

Jeff straightened. "JR told you?"

"Yeah. That man was already dead when Johnny Ray found him. One of them panthers had attacked him. There was blood everywhere. The lock on the cage had been meddled with and my po' JR's fingerprints were all over from trying to get the damned thing open so he could get the man outta there."

Tipping backwards in his chair, Jeff stared at the tiled ceiling and pressed his lips in thought. "The murdered man, Alexander Beatty, worked for him?"

"Yes, sir. He was one of the keepers. Took care of the big cats."

"So it wasn't surprising he was in the cage, then." Jeff looked at me. "Can't really go further without knowing more. Still, even if this is true, how does it tie in with Wright and his murder?"

"It just plain don't," she grumbled, staring at her toes. Then her gaze shot up, searchingly. "Don't ya'll see? JR didn't run away 'cause he killed Mr. Wright, he ran 'cause he knew the police would find out about Florida when they checked up on him."

I thought about last night. The ball. All the well-heeled patrons. JR had been so concerned about the crocodiles, going as far as skipping dinner. Shari hadn't been too happy about that. In fact, they had been arguing quite a bit that evening. So I asked her about it.

She denied it.

"Shari, we saw you. Half the people at the zoo saw you. In fact, I thought Melanie Wright was going to walk over and ask the two of you to leave."

Her mouth formed an angry line but I persevered. "We're your friends, Shari. You came to me this morning because you wanted my help. Well, if you want it, you have to be straight with us. If you really care about JR, then don't tell us something we know isn't true."

"This thing is between me and Johnny Ray." She raised her nose a little higher and pushed Kow away as the cat brushed against her.

"Don't you mean Jimmy Bob?"

She frowned, looking like a petulant teenager.

"His real name is James Robert O'Malley, isn't it?" I pointed out.

She winced but had no reply. After a moment she struggled to her feet, her face swollen with tears, and announced she was going home. She refused to say more.

Jeff and I looked at each other. What was Shari up to? Of course she might not have been up to anything, I realized, the occasional childish outburst being one of her less endearing character traits.

In the end it was decided it was best if I drove her home in her car and Jeff followed in our truck. It wasn't my first choice, but for some reason Jeff thought she'd be more likely to confide in me. Except that I was tired, worn out and not in the mood to suddenly become Shari's best friend.

JR and Shari rented a small townhouse just east of the interstate in Burnsville. The ride seemed longer than usual, my attempts at small talk falling on deaf ears. She refused to talk, staring out the window at the neon retail lights that lined the freeway, adding color to the dark, starless night. Even the crying had stopped. The uneasy feeling that she knew a lot more than she was telling weighed on me. Even with all that had been revealed this evening, I couldn't believe JR was guilty of two murders. There had to be more to it. Call it curiosity or loyalty to a friend, but I needed to know. For my own peace of mind, if nothing else. How could I ever trust my own judgment again, knowing I had befriended a killer?

"It's not going to take the police long to learn the truth," I said as we reached the outskirts of Apple Valley, repeating Ole's warning that they would have an easy time checking out her story. "If you're hiding something, the police are going to find out."

"Just like they found out about JR?" she asked, speaking at last, still staring out the window.

"You'd be better off telling them whatever you know, or they could throw you in jail for obstructing justice." I didn't know that, but it sounded good. I was desperate to get the woman to talk—ironic, as you usually couldn't get her to shut up.

"At least I'd be safe there."

A muscle caught in my neck as I turned my head too quickly. "Safe from who? JR?"

She faced forward for a moment, twisting a tissue around her finger, her stricken face lit in the light of an oncoming car. "My husband."

You can't imagine my relief when I was back in the truck with Jeff and heading home again.

"Odd, isn't it?" he mused as he shifted the old Ford F-series into gear and peeled out of the townhouse's driveway. "As fiercely loyal and protective as she is—"

"Possessive, you mean."

"Yeah, that, too." He grinned in the darkness. It was only the two of us now, alone, away from Shari and the police, able to be ourselves. "I'm surprised she didn't give JR an alibi for the night Wright was killed."

"She had her reasons."

We were stopped at a streetlight, brightly lit strip malls stretching out in each direction. Behind us a car had its bass speaker at full volume, blasting us with the vibrating beat of gangsta rap.

"Snake, what's up? You know something, you little ripper." He gave me a gentle poke.

Ticklish, I instinctively flinched away, grabbed his hand and squeezed it. Shari had told me more than I wanted to know. Once she had started talking, she couldn't stop. I felt sick, the knowledge constricting my chest like a vise. I had never been overly charitable toward Shari, her neediness and dependence on JR something I didn't understand. Or try to understand.

"Shari was in Florida with JR," I began, knowing this would come as no surprise to Jeff.

The light changed and we headed south on 35W.

"I figured as much. Why didn't she tell us that in the first place?" Jeff slapped his hand against the steering wheel. "Crikey, what's the big to-do?"

Putting myself in her shoes, I thought of what she'd told me and tried to imagine the kind of life that would fill her with so much terror she would rather see her man go to jail for murder than give him an alibi.

"She was running away, too."

Jeff was startled. "Shari's running from the coppers as well?"

The truck had no air-conditioning and I had to raise my voice to be heard over the rush of summer air that was our cooling system. "Her husband."

"Whoa!" The lights of an oncoming car shone in Jeff's wide eyes as he momentarily took his gaze from the highway to look at me. "She's married?"

"The broken cheekbone, the scar on her lip. All his gifts to her."

Jeff let out a groan and I scooted as close to him as I could under the restraints of the seatbelt, resting my head on his shoulder as he steered us through the night. For a moment we both stared straight ahead, the oncoming traffic on the highway a long succession of white and yellow orbs heading for the city. Shari's dependency and devotion to JR all made sense now.

"JR rescued her," I said softly, feeling the warmth and comfort of Jeff's presence. "He took her with him when he ran off to Mexico and helped change her identity when he changed his. He saved her from an abusive husband who'd hunt her down and beat her—if not kill her—if he knew where she was."

"So checking into her background might tip off the hubby and he'd come after her—"

"Which is why she didn't give JR an alibi. If they suspected him, the police were going to check her background, too. She tried to distance herself from him."

I hoped I would never forget how lucky I was to have a man like Jeff in my life. That I would never take him for granted. I couldn't imagine what Shari's life had been like with her husband, filled with fear, not knowing from day to day if he was going to be kind or violent. And now I felt the need to make up for my uncharitable thoughts toward her and try to help clear JR.

Chapter 10

It was Monday and the zoo was closed again. Sometime during the night someone had capsized most of the trash bins along the Walkabout Trail and strewn the garbage along the paths. The bins were big, heavy things with concrete bottoms, not easily moved or tipped over. Security had immediately called the police and the police had chosen to shut us down for yet another day. Whether this incident was connected to the murder or was an unrelated act of vandalism was under investigation.

I jumped on this small shred of hope. If the murderer had been in the zoo last night looking for something, then JR couldn't be guilty. And my old friend Ole Sorenson would have to look for another suspect.

The thought buoyed me as I dragged out the hose to wash down the enclosure our small-clawed otters called home. It had been a long night for Jeff and me, talking into the wee hours. After sorting through our mixed emotions, we had decided that we still believed in JR's innocence, and that, given the facts, we could understand his reluctance to tell us the truth about his past when we'd first met him. You don't blurt out to just anyone that you're wanted for a murder, regardless if you didn't commit it. But it didn't look good. The deck was truly stacked against him, but Jeff and I believed our friend couldn't have killed anyone. It just wasn't in him. Equally clear last night was the fact that the police were not going to look much further than the man they had already arrested. Hopefully, the vandalism on the Australian Walkabout would change their minds. Otherwise, I'd have to start poking around on my own.

What that meant, I wasn't sure, but neither of us could sit on the sidelines and do nothing. Shari had made me promise to help JR before she let me leave her townhouse the night before. I was prepared to stick my neck out and see what I could unearth; for JR's sake, not for Shari's. And most certainly that meant having to figure out who had really killed Anthony Wright. I didn't read mysteries and rarely watched the popular police dramas on TV. But zookeeping often held an element of detective work. Dealing with animals that couldn't speak for themselves involved looking for clues to their health and behavior. How much harder could it be to find clues proving JR's innocence?

A sparkle at the bottom of the exhibit's small pool caught my eye. The otters had missed a quarter and a dime. Visitors to the zoo seem to think every pond is a wishing well and so they toss in money. The otters dive in, grab a coin, waddle up to the closed door hidden in a crook of the faux rock and slip their treasures under the door to the keepers. We told the little guys we couldn't be bribed and that they'd have to wait until the zoo closed to be fed, like everyone else, but they kept retrieving the coins for us anyway.

I scooped the money from the bottom of the pond and pocketed it until later. There was a jar in the kitchen that held the coins our entrepreneur otters collected. Someone had taped a note to the jar that said "College Fund." Yesterday someone had crossed out "college" and wrote "retirement." Which really wasn't that funny considering the zoo had now missed two days of revenue due to the police investigation. It wasn't helping our already strained budget.

I put down fresh straw and let the otters into the exhibit. Later I would give them a special treat and add some live minnows to the pond for them to swim after and snack on.

I looked up to see Jeff on the visitor side of the fence, leaning against the top rail and grinning at me.

I treated him to a gentle sprinkle from the hose. "How long have you been standing there?"

"Long enough to see you talking to yourself."

It was a bad habit of mine. I moved up to the fence and planted a kiss on that grin.

"Want to go to Dr. Steve's with me?" he asked, not at all offended that I had gotten him wet. "He's X-raying Rocky this morning. Wants me to have a bo-peep at him."

Rocky, our five-and-a-half-foot Komodo monitor, had been feeling poorly, and the decision had been made to sedate him and take some X-rays. I was thrilled at the invitation to join Jeff. I had never seen the insides of a Komodo dragon before.

"How's the clean-up going?" I asked as we left the building and took the utility path to the animal health center.

It wasn't quite as humid outside as it had been in the Tropics building. It was warm, the sun high in the sky, but a slight breeze kept it from the stifling heat we'd be in for in a month or two.

"Not as bad as security made it sound," Jeff said, slipping on a pair of sunglasses. "The trash bins had been emptied before the fundraiser, so there really wasn't that much trash to scatter. Still, I'd like to get my hands on the rotter who'd do something like that."

"The police have any ideas?"

"Not really. They said it could be kids."

"Kids!"

"Or pranksters."

"At least they can't say it was JR."

"He could have had an accomplice, luv—not that I believe that of course," he added after seeing the disappointment in my face. "It's what the police are thinking."

"Well, they'll have to find this person and prove he's connected with JR. And if they can't find him, that opens up the possibility JR didn't do it. That's something at least."

The zoo's animal health center was built on the far side of the African Trail, bordered by a wide stand of trees and shrubs that made you forget there were upper-crust townhouses being built on the other side. The wide windows of the hospital ward faced this woodland, giving the animals under veterinary care something to look at besides concrete and bars. There was also a quarantine area, a necropsy room, an animal commissary and a laboratory. The once state-of-the-art surgical room was in need of some updating, and there were those who felt it should have taken priority over a new Australian trail.

Dr. Steve Coen was waiting for us in his office. A fixture at the zoo since it had opened twenty-five years ago, the veterinarian had never lost enthusiasm for his job. Despite the fact that he had to be in his early sixties, Dr. Steve's longish blond hair was untouched by gray and his sky-blue eyes were crisp and clear behind the oversized tortoiseshell glasses that slipped to the end of his long nose.

The Komodo's X-rays were clipped to the light box on the wall. Looking at the film, the relationship between birds and reptiles was easy to see. The shape of the skull, the limbs as they were spread from the body. It wasn't too hard to imagine the outlined shape covered in feathers.

What was surprising was a large mass in the bottom of his stomach. A shape with two black unblinking eyes and long fuzzy ears.

"A toy? He swallowed a toy?"

"A bunny," Dr. Steve intoned.

Coins weren't the only thing zoo guests dropped into zoo exhibits. Small toys were another favorite. As were baby bottles, pacifiers, mittens and the plastic animals the zoo sold in the gift shop. And a Komodo's jaws could stretch and unhinge, allowing them to accommodate even the largest Teddy bear. They usually ate wild boar, goats and deer. At the zoo they're fed rats, chicken, fish and quail. Not toy bunnies.

"What do you think, Jeff? Can he can pass that through?" Dr. Steve studied the black-and-white radiograph intently, a measure of uncertainty in his voice.

"Hard to say." Jeff moved in closer, squinting at the X-ray. "We had one down in Sydney a couple years ago, swallowed a ring of keys. Came out the other end a few days later."

"Could do an ultrasound on him," the vet considered out loud, "but that probably wouldn't tell us much more. It'd be a lot easier if we had an idea when he ate this." Dr. Steve pushed his glasses back up his nose. "I noticed a slight change in his behavior three days ago. We've been monitoring excrement and so far everything looks normal. Last night he seemed a bit more lethargic and there's been no improvement today."

"Is he eating?"

"Not as much as he had, but he's still passing it."

"That's a good sign."

I couldn't help but think Gary Olson would have enjoyed this discussion, remembering his fascination with crocodile excrement last night. Then again, my mother could say the same of me. She never tires of telling the story of how I came home from grade school and showed her the cool rock I had found. Rather, it was a rock-hard, aged-over-the-winter genuine dog scat. She had turned her nose up in disgust, got a very large piece of paper towel to pick it up with and threw it out the door.

We walked back to the hospital ward to look in at the sleeping Komodo, which lay on a stainless-steel exam table, under the watchful eyes of Dr. Steve's assistant, Carol. The anesthesia machine was mounted on a mobile stand next to the electronic monitors that tracked the lizard's vital signs. Rocky's color was still good and his breathing was normal.

Jeff got down low and peered in at him. "You might try some mineral oil, see if that has any effect. Otherwise, you'll have to go in and pull it out."

With no clear-cut solution on our Komodo but to wait and observe a while longer, I went back to the Tropics building where I shared office space behind the nocturnal exhibit with the other keepers. It was a cluttered bunker of whitewashed cinderblock walls and one small casement window. Stacks of old zoo bulletins and newsletters were piled on top of a row of filing cabinets, bending Tower-of-Pisa-like toward the coffee maker. Wire-framed In and Out baskets along the metal desk were stuffed with mail, reports, inventory forms, and packing slips. Clipboards with health data sheets hung on the wall beneath a large erasable monthly calendar marked up in a profusion of black and green ink. In the far corner were two sturdy tables hosting several aquariums that housed a green boa, geckos, and several dart frogs. The lingering tang of dry animal feed hung in the air.

There, at our cramped little computer area, I found Mitch Flanagan staring into the monitor.

"Got spam?" I asked, noticing the sour look on his face.

"E-mail's going to be the undoing of family life," he grumbled, his handlebar moustache seesawing over a discontented frown. "My own mother doesn't hear from me for three weeks. Does she call to see if I'm still breathing? No. She sends me an e-mail."

I should be so lucky. I still hadn't returned my mother's several phone calls.

Mitch was well-known around the zoo for his less-than-sunny

disposition. If there was something to complain about, he'd find it. Except when it concerned his birds. He never complained about the care and feeding of his birds. They were his life.

"Other than that, how's it going?" I hoped I wasn't opening a can of worms. Asking Mitch how he was doing was like giving him an invitation to unload on the ills of the world. He might not volunteer his opinions outright but, hell, if you were rash enough to ask him what he thought about things he'd give you an earful, usually negative.

What I didn't expect from him was unabashed optimism. The bright smile took me aback. "The raptor center is a distinct possibility again."

"Really?" The night of the Beastly Ball it had been a dead issue. "What'd you do, take my advice and sweet talk some rich donor?"

Mitch snorted. "Not exactly. But change is blowin' in the wind, kiddo. Mark my words, if Butler Thomas gets his hands on the operations budget, I'm sure he'll be the first to write a check."

It was my turn to frown as Mitch got up and I took his place at the computer and logged in. "What has Butler got to do with this?"

"Ding dong the witch is dead, woman. Can't you feel the difference? It's like the collapse of the Berlin Wall, like the fall of a tyrant."

"Wright wasn't that bad, Mitch."

"Maybe not for you. You got your Walkabout Trail, Snake. Other projects around here were put to death under the Wright regime. The man was so damned shortsighted. But that's changed. Butler's in charge now and he's always been one hundred percent behind the raptor exhibit."

The shock on my face must have shown. He threw his hands in the air and plopped down in the room's only other chair.

"Hey! Just because the guy is dead, I'm not going to start pretending I liked him. Anthony Wright was an asshole with a capital A. And plenty of others around here would agree with me."

It wasn't his callous comment about Wright that shocked me; it was what he had implied about Butler Thomas. "Butler reversed Wright's decision on the raptor center?"

"Not yet. But as soon as the board of directors appoint him zoo director, he will."

As far as I was concerned, Butler was the best choice for the now vacant position of zoo director, but all of this seemed a bit premature. Wright hadn't even been buried yet.

I eyed Mitch skeptically. "He told you that?"

"What? That he's going to be the next director or he's going to give me my raptor center?"

"Both, actually."

Inexplicably, Mitch bolted out of the chair and headed to the door like a man with a fire lit underneath him. He paused momentarily at the threshold. "Who else are they going to pick, kiddo? Butler's been working as assistant director at the zoo for ten years now. He's already been passed over once. If the Board does that again, they're going to lose him, and that would be a crime."

Mitch was out the door before I could press him for details. I wanted to know exactly what Butler had told him. I couldn't believe he'd make a promise like that. And given the way Mitch could blow things out of proportion, I doubted he had.

CHAPTER 11

"You've got chocolate on your chin." Billie Bradshaw glanced at me before opening the oven door to slip in another cookie sheet covered with evenly spaced rows of uniform lumps of chocolate chip cookie dough. Who would have thought our tough-as-nails producer also had a domestic side?

Busted. I was hoping she hadn't seen me sneak a warm chocolate chip cookie off the counter. An attempt to lick the chocolate from my chin was interrupted by a prolonged yawn. It had been a long, hard day at the zoo and I was beat, but instead of going home at the end of our shifts, Jeff and I had ended up in Billie's kitchen for a *Zoofari* production meeting.

Despite the luscious aroma of fresh-baked cookies, Billie's Apple Valley condominium was not what you would call warm and fuzzy. I pictured her walking into the model condo and buying it, display furnishings and all. It lacked the personal touches: photographs, favorite paintings, ugly but treasured knickknacks, or the old beat-up chair that has been carted from place to place. All of the things I looked forward to going home to were missing from Billie's place.

The kitchen was small and windowless with little ornamentation other than a quartet of framed fruit photographs symmetrically arranged on the wall, breaking up the monotony of white. The round glass table beneath the photographs bore the only stamp marking this as Billie's territory: piles of paperwork for future installments of our cable TV show.

"I never would have guessed you were such a domestic diva, Billie," Jeff said as she plopped a plate of freshly baked cookies on top of the paperwork, effectively screening me from reading her notes on tonight's meeting and getting a hint of why she had called us together. Although Jeff was the executive producer of *Zoofari,* his curator duties at the zoo took up most of his attention, so Billie's job was to oversee the day-to-day production chores of the show.

There was a knock at the door and Shaggy wandered in, not waiting for an invite. He sauntered into the kitchenette, helped himself to a still-warm cookie and leaned against the doorframe. "Bodacious!" He held up the remnants of the morsel, nodding with approval. You would have thought he'd found Nirvana. Then his attention was diverted. "Somethin' bugging you, Bill?"

Shaggy had a nickname for everyone. Billie was just Bill. Jeff was The Man. Gary was The Kid. And I was still Snake.

Billie glowered at him, her dark hazel eyes shadowed by overlong silver bangs and generously penciled-in eyebrows. It was a middle-aged face etched with the creases of experience and adversity. She had toughed her way through life and the hard shell she had developed along the way seemed to have become her nature, though I had once heard she had been sweet and somewhat innocent as a young woman.

That had been a long time ago.

"She only bakes when she's pissed about something," Shaggy confided in a stage whisper. "Kind of like therapy, y'know."

Shaggy had worked with Billie on several documentaries over the years. He was her first choice as cameraman for *Zoofari,* his laid-back outlook on life impervious to her drill-sergeant sensibilities. Our other camera operators were temps, friends of Shaggy who came and went each couple of episodes, depending on their availability.

I smiled back at him. "If I'd known she made such fabulous cookies, I would have upset her a long time ago."

Billie was not amused. She shook a long wooden spoon at me. "Snake, this isn't funny. Dammit, this murder scandal could ruin us."

"As to that," Jeff said, helping himself to a cookie, "I talked to Butler today and he fully expects attendance to increase as soon as we're able to open our doors again. Judging by the calls he's been getting, people are very eager to see the new Aussie Trail and its killer crocodile." He took a savage bite of chocolate chip. "It's morbid, I grant you, but the publicity may be the one positive thing to come from this tragedy."

Billie huffed. "Butler is a marketing guy. Leave it to him to find a positive spin on this."

"What I'm saying, Billie, is this may not be the disaster you seem to think."

"You don't get it, do you? Have you read the papers?" She grabbed a copy of the *Minneapolis Star Tribune* and tossed it on the table. "They're talking about a murder in Florida that could be connected to Wright's death, one that involved the sale of endangered animals. Not something any zoo wants to be connected with. And you hired the man at the heart of it all. *Zoofari* is going to be implicated and our credibility ruined."

The spoon waved between Jeff and me. Ignoring it, I looked her squarely in the eye. "Billie, the show's important to all of us, but have a little compassion for JR. Think of what he's going through."

"Yeah, Bill," Shaggy chided, leaning against the breakfast counter, as he rubbed his chin whiskers. "The dude could be heading for death row, man. That's some pretty heavy shit."

The spoon was about to speak but slowly came down as Billie lowered her hand.

She plopped down in the chair next to me, her gruff exterior softening as she regarded the rest of us contritely. "Sorry. That was harsh."

She swallowed hard, then seemed to struggle a moment as she collected her thoughts. "Our show means everything to me. We're on the brink of going national in a year. I just don't want to blow it." Her eyes flared and her face hardened. "We've all worked so damned hard over the past ten months. Opportunities like this don't come along every day, and just when we were about to get great exposure, this . . . this incident had to—!" Billie choked off her words and turned away.

She was a passionate woman and a bit of a perfectionist, and working with Jeff and me must have driven her a little crazy, since we were anything but that. Pressing her lips together, she seemed to be willing herself to remain calm as the rest of us watched her. "Anyway," she continued softly, with restraint, "I feel like the rug is being pulled out from under us. I know JR is hurting. It was a shock hearing about his arrest. I like JR as much as you guys. But—" her eyes swept the room—"what if he's guilty?"

The kitchen fell silent.

Behind her the rhythmic ticking of the wall clock beat out each passing second. None of us really believed JR was guilty; yet much of that faith was probably a knee-jerk reaction, friends rallying around someone we cared for. That he might actually be guilty of the crime was too sensitive a topic to explore, like ripping the bandage off a fresh wound. Nobody really wanted to look.

Finally Jeff stirred. "There was a swarm of people at the zoo that night," he offered. "Anyone could've crept in and out again. Security wasn't ironclad."

"My moola is on that gnarly politician dude." Shaggy nodded toward the photograph of Senator Ted McNealey on the front page of the newspaper, his look of shock and dismay seeming rather overdone.

I scanned the article, Jeff reading over my shoulder. It hadn't taken McNealey long to exploit this tragedy for his own self-interest. The article showed him taking a very public stance. On one hand, it said, he supported the zoo and knew in his heart none of our dedicated staff could be implicated in this misfortune. On the other, he intended to "get to the bottom of the situation" and would spearhead a thorough investigation of the matter, promising to bring any wrongdoer to justice.

"He did seem a bit upset at dinner that evening," I tossed out tentatively, not wanting my dislike of the man to cloud my judgment. I needed to retain some objectivity if I were going to help JR.

"That's putting it mildly." Billie snorted. "Wright must have reamed him over pretty good to get him that bent out of shape."

Jeff and I exchanged a puzzled look, then turned our attention back to Billie.

"Didn't you know? Wright and McNealey had an argument just before dinner." Billie picked up the mixing bowl and helped herself to a chunk of cookie dough. "And no small tiff, mind you. It was a barn burner."

"You saw them arguing?"

"Not me. Shaggy."

Our heads swiveled back to our head cameraman.

The Shagster gestured vaguely. "I was coming up the trail, filming from the visitor's POV, ya know?" He waited until we nodded our understanding and went on, his hands up to his face, mimicking a camera viewfinder. "Senator Ted and Mr. Zoo Director were in the heat of it at the head of the trail, but it was mainly our head honcho doing the talking. I couldn't hear what they were saying, but he was mondo pissed! It looked like our senator was getting in some verbal licks of his own, but it was all Wright's show. The vibes were a total downner, man, so I husked it back down the path and ducked into the service tunnel."

I rested my arms on the table, leaning in Shaggy's direction. "When was this?"

"Just before eats."

"You've no idea what they were arguing about?"

"Negatory." He snagged another cookie from the plate on the table, his fourth. "You'd've needed a machete to cut through the tension around those two. Anywho, the rest of the gala was too bitchin' to think much about them. Had to get back to the main event. Retreat is the better part of valor, y' know."

"I can only hope they were discussing the shoddy workmanship of the construction crew," Jeff said.

Now I was confused. "Why would that concern McNealey?"

Jeff reached out and patted me on the back. "Carruth Construction is owned by the senator's mother-in-law. I've no doubts that getting the construction contract and McNealey's sudden support of the zoo are readily connected."

They were all smiling at me. Was I the only one who didn't know this? I'm not proud of my disinterest in politics, but there's way too much double-talk, back-stabbing and changing partners going on for me. I can't keep up with it. The only time I take an interest in the workings of the government is when it involves the environment and protecting our wildlife.

I looked back up at Shaggy. "Have you told this to the police?"

Shaggy nodded. "Yeah, the fuzz grilled me pretty good on that one."

"And yet McNealey's not a suspect."

"Probably has an alibi," Billie said getting out of her chair. "You don't mess with a man of his stature unless you have some very solid proof."

My cell phone chose that moment to go off.

Gary Olson stuttered through a greeting, then hesitantly

asked if I had some free time.

"I'm pretty busy right now, Gary."

"It's just that, well, I have some information you might want to see."

I got up and walked out of the kitchen, cell phone to my ear. "Information about what?"

"Mr. Wright."

"What about him?"

"I think you should see it."

I held my temper. I wasn't in the mood for any cryptic talk. Gary could be slow getting to the point. "Okay. I'll bite. Where are you?"

I arranged to meet him at his house as soon as our meeting was done. When I returned to the kitchen I got the feeling another shoe was about to drop.

Billie had picked up the bowl of cookie dough and was depositing rounded spoonfuls of dough onto the metal baking sheet with short, agitated plops.

"The police took all the video we shot on Saturday," she blurted out. "We don't have a show." The wooden spoon tapped the edge of the bowl. "Unless—" she grunted sarcastically—"our resident croc wrangler wants to take another plunge in the billabong with Sebastian so we can re-shoot it."

My heart sank. Even with five shows in reserve, it would mean stepping up our filming schedule, researching locations, contacting people and rearranging our calendar. Normally, I'd welcome the challenge; but, given recent events, I just didn't have the energy. I was more focused on JR's woes than the show just now.

"What do they expect to find on the tapes?" I asked, looking from Billie to Shaggy.

"Evidence," Billie said.

"But none of the crew was anywhere near the crocodiles at

the time Wright was supposed to have been killed. They were filming the gala."

"That's what I said." Shaggy savored another cookie for a moment. "I was pretty much zoned in on the plumbing thing after Jeff and Sebastian were rockin' and rollin' in the pond and Mr. Wright getting all stink-eyed over the exhibit not being up and running."

"And?"

"So, just maybe our cameras caught something," Billie chimed in. "An argument, a hostile look, greed, jealousy."

Or someone missing from the gala.

I suddenly wanted a look at those tapes myself. I knew about the argument, but would they also tell me why McNealey and Wright had been so upset? Had Wright tossed the senator a curve ball? Could he have been angry enough to commit murder?

"How long are the police going to keep the tapes?" I asked.

Shaggy shrugged.

"Did we make a copy?"

"Didn't have a chance, man. They confiscated them right there at the zoo."

"Maybe those tapes could help clear JR," I said, feeling more upbeat.

"Maybe you could sweet talk your ex-boyfriend, Detective Sorenson, into giving them back to you," Jeff teased, making a kissy-face.

"Maybe." Since they were *Zoofari*'s property, I was hoping that wouldn't be much of a problem.

Billie suddenly grew wary, giving me the evil eye. "What for? To look for clues?" She extended a forefinger and poked it in my direction. "You shouldn't be messing with this, Snake. What if you're right? What if JR isn't the murderer? That means he's still out there. It may even be someone we know. If the killer finds out you're sticking your nose into this, he may want to do something about it. Did you ever consider that?"

Gary lived with his mother in one of those slab houses that was built right after WWII to accommodate the returning servicemen. The North Minneapolis house was small, just two bedrooms, a living room, kitchen and bathroom. But Gary's mother had packed enough furniture and knickknacks into it to furnish three more its size. It hardly seemed the ideal place to raise an ill-at-ease, less than graceful son.

"We used to have a bigger place," Gary said, as if apologizing for the size of the house.

"When your stepfather was alive?"

I weaved my way through floral-and-striped-patterned furniture, catching my knee on the corner of a green-painted end table, upsetting one of the framed photographs that monopolized its surface. It was a picture of Betsy Olson and her late husband, a man with classic Hollywood good looks I recognized from the wallet-sized photos she had shown me on one of her visits to the zoo to see Gary.

"Your stepfather was a good-looking man," I said, righting the photo I had upset.

Gary turned and glanced at the picture. "He wasn't really my stepfather."

"But your mom told me—"

"She likes people to think they were married."

I wondered at the lifestyle they must have lost when he died. Two incomes, a larger house, better neighborhood. Unless he had left a will, not being married would have left her nothing when he died.

I picked up another photo from the table. It was a faded, colored picture of a man in a zookeeper's uniform holding a small American alligator in his arms. I squinted at the patch on his sleeve. It looked like SCWR, a zoo logo I didn't recognize. A much younger Gary appeared to be disengaging the gator's jaw from the man's metal watchband. Nearby, a fretful Betsy looked on with double concern. It was a charmingly candid shot.

"What's the story here?"

Gary smiled thinly. "We were posing and the gator decided to take a nip out of his arm. Instead it got his watch and the gator's tooth got stuck."

"Pretty fearless of you to help out like that. This your stepdad?"

I waited for him to answer, to give me a name, some other way to refer to this faux stepfather. But he said nothing. So to ease the strained silence I asked, "How old were you?"

"Twelve."

There was a certain familiarity about this photograph that appealed to me, even though I'd never seen it before. It reminded me of something, but I wasn't sure what. Most likely it stirred an old memory of Jeff and his father in the Outback, one of many adventures I'd heard when I was Down Under and being welcomed into my new extended family.

"You look a lot like your mom."

There was a strong resemblance in her son: the bright blue eyes with dark lashes, the small, upturned nose and thick black hair. It was a young face, uncertain yet full of hope.

Gary shrugged and it was hard to tell if he was embarrassed by his resemblance to his mother or was just tired of hearing about it. I didn't know Betsy Olson well, although she came down to the zoo on occasion to see Gary. She was an overly talkative woman whose main topic of conversation revolved around Gary and his deceased "stepfather."

"Where's your mom? She hasn't stopped by the zoo for a while."

"She left yesterday to visit some relatives for a couple of

weeks." He headed down the small hall toward the back of the house.

Not knowing if he wanted me to wait or follow, I chose to follow, curious about the rest of this young man's natural habitat. Basically I'm just nosey.

If Billie's home was an advertisement for sterile condo living, Gary's was like a two-page spread for Sloppy College Dorm Magazine. There was a bed—somewhere under piles of clothes—a computer desk rife with several CPUs, monitors, peripherals, and attachments too numerous to fathom. Posters of animals and organizations covered the walls: timber wolves from the International Wolf Center in Ely, Minnesota; Humane Society membership calendars; and a PETA anti-fur message with baby seals. And right smack in the middle of it was a psychedelic green-and-black poster of Led Zeppelin.

National Geographic DVDs shared space on a makeshift wall shelf with an impressive collection of science-fiction films and young-adult comedies only a college student would find funny. Below was a shelf of books on the natural world, comic books and an *X-Files* compendium.

With his foot, Gary adroitly nudged some previously worn socks and underwear into a nearby closet, hoping, I'm sure, I wouldn't notice the maneuver.

The desk area was virtually buried under magazines, papers, and a dirty plate with a leftover pizza crust still on it that probably had been there for some time. How long, I didn't want to think.

Gary rummaged through the piles of clutter, tossing some textbooks behind him onto the bed. At last he handed me a ragged pile of computer printouts.

"This is all stuff on Anthony Wright?" I asked, impressed.

"He was a pretty public guy."

"With all this, you could've written the article without

interviewing him," I smiled, scanning the top sheet about Wright's appointment as director of the Minnesota Valley Zoo.

Gary looked pleased. "There's a lot of stuff out there, most of it recent. I had to do some digging to get into the man's past."

"This is a side of you I haven't seen before. I'll have to tell Billie we have a born researcher on the team."

"It helps if you put the right words in the search engine. And not everything on record is cross-indexed the way you'd think, so it pays to do searches for archives that could be related in some obscure way. Sometimes unexpected things'll pop up."

"Uh-huh . . ."

I flipped to the next page, skimming through a bio the *Star Tribune* had printed after his appointment had been announced. What I was looking for, I didn't know. Maybe something would jump out at me, some little thing I could use to point the police in the right direction, a name, a place, something I could connect with Anthony Wright that shouldn't have been there. Anything.

Gary reached over and rifled through the pages. "There's one in particular I wanted you to see."

He took the stack from me and thumbed through the pile twice before pulling out what he wanted. He handed it to me with a flourish.

It was a photograph of Melanie and Anthony Wright. The black-and-white printout had frozen them in another time, much younger and, as far as the stocky Mr. Wright I'd known was concerned, at least fifty pounds lighter. It was a society column announcing Wright's promotion to full partner at the Adams, Crombie and Gallaher law firm. Under the photo, the caption referenced Melanie's fundraising endeavors for the ailing Sweetwater Creek Wildlife Rehabilitation Center where she volunteered her skills as a zookeeper.

Gary was waiting for my reaction. A self-satisfied smirk curved the corners of his mouth. “Sweetwater Creek is where JR had his animal park.”

Chapter 12

"He lied to me. The bastard lied to me!"

I don't usually lurk in dark hallways eavesdropping. I don't even peek out the window when my neighbors come home. My mom is better at that sort of thing. Every slam of a car door, every outdoor light that winks on sends her running to the window, peeking through the slats of the blinds. It was a wonder she got anything done.

But it was hard to ignore the voices that came from Butler Thomas's office.

"It was a business decision, Senator, based on economics. Don't take it personally."

The consoling voice belonged to Suzanne Terak, the woman who had been Anthony Wright's personal assistant for the past four years.

"Business!" Senator Ted McNealey spat out sourly. "Wright was stringing me along on this one. He did it to spite me—I know it! He got what he wanted and didn't give a damn about keeping his promises." McNealey was on the boil, his emotions overflowing. "Goddamit! It's a good thing the bastard's dead, because if he were here I'd kill him myself!"

There came an uncomfortable pause as the words hung in the air.

Butler Thomas's response came from the corner of the room, his voice detached, his manner all business. "Then Mr. Wright still wouldn't be able to bail you out of this mess, would he?

And you'd be in prison."

It was not a happy scene I had stumbled onto. From where I stood, hidden by the half-opened door, I could see the senator's reflection in the glass of a framed zoo poster of a pygmy marmoset. The bright unflinching eyes of the primate looked out from the guarded face of an aging politician. It was an oddly conflicting image.

Uncomfortable with my new role of snoop, I debated whether to fade quietly away or make my presence known. I had come up to the administrative wing looking for Melanie Wright, not to stumble on a private meeting I wasn't meant to overhear.

I wanted desperately to talk to Melanie about the information Gary had given me last night, but open for the first time since Anthony Wright's death, the zoo had been—literally and figuratively—a zoo. Our attendance had been almost double what it normally is on a Tuesday in June, and all the keepers had scrambled like a colony of ants—taking care of the animals and fielding questions from visitors intent on knowing the truth behind the grisly murder that Saturday night.

Then there were the behind-the-scenes crises. The Komodo still wasn't feeling well and had to be closely monitored. Our binturong, usually asleep in his tree in the tapir exhibit, had become curious, climbed down from his perch and went for a walk along the Tropic Trail's path. And Edna, our white-cheek gibbon, had decided to slam dunk her newborn baby on the floor of the nursery. Happily, the little tyke had been rescued, but hand-raising it was going to take man hours and I had pulled the first shift. In between feeding the newborn, keeping an eye on the Komodo and capturing the binturong, I had tried unsuccessfully to track down Melanie to question her about JR and her work at the Sweetwater Creek Wildlife Rehabilitation Center.

In light of what Gary had discovered, I was determined to

find out what she knew. That she had lied to me—or, at best, been less than forthcoming—was upsetting. I had thought we were friends. I was hurt she didn't trust me enough to tell me the truth, to confide in me. Between Melanie and JR, it seemed it was a week for friends keeping secrets.

Earlier in the day I had tried to recall some of the things Melanie had told me about her past. I knew she had lived in Miami and worked as a zookeeper at a small facility down there. How long ago was that? She had joined the Minnesota Valley Zoo staff about five years ago. Wright became director a year later. I had no idea how long they had lived in Minneapolis prior to their careers at the zoo. As far as I knew, she had never mentioned JR or James O'Malley or anything about a zookeeper being murdered in Florida.

By the time the lunch hour rolled around and I was dribbling honey on the climbing tree in the Malayan sun bear exhibit, I was giving Melanie the benefit of the doubt. Maybe she hadn't known. Was that possible? Had I gotten it wrong? Had she returned to Minnesota before all of that had happened?

It was late afternoon before I heard the news Melanie had been invited to attend an emergency board meeting. By the time I found a free minute to get up to the administrative wing, the boardroom was empty. There was not so much as a cup of coffee left on the large oval table that dominated the center of the room. Most of the department doors were closed as well, leaving the hallway empty and dimly lit.

The only open office door along the lengthy hallway belonged to Butler Thomas, assistant director. The heated discussion in his office had drawn me to them like a sun bear to Gatorade. I hadn't wanted to barge in on them, so I waited outside for things to quiet down. Only they didn't. Which meant I stood outside for a bit of uncharacteristic eavesdropping.

It was obvious Senator McNealey was not a happy camper.

Whatever news Butler may have brought back from the board meeting, McNealey was making no bones about his displeasure. I'd kept silent, watching the senator's reflection in the glass as he paced and ranted. I don't know what I expected to hear. A heartfelt confession to Wright's murder? Ha! But I had to wonder if his anger was an extension of whatever he and Wright had argued about the night of the Beastly Ball.

I might have listened indefinitely were it not for the sound of a chair being moved, alerting me that someone might pop out and discover me looming near the doorway like a vulture. I tried a dramatic clearing of my throat and slipped through the open door where I had been lurking unnoticed for the past ten minutes. The room's three occupants turned as one in my direction, their eyes boring into me.

"Hi," I said cheerfully, trying to make the best of an awkward situation.

Suzanne Terak, Butler Thomas, and Senator McNealey presented a cozy triad, and I said as much as I leaned casually against the doorjamb, putting up a brave front. I was feeling anything but brave inside and hoped they wouldn't notice.

"Snake," said Butler with a pleasant, if slightly less-than-welcoming, smile. "Can we help you?"

"How long have you been standing there?" McNealey demanded, lines of worry lowering his receding hairline.

"Long enough," I finally answered. Sure it was a cliché, but clever repartee is not my strong suit, particularly when I'm in the hot seat.

Butler's dimples deepened as he turned a cajoling, fourteen-carat smile in my direction. "Come in." He motioned. He sat behind his desk, an overly neat oasis in the hustling administrative wing of the zoo, a sharp contrast to Gary Olson's wild idea of functional workspace.

If Butler was amused by my presence, the senator was

anything but. He flushed, turning a darker shade of red, fuming in silence. His head withdrew into his shirt collar like a tortoise retreating into his carapace. He had lost control of the situation and didn't like it.

"Well, Mrs. Jones," he said with a flinty edge to his voice, "just how long is 'long enough'?"

The three of them exchanged wary glances, uncertain what I'd overheard. Silence hung in the air like humidity in August.

"I was looking for Melanie." I decided to avoid his question, not quite sure how to proceed. "Someone said she was at the board meeting."

McNealey jammed his hands into his trouser pockets. I'm sure at this point he would have preferred to strangle me with them. His head protruded forward, suspicion in his eyes. "The board meeting has been over for quite some time."

The ever-composed Suzanne spoke calmly, her body language unusually tense. "We were just discussing the Board's decisions to move forward now that Mr. Wright . . ."

She faltered over Wright's name with a nervous twitter. And that was out of character, too. Although she was trying her best to remain calm and businesslike, there were cracks in the performance. For the first time since I'd entered the room I took a close look at her.

Suzanne Terak, who had so coolly and competently taken charge of the panicked crowd on the night of Wright's death and herded the zoo patrons away from the billabong, now looked agitated and somewhat lost. Known as the Ice Princess by some, she was clearly struggling to maintain an emotion-free exterior. I had assumed she was handling Wright's death as she handled his business affairs, with smooth efficiency and dispassion.

I had not expected to see her sporting a pair of puffy, red-rimmed eyes. Grief for her employer? Why not? Why shouldn't she care about a man she had worked closely with for over four years? Or could it be more than that? A few people had gossiped about the true nature of her relationship with Wright: the powerful older man and his hot-looking executive assistant. Just how personal was she? Or so went the jokes passed around the zoo in low murmurs.

Whatever her reason, she was the only person in Wright's tight circle showing any visible signs of grief. Even Melanie Wright, the dead man's wife of twenty-five years, had been more detached and poised in her grief than his administrative assistant.

Moistening her lips, Suzanne straightened up and smoothed the white linen jacket of her tailored suit. "Butler has received the official nod to act as director until Mr. Wright's position can be filled again." This time there was no stumbling over his name, but her eyes were fastened on a nonexistent piece of lint on her blazer that she picked at with elegant fingers.

"And I sincerely hope you'll stay and help me through this, Suzanne." Butler tilted his head to the side, studying her with some apprehension.

Butler had been assistant director during the administration of our last zoo director. He had been upset at the Board's hiring of Wright and not too happy about the new direction he had taken the zoo.

Wright had sidestepped the plans set down by his predecessor, running full steam ahead with his dream of a building dedicated to the unusual animals of Australia. This hadn't made him popular with personnel whose pet projects were shelved. Not everyone thinks koalas are adorable, and the challenge of housing two full-sized crocs was considered a waste of resources. But Wright's strong personality and silver tongue had won over the board of directors. And to keep them happy, he micromanaged every aspect of running the zoo.

Nothing slipped past him, and he often made deals and decisions without the knowledge of our staff and field experts. Even the delivery of feed and fresh produce was marked by this man. No one would have a better understanding of what deals Wright was in the middle of than Suzanne Terak. "Organization" was her middle name. She'd be an asset to anyone who made the decision to fill Wright's shoes.

"What exactly did the Board have to say?" I asked, knowing that there'd soon be a memo out to all zoo personnel telling us all we needed to know, and nothing more.

McNealey grunted, wanting to say something but clearly inhibited by my presence. I had to wonder why he was here at all. He wasn't a member of the Board or an employee. At best, he had been a reluctant supporter of the zoo. Without Wright's guiding hand, I doubt he'd vote for zoo funding over any new stadiums being debated in the Minnesota Senate.

I must have been staring, as he turned his back to me, taking an inordinate interest in the piglet poster hanging behind Butler Thomas's desk. I thought about what had been said last night about McNealey's connection to the firm that had managed the construction of the Australia building and Walkabout Trail.

"I assume all construction projects have been put on hold," I said, watching the back of McNealey's shoulders tense.

Butler leaned back in his chair and closed his eyes as if the dim light in the office was causing him pain. "There will be some cutbacks, yes. Hopefully, temporary."

"Or else the senator will withdraw his support?"

The senator whirled around to face me. "Exactly what are you implying, Mrs. Jones?"

I squared my shoulders and fought the nervous urge to curl the end of my ponytail around my finger. "Just that I heard Carruth Construction is owned by your family, Senator."

Or, more pointedly, by Hannah Carruth, the senator's

hammer-wielding mother-in-law. She had started the company on her own and married her senior foreman. Neither marriage nor four daughters had forced her to loosen the reins of control. Since she now suffered from poor health, that was about to change. McNealey's wife was the only daughter still living in the area, and I couldn't picture anyone less likely to head her mother's company than the senator's overly pampered wife. It didn't take a brain surgeon to figure out Ted McNealey was a big player in the line of ascension.

"Carruth Construction bids on all zoo projects just like anyone else."

"And Carruth always seems to come in as the low bidder. By quite a bit, from what I've been told." And the state always awards the lowest bid. "Why is that, Senator? They're certainly adept at cutting corners, aren't they? Is that why the plumbing got mucked up in the croc exhibit and Jeff was almost killed trying to fix it?"

"If the plumbing subcontractor used substandard materials, they will be held accountable."

Now McNealey sounded like the politician he was. I wondered what Mother Carruth would say if she suspected shoddy workmanship on her construction sites. The loss of a zoo construction project might be motive enough for murder. Being the zoo's construction company of choice was a lucrative contract and a high-profile project that could bring in a lot of free publicity. And in Minnesota the job of state senator was a part-time position; McNealey's full-time job was in the family business.

"Is that why you and Wright were arguing the night he died?"

Both Butler and Suzanne looked surprised. McNealey's eyes narrowed and his lips tightened into a thin, pale line. "Exactly what do you know about that?"

"Later that evening, you looked pretty upset when you got up to talk. Why was that, Senator? Guilty conscience?"

"What the—!" McNealey spluttered, and I thought his eyes might bulge right out of their sockets.

"Snake—" Butler stood up, the color drained from his face. "That's out of line."

I turned round to face him. "I'm sorry, Butler, but something happened between him and Wright that night. And from what I just overheard, it sounds like there was some breach of a promised business deal. And you heard what he said. 'It's a good thing the bastard's dead, because if he were here I'd kill him myself!' "

Nearly apoplectic, the senator struggled for control. He raised a warning finger at me. "That's not what I meant. It's merely a figure of speech, nothing more. Wright was a friend."

"And friends disappoint us, don't they?" I knew that first hand. "What did he do? Cheat you? Break a contract? What made you so angry?"

"There is no contract, Mrs. Jones." McNealey's voice went icy. He moved toward the door, pausing a foot in front of me, staring down with a smirk of satisfaction. "The board of directors has seen to that." He leveled a cold, hard smile at me. "And it seems you're also out of a job, Mrs. Jones. G'day."

For a moment I was stunned. Then I swung around to the two remaining people in the room. "Butler?"

This was no way to hand out pink slips, and Butler glared at McNealey's departing back.

"Sit down, Snake." He waved me toward the chair in front of his desk, a bit dazed himself, drawing in a troubled breath. So this was official then.

"I think I'd better leave as well," Suzanne picked up her purse and made for the doorway. "I'll be in my office should either of you need me." Her eyes lingered on me sympathetically for a moment before she left the room.

Butler waited until Suzanne had gone, shutting the door behind her.

"I wanted to wait until I could speak to you and Jeff together."

"Jeff's fired, too?"

"Absolutely not. You and Jeff are valuable members of our staff." He stopped to take another deep breath. "I'm afraid it's *Zoofari* we have to put on hold. Production costs are just too expensive for the return we're getting—"

"But we're just beginning to get some national attention—"

"I realize that. And don't think the zoo doesn't appreciate your efforts. We just can't justify the monetary expenditure right now. Cuts have to be made somewhere, Snake. Even with the senator's support, we're unlikely to get all the monies we've asked for."

He sat behind his desk. "It was the Board's decision." He locked eyes with me, as if daring me to protest. "They felt it would be foolhardy to continue the show when we've got no idea what the state legislature is going to do, especially after a stalled session that ended without passing a budget this year. Governor Wolfe is cutting state agency budgets by three percent. That's over $200,000 for the zoo's baseline budget. Along with that, our projection for attendance this year hasn't met expectations. We're already increasing admission fees and may think about charging for parking, and charge admission to the butterfly exhibit. More fee increases could adversely affect us. We've trimmed all we can without laying off staff. The Board recommends we dip into our emergency reserves, hoping it will send a message to the government that there's no fat left to cut. Snake, I'm sorry, but that's the way it has to be."

I was crushed. *Zoofari* was our baby. And now its future was on hold. Just when we were building momentum. I was only half listening to his talk about budgets. I slumped down in my chair feeling like I was ten years old again. My family was visiting my mother's sister in Arizona. Left to my own devices on the fringe of the desert, I'd spotted, tracked, and captured a Gila monster. As Jeff would say, he was "a beauty." I'd never seen such a large lizard and was busting with pride until Mom freaked out, lecturing me that proper young ladies didn't crawl around in the sand and pick up filthy animals. She robbed me of my accomplishment and made me feel like something was wrong with me. She'd made me cry.

But I wasn't ten years old any longer. I knew how to fight back. I sat up a little straighter and gripped the edge of the desk.

"Butler," I challenged, "*Zoofari* makes money—at least recently. We draw people to the zoo. We promote this place. Why do you think some of those donors came to the Beastly Ball? To see Jeff Jones, the cable TV guy. And some of them wrote rather large checks if I'm not mistaken."

He shook his head. "I've seen the numbers, Snake. For the past six months the show has generated a tiny profit—with the emphasis on 'tiny.' It's still not enough to justify the production costs under the present circumstances. That money could be better used to upgrade our veterinary care, for example."

"But we *make* money! We pay for ourselves now. What costs?"

"I know, it doesn't seem fair. You know I'm a big fan of the show. I hope this decision's temporary. We're contractually obligated to the cable company to do six more programs. After that we're putting the show on hiatus for the rest of the year, then we'll see what we can do after that."

My mouth opened to protest but I closed it immediately. I couldn't win this argument, so there was no point in riling him further. Butler wouldn't arbitrarily shut us down without reason.

When he got no protest from me, he sat back in his chair, steepled his fingers and spoke his next words carefully. "You know, Snake, most of our operating budget comes from the state. Senator McNealey has been an ally of the zoo—"

I made a derisive noise, crossing my legs. My hiking boot accidentally smacked the leg of his desk.

"He can still be a powerful friend. And you insulted him. How do you think that will play with the Board? I hate to say this but you may have just shot yourself in the foot. You could have been more civil to him. In fact, you might have helped your cause if you had."

Christ! I had a flashback to the Beastly Ball on Saturday. There I was preaching to Mitch Flanagan about sucking up to the rich patrons in hopes of helping his raptor birds. Yeah, I was great at giving other people advice, but not very good at taking it myself.

I felt like an idiot. Adding insult to injury, Butler Thomas added, "If you care anything about the future of this zoo—about *Zoofari*—you should apologize to him."

"Apologize?" The word almost gagged me. "For what? The man could be a murderer."

"That's the most absurd thing I've ever heard."

"What makes you think he couldn't have done it? He was arguing with Wright just before dinner. In fact, I have a witness who saw them walking down the Aussie Trail alone just before the murder." I wasn't going to tell him my big witness was Shaggy.

"You have a witness?" Butler raised a skeptical brow at me. "I hadn't realized you joined the police force."

I let that one pass without comment, for as much as I cared about our TV show, a man's life was at stake. That's what had brought me to this office originally. I had to remember that, had to focus on my purpose and not get sidetracked. Measuring my words with care, I leveled my eyes on Mr. Thomas like a cannon. "I'm not going to let JR go to prison for something he didn't do. The police have the wrong man."

"The evidence against JR is pretty bad."

My eyes hardened. "What evidence? JR ran away after Wright's death. That was the only reason the police suspected him in the first place. Not exactly a rock-solid case."

"What about that murder in Florida? You can't pretend that didn't happen."

"Alleged murder."

"Well," Butler continued, undeterred, "it doesn't really look good that JR ran away and changed his identity after a man was killed in the animal park he owned, does it?"

"Okay, but how does that tie JR in with Wright's death? What have the police told you?"

"I don't know the particulars, Snake. Maybe Wright knew him, recognized him, and was going to call the police. JR found out and killed Wright to protect himself." The acting zoo director gestured broadly as if to say "There you have it."

"If Wright had threatened to expose JR, he might have run off, but he wouldn't have killed him. He's disappeared before. That's his history, not murder."

"He murdered a man in Florida. Then he ran. *That's* his history." Butler emphasized the end of the sentence with an unusual amount of acrimony.

"They have no proof of that, either."

"Only his fingerprints all over the cat's cage."

I surged to my feet, my voice intensifying. "He's a zookeeper, for Chrissakes! All the keepers' prints had to have been on that cage, but no one else is a suspect."

He smiled back cryptically, amused. "Okay, okay," he motioned me back into my seat, "don't blow a fuse, Snake. Suppose for an instant I agree with you. If JR isn't the killer, then who else could have done it?"

"We had hundreds of guests here that evening."

"It's hard to believe anyone at the fundraiser would have done this."

"Why not? Most of them had financial ties to Wright in one way or another." At Butler's scowl, I tried another theory. "Or maybe it wasn't one of our guests. Couldn't someone have slipped into the zoo during the ball—with all that music and confusion—killed Wright, merged with the crowd and got out again?"

Butler shook his head, a lock of his immaculate hair dipping down across his eyebrow. "That's a bit of a stretch."

"But possible. Security was loose that evening. People were wandering around all over the place."

"True enough," he acceded. "But there were security cameras, Snake. We gave those tapes to the police. The police have gone over every one of them and saw no one coming in or going out who wasn't accounted for."

I wasn't ready to give up. "The zoo's a big place, with lots of places to hide. Not every inch is under the eye of the camera."

I could tell he didn't want to, but he was forced to agree with me. The zoo security cameras were placed in order to keep track of the exhibits and paths near them—and not all of them, at that; but they weren't aimed at the perimeters to catch gatecrashers.

Butler fidgeted, covertly glancing at his watch, obviously needing to be somewhere else. He was a busy man, busier than usual given what had happened, but he was putting up with me because he liked me.

"The zoo is in a pickle right now," I said. "Wright is dead and a zoo employee is being charged with the crime. On the one hand I can see how that wraps up things neatly for everyone. You take your lumps and move on. I know where you're coming from, Butler." I took in a breath, steadying myself for what I was about to say. "Maybe we're asking the wrong questions."

"What do you mean?" His brow furrowed with concern.

"Instead of asking who, maybe we should be asking why. Why would someone want to kill Wright?"

The face across the desk from me looked surprised, then angry. "The police have already asked that question, Snake. Anthony Wright was a highly regarded member of the staff, a respected member of the community."

"Yeah, a real Boy Scout," I came back. "There's still the question of McNealey and Wright. What do you know about those two and their business deals?"

"That's private information, Snake. Sorry."

It was a charming blow-off, but a blow-off nonetheless. I didn't take offense. He was right, I had no business pressing the issue, but I was going to for JR's sake.

I thought about what I had overheard this evening and of Jeff's complaint of shoddy workmanship by the subcontractors Carruth Construction had hired to work at the zoo. "Are you worried Wright did something unethical? Something that could hurt the zoo?"

That was it! I could read it in his face, even though Butler tried to conceal it; for an instant he reacted to my words.

Carefully, the man spread his large, well-manicured hands in a sort of open gesture, as the handsome face regarded me with an empty smile. "We are cooperating fully with the police."

"And the police have the wrong man! Help me on this, Butler. I don't want the zoo to suffer any more than you do, but we have to find out who murdered Anthony Wright—and it isn't JR."

"We're handling it, Snake. That's the bottom line. The board of directors is launching a full investigation of its own into Wright's death. The zoo wants the answers as much as anyone else."

"And McNealey is heading up the investigation? That's sweet."

"We're a state institution. McNealey won't be the only legislator sitting on the Investigative Committee."

"Let me help, Butler. I know the people who work here. They might be willing to tell me something they wouldn't tell the police. I can be discreet. The Board doesn't have to know."

He grunted. "I saw how diplomatic you were with Senator McNealey." He seemed to gather himself inwardly, his gaze taking me in for a moment. When he spoke it was unequivocal. "I know you think the police have the wrong man. Maybe they do. But they're the professionals. Who am I—or you, for that matter—to say they're wrong? We have to let the law run its course. I'm sorry, but I have a lot of work to do. So do you, if I'm not mistaken."

Butler sat forward again, grabbed a folder from the pile next to him, opened it and began reading. I had been dismissed. I started to say something else, but the withering gaze that bulleted at me from across the top of the folder ensured my silence.

Out in the hallway, I leaned against the wall and tried to assimilate what I thought I had learned. Butler's attitude explained all the tension earlier, the reason for his reluctance for full disclosure; he was protecting the zoo from a potential scandal, but he was also covering his own ass.

Chapter 13

The late-evening sun was glowing through the windows as I left Butler's office and headed toward what had been Anthony Wright's home away from home. The outer office where Suzanne Terak had stood sentinel for Anthony Wright was dark. I found her next door in Wright's office, sitting behind the oak desk with only the green-shaded lamp for lighting.

For a moment, she didn't see me. She stared blankly at the contents of a manila folder, one of a stack on his desk. Behind her was a Monet print of Paris, flanked on either side by potted ferns on top of a black-lacquered credenza. Her long, lustrous hair hung around her shoulders, her dark eyes focused a million miles away, or maybe on a more certain memory of the not-so-distant past.

For the first time I thought of what Wright's death would mean to Suzanne. She had been his right hand during his tenure at the zoo. His Girl Friday. Although an outdated title, it took in more than the average executive assistant. She was his appointment book, his travel agent, his sentinel, his organizer, and his private shopper. I was also hoping she had been his confidant, knowing more about his affairs inside and outside the zoo than even his wife.

Suzanne looked up with a slight start, suddenly aware of my presence.

"Snake, you have to stop appearing out of nowhere."

"Sorry," I said with a tentative smile, hoping for a smooth

transition into what was on my mind. "Got a minute?"

She stood, her trim and shapely figure wrapped in a white linen suit. Suzanne wore little makeup. She didn't have to. On a physical level, she made me feel like an also-ran without even trying. Dressed in hiking boots and the zoo's khaki shorts and short-sleeved shirt uniform, I felt like the scullery maid before her lady.

She let the folder fall closed, then set the stack of folders next to it on top. Her soft brown eyes regarded me kindly. "That was quite the scene you stumbled onto."

"It was a bit awkward," I confessed.

"Are you all right? McNealey had no right divulging the fate of your cable show like that. It was a cheap shot. And something he had no business knowing about in the first place."

I had almost forgotten *Zoofari* in my zeal to play Nancy Drew. "Hopefully, it's a temporary setback. Maybe we can find a new sponsor, though I hate to take it away from the zoo."

Jeff would take it in stride, I knew; maybe even come up with an alternative solution to the cut. Billie was the person I worried about telling. *Zoofari* had been her brainchild. After seeing Jeff and me showing off Australian reptiles on the ten-o'clock news one night, she wanted us to host a documentary on zoological gardens and aquariums. Under Jeff's tutelage and funding from the Minnesota Valley Zoo, it had become a weekly series with Billie at its helm as director and assistant producer.

Suzanne nodded her understanding. "It's a wonderful program. You and Jeff have brought our mission into the public's living room. We're more than just a receptacle for exotic animals."

It was the one thing Jeff and I were proudest of. Bringing to the forefront the importance of zoos around the world as active participants and promoters of conservation; reintroducing endangered animals to the wild, captive breeding programs, adopting wildlife parks in countries not able to manage the funds necessary to keep them open, hosting international training workshops in conservation education. The list went on.

I swiveled around in the leather chair across from her and took in the paneled office. I had never been in Wright's office before, which seemed rather odd now that I thought about it, but it seemed he always came to me if he wanted something, showing up on the trail or in the kitchens at the oddest times.

An assortment of beat-up packing boxes was stacked along the back wall. The east wall was bare, but the west wall was still decorated with photos of Wright with various zoo celebrities.

"I thought it was time I started putting his things away and getting things in order. I'm sure Butler will want a full report as soon as possible." There was no rancor in Suzanne's voice. Only sadness and a touch of the inevitable.

As acting director of the zoo, Butler Thomas would make the transition for the new director as smooth as possible. Would Butler be the Board's permanent choice as well? He had been one of the top contenders when the position had been handed to Wright. And he had been vocal about his disapproval of the Board's decision. Wright's zoo experience was mostly on the business side. Wright was a lawyer and a businessman, not a zoologist. He hadn't mucked out an exhibit in over twenty-five years.

I took a closer look at the photos that still hung on the wall. Wright with Jack Hannah, another with Marlin Perkins. An old-time eight-by-ten, sepia-toned photograph of two men in pith helmets and safari shirts, one holding a baby gorilla in diapers immediately drew my gaze. I leaned forward in my chair and read aloud the name of the autograph sprawled across the photo.

"Frank Buck?" I turned my chair back toward Suzanne. "Frank 'Bring 'em Back Alive' Buck?"

She nodded. "And the man with him is Jungle Jack, Mr.

Wright's father. He traveled with Frank Buck on animal collection safaris to Africa and India. Even saved his life once, I'm told."

I tried not to show my distaste, reminding myself it had been a different world back then. For zoos at the turn of the century the only way to obtain a collection of animals was to take them from the wild. And in the early 1900's Frank Buck was the most well-known and successful animal collector of his day. Where he got the moniker 'Bring 'em Back Alive' was beyond me. Lion and tiger cubs were stolen from dens while their mothers were out hunting. Female rhinos and elephants were killed in order to obtain their calves. Half the animals he collected died before they reached their destinations. Those that survived had little to look forward to. By today's standards, zoos were bleak places back then and little was known about diets and habitat. In the 1920's the average life span of a gorilla in captivity was one year. Today, they often outlived their wild brethren.

"I never once heard Wright apologize for what his father did," Suzanne said as she removed the picture from the wall and placed it in an open box. "He seemed even proud of it at times, often regaling an audience about his father's escapades."

"Frank Buck was certainly the action hero of his times. I guess hunting animals in Africa and Asia was a big adventure, no matter how brutal we may think it is today."

"It was also big business. And when his father finally decided to settle down, he began his own zoo from the menagerie he had collected."

I sat up in my seat. "In Texas? The one he and Melanie ran?"

Suzanne nodded, sitting back down in Wright's chair behind the desk. "It was a family business. One that his sister now wants to sell." She swept her arm toward the pile of boxes against the wall. "She's sent all of the paperwork and records for Melanie to sort through."

"Which you've inherited, no doubt."

She smiled thinly, with all the mystery of the Mona Lisa, neither confirming nor denying the statement.

I pressed forward. "Was Melanie at today's board meeting?"

"As a matter of courtesy. They wanted her to know the stand they were taking on her husband's death." She shut her eyes, as if the last words had managed to crack through her defenses. It took her several seconds to gather herself again before she could face me with her usual steady gaze. "With Mr. Wright's death on zoo property, particularly in such a public manner, and with a zoo employee charged with the crime, the board of directors is naturally . . . *concerned.*" Her voice, though quiet, rang with clarity and purpose, as if she were doing this against her better judgment. Her slender hands were clasped together on the desk, albeit a bit too tightly.

"The Board is worried about bad publicity," she went on. "Times are tough, revenue for the state is down, and more cuts are coming. It would be politically easy to take our funding away if we have a scandal. The Board wants to avoid anything that would reflect badly on them or the zoo."

"That's understandable. Nobody wants that," I said.

"Mrs. Wright has a fair bit of clout herself, not only because she was married to our zoo director, but because she's a rich woman. The Australia Walkabout was largely funded by her donation."

That I knew, though it had slipped my mind. Melanie had a way of making you forget she was born with a silver spoon in her mouth. Anthony Wright, on the other hand, had missed no opportunity to let Jeff know that his wife's money was footing the bill for all his hard work. The Hanley-Holm retail chain, of which she was heir, was profitable and in need of a good tax write-off.

Obviously the Board knew this, too, and no doubt wanted to

avoid making any moves that would jeopardize the close and personal relationship they had with her checkbook.

"Melanie made one thing very clear at the meeting," Suzanne continued with admiration, "that she wanted everyone to fully cooperate with the police to make sure the killer was brought to justice. No special favors, even if the facts didn't reflect well on her or her husband."

Really? Once again Melanie Wright surprised me with the unexpected. While she was laudable in taking a courageous stand in the name of Truth, I was still troubled by her lack of candor with me, and unable to shake the feeling that she knew a lot more than she was telling.

Suzanne misinterpreted my look. "I got the feeling she doesn't think Jeff's friend committed the murder."

"Well, that makes two of us, anyway." I clasped my hands in my lap in order to keep from clenching my fists. My nerves were on edge. Something was going on with Melanie and I needed time to sort it out. In the meantime I had to keep cool, stay on track. I smiled at the lovely Suzanne. "What about you? Any ideas who might've killed Anthony Wright? Not including JR, of course."

She studied the desk blotter, deep in thought, before letting her eyes rest on me. "I don't know JR," she said philosophically. "Our paths never crossed. If he didn't do it then . . . well, I don't know. And I've been thinking about that quite a bit." She looked natural ensconced in Wright's big leather chair. The power behind the throne. "Mr. Wright has made enemies. Men in his position do. Would any of them profit from his death?" She pondered that for a moment then shook her head. "Unlikely."

"Maybe it was personal, then, not business. Profit isn't the only motive for murder, is it? Passion's always good, so's revenge. Self-preservation."

A neatly tweezed eyebrow rose in speculation. "Your implication being?" she asked pointedly.

I hesitated, realizing how delicately I had to tread. There had been rumors about Wright and Suzanne. Snide remarks chortled around the water cooler when Wright and his assistant were seen together. At first many thought he'd taken her along to his high-powered meetings merely as eye-candy, to soften up the hard-core fogies by dangling a shapely young thing in front of them. In time, people learned she was a damned efficient, intelligent woman with a genius for understanding a situation and acting accordingly. When the wheels fell off a business deal, no one was better at putting them back on. That she could also perform her job with charm and grace only seemed to draw more attention to her. And some of that attention was filled with innuendo about her personal life—with her boss. Whether true or not, I'd always thought it unfair. I'm sure she was aware of the talk, but it wasn't a line of questioning I wanted to pursue right now.

"McNealey. What about him?" I asked quickly. My money was still on our dear senator, and I didn't want to alienate her with questions that were really none of my business—yet. "He was pretty pissed off at Wright."

"Not enough motive. He has a reputation to think of. Do you think he'd risk that?"

"I've seen politicians risk more for less." I looked at her meaningfully, hoping she would shed some light on why they were fighting.

"If Senator McNealey had killed Mr. Wright, I'm sure he would have been much more guarded earlier this afternoon, don't you think?"

"You mean not threaten to kill a dead man?"

"Precisely."

She was probably right. But what did I know about human

psychology? I was much better at deciphering animal behavior. Yet one thing had been clear from McNealey's outburst.

"It sounded like Wright had backed out on a promise he had made to the senator. What? A construction contract in exchange for support for the zoo?" I asked.

She became immediately guarded. "The board of directors has put a moratorium on any further construction."

"And Carruth Construction in particular?"

Suzanne looked at me with weary eyes. "That isn't my news to tell, Snake. What you're asking is confidential. Mr. Wright may be dead, but I still owe him my loyalty."

"And there could be a lot of negative feedback if the public found out there were any improprieties taken in our construction practices. Even if they were done with the best of intentions."

"I assure you, there have been no under-the-table deals where the zoo is concerned. Everything has been aboveboard and legal." Suzanne drew herself up, her back ramrod straight. I could feel the sudden chill in the air. Not surprising that she had taken the merest hint of impropriety against her boss personally. "The police are confident they have the killer," she reminded me with vigor. "It's your friend John Erling. If your husband hadn't hired him, Mr. Wright would still be alive."

I stood up. It was a zinger and one I probably deserved. Maybe I had been rather insensitive to bring this up so soon after Wright's death. Clearly, suggesting any wrongdoing from this office wasn't going to go over well. Another approach was necessary. I paced across the carpet, tugging thoughtfully on my ponytail, a nervous habit of mine. If I was wrong and JR had killed Anthony Wright, then Jeff would be partly to blame for hiring him. That's what people would say behind our backs.

After a moment I stopped and turned to Suzanne, who sat quietly watching me. From the way her lips pinched together I could see she was hoping I'd leave. Not just yet.

In a calm, determined voice I said, "JR didn't kill anyone. The police haven't found a link between Wright and JR yet. They're going to dig into every nook and cranny of Anthony Wright's life until they do. I don't know what they'll turn up, but if we can prove someone else did it—someone not connected to the zoo—we can deflect some of the bad publicity that's bound to come out of this whole mess."

I fell into the chair opposite her, eyes locked onto hers, hoping my sincerity would appeal to her sense of integrity and would win some cooperation. I crossed my legs and rested my hands lightly on the armrests, trying to project an aura of composure and professionalism. Maybe if I had been wearing black, low-heeled pumps versus hiking boots I would have presented a more convincing image.

Finally, she said in an icy voice, "I don't know how I can help you, Snake. I've already told the police everything I know."

I released the breath I had been holding and worded my new question carefully. "Can you give me any reason at all why Senator McNealey and Anthony Wright would have been arguing the evening of the Beastly Ball?"

"You heard what the senator said about the contract."

"No, not what. *Why?* Why then? Just before the big opening? The timing seems strange. Whatever their differences, this was a big night for both of them. They both had a lot to gain. That's what I'm curious about, Suzanne. Do you know a reason this would've come up that night?"

Her gaze clouded over briefly as she said in a distant voice, "No, no I don't. You'll have to ask the senator."

I deflated a bit and tried another tactic. "Did Wright have any arguments with anyone else recently?"

"Mr. Wright was an argumentative man. Where would you like me to start?"

I didn't like the hostile vibes I was getting from her, but pushed forward, not ready to give up just yet. "Does any one stand out? Something at odds with his usual behavior."

For a moment she grew frosty, then thawed as if remembering something. I waited while she carried the thought through, slowly smiling at me. It was a superior, predatory smile.

"Well, there was that young protégé of yours. The one with that awful head of hair."

"Gary Olson?" I put my leg down, edging forward in my chair. "Gary spoke with Wright?"

Suzanne nodded. "He wanted to interview him for some website he had. He wasn't in Mr. Wright's office for fifteen minutes before he came cringing out of there like a whipped dog. Mr. Wright was livid. I'd never seen him quite that angry."

"What did Gary do to set him off?" Gary had told me he hadn't interviewed Wright. That he had never gotten the chance.

"Mr. Wright didn't confide that information to me. He did say he wanted the boy off the premises and never wanted to catch sight of him again."

I was fuming. "When was this?"

Suzanne shrugged. "A couple of weeks ago."

That little weasel. Gary had lied to me. And the day Wright had come storming down to the crocodile exhibit, he had ducked behind JR and disappeared. No wonder. Wright would have tossed him in with the crocodiles if he had caught sight of him.

"Anyone else?" I croaked, my mind dwelling on what I was going to do to Gary when I got my hands on him.

Suzanne stood up. "That's all I have. Now, if you'll excuse me, I have boxes to pack."

I thanked her for her time and left, disappointed I hadn't gotten any real clues. Now I had to deal with Gary.

I pulled out my cell phone and called him. Standing in the

empty corridors of the administration building, I felt closed in by the darkness that now clung to the windows. It was as if I were in a box with no air holes.

On the fourth ring I heard Gary's tentative greeting.

"We need to talk," I spat out, skipping the preamble. "Where are you?"

"I'm in the zoo, with the film crew. We were just packing up."

Of course, how could I have forgotten? They were reshooting some of the scenes we had to surrender on the tapes we gave the police. Needlessly, if the zoo was shutting us down.

"You're on the Aussie Trail, then?"

"Yeah . . . near the lizards—the goannas."

"Meet me at the crocodile billabong." I'd drag him into Jeff's office behind the exhibit where no one could overhear us.

I signed off without waiting for his reply.

CHAPTER 14

I was in a foul mood, so I took the long way from the administrative offices to the crocodiles' billabong. The zoo had been closed for a couple of hours and few people roamed the concrete corridors. A custodian, making the last sweep of the area with a push broom, ambled by with a friendly nod. Turning a corner, a security guard shot me a hard look as I hurried by, more focused on the chatter coming out of his radio than me. I didn't know either one of them, but they seemed to recognize me, though whether from my presence in the Tropics Trail or from TV, I didn't know.

The overhead halogen lights used to simulate tropical sunshine had been turned off in the building. Only the lights in the plaza and trail-marker lights were still illuminated for the sake of the night staff. It was like taking a walk under a full moon, the bright stars easily seen through the glass-paneled ceiling.

The sweet smell of jasmine greeted me from the flowering trees that accented the plaza connecting the Australian Walkabout with the Tropics Trail. A few squabbling birds broke the silence, then whirled into the dark to perch on a support structure at the top of the dome.

At the kangaroo compound I made out the figure of Boomer, our delinquent alpha male, watching me as I went by. The rest of the mob were in their night enclosures along with the other mammals, where they had been fed and checked over before their keepers left for the evening. Boomer was a holdout, apparently. No surprise. Wily to the ways of humans, the big red roo wasn't always easy to entice into his holding area; rounding him up forcibly would have been a struggle. Sometimes it's easier to let well enough alone: he was safe enough on his island.

Boomer hopped up to the edge of the dry moat that surrounded his enclosure and stood up on his hindquarters, sniffing the air as I hurried by, no doubt looking for the roo bar I usually tossed him when I came this way for a visit.

I took the time to stop and displayed empty hands. "Sorry, I don't haven't anything for you," I explained, forcing down my anger toward Gary and using my sweetest tone of voice. "I owe you, big guy."

Boomer was not pleased. I heard an irritated thump as I continued on, then a soft bark that was answered by a dingo, no doubt wishing he could get a taste of the kangaroo he kept smelling.

The arid scrubland that was Boomer's home gave way to the lush vegetation of the billabong. I could smell it before I actually stepped into the new environment. A fine mist fell from above the trees, adding moisture and humidity to the fetid aroma of decaying vegetation.

No one else was there. The film crew was gone and there was no sign of Gary. The reptiles were sleeping on the warm sand at the edge of the man-made lagoon. Seeing them at rest, I was reminded of a report Jeff and I had read regarding keepers who had trained crocodiles to crawl willingly into a holding pen for examination. The crocodiles even responded when their names were called. We didn't know if these had been hand-raised animals or captured in the wild. Regardless, this was something Jeff was keen on trying with Sebastian. Whether he pulled it off or not, it would make a great episode of *Zoofari.* If there were any more episodes of *Zoofari.*

Stepping off the main trail I approached the waist-high wall at the top of the enclosure and looked down. At the sound of my footsteps, Sebastian's eyes flashed open and I saw the reflection of the trail lamplights glisten in those primeval irises. The jaws hinged back to display an impressive array of razor-like teeth and he expelled a long warning hiss. I was at the edge of his territory and should come no farther.

"Hey there, Sebastian," I spoke softly, wondering if he'd respond to my voice.

Before I had met Jeff I hadn't thought much about crocodiles as endearing animals. It was the cuddly, furry creatures that captured the whole of my attention. Jeff changed all that. Crocodiles were his life, his passion. He had taught me the beauty of these magnificent creatures and the simple majesty of their ways.

Maybe it was my nearness or even that he associated my voice with Jeff, but Sebastian seemed to interpret my proximity as a threat. Silently he left the sand and slipped into the water, exposing the big dinosaur-like plates on the back of his head, then his entire back. This was a threatening posture to let me know I was in his territory and he was not happy about it. He swam slowly around the pool and then submerged himself among the mangrove roots. Babe, on the other hand, was practically mellow, barely acknowledging my presence with a languorous lift of her head.

From behind me came a scraping sound along the path I had come on. I called out Gary's name and there was silence. Landscape ferns, palms and shrubbery obscured my view of the trail and the man-made twilight didn't help either. I angled my head but the air remained still, with only the distant rhythms of a bullfrog and a few crickets that had managed to escape their fate as dining fare for the free-flying birds that populated the area. Most likely a hornbill scraping his beak along a tree trunk.

To be honest, I was glad for the time alone before Gary got here. I needed a quiet moment to sort things out. Closing my eyes, my elbows resting on the wall, I drew in a deep, calming breath. The zoo was a comforting old friend; one I could count on, a place of sanctuary after the crowds were gone and the animals were fed and bedded down for the night. With the events of the last few days, it felt good to be in an environment I understood and felt safe in. Nature—even canned nature—had a renewing quality, a way of transporting me to those things that really mattered in my life, made me appreciate the beauty and diversity of this fragile little planet. Most creatures on this earth live simply, going about their business in an effort to survive, part of nature's delicate balance, their existence dependent on the equilibrium of Mother Nature's scales. Only humans complicated their existence by constantly overreaching, taking more than they needed with little thought about its effect on the future.

I didn't want to open my eyes, didn't want to let recent events invade my peaceful little world. Jeff and I had harbored an accused murderer, a man we had both called friend. Did we believe JR had murdered that man in Florida? No. But it didn't look good. And despite his innocence, the reality of his past now changed JR in our eyes, as events had changed my feelings toward Melanie.

Melanie's alleged betrayal was the hardest thing to swallow. I'd trusted her. She'd looked me in the eye and hidden the fact that she'd known JR before, both she and her husband. Why? If she had told the police JR had known her husband in Florida, it would have been damning evidence, one more knot in the hanging rope. And it wouldn't be long before the police found this out. With the way things were now, if Detective Ole Sorenson hadn't figured out the connection between the Wrights and JR, I'd have to tell him.

And what should I make of Senator McNealey? From what I had overheard outside Butler Thomas's office, Senator Ted was hiding some unethical business dealings with Wright, if not outright illegalities. Suzanne Terak refused to admit it, but I smelled a cover-up of some kind.

Too severe? Maybe. I could see the vested interests of the senator, Butler Thomas, and Suzanne Terak. Hell, even I had a vested interest in Wright's murder investigation. Bad publicity could adversely affect the whole zoo. It might even curtail future expansion plans. Neither Jeff nor I wanted that. Yet we believed in JR, even if our confidence was on shakier ground these days, and we wanted the truth.

A gurgle brought me out of my reverie; air bubbles from the billabong. Sebastian lumbered back on shore and plopped down next to his dozing mate. Wary, but more accepting of my presence now, he kept a watchful eye from the beach.

I didn't hear the scuffle of footsteps until it was too late. My eyes flew open as I was struck violently from behind. I pitched forward, arms flailing, to grab hold of empty air as I hurled over the low wall, bounced off the sloping embankment and into the murky water with a huge splash.

A wet muffled world enveloped me. After the immediate shock of immersion, I jerked my head around in panic, eyes wide, raking the water round me, my only thought being that I was in the territorial pond of a fifteen-foot saltwater crocodile, a cold-blooded killing machine.

I kicked my arms and legs, propelling myself to the surface, gulping in a lungful of air. Desperation clutched at my heart. Sebastian would already be propelling himself toward me. They might be lumbering creatures on land, but crocodiles are amazingly agile and frighteningly swift in the water. And very strong. All muscle.

The water splashed and surged around me. I scrambled to

the edge and found footing below me in the shallows. My hands shot out and touched grass. My fingers clutched at the ground as I tried to hoist myself up. Instinct, though, made me turn at the last second, just in time to see the deadly jaws lunging at my foot. I jerked it back but the lightning-fast mouth chomped down.

A scream choked in my throat as I waited for my foot to be sliced off. It wasn't. The thick sole of my hiking boot was wedged into Sebastian's jaws vertically, jammed near the back of his throat. I tried to pull my foot back, but the powerful vise that held me only tightened. I felt the bottom row of jagged teeth pinch into my calf.

My heart turned cold. At any moment he could realign his mouth to find soft leather the only impediment to my flesh. Or, if he went into a death roll, he could snap my foot off like a toothpick. Crocodile teeth aren't made for chewing food, they're made for ripping and tearing. My other foot lashed out. Fighting back was the only defense I had. In panic I kicked his snout again and again with my hard-soled boot. Suddenly, the pressure released from my foot and I jerked it away. Sebastian's jaws opened and snapped shut as he surged toward me. Water violently splashed away from his mouth but it was empty.

I was stunned. Sebastian had missed. How was that possible?

Then I heard Jeff yelling at me.

"Move! Snake! Move yer arse!"

There he was, half submerged, holding on for dear life to Sebastian's tail and rear quarters.

"Move!"

He struggled as Sebastian thrashed around him. The angry croc nearly got his arm.

I found my footing, lurched onto the grass embankment and realized there were people around. Dangling over the edge of the wall, Gary Olson's left hand was extended toward me.

"Snake, quick!" he called, staring with alarm at the water.

Hobbling up the grass, I clambered up and reached for Gary's open hand. I overshot, grabbing his wrist instead. My wet fingers couldn't find a grip on his bare skin. Just then his fingers tightened on my arm and he hoisted us both up. Once in range, a jumble of arms helped me over the wall.

"Jeff!" I called, gripping the rail.

I saw him roll out of the water onto the bank. Sebastian came right after him; angry jaws lunging out of the water for a strike, barely missing his thigh. Jeff rolled and jumped aside just as Sebastian veered and rushed in for the kill. Another near miss. On land now, Jeff had the advantage. He scurried behind a tree, then, using the moment's hesitation, ran wide to the fence and safety.

"Hoo—eee!" An exhausted, but triumphant, Jeff pumped his fist in the air. "Did ya see that? Crikey! That was close!"

Way too close. And I had seen the terror in his eyes as he had held onto that croc's tail. Terror for my safety. Battered but intact, he was breathing hard, rubbing a bright red welt on the side of his thigh where Sebastian's tail had whipped him.

I ran over to him and fell into his arms. Jeff cooed soothingly into my ear, as he would any frightened animal, which was what I was. I clung to him, sputtering water and shaking.

"I've never been so scared in me life," he confessed, crushing me against him. "I thought you were a goner for sure." The raw emotion in his voice reached deep into my core and melted away the fear. I felt safe, enveloped in the love of this man.

Pulling away after a moment, he looked down at my upturned face, smiling brilliantly. "It's a good thing I married a woman who wears sensible shoes!"

He pulled my right leg up taking a closer inspection of my boot. There was a nasty two-inch gash along the sole and another chunk missing from the heel. Then and only then did I notice the shallow cuts and minor puncture wounds on my shin and calf.

"Thank God you were still here," was all I could muster, though there were many things I wanted to say.

"Thank Gary, y'mean," he said with a wink at the young student, who, along with Billie Bradshaw and Shaggy Lutz, stood nearby. "He heard you fall in and called out for help." Jeff tenderly smoothed the wet hair away from my eyes.

"I didn't fall in," I managed to sputter, "I was pushed."

"Pushed!" Jeff held me at arm's length.

"Pushed?" Billie echoed Jeff's disbelief.

My wet clothes hung like a lead overcoat but I swung around excitedly. "Gary, where were you? Did you see anybody?"

"I—I was in the tunnel, on my way to meet you, when I heard you yell. I came running, but didn't see anyone else around."

Indignant now, I inhaled sharply. "This was no accident," I told them. "It was deliberate. Whoever it was came from behind and bulldozed me like a football player."

"Man, who'd do something like that?" Shaggy asked of no one in particular, scratching the scraggly hair on his chin.

"You've been poking around, haven't you?" Billie jabbed a finger at me, her gravelly voice accusing. "Didn't I warn you? Now look what's happened!"

"Which only supports what I've been saying. JR's not the killer."

I didn't tell them about the conversation I had overheard in Butler Thomas's office with the senator, or the implications of McNealey's business dealings, as well as Wright's. I didn't even mention Melanie's duplicity. That was for later, when Jeff and I were alone.

"JR could still have an accomplice, y'know." Billie arched a warning eyebrow at me.

An accomplice. Yeah, that seemed a popular theory. But I had my doubts. Was my attacker our trashcan marauder? Could it be someone was working with JR?

Before I could second-guess myself again, Jeff stirred.

"Either way, someone doesn't want Wright's death looked at too closely," Jeff said in a hushed voice. "You must be ruffling someone's feathers, luv."

Jeff grasped my arms again, his eyes full of worry. I braced myself for a lecture, for the warning to let well enough alone and to let the police do their work. It was what any loving husband would have said if his snooping wife had endangered her life. But Jeff Jones was not just anyone's husband, he was *my* husband. And he was a right scrapper. Danger was part of his work; and taking a calculated risk for a worthwhile cause was something we both had done before. When I saw in his face that no lecture was forthcoming, I realized there was no stopping now.

I wasn't going to be coddled or kept out of harm's way owing to some marital power play. Jeff respected me too much for that. Whatever was to follow, I knew he would be there to shore up my backbone.

Jeff's eyes narrowed as his voice filled with determination. "This just got personal, luv. Nobody messes with my green-eyed sheila!"

Grinning with pride at his Aussie resolve, I suddenly felt my path was clear for what I had to do. But first things first. I turned to the others.

"Gary," I said. "We have to talk."

Chapter 15

You'd think by this time I'd know enough to keep a spare uniform in my office. My wet clothes were chafing and my boots were done for, sliced up nicely thanks to Sebastian. So instead of grilling Gary about his interview with Anthony Wright, I retreated to the women's rest room to rinse off and stand in front of the hand dryer. Or, rather, wobble in front of the hand dryer.

I was still shaking. Looking down the throat of a fifteen-foot crocodile was not something I ever wanted to do again. If Jeff hadn't come when he did I doubt I would have made it out of there—at least not with all my body parts intact. I couldn't believe someone would actually want me dead. What had I found out that I wasn't supposed to know?

I focused the dryer downward and sank to the floor, letting the warm air blow on the back of my head. I pulled out the elastic band that held my ponytail and ran my fingers through my hair. The only person I could think of that had gotten angry enough at me to shove me into the crocodile pool was our good senator. Had he and Anthony Wright connived in an exchange of favors? McNealey's vote in the legislature in exchange for an exclusive construction contract at the zoo? But the legislature had recessed without voting on the bond issue. As a consequence, the zoo would have to tighten its belt yet again. And that meant no more construction. That was hardly Wright's fault. McNealey was smart enough to know that. What then?

By the time I had myself reasonably dry and returned to the Aussie Trail, the overhead lights were ablaze and Detective Ole Sorenson was sitting on a bench with Jeff. The night sky hung like black canvas beyond the glass roof, and the two men were washed in lights like actors on a stage. Shaggy, Billie and Gary were nowhere in sight, so I assumed they had gone home.

Jeff immediately got up and strode over, his expression tight. Obviously he had not been enjoying his talk with Ole. As he neared I heard him mutter "wanker" under his breath with a sidelong glance at the detective. Concern for me overruled all other sentiments, however, and the big lug draped an arm around my shoulders and asked me if I was all right. "You look a bit pale."

I was. I had stopped shaking, but now that the adrenaline had stopped pumping, I hurt. Whoever had pushed me had come at a great force and a huge bruise was already visible on my back. If it hurt now, I knew it would be agony in the morning.

"What's he doing here?" I whispered, leaning toward Jeff and rolling my eyes in Ole's direction.

"Security insisted on calling the police after what happened. He's already talked to the rest of the mob."

I sighed. All I wanted was to go home with my husband and take a long soak in our big old claw-foot tub. But Ole had a right to know what had happened. Maybe it would make him a little less certain about having the right man in custody.

Ole echoed Jeff's concern, but his body language didn't reflect it. He was annoyed and wasn't hiding it.

I forced a smile. "You wouldn't have any aspirin on you, would you?"

"Antacids." He rattled a tin in his pants pocket for emphasis. "Lots of antacids."

Jeff gave me a kiss on the forehead, relieving me of my ruined boots. "Ought to have these bronzed. I'll be in my office if you need me, drying off." Although his hair was dry and neat, Jeff's bush shirt hung like a wet sheet. He inclined his head toward Ole. "Your friend wants a private chat with you."

"You don't have to wait. My Jeep is here—"

"I'd feel a lot better driving you home myself." He spared a warning glare at Ole and headed across the bridge, disappearing into the tunnel.

Ole stood, fists on hips, chomping down on a wad of gum, making it crack. "I hope I can talk more sense into you than I could that bull-headed husband of yours."

Time flew back twenty years. Ole Sorenson was the buff linebacker he used to be and I the rival team he was sizing up on the gridiron. The football hero and the snake girl. How he had ever picked me out of the bleachers was beyond me. I didn't even like sports. But then all of my friends squealed with delight when he asked me out and I couldn't say no. I was instantly transported into the popular clique of kids and found my mother squealing with delight, too. I felt like I had finally found some approval in her eyes. I was no longer the tomboy who found bugs more fascinating than boys. Dad, on the other hand, would have preferred I stayed with the bugs. Dating jocks wasn't high on his list of things he wanted for his teenaged daughter.

"You nearly got yourself killed tonight," Ole said.

"I was pushed," I pointed out. It wasn't like I had decided on a leisurely swim with a couple of crocodiles for grins and giggles.

He took a step closer, invading my personal space. "You were sticking your nose in where it don't belong."

I lifted my chin. I'm sure he recognized the stubborn gesture, as he didn't wait for my reply but barreled ahead as usual.

"Wanna tell me what the hell you think you're playing at, poking around here after hours in the dark?"

"Gary was supposed—"

"Gary!" Ole snorted. "That overeducated twit. A bit young for you, isn't he?"

"Very funny." His snide sense of humor hadn't changed any. "I wanted to talk to him."

"About what? No, no." He took a step back and held up his hands to ward off my response. "Let me guess. You think you can do better than the police. You think just because these are your friends and this is your turf that you can ask the right questions and you'll solve the crime and Erling will go free. Well, I've run into people like you before, and it don't work that way."

I started to protest, but he waved me off.

"I worked hard to get where I am, Lavender. I didn't do it by being an idiot or calling in favors. I worked damn hard. How'd you feel if I came in here and started telling you how to take care of your animals?"

Right, like he had ever given a damn about anything with more than two legs. But he was right—up to a point. I'd be furious at anyone trying to tell me how to do my job. I gestured vaguely, not willing to concede. "At least now you know the killer is still loose and JR didn't do it."

He pushed his baseball cap farther back on his head, a thin tuft of orange hair erupting next to the brim. "What I know is that you asked someone the wrong question and whoever it is wants you out of the way." A finger jabbed at me. "Like I said when I was here the first time, this was no accident. Someone struggled with Wright. They put their hands around his throat and tried to squeeze the life out of him. The bruises were on his neck. The two of 'em wrestled some and then the killer shoved Wright hard—hard enough so he broke through those temporary boards on the footbridge. Then the bastard let the crocodiles finish him off. But he was already dead before that big guy over there got to him."

"Is that true?" Optimism rose in my voice. If it was, then Sebastian couldn't be blamed indirectly for Wright's death. That made a huge difference.

Ole grunted assent. "The medical examiner says there was very little water in Wright's lungs, yet he drowned, though not in the usual way."

"I don't follow."

"It's weird. The ME said the brain was partly congested, a sign of death by suffocation; but his skin had signs of what's called 'goose-skin' which sometimes occurs in cases of sudden death, usually in drownings—"

"So which was it? Suffocation or drowning?"

"Both, I guess," Ole offered tentatively. "It happens when you're suddenly submerged and the water rushes up your nose. It can cause severe shock, you can even pass out. Like this, you're gone." He snapped his fingers. "Wright was already half dead from being choked. The plunge finished him off. Hell, there was even a famous case like this once. It happened in London around 1914. 'The Brides in the Bath' murder case. A guy kept knocking off his new brides for the insurance money. Jerked their knees up while they were in the tub, suddenly submerging them and they'd die just like Wright. Nasty." He shook his head.

I looked at Ole with new appreciation. That sounded like research. This, from the guy who paid someone else to do his homework. He saw my reaction and drew himself up.

"Yeah, I did some reading. Don't make a big deal out of it. The point is, Lavender, we're not just pissing in the wind here. We know what we're doing."

Ole motioned us back to the bench, where he flopped down, drew up a knee and rested his foot on the seat, as he regarded me circumspectly. "And now I have to figure out exactly what you've gone and dug up that would make someone mad enough to try and kill you."

I sat down on the other side of the bench, my damp shorts squishing as I sat. The earth-like concrete path under my bare feet felt cool and rough. I was beginning to smell like a bad day on the beach. My mind boiled over with lies and cover-ups. It was the same reaction he would have gotten from me in high school. Make up some excuse and then do exactly what he didn't want me to. Which in this case meant refusing to leave JR to the tender mercies of our judicial system.

Ole had every right to be irritated with me. I tried not to deny that. My snooping around could mess up his investigation, too. But how much information could I trust him with? If anything I suspected about McNealey and Wright got out, the zoo would suffer. And what I had found out about Melanie was more likely to hang JR than save him.

I could feel Ole's eyes boring into me as we sat in silence. Finally, he said, "So, you were coming down here to meet Gary. Which direction did you come from?"

I pointed down the trail, toward the curved path that led to where the kangaroos and koalas were housed.

"And you didn't hear or see anyone?"

I shook my head.

"You were coming from the administration offices upstairs. Who were you cross-examining there?"

I folded my arms across my chest and stared at my bare toes. "If you're going to continue to be your old charming self, I'm not going to tell you anything."

He leaned toward me. "Then I can take you down to the police station and keep you there until you do. I can even arrest you for obstructing justice."

He wasn't kidding either, much to my annoyance. After zinging him with a frosty stare, I capitulated. There wasn't much fight left in me. Slowly I went over the events of the day, my meeting with Butler Thomas and Suzanne Terak. I left out some of my suspicions and the fact that I had been eavesdropping outside Butler's door.

"What was McNealey doing there? Seems a long way from Capitol Hill."

"He's been a solid supporter of the zoo—"

Ole guffawed, screwing his face up in distaste. "McNealey's never been a strong supporter of anyone but McNealey. Pull the other one."

I found myself defending a man I detested. "Okay. Not always a solid supporter, but he's turned around in the last few months. If the legislature had kept their minds on business instead of arguing about the legal definition of marriage, he might have gotten a chance to vote in favor of that bonding bill and we wouldn't be faced with more budget cuts."

He didn't comment. Instead, he pulled a pack of Juicy Fruit from his pocket and began unwrapping a stick of gum to add to the collection in his mouth. He changed the subject.

"How well do you know Melanie Wright?"

"She's a good friend."

Ole wadded up the gum wrapper and pitched it into the nearby trashcan. "Does she confide in you? Talk about her personal life?"

I considered him carefully. It was possible he already knew what I had found out yesterday. It would make sense. He was a cop. He had access to other cops and a ton of information I could only guess at. It was time I quit thinking of him as that scholastically challenged high-school football star and started admitting the possibility that he had matured and changed as much as I had.

"What are you getting at?"

"Just routine questions. The spouse of a victim is generally where suspicion first falls."

"I thought you had your murderer?"

"Just double-checking my facts."

"Which are?"

He pulled a palm-sized notebook from his inside pocket and flipped through the pages. "You visited Mrs. Wright the day after the murder. How did she seem?"

Who told him that? Not that I had anything to hide. It was a condolence call. And I said as much.

"Was she distraught? Hysterical? In shock?"

"Everybody reacts differently to their grief. Her husband had just been murdered. What kind of shape do you think she was in?"

He changed tactics. "Did she know John Erling?"

I tried not to let my gaze shift from his. If he found out JR and Melanie knew each other in Florida, it would only make JR look guiltier. I answered with the truth. "I didn't ask her that."

And I hadn't. I had assumed from her reaction to JR's arrest that she only knew him as being one of the keepers on the Australia Walkabout.

"What about your husband? Where was he that evening?"

I tried not to let my mouth drop open. "You can't be serious?"

Ole lifted his shoulders. "He and Wright had a disagreement the night Wright was murdered. And not for the first time, I hear."

"Jeff did not kill Anthony Wright." I bristled, indignant and alarmed at even the suggestion. "He was with me all evening. And we have lots of witnesses to prove it."

"Maybe you were in on it. Didn't the two of you disappear for a while just before dinner?"

I started to protest, then remembered Jeff and I ducking behind the backdrop of the aboriginal band to grab a couple of moments alone together. We hadn't been gone long—just long enough to commit murder. But how could anyone think either Jeff or I—or both of us—would be capable of such a thing?

That's when I noticed Ole's sly smirk as he adjusted his hat. Then he chuckled self-indulgently. "See how easy that was?" He met my eyes, the smirk breaking into a lopsided smile. "Things aren't always the way they look, Lavender. Leave the detecting to the professionals."

Chapter 16

"We've got a traitor in our midst."

It was the last thing I expected to hear. I stood in the doorway of Jeff's tiny office just behind Crocodile Island. Aussie Trail Central we sometimes called it. It was a tight space. You couldn't open the door without banging it against one of the two desks that filled the room. But it served its purpose. The real space was allocated to the animals. We humans just had to make do. An alert bearded dragon pressed his nose against the glass of his condo in the reptile hotel, a vertical stack of aquariums wedged into the tight space behind Jeff's desk.

"We've what?" I stared at Jeff for an explanation.

He motioned toward Gary Olson, who sat on an up-ended plastic bucket, leaning forward with elbows on knees. He looked miserable, anxiously shifting his eyes away as I entered. I stifled a yawn. I was still damp from my unscheduled swim in the billabong and exhausted from my sparring match with Detective Sorenson.

Jeff didn't look like he was joking; there were signs of a storm brewing behind his intense blue eyes. And it was directed at *Zoofari*'s young intern. Considering the way I felt toward Gary at the moment, it looked like he was going to catch hell from both of us.

And yet something about his tone didn't sit right with me. After all the time I'd been with Jeff, you'd think I'd be able to read him like yesterday's newspaper; but he could still catch me with his damned Aussie sarcasm.

My body, which had tensed up, relaxed. "You're putting me on, right?"

"Only a little," he admitted, still in ill humor. "Gary's shown his true colors and they aren't pretty."

"What're you talking about?"

"This." He waved a computer printout he'd snatched from his desk. "They're the research articles he gave you. Have a look."

I took the papers and was immediately drawn to the top sheet, which was an article from Gary's website. I hadn't seen it during my initial glance at the material. Now that it was on top of the pile I was taken aback. A collage of animal photos formed a vertical border on the right and on the left were hyperlinks to other pages on his site. Dead center was an article titled "The Wolf Among Us." I raised an eyebrow in Gary's direction as I perched on the corner of Jeff's desk and began scanning the contents.

> *Where Anthony Wright goes, death and destruction follow. He uses his rank and position to destroy what he professes to save. The selling of exotic species for profit is a million-dollar business. Asian medicines, fenced trophy shoots, exotic pets. Anthony Wright fed them all. The death of innocents. The destruction of trust.*
>
> *He got his start in the state of Texas, where every man and woman has a gun in the pickup and where there are more tigers on the back forty than there are left in the wild.*

It was melodramatic and over the top. I found myself rereading whole paragraphs in disbelief. According to Gary, Wright put himself through college writing phony death certificates for exotic species and then turned around and sold the very much alive animals to a private dealer, who in turn sold them to another dealer and so on. Until there was no paper trail left to trace. If the U.S. Fish and Wildlife Service caught up with a dealer, the suspect only had to claim it wasn't his animal, or that the sale he'd made was legal. He claimed to have no idea how that lion ended up in an exotic meat market in Chicago. It wasn't one of his.

And a zoo was the perfect place to line his pockets. Overbreeding leads to overcrowding. What do you do with the cute crowd-drawing babies that grow into adults? The surplus is sold to private dealers, breeders, ranchers, whoever will take them—at a tidy profit.

Jeff waited patiently until I looked up from my reading, his arms folded across his chest. He nodded at my startled expression. "Leaves you kind of gobsmacked, doesn't it? Total character assassination."

I turned on Gary. "And you think Wright was selling off our surplus stock? When was the last time you saw a surplus of baby animals around here?"

"Well, I—"

"We've got a newborn gibbon that has to be fed six times a day, around the clock, that the public won't be able to see until he's old enough to fend for himself. By that time he won't look much different from mom and dad. And the new tiger cubs—have you seen the public oohing and ahing over them?" Before he could stutter out an answer, I answered for him. "No. Because we don't have anyplace to put them on display. Our tiger nursery was turned into an exhibit for the new aardvark. All we can provide is a web cam from the nursery in the healthcare building."

Gary averted his eyes, painfully ill at ease. "There are other zoos—"

"There are no other zoos—Christ! Gary. It's been ten years

since a gibbon was born here. Four years since we've had tiger cubs, and fifteen years since we bred one of those cute little Przewalski horses. I don't see a surplus of baby animals bringing the crowds in, do you? We have an SSP that dictates when, where and with whom an animal can be bred. All accredited zoos follow these recommendations. If we don't have another accredited zoo looking for offspring, we don't breed them."

The SSP was our Bible, the Species Survival Program. This was the database that organized scientifically managed breeding programs to try and maintain a self-sustaining and genetically diverse captive population. In some cases, the hope was to someday reintroduce these species back into their native habitat—if there was any habitat left. It was just one of the many tools zoological parks and aquariums around the world used to ensure a species' survival.

That Gary would have the sheer balls to write a libelous, vindictive exposé of Anthony Wright left me speechless. That he would ruin the reputation of zoos everywhere in the process made me livid. It was reckless and irresponsible. He had obviously missed the chapter on ethics in his journalism classes at the university.

"Snake, I'm sorry," Gary implored, sitting up. "But . . . but it's the same stuff I handed you last night. I didn't hear any objections then. And the stuff about Wright is right on."

I frowned. Last night I hadn't been able to get past the fact that Melanie had worked at Sweetwater Creek and hadn't told me. I had never bothered to read the stack of information Gary had given me, never guessing he'd come up with this crapola.

"You haven't got squat," Jeff said. " 'Cept maybe an expensive libel suit. Does the article you're doing on me look anything like this?" he asked with justifiable concern.

On the defensive, Gary stood up, snatching the other printouts from Jeff's desk. "I'd never do that to you," he said, sounding hurt. "You're the real deal. You really care about your animals." Turning over several pages, Gary found what he wanted. "Anyway, it's not libel if it's true! Read this." Gary jabbed a finger at a reprinted article from the *Amarillo Herald.*

It was dated 1965 and reported the arrest of a man for dealing in the sale of endangered animals. The accused had a ranch near Hereford, Texas, a small town in Deaf Smith County. Several ill and poorly cared for animals were found in the man's possession, including a pair of golden tamarins and a Bengal tiger cub.

It made me sick to my stomach.

I glowered at Gary. "What does this prove? Lots of people are arrested each year for mistreating and selling endangered animals. I don't see Anthony Wright's name in this article."

"It should have been there," returned Gary with youthful intensity. "He was living in Deaf Smith County back then. His father's zoo was there. It's less than ten miles from Hereford."

"Mate, that's a bit of a leap," Jeff said. "If the coppers didn't draw that conclusion back then, what makes you think you can now? You need proof."

Gary's bright blue eyes shone with triumph as he turned the papers to another article. It came from one of those weekly newspapers that abound in small communities across the country. It was another one from Texas, and it alluded to the financial problems of Deaf Smith County Zoo, a privately owned zoological garden near Amarillo. Highlighted in yellow was a sentence regarding the unexpected deaths of some prized animals—a pair of golden tamarins and a Bengal tiger cub. It had been a blow, but with the help of his son, the zoo's owner was able to dig in his heels and managed to turn the zoo around financially. The son was Anthony Wright.

Jeff was not swayed. "Wright had a knack for turning around failed enterprises. That's no secret. He's always been good at cost cutting, efficiency, and raising cash. If I'm not mistaken—" Jeff screwed up his face, recalling, "Wright created some quite novel fundraising ideas in his youth. The zoo's financial success didn't come from illegally selling its animals."

"That's because he doctored the books and made it all look legit! The hide of a big cat can bring in two thousand big ones, the meat another thousand bucks. That's a big temptation for anyone."

"Proof, Gary," I said. "You need proof, not innuendo."

"It's not innuendo."

"Until you back it up with evidence it is."

"Okay—okay," he conceded.

Our eyes met. "This website piece is a hatchet job, Gary. You could do a lot of harm to reputations with this, to good people who've worked hard. I'm disappointed in you. I want it down. Now!"

The college student opened his mouth to speak, but stayed himself, floundering in his own turmoil. At last he gave up and hung his head, staring glumly at the floor as he let out a frustrated sigh. It was then I noticed the marks on his left arm. Two six-inch scratches jagged down his bare forearm to his wrist where my nails had dug into him as he'd pulled me away from Sebastian's snapping jaws. He'd saved my life, along with Jeff, less than two hours ago.

I felt a pang of guilt—and something else I couldn't understand.

"Gary . . ." I softened, trying a different tack. "Don't you see how bad this article makes you look? It makes you a suspect. It shows you had it in for Wright."

Gary's head shot up, fear in his eyes.

"And you had direct contact with Wright," I pointed out. "Like the rest of us, you could have ambushed him. Now you've given the police a motive. Yeah, it's a pretty weak one, I'll admit.

You disagreed with Wright's stand on conservation and animal issues. Hardly a reason to kill a man, but the police might not be so charitable. What's more, it just looks bad when you publish crap like this, not just for you but everyone associated with you. And that includes Jeff and me. You've got to be more careful."

Frankly, I saw Gary as a paper tiger, ferocious behind his keyboard, but hardly one to get involved in a face-to-face confrontation. Nonetheless, he could still do a lot of damage from the safety of his bedroom office.

He nodded back, still looking concerned. "Guess I didn't see it that way before. Sorry." Then he considered his next point with care. "But I didn't manufacture that stuff. It's based on solid research. You wanted proof, Snake. It's in there. There's that bird sanctuary Wright worked his financial magic on. What happened to a suitcase full of hyacinth macaws the U.S. Fish and Wildlife Service confiscated from a smuggler and then entrusted to the sanctuary?"

"You tell us."

"Half of them died—supposedly." Gary Olson stood back with satisfaction, pushing his glasses back up on his nose.

"The trauma of having their beaks and legs taped and getting stuffed into plastic tubes and packed in a suitcase for God knows how long with no food and water will do that to a bird," Jeff pointed out with more than a little sarcasm.

Gary wasn't ready to give up. "The rest of the birds disappeared. And a hyacinth can bring ten grand on the black market. Enough to put a guy through college back then."

"Was an arrest made?"

"They assumed it was an outside job. Someone broke in and took the healthy ones. It had to be—"

"Time out." Jeff put out a restraining hand, surging to his feet. "I think that's enough wild speculation for one night, Gary.

By tomorrow morning this flaming article of yours had better do a permanent walkabout from your website. And let's hope no one else has seen it and taken it seriously."

"It just went up today. I thought when Snake didn't say anything—"

"Don't shift the blame to Snake, mate. You're old enough to know better."

Gary tried to protest.

"Back off." Jeff indicated the door with a stern tone. "End of discussion. It's been a long, hard day. I'm taking Snake home and putting her to bed." His voice grew affectionate as I stifled another yawn. "Poor sheila's knackered."

Gary desperately rifled through his papers as he moved toward the door. "Wait! You got to look at this. There's an outfit called International Wildlife Supply—"

"They're an accredited middleman, Gary. They've got the equipment to transport larger animals. A zoo can't afford to keep equipment like that." Jeff held the door open.

"Yeah, but they subcontracted to Wild Acres, Incorporated. And it has ties to the South American suppliers the smuggled macaws were traced to."

"Right," Jeff agreed, leaning against the doorframe, "but that implicates Wild Acres, not Anthony Wright."

Agitated, Gary looked from me to Jeff, hoping to convince us. He thought he had carefully pieced together a solid case and here we were poking holes in it. "Okay. It's not a smoking gun. There are links, though—too many to be coincidence. Individually, they don't mean much. But string them all together and they smell pretty fishy. Doesn't it seem funny to you that JR is accused of selling Florida panthers at the same time Anthony Wright is in the same city in Florida and his wife—his *wife,* for crying out loud!—works at JR's animal park?"

I slammed the door shut and faced Gary. "Now you're accusing Melanie?"

"No!" he denied vehemently, his voice starting to fray. "All I'm saying is that it's another link. Something very irregular happens and there's Anthony Wright with a connection through his wife." Gary's hands clutched the top of his head. "There's a multibillion-dollar exotic animal trade out there and Wright was part of it! Somehow, some way, he was involved!"

In the aftermath of that brash statement, Gary slumped down on the edge of Jeff's desk, his troubled expression urging us to believe him. It was then, while he was unprepared, that I decided to drop the other shoe on him.

"Is this why Wright threw you out of his office? During that interview you didn't have? Did you try all these wild accusations out on him?"

I repeated what Suzanne Terak had told me about Gary's visit to Anthony Wright's office, filling Jeff in on our intern's little lie.

Jeff gave Gary a cold stare. "You told us you hadn't spoken with him."

Gary's dreadlocks wilted around his face. "I'm sorry. I didn't want to lie to you." He pushed his glasses up on his nose, eyes cast down. "I was afraid you'd be mad . . ."

"You got that right, mate. I'm mad now. What exactly did you say to him?"

Our intern sank further into himself under the pressure of Jeff's glare. "I just—I guess I got a little carried away. He was expecting some dumb student to ask him a lot of fluff and I gave him the hard stuff. I wanted to know why Senator McNealey had suddenly changed his mind about the bond issue for the zoo." He drew in a deep breath. "I wanted to know why it coincided with a sizeable contract between Hanley-Holm and Carruth Construction."

I blinked. "Hanley-Holm? Melanie's department store chain?"

Gary nodded. "Actually, it's her family's business, though she'll inherit a hunk of change when the old man retires."

"I know that, Gary. Tell me about the deal."

"They just bought out that chain of discount stores and were going to do some expanding out west. Carruth was hired as construction manager for the project—"

"But the deal fell through," I finished for him.

"Yeah, but I didn't know it at the time. I don't think the senator did either."

"Until the night—"

"—of the Beastly Ball." Jeff and I completed in unison.

So I had been partially right about Senator Ted McNealey and Anthony Wright. That night they had been arguing. I had assumed it concerned McNealey exchanging political favors for Carruth Construction receiving the Phase Two construction contract from the zoo and Wright backing out of the contract. If it didn't involve an illegal under-the-table deal between Carruth and the Minnesota Valley Zoo, that would explain why Suzanne Terak had dodged my questions by telling me it wasn't her secret to tell. It wasn't. While the zoo might have profited from the deal, it was off the hook.

Anthony Wright could have easily influenced his father-in-law into hiring and firing Carruth Construction. Phase Two zoo construction could have netted Carruth thirty million dollars, tops. For a chain of retail stores you were probably looking at sixty to a hundred million dollars per store. That was a hell of a contract to lose.

And more than enough to commit murder over.

Chapter 17

Jeff insisted I sleep in the next morning. He called the staff and asked if someone would mind staying a little later to cover for me. Considering this involved another turn at bottle-feeding Little Jack, our baby gibbon, just about any keeper at the zoo would be only too happy to oblige. As for me, I was thankful for a couple of extra hours in bed, where unconsciousness allowed a respite from thinking about what I'd gone through in the past twenty-four hours.

I sent Jeff off to the zoo, despite his wanting to stay home and keep an eye on me. There was too much going on for both of us to be late that Wednesday. After a sleepy goodbye kiss I buried my face back into my pillow and was out in a nanosecond. By the time I finally hauled myself out of bed it was almost nine a.m. I bumped and shuffled my way around like a decrepit old crone, hunched over and barely functional. My back ached from last night's blow and every muscle in my body throbbed from my struggle with Sebastian. My ankle was tender from nearly being bitten off and Technicolor bruises had already flowered around the puncture marks on my calf.

Someone had tried to kill me last night. The seriousness sank in despite my efforts to brush it aside. Now that I was awake and the events had played in my head for the umpteenth time, emotions churned in a jumble of feelings: apprehension, vulnerability, indecisiveness.

And anger, lots and lots of anger.

Kow bolted for cover with feline indignation as I limped around the kitchen, slamming cupboard doors and venting my frustration by chipping dishes and denting a frying pan. Someone wanted me dead. And they'd almost succeeded. I was furious. I wanted to scream. Instead I slammed another cupboard door.

How *dare* they?

My teeth ground together as I searched for something else to hurl across the kitchen. As if reading my mind, Kow beat a hasty exit out of the room while Bagger kept his snout buried in his food dish, oblivious.

It was no good. A barrage of mental images ricocheted in front of me, each plucking one emotional string after another until I didn't know what to feel. A stab of pain through my lower back sent me to the bathroom for more aspirin. After downing more than the suggested dosage, I decided on a long, hot bath to ease my protesting muscles and, I hoped, to soothe my raw emotions as well.

An hour later I emerged from the bathroom in my terrycloth robe, wide -awake, less achy, but no less conflicted. With a growing sense of futility, I wandered into the living room and slumped onto the sofa, leaning forward with my head in my hands. A dark, wet curtain of hair hung in front of my face and shoulders. I wanted to draw that curtain closed and hide behind it.

What was I suppose to do? Just cave in to threats? Give up because someone wanted me to? God! I was pissed. Really, *really* pissed. My sense of outrage began to boil over.

The last time I'd felt this riled up, I'd been driving along 35E in Mendota Heights. It was an early Sunday morning and the road was free of its usual congestion when a shiny Dodge Ram pickup raced up from behind, sped past me and shot ahead. It soon angled closer to the right shoulder, where a black trash bag flew out the passenger's window and landed in the grassy ditch.

"For crying out loud, Studly," I grumbled, reading his vanity plates, "find a damned garbage can next time!"

A moment before I passed the trash bag, it moved.

Something inside was alive.

I veered to the shoulder of the road, kicking up gravel as I squealed to a stop. Jumping out of the Jeep, I raced to where the bag had been tossed, terrified of what I'd find inside. Ripping open the plastic I was immediately greeted by the wide, frightened eyes of a puppy. The golden retriever's high-pitched whine melted my heart. He yelped as I picked him up, but eagerly licked my face when I hugged him to me.

Son of a bitch! My eyes seared down the highway. Heartless bastard. How could he? Running to my Jeep, I made sure the puppy was okay, set him down next to me, slammed the door shut, ripped the gearbox into drive and jammed the pedal to the floor. I must have gone twenty miles over the speed limit but I was hell-bent on catching that pickup. Five minutes later I felt a jolt of satisfaction when my target appeared a quarter mile ahead of me and I slowed down to follow. Within two minutes he pulled off onto Pilot Knob Road and into a Holiday station. I squealed in next to him and was screaming before my feet hit the ground.

Fortyish-looking with a big gut and flat-top crew cut, he was at least a head taller than me and easily a hundred pounds heavier, but I didn't care.

"What the hell's wrong with you?" I shouted, tossing the empty garbage bag at him. "You don't throw an animal out of a moving truck like he's a sack of garbage!"

"Lady, I don't know what you're talking about."

"I saw you!"

"You got the wrong guy."

I was in his face now. "Let me give you a piece of advice, *Studly;* next time you plan on doing something illegal or just plain stupid, take off the vanity plates."

His jaw tightened, his face turning red right up to the crew cut. "Not your fucking business."

"I'm making it my fucking business! If you didn't want the animal take it to a shelter—that's what they're for! You don't toss a dog away like an empty beer can—on the freeway!" I was shouting, my body shaking. Other customers looked over with curiosity.

Studly made a threatening gesture, flexing his thick biceps. I didn't care.

My hands were balled into tight fists, ready to fight. "Go ahead, chump. Just try it. You know how many witnesses I've got? Add assault to your troubles, too, why don't you?"

His eyes shifted, and he noticed the others. He backed off reluctantly, his face turning red. "Piss off," he said through clenched teeth.

"Don't worry. I'm leaving; but you're not getting away with this. I'm reporting you for animal cruelty—and that's letting you off easy, pal. If it were up to me, I'd put you in a trash bag and throw *you* out a speeding car down the highway!"

I turned and marched away. My throat hurt, and it took my heart twenty minutes to settle down after I realized what I'd done, but I didn't regret it. Not for a moment.

That day it had been easy, I knew what I had to do. I never thought of the consequences. I was fearless because I was incensed by that bozo's blatant act of cruelty. This time things weren't as clear. I didn't have a name and a face to direct my outrage at. It all felt so useless, like cursing at the wind. In the end, the only tangible things I had were my emotions—my anger, frustration, and doubt.

Just who did I think I was? Did I really believe I was going to solve Wright's murder and clear JR? Was I really that naïve? Or stupid? And what about the murder in Florida? How did that connect?

It seemed hopeless. Tears gathered behind my eyes. No! No, you won't cry, dammit. You won't!

But I did.

The next thing I felt was a cold nose nuzzling against my arm and a wet tongue slopping across my hand. Bagger regarded me with wide, anxious, caring eyes. They were nearly the same as the day I'd first found him inside that plastic bag by the freeway, just bigger. He snuffled past my wet hair and licked my face with abandon. Overcome, I grabbed his beautiful head and pressed it against me, hearing his huge tail thump happily against the carpet.

It was almost noon before I dragged myself to the zoo, just in time for little Jack's next feeding. The health-care center smelled of cat hair, alcohol and ripe bananas. Dr. Steve was in the nursery room, hunched over an incubator, the tag of his white lab coat waving over his collar. He looked up, motioning me in. If he took any notice of my bandaged leg or the limp, he made no comment. But that was Dr. Steve for you. By now my narrow escape in the croc pool must have hit the rumor mill, the story growing with each new telling, but our senior veterinarian typically ignored most gossip and got on with what was most important to him—the health and welfare of the animals.

I donned a lab coat, face mask and gloves and went in for a closer look. My heart melted. The cute meter was off the charts with this little guy. Three days old, the baby white-cheeked gibbon weighed only a little over a pound. His pink, wrinkled skin was covered in a soft fuzz that would soon grow into a smooth buff coat like his mother's. Blending in with mom was good camouflage in the wild. In six months he'd darken, taking on the black coat and white cheeks of his father.

Clutching a fake-fur pillow with hands that seemed much too large for his tiny body, Jack stared up at me with deep-brown eyes that dominated his impish face. He should have been clutching his mother, a first-time mom who had never had the benefit of growing up with siblings. She simply didn't know what to do with him and so she had rejected him.

"We showed him off to Ma and Pa this morning," Dr. Steve's voice was somewhat muffled from behind his face mask. "Neither of them took too much notice of him. They were much more interested in the fresh grapes and figs we brought them."

Understandable. In time, it was hoped, the two adults would associate the pleasure of these treats with the appearance of their offspring and hopefully show a bit more interest in him. Meanwhile these visits were important, even if there was no physical contact. We wanted Jack to relate to other gibbons and be comfortable with them.

"How's the Komodo doing?" I asked reaching into the incubator to pick the young gibbon up along with the pillow he clung to.

"No better, perhaps slightly worse," the doctor answered, as he prepared a bottle of formula for Jack. "But I'm concerned we're running out of time. If things don't improve in the next day or two we'll have to go in and get the toy."

"Jeff would like to be part of that."

"Wouldn't think of letting him miss it. If nothing else, he'll want to watch. That is, if he can tear himself away from his crocs. Though if I know Jeff, he'll want to lend a hand."

For a moment it was like having an out-of-body experience. I don't know why, just the odd sensation that a veil had just been momentarily whisked away from my eyes and I'd seen the world more clearly. Except it flashed by so fast I couldn't grasp it.

"Snake?" Dr. Steve spoke my name and I snapped out of my

reverie. He handed me the warmed baby bottle and went off to check on his other patients.

Mentally I was wandering and needed to focus on the task at hand. Jack accepted the offered bottle and sucked greedily on the nipple while clinging to the comfort of the faux-fur pillow. I covered him with a square of sheepskin and tried not to rock as I fed him. Mother gibbons don't rock their babies. The less he imprinted on humans, the better. An adult gibbon without a healthy fear of humans could be a dangerous animal. And we wanted him interacting and breeding with other white-cheeked gibbons. I forced myself to relax. Focusing on this task helped ease my nerves, letting me forget last night's attack and other issues I needed to grapple with once away from the soothing confines of the health-care center's walls.

But not for long.

A tap on the nursery window made me look up. Melanie Wright waved with an "oh, isn't he cute" expression at the suckling baby on my lap. It was the first time since the death of her husband that I'd seen her at the zoo. Her keeper's duties had been taken on by other staff in deference to her loss.

It had always impressed me that this well-to-do wife of the director of the zoo had wanted to work a regular lower-level staff job when she could have taken on more prestigious assignments. Working with animals was what she liked to do and you don't get that daily, hands-on gratification in Mahogany Row, as we called the executive suite.

Melanie wasn't in uniform and despite her thin smile, she looked drained. Maybe her husband's death was finally taking its toll. I found myself feeling sorry for her and rethinking what I wanted to say. You couldn't lay into a woman who had just lost her husband. Especially when that husband had been murdered.

"Snake," she said as I came out of the room after leaving the gibbon sleeping peacefully in the incubator. "Are you all right?" Her eyes fell to my bandaged leg. "I heard about what happened last night."

"I'm fine." I wasn't, but I was tired of rehashing it. "Is that why you're here?"

"I wanted to talk." Her eyes shifted to the side, avoiding mine.

We left the cool comfort of the health center and walked slowly along the utility road toward the African exhibits, keeping under the shade of the trees. The health center sat in what we called "the private sector," a part of the zoo the public wasn't allowed to visit except by special invitation. Under the shelter of the trees and surrounded by outbuildings, holding areas and dense native vegetation, it was easy to forget this wasn't a private little world reserved for the dedicated few who worked here.

Melanie rubbed her hands together, stopping to twist her wedding ring around her finger. "I don't know where to start."

"Why don't you start with JR?"

She nodded. "JR." She said the name with amusement, watching her feet as we walked along the unpaved path. "I didn't know him as that. To me he was always Jamie."

Jamie? Ah, James Robert O'Malley, I remembered.

"I should have told you before that I knew him. I wasn't thinking straight when you came to call. I was still numb over Anthony's death. Besides, what would have been gained by telling you I'd known him before?" She folded her arms across her chest as if to ward off a chill. "I'm sorry I lied to you, Snake." Her eyes flicked up to me in earnest. "Really I am. But Jamie was in enough trouble as it was. I didn't want to make things worse for him."

"I think you already have. Now the police will think you were hiding something. Wouldn't telling the truth from the beginning have been better?"

Melanie shook her head. "Not necessarily—"

We hurriedly stepped aside to let a golf cart pass. Golf carts were zoo personnel's main means of transportation from one end of the zoo to the other. Mitch Flanagan waved from the driver's seat, but didn't stop to offer us a lift.

On the trail again, Melanie continued, "I didn't want the police to draw any connections between Jamie and Anthony. They're already convinced he's the killer. They're like a dog with a bone. They won't let go."

"Was there a connection?"

"If you're asking me if Anthony knew him, no. He never had enough interest in my life away from home, never visited the parks where I worked. And at this zoo . . . well, until last week I didn't even know Jamie was in Minnesota, let alone that he worked here! He looks so different without the beard." She smiled slightly at the memory.

We reached the security entry that separated the utility path from the African Trail and kept the public out of our private domain. Melanie Wright turned away from me to swing the wide gate open and I thought I saw her shoulders sag marginally, as though that instant away from me allowed her emotions to surface briefly. Our shoes crunched on the gravel before we transitioned to the asphalt of the public trail, the gate clanging shut behind us.

"How well did you know him?" I asked, not liking the sudden suspicions crowding my thoughts.

I felt the tension crawl up my spine as a flush of emotion gently washed over her features like cumulus clouds casting shadows. She was an enigma at times. The woman had such poise and dignity; I admired her for that.

When Melanie spoke again, it was in a thoughtful, forthright manner. "No one has more of an interest in finding Anthony's killer than me, Snake. And I know Jamie didn't do it." She paused for emphasis. "He's a good man. What happened to him in Florida was shameful. He worked hard, very hard, for those animals, building his reputation. And then to be accused of murder . . ." She sighed. "I can't imagine the hardships he's gone through since then, running, hiding out in Mexico. . . ."

Her voice trailed off and we walked in silence, the smell of manure and hay cutting through the humidity. We stopped to watch one of our reticulated giraffes scratch his long neck along the red brick of the giraffe house. Taiyko was a big guy, almost sixteen feet tall, and still growing.

"Melanie," I said, "did JR know who Anthony was?"

"Personally?" she dipped her head and looped a lock of hair behind her right ear. "No. Jamie only knew him as a signature on the checks."

"Checks?" I made her turn toward me.

She managed a wan smile at the uneasiness in my face. "I guess Anthony did listen to my work stories—once in a while. That was in the early days," she amended, "when he was still at the law firm. When things got tough for the park and he was tired of my complaining, he'd bully his law partners into making a sizable tax-deductible donation. Or he'd collar one of his rich cronies. He was good that way. But come down to Sweetwater Creek and check it out himself? Never! In those days he was very hands-off. He never met Jamie. There's absolutely no connection between the two."

My leg began to throb and I sat down at the observation point that had been set up in front of the giraffe exhibit. A wooden bench sat beneath a shady canopy of thatch, simulating the roofs of an African hut in Kenya where wild populations of giraffes still struggled to survive. Only this was a hut with a single wall that posted biofacts on giraffes and a video that could be turned on to watch the birth of a giraffe.

Another giraffe rambled into the bright sunlight, closely followed by a smaller carbon copy of herself. The little one couldn't have been more than a couple of days old, but was already six feet tall.

"We've certainly had a rash of births over the past week," I commented, watching the little one nuzzling his mother's dappled underbelly, sucking loudly when he hit pay dirt.

Melanie pressed the toe of her shoe against the bench support, her eyes downcast. "We've been lucky."

Had we? Jeff and I had discussed the other "facts" Gary had tossed at us last night. Neither of us wanted to consider the possibility that Anthony Wright was dealing in the illegal sale of exotic animals. The possibility he could have done so at our zoo was disheartening.

"I wish I had been here when Uhura gave birth," Melanie said, indicating the new mom. "It's quite a sight. Have you ever witnessed the birth of a giraffe?"

I had. It had been the first birth of a giraffe at the zoo and our director wanted to take full advantage and publicize it as widely as possible. The *Zoofari* crew had been on hand to record Savannah's entry into the world. While on this topic, the latent sadness that had hovered around Melanie was lifted, a lightness returned, easing the delicate lines creasing her brow; yet I felt compelled to steer her back on course, even if we both enjoyed the diversion.

"Suzanne Terak told me what you said to the board of directors yesterday."

"What did I say?" she asked, a wary tone creeping into her voice.

"About not wanting the zoo to cover up the truth about Anthony's death in order to protect you or his reputation."

"Those weren't my exact words, but yes. I didn't want Jamie being railroaded for something he didn't do. Nor do I want a whitewash. Let the chips fall where they may. I didn't want the

Board to use Jamie as a scapegoat for anyone else's wrongdoing."

The giraffes were quietly scavenging through the salad bar that hung from a feeding post planted near the front of their enclosure. Baskets of fresh greens and carrots were hung over their heads, forcing them to stretch and work for their supper like they would in the wild. Cow and bull used their long prehensile tongues to yank lettuce leaves from the baskets above, while their young calf got his meal a bit closer to the ground.

I picked my next words carefully. "What happened to the calf that was born last year? Is she still here?"

"That was almost two years ago, Snake. And no she's not. Savannah was loaned out to Lincoln Park Zoo in Chicago."

"Is she still there?" I asked, trying to sound casual, crossing my fingers. "You were in Chicago for an AZA conference a while ago. Did you stop by the zoo to see her?"

Melanie shifted, turning with a puzzled look. "Last month I gave her keeper a call. I like to keep updated on how other zoos are managing our stock. She was doing well."

I let a relieved whistle under my breath. Gary's accusations were clouding my judgment. But Melanie was staring at me, expecting an explanation I wasn't prepared to give.

"Can I ask you a question?" Melanie took a step in my direction, her body a gray shadow backlit against the bright sun.

I raised my hand to shield my eyes, but couldn't see her face.

"Why were you attacked last night?" she asked. "Why would someone do something like that?"

I looked down at my leg and picked at the bandage that hid the damage Sebastian had done. "Someone wanted to shut me up. I guess I stuck my nose where it wasn't wanted."

"You've been playing detective?"

"And not very well, I guess. I come up with more questions than I do answers."

Melanie stepped out of the sun. She regarded me briefly, then directed her attention toward the giraffes again. "If someone tried to kill you for asking the wrong questions, I'd think it's fair to say the person who killed Anthony might still be out there. That means Jamie's innocent."

"You'd think. The idea of an accomplice seems to be a popular theory with the police right now."

Melanie turned and made a face. "That doesn't help Jamie much."

No, it didn't. Nothing I learned seemed to help JR much. At least nothing I could prove.

"You're lucky you didn't get seriously hurt, Snake—or worse," she added with caution.

"I know."

"Any ideas who pushed you?"

"Ted McNealey," I blurted out, only half-seriously. It was the first name that came to mind.

"The senator?"

"Well, I don't know that for a fact. But less than an hour before the attack he was royally pissed off at the world, ranting to Butler how unfairly he'd been treated by Anthony. Didn't like me asking him about the argument they'd had before dinner. Even threatened me."

"Oh?"

I nodded. "Yeah, I admit I was a pain in the ass. But if looks could kill, he was visually assassinating me in Butler's office. And how do we know he left the zoo afterwards? He could've hung around to get me at the right moment."

Melanie frowned thoughtfully. "I suppose . . . but that doesn't seem his style. I've talked to Ted more than you have, Snake, and I'm not sure he'd be capable of something like that. A man in his position has a lot to lose."

Only if he gets caught, I almost said, then reconsidered. Melanie was my friend, but she also knew McNealey. How close they were I didn't know. It's too easy to assume your friends feel the same way you do about another person. Often they don't. I had to be careful. I recalled what Melanie had said the day I had come to pay my condolences and found the senator on his way out. She had voiced concern that Wright's political cronies would be lining up to make sure she lived up to the commitments he'd made. That alone made me believe she found the idea distasteful and that I could trust her. Did McNealey think she would be ignorant of what had transpired between him and Wright?

"Mel, you knew Anthony was going to cut McNealey out of the Phase Two construction contracts, didn't you?"

"Yes." Her voice seemed distant. "What with the budget cuts, Phase Two is pretty much on hold."

"Is that the only reason?"

Her lips pressed together then parted. "A few of the subcontractors hired by Carruth are suspected of using materials that aren't entirely up to standards. Regardless, Carruth was the general contractor and responsible for everything. It's their job to make sure the project is done to code. Anthony believed it was intentional—bid the contract with materials that more than meet building regulations; build it with lesser-quality materials and pocket the difference. Not acceptable. Anthony was livid."

"And the senator's been putting the squeeze on you to honor the Hanley-Holm contract?"

"Oh, yes." The corners of her mouth stretched. "Ted underestimated me. Thought he might charm me, I guess, or help me through my grief. I saw him yesterday just before the board meeting. He was here lobbying his case. I told him there was no chance we'd reconsider. Carruth was out. He nearly had an aneurysm. So I'm probably the one who set him off before you saw him, Snake. I lit the fuse, but you were there for the explosion. Sorry."

My mind was spinning. So while Ted McNealey was venting at me yesterday, was his anger really aimed at Melanie? On the other hand, I had more or less accused him of exchanging favors to further the family business. Not the best motive to go after me, since the senator's business dealings seemed to be becoming public knowledge. I wasn't as positive he'd been my attacker as I had been a minute ago.

Perhaps sensing this, Melanie asked, "If Ted McNealey didn't attack you, who else could have?"

To be honest I couldn't think of anyone else. Ole had warned me about jumping to conclusions, and I was glad he wasn't here now to lecture me again. Yet I had been attacked, and not far from where I'd been knocked into the billabong was another overturned trash container. What was our trashcan bandit looking for? I knew I shouldn't jump to conclusions but the two incidents certainly seemed connected.

"Have you talked to Shari yet?" Melanie asked, turning her face away from me, watching the giraffes with renewed interest. "She's pretty devoted to him."

Oh Lord! I straightened up. My fingers gripped the edge of the bench. "If you worked with JR, you worked with Shari, didn't you?" At her reluctant nod, I sallied on. "Which means she knew you, too. So why didn't she say something to me about this?" *Or you for that matter,* but I bit my tongue and didn't say it.

Shari had asked me to help JR and clear his name. I thought she had told me everything the night I had driven her home. How much more was she hiding?

"Maybe she thought she was protecting Jamie."

"Maybe." Melanie and Shari had that in common. What was I missing here? "How well did you know her?"

Melanie chuckled at some vague thought. "I'd watch myself around her, Snake. She's not all that she seems. Inside that soft Southern-belle exterior lurks the iron will of Scarlett O'Hara." She slapped at a mosquito that had landed on her bare arm, a sour expression on her usually sweet face. "You have no idea how far that woman will go to get what she wants. She threw herself at Jamie in Florida, when it was apparent to everyone else at the park he had no interest in her. It was embarrassing for everyone, especially Jamie."

"And what the hell would y'all know about it!" A shrill new voice burst in from behind us.

Speak of the devil.

Chapter 18

Shari Jensen confronted us, hands on hips, her full lips set in a grim line. The electric pink cowboy shirt she wore had one too many buttons open, while the rest of her was tightly belted into a pair of brushed-on Western jeans. Her footwear was what got my blood boiling. Snakeskin boots. And from where I was standing, they did not look like fake rattlesnake. She must have gone on a little shopping spree after JR was arrested, because if she had brought those home while he was around, they would have been tossed in the dumpster.

"Well, if it ain't Little Miss Goody Two-shoes." Shari swept her mass of curly blond hair behind her shoulders, eyes narrowing like a cat who'd found a new toy. "I thought I'd find you here. Good thing, too, from what I'm hearing. Talking about me behind my back." She wagged her finger at Melanie and for a moment I thought she might be drunk.

"Don't you dare try to pull your shit here," Melanie lashed out, her eyes firing daggers. "I'll call security and have you tossed out on your ass."

"My, my, the lady swears." Shari's eyebrows raised in mock surprise.

Her contempt was nearly palpable. But it was Melanie's reaction that surprised me. Usually calm and restrained, I had never heard the woman swear. Even on one of our outings together, when we talked about zoo politics, men and husbands, she never swore. She never disapproved of or was shocked by anything that came out of my mouth after a few wine coolers, but she was never tempted to join in.

"What do you want, Shari?" I asked, suddenly very tired. It was hot and humid, and I didn't have the energy to deal with any of her histrionics. That outward calm couldn't last, and I didn't want to be here when the habitual "poor li'l old me" whine set in.

Shari's smile was triumphant as she turned toward me, the rhinestone buttons of her shirt catching the rays of the sun like tiny prisms. "I'll bet her majesty here hasn't told you the whole story, has she?"

"You haven't told me the whole story," I pointed out.

She lifted her shoulders as if that wasn't the point. "You'd never believe anything I had to tell you anyway. I ain't the poor grieving widow, am I?"

Melanie was frigid, hands clutched at her sides. She never took her eyes off Shari, turning as the other woman circled around the bench slowly, deliberately, her cowboy boots clicking on the boardwalk. While I had been wondering about Melanie's relationship with JR, maybe I should have been thinking about her connection to Shari.

Shari's gaze swept across Melanie with the discriminating eye of a real-estate agent sizing up a property. "You got just what you want now, don't you? I've seen that house of yours in that fancy-spancy neighborhood. And now it's all yours. Just like you planned."

Melanie's nostrils flared. "It was always all mine."

Shari snorted. "Know the right lawyers, do you, hon? A fancy prenup? Didn't know they had them kind of things back in the Dark Ages."

"No. I know the right bankers."

Shari hesitated a moment and Melanie relaxed, giving Shari the once over. "You've never been shopping at Hanley's, have you, Shari? No. Not your style. You're more the Save Rite type, aren't you? Not to worry. Even someone with your taste can pad my retirement fund."

Meow. Hanley's was the upscale exclusive department store of Hanley-Holm Companies' empire. Safe Rite was for discount shoppers. Both part of the sizeable retail conglomerate Melanie would one day inherit. But it wasn't a fact she normally pointed out to people.

Ignoring the slur on her taste, Shari let out a whistle, impressed. "Was I wrong, then? Maybe Johnny Ray was after your money."

"You are pathetic," Melanie said, turning away to watch the giraffes as they made their way back into the barn.

Shari's voice got louder. "Am I? You're the one that lured him here." She turned toward me again. "I tried to talk him out of moving up here, y'know. We were safe in Mexico. The police would never find us, but JR said it was the chance of a lifetime to work with Jeff Jones and them damned crocodiles. Worth the risk. I thought he was being stupid. But it was her."

A mother and father dragging their screaming child passed by us.

"It was always you!" Shari shouted at Melanie's back.

Melanie twirled around. "And why wouldn't it be? He never wanted you. I didn't have to lure him here. He left because he wasn't happy. He wanted his old life back. And if you ever thought about anyone but yourself, you would have helped him."

More visitors were coming down the path. I grabbed Shari by the arm, hoping to send her on her way. We didn't need an audience for this little altercation. The zoo had enough problems, having a murder on site. We didn't need the public to see the widow brawling with the accused murderer's girlfriend.

Shari pulled away from me, her eyes still fixed on Melanie.

"He wanted you!"

Melanie waited until the next group of visitors had glanced our way, saw no giraffes in the paddock and went on their way. "I didn't even know he was here until a couple of weeks ago."

Shari was undeterred, stiffening her back. "How dumb do y'all think I am? I saw you."

"Saw me what?"

"I watched you. You were always following him around, bad-mouthing me. You thought you was so smart. This is what you wanted. To be free of that husband of yours. So you planned the whole thing. You murdered your husband plain as day and let my poor Johnny Ray take the blame."

In all the scenarios I had gone over in my head, I can honestly say this had not been one of them. Even Melanie was stunned. Disbelief swept across her soft features, quickly giving way to scorn.

I stepped forward again. "Shari, stop. I think you've said enough."

"I haven't even begun. You never saw them together, saw the way they looked at each other. They were more than friends. Her husband knew! That's why he quit his job and dragged her up to Minnesota, away from JR."

"You bitch!" For a moment I thought Melanie was going to strike her. "You told Anthony I was having an affair!"

Shari took a step back from Melanie's murderous look, a little less sure of herself. "He already knew. I just confirmed it for him."

Despite all their problems, Melanie was not a woman I would ever have suspected of cheating on her husband. It didn't seem in character. But it made sense. Why else would she hide the fact that she knew JR? Even before the murder, I would have thought she would have mentioned knowing him. And JR hadn't said anything to Jeff or me about knowing Melanie either. Why the big secret? Unless Shari was right.

Melanie's reaction to this charge was to regard the younger woman with utter derision. "You're delusional, Shari. You went to a lot of trouble for nothing. JR and I were never lovers. Almost," she amended with some regret, "yet somehow in that twisted little mind of yours you thought getting rid of me was going to make JR love you. Did it work? Was all your scheming worth it?"

"I'm the one he took to Mexico," Shari shot back, looking superior again.

"Did he? Or did you chase him there? Nothing changed for you in Mexico, did it?" Melanie stood tall, sporting a cruel smile. "He still treated you like some love-struck little girl who slobbered all over him. I don't doubt it was flattering . . . at first."

Shari was at a loss. She shifted her weight, her chin angling upward slightly so that the disfigured cheekbone was more prominent in the full rays of the afternoon sun.

"A lot you know," she muttered.

"I know more than you think."

Their eyes locked. I didn't exist. It was like being in grade school again, trying to stare a classmate down and not be the first to blink. In this contest of wills, my money was on Melanie. Shari's exterior began to splinter as her posture grew unsteady, her resolve slowly crumbling. I braced myself for the usual spectacle of tears that were sure to follow. None came. Without another word she spat on the ground, turned on her heels and stomped away, disappearing as the trail turned a corner, and was lost in the landscape of trees and shrubs that bordered it.

Melanie and I stood alone. A house wren called for a mate in the oak tree above us. The humidity weighed on me, and I wiped the moisture from my forehead with the back of my hand. I had no idea what to do or say. I was filled with questions. I had seen a new side of Melanie and had yet to assimilate it.

She gave me an empty smile. "I'm sorry, Snake. I haven't been honest with you."

"No. You haven't."

We began walking back toward the main building, not hurrying, each of us lost in our own thoughts.

We came abreast of the next exhibit. Our small family group of okapi stood near the tree-lined border at the back, taking little interest in passersby. The only other member of the giraffidae family, they were so timid, their existence had been unknown until the turn of the last century.

"Did you love him?" I finally asked.

"Jamie?" She nodded slowly, remembering. "We had so much in common. He was such a gentle, unambitious soul. Not at all like Anthony."

Her eyes were bright as she turned toward me. "But you know the best part? He knew how to listen. Talking to him was like talking to my best friend. He listened and he remembered. We'd be having a conversation and he'd remind me of something I had said two months earlier, some little insignificant thing I had totally forgotten."

Her smile widened at the memory. "But there was no affair. If I had stayed, it might have happened . . . if Anthony hadn't whisked me away, suddenly eager to live near my parents."

"Because of Shari?"

"It would seem that way. Now it makes more sense. Our lives in Florida were good, and then suddenly Anthony starts talking about moving on. I felt like a traitor. Jamie's world was falling apart. He lost his wildlife license. And then Al was murdered."

"Do you think JR killed him?"

"God, no." Melanie's face registered shock. "They were

friends. Alexander Beatty was trying to clear Jamie's name. We all were."

"Did anyone find anything?" It seemed like a lame question. I knew the answer.

"I don't know. Not while I was still there."

A lion roared from the exhibit across from us and a cub scampered back to the safety of his mother.

"And what about now?" I asked. "Have you been seeing JR—Jamie?"

"We talked. Just once or twice. And he still listens." She shook her head in wonderment. "After all that has happened to him, he could still listen to me and my problems."

"He's a nice guy."

"And he's no murderer."

But someone was. Melanie knew JR better than she had let on. A lot better. I wanted to believe what she had told me, but why hadn't she admitted this all earlier? She said she was protecting him. Was there more to it than that? How much was she keeping from me this time?

I thought about Shari's accusations again. If I were to give any credence to her at all, was it possible Melanie had killed her husband to be with JR? Or had JR been the perfect patsy? Was Melanie capable of setting him up?

The night of the Beastly Ball she had arrived at the dinner late, slightly flushed. It hadn't seemed odd at the time. By then everyone knew Anthony Wright was missing, and I had assumed she had been looking for him. Had she found him and pushed him in the crocodile billabong? Did she want to be free of Anthony that badly? Could she have done it? How much strength would it have taken to send a man Anthony's size through the bridge railing and into the water?

Melanie, Shari, JR. A tangle of deceit. They had kept their knowledge of each other a secret. They had each lied about their pasts and their relationship to each other. I had to wonder what else they had lied about.

Chapter 19

"Someone tried to kill you, Lavender. Isn't that reason enough to keep your nose out of police business?"

Not this again! I think I stopped myself before my eyes rolled. Instead I sat attentively like a schoolgirl in front of the principal, trying to look mildly contrite while mentally sticking my tongue out at him.

Detective Ole Sorenson's cramped office reminded me of his old college dorm room, with framed photos of his football fame at Roosevelt High and Mankato State ornamenting the walls like fine art. Where once they had hung next to posters of KISS and Aerosmith, they now shared wall space with a pad of the FBI's most wanted.

Even his desk looked the same: a mountain of paper and file folders stacked with no sense of order, leastways not to the casual observer. A clear plastic bag bulging with the contents of a man's pocket teetered on the edge of the desk. It may have been evidence, or some poor slob's personal effects. The wallet inside looked expensive but worn, and the corner of a fifty-dollar bill that peeked out looked as if it had been soaked in water. At least the Timex in the bag was still ticking.

Ole, ensconced behind his desk, swiveled toward Jeff and leveled a reproachful gaze. "After the other night, I'd think you'd want to discourage her as well."

"Snake's a battler, mate; a fair dinkum sheila who can do the yakka on 'er own."

Jeff was intentionally laying on the Aussie gab a little thick here, probably to put off Ole, who blinked back at him without comprehension. However, the pride in Jeff's voice was unmistakable. I smiled affectionately at the big goof.

"Nearly getting killed kind of makes it my business, too, doesn't it?" I reasoned.

"I know, I know." Ole held out a hand in defeat. "I'm not going to convince you to back off. You were always stubborn that way. Just thought I'd give it one more shot." His shoulders slumped with resignation.

I inched forward in my chair. "Look, JR is our friend. I can't sit around doing nothing while he sits in your jail, Ole. No matter what you think, he's innocent. I know it. And we need to find out who the real killer is before—" I clamped my lips shut, silently cursing my big mouth.

Ole gave me the evil eye, arms folded across his chest. He chomped hard on the wad of Juicy Fruit gum that had built up in his mouth over the course of the day.

"Before what?" he asked.

I stalled, not ready to tell him Melanie and JR had known each other in Florida, nor the fact that Shari had told Anthony Wright that JR was having an affair with his wife. Didn't matter that Shari was wrong; it sounded bad. Really bad. Ole also didn't need to know about Gary's allegations that Wright was profiteering from the sale of surplus zoo animals to unsavory buyers. Not yet; not until I had some solid proof. For the time being all I had was a string of coincidences, which might or might not be connected. And this information would be like fresh meat to the wolves. Once the police sank their teeth into this, it wouldn't take long before the news leaked to the media. And the zoo didn't need that kind of publicity. Moreover, Butler Thomas would have my head on a platter if the press or animal rights groups got wind of a scandal like that.

"Before what?" Ole repeated, when I took too long to answer.

"Before you hang the wrong man," I said at last, knowing it would get his goat. It was a good save. Not particularly tactful on my part, but the red-faced reaction from Ole told me I had struck a nerve. It was enough to make him forget my slip of the tongue.

"Unlike you, Lavender, I'm not working on a hunch or gut feeling. I'm working on facts. And right now the facts point to your friend being guilty of killing Wright."

"Doesn't the attack on Snake raise some questions?" Jeff jumped in.

"Perhaps . . . but they can easily be explained by an accomplice. We've already talked about that."

"So," I came back, "why aren't you looking for that so-called accomplice?"

"What makes you think I'm not?" Ole raised an eyebrow and looked down his crooked nose at me. "Just because I don't check in with you, Detective Jones?"

I sank back into my chair. Point taken.

Ole seemed a little too self-satisfied as he went on, "Give me some credit, Lavender, we're making progress there."

"What? With the accomplice?"

"Yes. For instance, this morning your friend Mrs. Wright was here. She gave O'Malley an alibi."

"For the night of the murder?"

"That's usually why people need alibis." He gave me a smart-ass smirk. Some things never change. Back in high school Ole was the inveterate wise guy, born with a sarcastic spoon in his mouth.

Jeff was excited, clamping his hands on top of his head. "Crikey! An alibi. If that's true, then that changes everything."

Then why wasn't I excited? Something didn't feel right. "Wait—wait . . ." I narrowed my gaze. "Are you telling me Melanie told you she was with JR when her husband was killed?"

"Yes."

It was as if he had dropped a bomb.

Jeff and I stared at each other. If Melanie was with JR at the time of the murder, then why the hell hadn't she said so in the first place? This made no sense.

Ole continued, "Mrs. Wright claims she and O'Malley were at the Beastly Ball talking about that crocodile exhibit. Can either of you back that up?"

Again Jeff and I swapped glances. No. We'd both been too busy to notice JR and Melanie in the crowd. The evening of the Beastly Ball was mostly a blur. According to Ole, Anthony Wright was murdered some time during or just before dinner. And dinner was over by the time Melanie had sat down at her table.

"Could she have been with O'Malley?" Ole prompted.

I shook my head. "I don't know. It's possible. But with Shari hanging on to him every minute like she does, it seems unlikely."

"She's a bloody octopus," Jeff agreed.

Ole nodded in concurrence. He'd had a good dose of her the night he had arrested JR. "Then Shari wasn't at dinner with you?"

"JR said he was going to stay with the crocs and Shari offered to take him a plate of food," Jeff offered.

"And did she?"

"Can't be sure. She never came to dinner. The last I saw of her she was arguing with JR in the Biodiversity Center. That was before dinner."

As they talked, a thought rumbled through my head. Could Melanie and JR have been together during the dinner? Knowing what I knew now about Melanie and JR's relationship, maybe they had been able to ditch the ubiquitous Shari Jensen, after all. If true, that seemed to raise more questions than it answered.

A worn brown blotter covered most of Ole's desk, stained with dried rings of long-ago coffee mugs. Ole drummed his fingers on the blotter. "Basically, nothing's proved one way or another. Mrs. Wright says she spoke with O'Malley outside the exhibit, near the info kiosk."

"What's JR say?"

"He backed up her story."

Jeff ran a hand through his sandy-colored hair. "Bloody hell, why is she saying this now?"

Why indeed? Why hadn't she told me this yesterday when she was confessing to knowing JR in Florida? Why hang onto this juicy bit of information? Why hadn't she come out with her alibi immediately? I was mystified and angry at once.

"Good question." Ole cracked his gum as he studied us at length, as if searching to see how much we really knew. "Mrs. Wright said she was a little fuzzy about the time. First she thought it was just after the dinner, then it suddenly dawned on her—or so she says—that it was before that."

"Why did Melanie offer him an alibi?" Jeff said, thinking out loud. "He's still getting extradited to Florida on another murder charge. What's the point?"

"If it's true, that should be reason enough," I suggested. "I admit Mel's timing is odd. Maybe by showing JR couldn't have killed Wright, she thought it would help with the Florida case." Maybe Melanie and JR had been together. Maybe not. What'd Melanie have to lose? Now that Shari was mouthing off, there'd be no reputation left to save, so why not admit knowing JR? Why not offer help to someone she so obviously cared about?

Ole smoothed out his moustache and cracked a smile. "Whether it's true or not might not matter. What does matter is she's sticking up for O'Malley publicly. Now if she's backing him up that way, could be she's helping him out in other ways."

What the—?

"Ole?" I angled my head at him, leaning forward, not liking where he was going. "Are you saying Melanie Wright was his accomplice?"

He lifted his shoulders grandly. "Why not?"

Why not? Because it was stupid, that's why not. Except the words never got out of my mouth. Somewhere in the depths of my heart I realized something unnerving: Ole could be right. With all that I'd learned about Melanie in the past few days, nothing should have surprised me. I tried to grapple with that thought as Ole thoughtfully played with the edges of his moustache, watching me.

"She could be the accomplice," he added, "though it doesn't seem her style. And I won't make any accusations unless there's real evidence." His gaze fell to some folders on his desk. "When she was here she was upset, more emotional than I've ever seen her. She forgot to take this when she left." He picked up the plastic bag whose once-waterlogged contents I'd noticed earlier. "Anthony Wright's personal effects."

A lead ball dropped to the pit of my stomach. Here were the belongings he'd had the night he died. My chair squeaked as I leaned closer to the plastic. The pen had come from the zoo gift shop, the cell phone a pricey nickel-plated curio, ostentatiously sleek and small. A white water stain wiggled across a once fine leather wallet. The metal band of the Timex was dented, tarnished and broken, the wrist it had been attached to severed by Sebastian's scythe-like jaws. Not a pleasant image to dwell upon when I considered how lucky my foot had been the other day. If any of Wright's effects were missing, they were probably in Sebastian's stomach.

An electronic rendition of "Tie Me Kangaroo Down" went off near the vicinity of Jeff's belt.

"Sorry." He shot to his feet, embarrassed. "Back in a tick." He took the call out in the hallway, which left Ole and me alone.

Ole shut the plastic bag in the top drawer of his desk, sat back in his chair, folded his hands loosely in his lap and regarded me with the eyes of an old boyfriend instead of an officer of the law.

"How'd you ever hook up with an Aussie?"

"Jeff was hired by the zoo as a consultant on the design of the Australia House. We hit it off immediately. I was floored when he was ready to give up his life in Australia and accept the job as curator to stay here with me."

"A guy has to be totally in love to leave his country, family, friends."

"He was—is." I smiled back.

Ole nodded. "No kids, though."

"Not yet."

His eyes drifted to the photo of two young boys on his desk then came back up to me with a hesitant, even nostalgic shine. "Look," he added, visibly changing gears, "I don't mean to come down hard on you, it's just what you're doing could be dangerous, and I'd hate to see you get hurt. . . ."

What do you know? That was almost sweet. Now why couldn't he have done it that way in the first place instead of crashing down on me like the Grim Reaper the other day? But I already knew the answer to that: it was part of the miscues and missteps that had caused us to break up long ago.

Still, it was an olive branch of sorts, and I didn't want to seem unkind.

"I know," was all I was able to manage.

It was enough. Ole Sorenson drew his chair closer to his desk and rested his elbows on the stained blotter. "I'd like to talk you out of sticking your neck in danger, but since we know that's not going to work, I might as well take advantage of whatever info you've got. You've been talking to people. Have you learned anything?"

"A little."

"After that dust-up with the senator in Butler Thomas's office, I thought you might."

It was not my shining moment and, in retrospect, I was embarrassed at how harsh I'd been with the senator, whether he deserved it or not. I shifted uncomfortably in my chair. "You heard about that?"

"Boy, did I. You gave it to McNealey right between the eyes!" Ole was enjoying himself. "Reminded me of the time in eleventh grade when Warren Jablonsky put his arm around you outside biology class and you read him the riot act."

"Yeah, his hand was wandering and I told him if he wanted to keep it he'd better lay off." I summoned up dusty memories of a bull-necked, six-foot-two wrestler with a perpetual five-o'clock shadow. I swear, that boy could have grown a beard in a week. He was the one who'd bought the beer for parties. "Whatever happened to Warren?"

"He became a priest."

"Father Jablonsky," I said, testing the sound of it.

"Bishop," amended Ole.

"Oh . . ." Great. That made me feel old.

Ole cleared his throat. "Getting back to McNealey. What's your take on him and Wright? I have to tell you those two are bugging me. The videos your cameraman gave us shows them having a shouting match sometime before the banquet started."

I regarded him circumspectly. "Have you checked out Senator McNealey's business dealings with Hanley-Holm?"

"What do you know about that?"

Now that I was certain there was no under-the-table deal between McNealey and the zoo, I told him a little of what I had overheard in Butler's office and about the cancelled zoo expansion. "That's a motive," I suggested.

"Yes, it is, and we're gonna check that out. Look, if someone else really killed Anthony Wright, we'll find him. You gotta understand that O'Malley—JR—whatever you want to call him—didn't leave me a lot of choice when he ran off like that. Whether he's cleared or not, I'll still have to hold him for extradition to Florida."

"I was afraid you'd stop looking once you thought you had your man."

"Lavender, if there's compelling evidence pointing somewhere else, I'll investigate. But there isn't any."

We locked gazes for an awkward moment and I looked away. Neither one of us was going to budge. Toward the end of our relationship it had been like this, and the memory of those uncomfortable silences made me self-conscious, so I changed the subject.

"Could we get those video tapes back?" I adjusted my ponytail with indifference, trying to mask my discomfort at locking horns a moment ago. "We might still be able to salvage a show from them."

"I thought your show was over."

News travels fast, especially when it's bad. "We've got a few shows in the can. This one'll probably be the last." It hurt to say it. With everything that had been going on, Jeff and I barely had time to discuss it. And we still had to tell Billie, Shaggy and the rest of our crew.

"Sure. There's nothing on them to help our case—not that we've seen. Fresh eyes might spot something we've missed."

Was this an acknowledgement that I might be of some help?

Jeff's voice sliced between us from the hallway. Other voices joined his. Curious, Ole got up to see what was going on.

A small group of people had gathered outside Ole's door. Jeff had been recognized and his fans were creating a bottleneck in the hallway. I could just see the back of Jeff's head, his hair sticking out like the arms of a sea urchin.

"Say! You're that crocodile guy on TV," said a delighted female. "My son loves your show. Wait till I tell him I saw you today. He'll flip!"

Another voice: "Wow, Jeff, that episode with you and that cobra was amazing. My wife thought you were a goner for sure."

Laughter and agreement.

"That was an adventure to remember. Beautiful animals, a thrill of a lifetime."

"Say, if you're handing out autographs, could you make one out to Ralphie?"

Ole shot me a look and excused himself. "Back in a minute."

He made haste to join the fan club. It was laughable; I could hear Ole greeting Jeff like a long lost brother as he shut the door behind him. Yeah, I'm sure Ole wanted everyone in the station to know he and their favorite cable TV star were old pals.

It took me only a second to wrestle with my conscience and jump up and rummage through the files on Ole's desk. I shuffled through the top layer until Wright's name popped up at me. A bulging manila folder spilled over with scribbling on Wright's murder. I quickly flipped over some gruesome photographs and found a faxed copy of an autopsy report. Only it wasn't Wright's. The report was filled out by a Dade County, Florida, coroner.

I didn't understand the medical language yet the faxed photos told the story. I winced at the torso shot. Blurred and too dark, the image in the fax was still horrific. Gaping claw marks raked across the chest, shoulders and lower face, a face so swollen by bruises, contusions and lacerations, I could barely stand to look at it: the face of Alexander Beatty—as it was labeled—the man whom JR was supposed to have murdered. Or more accurately, was supposed to have beaten up and then put into the cage of a Florida panther who supposedly finished the job.

Depositions from co-workers at Sweetwater Creek proclaimed

JR's innocence. None of the people with whom JR—O'Malley as he was known—had worked with believed him capable of so brutal a crime. Just like me, except now with regard to Wright's murder. Melanie's name was nowhere to be seen, but then, she said she and her husband had left Miami the day Beatty was murdered.

Then my eye caught something on one of the fax sheets, a summary of the coroner's report, and my heart jumped. Beatty was severely beaten, it said; the cause of death due to internal injuries that resulted in organ failure. The beating killed him, not the panther attack. Supposedly JR beat up Alex Beatty then tossed him in with the panther with the idea of making it look like a horrible accident. I glanced at the autopsy photos again, then back at the report. Something was missing.

Bite marks. There were no bite marks.

The report detailed the bruises and lacerations and broken ribs, but no mention was made of bite marks, nor of injuries to Beatty's neck or throat. That was significant. Big cats tend to kill larger prey by pouncing on them and biting them on the nape of the neck. Or if it's too large, they'll grab their prey by the throat and suffocate it.

But there were no bite marks on Alex Beatty's neck or throat, none at all on his body. And he hadn't died of suffocation. If Beatty was already dead or dying when he was thrown into the panther's cage, the cat wouldn't have felt threatened by him, wouldn't have felt the urge to kill. Yes, Beatty got mauled, but the panther didn't kill him. A big cat expert like James O'Malley would've known that. Any other big cat expert would know it, too.

I straightened up, jolted by a thought: whoever threw Beatty into that panther cage knew little or nothing about the behavior of big cats. My God, the autopsy report might prove JR's innocence! Not for Wright's murder, but for Alexander Beatty's.

Before I could read more, I heard movement outside in the corridor, and quickly put everything back the way I had found it and jumped back to my chair, taking an inordinate interest in the wanted posters tacked to the wall. Seconds later, Jeff and Ole returned to the office, laughing like old bar buddies.

"Well," Ole said, hitching up his pants as he sat on the corner of his desk. He wore a look of satisfaction, as though being seen with Jeff had increased his stock in the estimation of his peers. He was in a very agreeable mood. "I'll get those tapes for you before you leave. Your camera crew didn't catch the murderer in action, but we got plenty of shots of other people. It helped us put together a timeline and establish where a few key people were. Thanks."

"Glad to be of service." Jeff turned on the charm, looking to parlay this cooperation into a personal favor. "D'you think we could see JR while we're here?"

A pause.

Then Ole tossed up his hands. "Why not? Everyone else has."

Our expressions begged for explanation.

"That overzealous girlfriend of his—or should I say one of his girlfriends—came in and made a scene this morning. It's not the first time."

"Shari Jensen."

"Yeah, her. If I were your friend, I'd pray for a conviction just to get away from her." Ole leaned across his desk to open the middle drawer, from which he pulled a fresh pack of gum. "Then Mrs. Wright shows up to make her statement, coughing up a belated alibi for him. She wanted to see him, too, but we wouldn't allow it. Can't have her tipping him off. We've got to cross-check her story."

He carefully unfolded the wrapper around another stick of Juicy Fruit, rolled it into a cylinder and popped it into his mouth with workmanlike ease. "Now if you'll excuse me for a minute,

I'll go placate the sergeant and see if I can't get you in to see your mate." This last with a wink toward Jeff.

Ole left the door open, so we kept our voices low. Jeff, who had taken the chair next to me, leaned closer, his rough hand resting on my shoulder. "Melanie's a puzzle. Why would she suddenly give JR an alibi?"

"To protect him?"

"Or to protect her husband?"

"I don't follow."

Jeff squeezed my shoulder. "Gary's saying Wright was into some shady business. What if the little blighter's right? What would that do to Wright's reputation, or to the zoo's? By giving JR an alibi, Melanie not only clears JR, but the police would have no reason to dig any further into a connection between JR and the Wrights."

"Maybe not but they'd still dig into Wright's background. If JR is cleared, that still leaves Anthony Wright's killer out there."

"True . . ."

"And I doubt if Melanie's too concerned about preserving her husband's reputation. What about that whole scene she played with the zoo board, telling them she wanted the truth?"

Jeff inhaled thoughtfully. "Perhaps she had a change of heart. Perhaps JR's just a bloody Don Juan with some magic voodoo over women."

I was reminded of the scene I had witnessed between Melanie and Shari yesterday. In a bizarre way, I wanted to agree with Jeff, although I had never seen JR behave in any way that led me to believe he was a womanizer. I said as much.

"Men like that can be very subtle, sweetheart. They just reel you in real slow-like." He pantomimed working a fishing reel and landing the big one. "When you least expect it they've got ya." Jeff jerked the line in.

"Exactly what are you catching?" Ole poked his head back in the room.

Before Jeff could reply, Ole stuck out his hand. "On second thought, I don't want to know. I'm sure it was reptilian, slimy and as ugly as my ex-mother-in-law." He offered a playful smirk that was meant to be funny.

I blew him off.

"Can we see JR?" I asked, my emotions all over the map, bouncing from concern over JR's mental state to wanting to make sure we got some straight answers from him. For that we might have to force a confrontation for which I wasn't eager.

And those criss-crossed emotions must have shown in my face, for in reply Ole Sorenson attempted gallantry—or something like it. Lord, he was in a good mood, for he threw the door open wide and made a sweeping bow as we passed. "Walk this way. His last visitor was just leaving. I gotta say this for your friend, he's got a real eye for beauty."

Jeff and I exchanged puzzled looks one more time.

"Long black hair, classy, great body—"

"Suzanne Terak?" I breathed.

"Yeah, that's the one."

What would Anthony Wright's assistant want with JR? In a week of rude surprises, this one might have surprised me most.

Chapter 20

I couldn't imagine why Suzanne Terak would come to visit JR. Nor did I have time to think about it, as Ole charged ahead of us, leading the way down an expanse of hallway comprised of industrial-painted cinderblocks and hanging fluorescent lights.

"You're lucky you came when you did," Ole told us. "He's getting transferred to County tomorrow."

Our footsteps echoed off the white concrete floors and walls, emphasizing the tomb-like quality of the space we had entered. No outside light penetrated this chamber, as though it too were restricted by court order. The pungent smell of burnt popcorn left too long in a break-room microwave hung in the air like swamp gas. We passed it and stopped at the last door, metallic with a narrow window protected with wire.

"Anything the prisoner says to you can be used as evidence," advised Ole before we entered. "There's no lawyer present and your conversation is not privileged. Remember that."

Jeff snorted. "JR's not bloody likely to tell us anything he hasn't already told you."

"What do you expect to get from him, then?"

"We're here to show we care. JR's a friend. At least I thought he was." Jeff's resolve faded marginally as he took in Ole's unflinching gaze. "He's in trouble. We're here to show he's not alone."

Surprisingly enough, Ole nodded with understanding. Our faith in the people we called our friends had been shaken to the roots over the past few days, and while we hoped to get some semblance of the truth out of JR during our visit, we still cared enough to show we had not abandoned him. It was a narrow tightrope to walk. Ole seemed to accept this explanation, and he opened the door for us without further comment.

Butterflies flitted in my stomach. Probably guilt. We should have visited days ago. But we were overwhelmed with work at the zoo and with *Zoofari*. We found other excuses. Maybe we just didn't want the last of our illusions about JR shattered. There was no way to know whom we'd find here, misunderstood friend or accomplished con man.

JR looked tired and careworn as he shuffled into view, his shoulders slumped in the orange prison jumpsuit, his head bowed. His hands and feet were cuffed, making movement difficult. When he saw us, his demeanor strengthened and his posture improved, as though he drew energy from our presence. A cautious smile spread across his face.

"Jeff, Snake. Great to see you," he said with subdued enthusiasm, then chuckled at a new thought. "How are the little ones?"

The "little ones," of course, were Sebastian and Babe, his beloved crocodiles.

"No worries, mate. They're doing fine. The ol' man is showing everyone he's king of the swamp, though Babe is a bit skittish from all the action lately."

JR nodded with satisfaction. "And the kangaroos? Boomer been behaving?"

"He's a little grumpy. Snake's been cutting back on his treats."

"Remind him he could still be boxing for his dinner at that two-bit carnival you rescued him from. Compared to that, he's living like a king now."

My laugh came out as a nervous twitter. "I'll tell him."

"And, guys, please tell the crew I'm sorry they have to work extra hours because of me."

"They understand."

JR turned to me, all signs of mirth wiped from his face, which was now heavy with concern. "I heard about the attack on you, Snake. Thank God you weren't hurt."

"I'm fine, thanks." I dismissed the incident, surprising myself. I felt awkward and annoyed at myself for sounding so remote. I wanted to trust JR, but my guard was up. My better nature told me to give the man a chance, while another voice whispered back, "He lied to you."

JR had lost weight in the past few days, probably from anxiety. His face was more gaunt, the high cheekbones sharper against his pallid skin. The fire that normally flickered behind his eyes had dimmed, struggling to shine in the darkness of his ordeal.

The three of us sat down at the scarred wooden table in the center of the small room, JR's cuffs clinking together as he tried to get comfortable. Not easy when you were hobbled hand and foot.

"It's good to see some friendly faces." He smiled thinly at us.

That might have been a bit of a stretch. I don't think either Jeff or I offered more than a polite, if not restrained, greeting.

Jeff's face hardened. "Is it, JR? From what I hear, there's been more'n a few friendly faces to see you today."

Melanie, Shari and Suzanne. At least JR had the good grace to look embarrassed.

"It certainly can't be your sterling charm, mate," Jeff dug in further. "What's going on? We've been finding out all sorts of things about you."

With downcast eyes, the prisoner said, "I deserve that. I'm sorry I wasn't completely honest with you. I didn't mean to get you dragged into this." His eyes came up now, earnest, searching for understanding.

I rested my hand on Jeff's arm and shot a clandestine look to the door. A uniformed cop stood outside. All I could see was the back of his head through the small window. How much could he hear, if anything? We had to assume he was taking down every word or that there was an intercom device nearby.

I had come to this meeting with my own agenda, but that had been trumped by Ole's news, which had to be addressed. "What's this about Melanie giving you an alibi?"

"I don't know. They wouldn't let her talk to me."

"If you were with her, you should know."

"Yeah," he struggled, "what I'm trying to say is I don't know what she told the police. I was with her during part of the dinner. We were catching up with each other. I knew she was in Minnesota, I'll admit that, but she had no idea until the week before that I was at the zoo. That's probably what she told the police. . . ."

"I talked to Melanie yesterday."

I tossed it out with emphasis, hoping to provoke a response.

JR shifted uncomfortably. "What did she tell you?"

"About Florida. About working with you at Sweetwater and *other interests.* Unfortunately, before she got into much detail, Shari barged in."

"Shit." JR covered his face with his hands. "Shari didn't say a word about it when she was here." His pained voice filtered through his fingers. "Not a word."

"Really?" I found it difficult to believe Shari wouldn't have bragged about it, wouldn't have lorded over the fact she had made the serene Melanie lose her temper.

JR dropped his hands, looking miserable, a man teetering on the edge of despair. "She was awfully quiet this last visit. I should've guessed something was up."

There were undercurrents here I couldn't follow. Suggestions of relationships too tangled to unravel. As if reading my mind, Jeff stirred. He cleared his throat.

"JR, what's up with the three of you?"

The prisoner parted his lips then hesitated, averting his eyes.

"JR," Jeff pressed, "we want to help you. That's why we're here. Snake was nearly killed trying to prove you're not the killer. You owe us some answers, some honest ones."

"I know . . . I know. And I'll tell you, even if it gets me in more trouble than I'm already in."

He paused to let the words sink in, then quietly forged ahead in a steady voice. "Shari's a hard woman to figure out, a real spark plug. I know you don't think much of her, but she's been good to me. Very good. She's stuck by me, protected me when it endangered her. I've always been up front with her." He looked down at his hands. "I've just never been in love with her, not the way she wants."

"She doesn't give up easy," I said.

Among other things, the woman was also deluding herself. You can't make someone fall in love with you. No matter how much you want it, how nice you are, how pretty. Love just doesn't work that way.

JR released a melancholy breath, as though it were trapped and only now could be let go. His body sagged like a scarecrow on a post. "At first I felt sorry for her. We all did. Shari's husband, Cradus Moseley, was a big Georgia country boy, built like the proverbial ox. Kinda looked like one, too." A smile teased at the corners of his mouth, then threw itself back in reverse. "He was a big man, hands like sledge hammers. Not the brightest bulb in the pack. The only future he could ever hope for was to run his daddy's gas station some day and it pissed him off. So he took it out on other folks, pushing them around, including Shari. You just never knew what was going to set him off."

A cold hand tightened around my stomach as I remembered Shari's tearful confession. "From what I heard, he did more than push her."

"The man was a brute," JR said flatly, his eyes distant, visualizing something in the past. "I even had to stitch her up once. He split her lip open. She was afraid to go to the doctor, afraid of the questions they'd ask."

"She wouldn't go to the police?" It seemed a simple enough solution to me.

"Snake, this was the South. Some old customs still hide under the guise of 'family values.' In some rural towns a little wife-beating is considered a good thing." The chains of his handcuffs tapped against the table as he shifted position. "Even if the law was sympathetic, it can take a while before a court order is issued. Shari was afraid of her husband. Hell, we were all afraid of him!"

"So you came to her rescue and decided to take her away from him," Jeff tried to comprehend. "Spirit her off to Mexico? That was the plan?"

JR regarded Jeff curiously, lowering his voice. "Don't you know what happened? It sounded like you did."

"Only the little bit Shari's told us. The police've said nothing."

JR discreetly swept the room with his eyes, narrowing them on the rectangle of glass in the door. There was no sign of our guard. I understood JR's caution, his fear of being overheard. Even the innocent can have something to hide, indiscretions that can be twisted into a stay in prison.

A moment's indecision hung on his face before he cleared it away. "You might as well know everything the police know."

With a sense of resignation he told his story, his voice low, at times animated. He was laying down all his cards. JR went back to Florida where it had all started, painting a lurid picture of deception and betrayal. He had already been under investigation for the suspected sale of an endangered species, his missing panthers supposedly having been discovered on a game farm in Texas. He was quick to point out it was a frame-up. No concrete proof existed, only the barest of circumstantial evidence trumped up by an anonymous tip to the U.S. Fish and Wildlife Service. JR and Alexander Beatty had been trying to figure out who would have made the accusations. Not until later did JR suspect that the accuser was in their midst. He began to suspect Beatty.

"I just couldn't believe any of our people would be capable of such a thing." He ran his cuffed hands through his thick dark hair, the short chain lightly riding up his creased forehead as he did.

"The Feds produced an invoice I hadn't seen, something incriminating. I found that out later. Not that it would've helped me at the time. There was an indictment with an investigation to follow. Well, the day after the news hit the papers, Melanie didn't show up for work. I tried calling her, but her phone had been disconnected. Beatty jumped on that as proof she'd been the source of the frame-up, which was ridiculous. We argued. It got loud. Several people overheard us. I'm afraid I was pretty worked up about it, too. I was having nothing but bad luck. That night I found Al. . . ."

"In the panther cage," Jeff prompted.

JR nodded. "He was dead. But it was no accident. Someone wanted it to look that way. Al would never have gone into her enclosure. Never. There was no reason to. It was after hours. Everyone had gone home. I came into the holding area and found Tasha, one of our Florida panthers, standing over him, her muzzle and paws covered in blood."

I leaned forward, my elbows on the table. "Beatty died of internal injuries." Off Jeff and JR's puzzled looks I explained, "I saw the autopsy report and photos in Ole's office. He was beaten to death."

JR nodded. "Yeah, the police claim I fought with him then put his body in with the panther to cover my tracks."

"You'd never do that."

"It'd be stupid. I'd fed the cats an hour before and they're usually pretty laid back after a meal. Whoever worked Al over must've stirred up Tasha a bit. She wasn't a vicious cat. Was hand-raised but—well, you know how wild animals are. She could kill if provoked."

"But she didn't kill Beatty. She mauled him then stopped."

"Probably because he wasn't conscious and she had a full belly. It was so obvious a frame-up."

Just what I wanted to hear. "Because she didn't follow through with the attack?"

"Yeah."

"Did you know there weren't any bite marks on Beatty's body?"

"There you are, then."

Continuing with his story, JR told how he had managed to secure the panther into the back of the enclosure and was hauling Beatty's body out when Shari burst into the holding area, crazed with fear, blood smeared across her nose and mouth, a raw jangle of nerves.

"Shari was terrified. Her old man was on another rampage, only this time he was after me. He thought she was cheating on him and I was the number-one suspect. He was going to rip me to shreds. Shari was hysterical. Her nose was bleeding and her eye swollen shut. She wouldn't stop screaming. There I was with blood all over my hands, holding Al in my arms, and she didn't even notice. She was that scared Cradus was going to charge in and kill us both."

JR tried to use his hands to punctuate what he was saying, but the handcuffs confined him. He stared dully at the table. "I panicked. I was already under investigation by the U.S. Fish and Wildlife Service. The only man who could help clear my name was dead at my feet. I could hear sirens in the distance, getting closer. It wouldn't take much for the cops to think I staged Beatty's death to dump the blame on him. And then Shari's husband was out for my blood. He knew where to find me and no amount of explanation or legal maneuvers was going to keep that old country boy from getting his big hairy paws on me. Everything was falling apart. I thought I could fight it but—but . . ." his voice surrendered to reality. ". . . I didn't have it in me. So I ran."

Defeat shrouded his words. He knew he had made the wrong choice, but was stuck with the consequences. Shari's hysterical screaming would have made a rational decision impossible. All that pressure and a screaming blond banshee to boot. I guess I didn't blame him for running.

"So the two of you went off to Mexico," I said softly.

He nodded dismally as his hands spread out along the surface of the scarred tabletop.

"A new name, a new start," he said.

"Where does Melanie fit in to all of this?"

"She doesn't." The answer came back quickly—too quickly—JR's eyes still fixed upon the table.

Whack!

Jeff brought his hand down sharply, causing both JR and me to jump. He glowered at the other man. "Don't lie to me anymore, JR. Snake and I both stuck our necks out for you. We deserve better. C'mon, sweetheart, let's go."

Jeff and I stood up as the guard outside the door came storming in, one hand on his gun. We were prepared to leave with him until JR stopped us.

"Wait."

The call was shallow, barely above a whisper, yet filled with quiet desperation.

"Please, stay," JR appealed. "You're right. I said I'd tell you the truth. I'm sorry."

The guard's gaze shifted between us, waiting.

JR drew in a harsh breath as we returned to our seats and the guard reluctantly returned to the hallway.

"I've stalled about Melanie for a reason. I don't want anyone else to get hurt. It's just . . . I loved her." JR's vision turned inward, struggling for the right words. "From the moment I first saw Melanie I was enthralled. Her voice, her manner, the way she carried herself, her heart. It didn't take long to completely lose my heart."

"Another married woman," Jeff pointed out.

"You can't control who you fall in love with. And the fact she was married isn't the point. We didn't do anything. Having those feelings isn't the issue. It's what you do or don't do with those feelings that matters. What made it difficult was that she had feelings for me, too. For months we fought our attraction, kept things on a business level. And we did it because she was married. Christ! She was so Goddamned unhappy with Wright. He treated her like some ornament he could put on display when it suited him. Yet, because he'd once been a great guy, she remained loyal. I never pushed the relationship. Nothing ever happened between us."

"So you turned to Shari instead?" Jeff's voice was edged with sarcasm, struggling to understand.

JR shifted uncomfortably in his seat. "I had to get on with my life. And Shari certainly wasn't interested in returning to Cradus." A half-hearted shrug moved his shoulders. "She was there. And she can be very caring and fun. I've been as good as I can to Shari. I won't let her down. But I've never led her to believe I felt something I didn't."

"Because of your feelings for Melanie?"

JR winced, but he answered honestly. "If there'd been any

hope for a future with Melanie, I never would have left Florida."

And there it was. As dangerous an admission as any he could have made. Even a hack prosecutor could easily connect the dots here, showing how the lovelorn JR saw a chance to finally help his lost love, Melanie, by eliminating her husband in a crocodile billabong one evening in a staged accident. *Another* staged accident, too.

With this in mind, I asked, "Did you stay in contact with Melanie?"

"Good Lord, no! That would've been idiotic. Besides, I didn't want to get her in trouble. She'd been candid with her feelings. In any case, the deck was stacked against me. For all I knew, she thought I had sold her beloved panthers so some trigger-happy hunters could slaughter them at close range. And now Al Beatty was dead. To the world I was guilty. And I had no way to prove my innocence. Anthony Wright had seen to that."

Jeff's face clouded. "Wright? Whatcha mean, mate? What did he have to do with it?"

JR laughed, a pathetic, self-deprecating guffaw filled with fatalism. His voice was almost a whisper now. "What you don't know—what nobody knows—is that the evening Beatty was killed I got a phone call, warning me there was trouble in the panther house. It's what sent me to the holding area. The caller didn't identify himself, even tried to disguise his voice, but it wasn't a voice I was likely to forget. I wasn't in Minnesota for two weeks when I heard it again. You and I were moving a truckload of straw. It sent chills up my spine. Anthony Wright was barking some orders to the maintenance crew and I realized he had been that voice on the phone. He had set me up." JR's face twisted into a scowl. "He had sent me to find Beatty's body. To link me to the murder and, I think, to keep me away from his wife."

Chapter 21

In the last four years at the Minnesota Valley Zoo, I'd had my run-ins with Anthony Wright. Quick to anger and not shy about throwing his weight around to get what he wanted, he could be a tough man to please. But this was too much.

"Wait. Wright set you up? You think he killed Beatty?"

"I don't know. But he certainly knew about it." JR pulled the chain between his handcuffs tight, curling his fingers around the metal. "Maybe I was getting too close to discovering who was stealing my animals. Maybe they were trying to send me a message by roughing up Al. I dunno, but it was Wright on the phone. Which can only mean that he was involved."

"You're sure it was Wright's voice you heard?" I still couldn't believe it.

"As positive as I am that you're sitting there, Snake. The man had a distinctive way of talking. Very memorable."

And I believed JR, although it pulled the rug out from under me. Anthony Wright had his rough side, but I never thought he'd stoop to setting another man up for murder. And for what? To keep him away from Melanie? Or to keep the police from discovering his own involvement with the illegal animal trade?

I felt a pang of dread. Whatever sense of hope the autopsy report gave me to clear JR was toppled now. This latest confession could only dig JR deeper into the hole he was in, giving him a clear-cut motive to kill Wright.

Jeff told him as much. "So Anthony recognized you. When he

threatened to turn you in, you pushed him off the footbridge into the billabong to let the crocs finish him off."

"No! I never went near Wright for that reason, Jeff. I was afraid he'd recognize me. I stayed clear of him. You've got to believe me. And if not me, then Melanie. She was with me. My alibi, remember?"

Desperation shaded his voice, while his beleaguered gaze darted between us.

"We believed you before, mate," intoned Jeff, the full measure of his disappointment leveled on the man in chains. "Melanie's alibi may get you off the hook here, but you're still going back to Florida to face the music. You've got no alibi down there."

His words stung JR, who balled his hands into tight fists and hung his head. "I know. But I'm positive it was Wright who was behind the trouble in Florida. As soon as I heard him, I knew." He looked up again, his dark-brown eyes bright. "I had suspected Beatty for some time, but knew he wasn't acting alone. Beatty must have been working with Wright. Maybe Wright had the contacts to sell my animals to some dealer who turned around and sold them to some damned canned hunt. I don't know."

I didn't want to believe it. Canned hunts. The very thought of them forced me to blink back tears. So-called sports hunters, who couldn't be satisfied shooting legal game, needed the thrill of the exotic, to track, shoot, and kill an endangered species. But a controlled hunt is no fair contest of skill, only a new variation of shooting fish in a barrel. The animals have no chance to escape. They roam in gated enclosures of several acres, ensuring a kill. And in some cases the animals don't even get to roam; they're chained to a stake in the ground, awaiting death. How could Wright be a part of something like that? How could anybody?

Jeff and I locked eyes and I'm sure he was thinking the same thing I was. Once again we were back to the accusations Gary had brought up against Anthony Wright. Could the kid be right? Had our late zoo director been living a double life?

"Beatty and Wright must have had a falling out." JR leaned toward us, his voice emphatic, urging us to believe. "Wright killed him and tried to blame me. Maybe he didn't strike the actual blows, but Al Beatty still wound up dead. He got two birds with one stone that way—making sure no one suspected him of the murder and keeping his rival away from his wife."

"Do you have any proof Wright was involved with Beatty?" I asked, knowing the answer.

"No. That's how these guys operate. A dealer sells an animal to a private zoo or animal park. Only it never gets there. Instead, it's sold to another dealer. Maybe the animal is transferred to a legitimate animal refuge before it goes on again. By the time that poor creature ends up in an exotic meat market or is sold for parts, the paper trail is so diluted the authorities can't prove it belonged to the original owner. He simply claims that's not his animal."

"You seem to know a lot about it," Jeff pointed out with misgivings.

"I've had a lot of time to think about it. For the last five years I've researched every shady animal dealer in the country, hoping to find some link, something to prove I'm innocent."

"Is that why you agreed to work for me, JR?" Jeff asked. "It was an awful risk you took. And it hasn't panned out too well, has it?"

JR ran a finger along the shackle that encircled his left wrist. "I won't lie to you again, Jeff. I never gave up hope of clearing my name. I wanted to come home. I wanted to be an American again. I was thrilled when you offered me the opportunity to work with you, to actually work with crocodiles again. Hell, I would have said yes if I had still been in Florida. It was the chance of a lifetime."

True as that sounded, I sensed there was more to it than that. "And . . . ?"

There was silence. An air conditioner turned on somewhere in the building, and a draft of cold air swept down into the stale, windowless room.

"JR?" I pressed.

JR swallowed and sat back heavily. "I read about Wright's appointment to the Minnesota Valley Zoo in an old AZA newsletter. I knew Melanie was here, too. So when you and Jeff came along with a job at the same zoo, it seemed like a sign. I jumped at it."

"A sign you could start something up with Melanie again?"

"No. That was never my intention. She was still a married woman. Nothing had changed. And I would never hurt Shari like that."

I let out an unladylike snort. "I bet Shari didn't believe that. That's why she's been so obstinate lately, isn't it? That's why you've been quarrelling so much?"

JR nodded. "She knows how I felt about Melanie. I try to reassure her, but nothing I say seems to help."

If it had been anyone but JR, I would have branded him as a swine, an unscrupulous Lothario, but I could see the turmoil in those puppy-brown eyes. I had never seen him treat Shari with anything but kindness and respect. I had seen him angry and upset with her, worn down by her unending demands, but he never aimed a cross word at her. Their arguments were mostly one-sided—she was arguing and he was listening.

"Weren't you worried Melanie would recognize you?" Jeff asked.

JR nodded. "I did my best to stay out of her way. Which wasn't too hard, considering she worked on the African Trail on the other side of the zoo. Our paths didn't cross until a week before Wright was killed. But I look different now. Back then I wore glasses and had a full beard. Few people had ever seen me clean shaven."

I remembered my conversation with Melanie at the zoo yesterday. "She said she recognized you a week earlier."

"Funny the way it works. She says she recognized my voice."

"And you told her your story."

"She knew I was innocent." A sappy smile crossed his face. "She's always known. After she heard my story, she was convinced of it. But there was no concrete proof of Wright's culpability. I think she wanted to see if she could find it."

"JR." I shook my head in disbelief. "This gets worse by the second. Now it sounds like you and Melanie were conspiring together."

"I know. Everything I can think of that might save me only seems to make things worse. And the last thing I want is for Melanie to be dragged through the mud because of her connection to me."

I stood up, feeling the need to move around. My ankle was still tight from nearly being a late-night snack for Sebastian. "There has got to be some proof. Somewhere, sometime, Wright has had to have gotten sloppy, left some evidence, something."

I turned to Jeff.

"Suzanne Terak," we said in unison. I sat back down, forcing myself to keep my voice low. "What did Suzanne talk to you about today?"

JR shook his head. "I'm not sure I know. I'm sure she was out to prove I had murdered her boss. That was fairly certain. She asked a lot of questions I couldn't give her answers to."

"Such as?"

"She asked about some zoo in Texas. I'd never heard of the place before."

"Deaf County Park Zoo?"

JR slowly nodded. "I think that was it. Why?"

For the first time since the murder, I felt as if I was on to something tangible, something that could at least clear JR of the Florida murder.

"Deaf County Park Zoo is owned by Anthony Wright and his sister. When I was talking to Suzanne on Tuesday, Wright's office was piled with boxes. His sister wanted to sell the zoo and had sent all the records from Texas for Suzanne to go through."

" 'S'truth." Jeff was taken aback. "Suzanne's gone and found something."

Now her visit made sense. Smiling with new understanding, I turned back to JR. "And she came here to get you to verify what she'd uncovered."

Chapter 22

It was too late to go back to the zoo and speak with Suzanne about what she had discovered, so we turned our attention to the *Zoofari* footage. Now that the Apple Valley police had returned the tapes, Jeff and I could barely wait to view the raw footage our crew had shot the day Anthony Wright was killed. Maybe I was being naïve, but a tingling in my bones told me there must be something there to see. Just no one had recognized it.

I wanted at least one private look at the footage, so without telling Billie Bradshaw or Butler Thomas, we rang up Shaggy from the courthouse and asked him to meet us at the production studio we rented. Like many small producers, we couldn't afford to own a full-time facility, so we leased space at one of the well-known production houses in Minneapolis. Sequestered in a small room surrounded by editing equipment and monitors, we reviewed the raw video footage Shaggy had shot during the day.

It turned into a long night's viewing, even with Shaggy's nimble fingers working the controls. The video images played like a bad home movie as we watched them; choppy in parts, chaotic, disconnected. The film was raw, unedited and without polish, just as it was shot.

We fast-forwarded through the tapes, using the shooting logs to find the scenes we wanted—anything that featured the people and places involved in the case, especially those scenes that caught Anthony Wright's last hours. Shaggy then transferred those scenes onto another tape for us to view later.

"Thanks for staying up to do this, Shag," I said, touching his sleeve as he handed me the video transfer.

"Hey." He glowed with accomplishment. "That's what the Shagster does. Filming is the process, but editing is the art."

And Shaggy is definitely an artist, behind the camera and in the editing room. Despite the raw footage, you could still see Shaggy's genius in the innovative camera angles and his ability to close in without disturbing his subject. Even the scripted segments looked natural and unrehearsed.

Although *Zoofari* was a part-time job and most of our crew took other assignments in the off months, it was going to break my heart to tell Shaggy and the others that the show had been put on hiatus, possibly canceled.

"When are we going to tell them?" I looked to Jeff once we got home. "We can't put off the bad news much longer. The crew's bound to hear it from someone else soon."

I popped the video in our VCR and took a spot on the carpet in front of the denim armchair, the one new piece of furniture we had in the house. Jeff sank to the floor behind me, trying not to spill the contents of his chipped Taronga Zoo mug. How he could drink coffee at this hour I never understood. I'd be up all night. Not Jeff. He rested his back against the base of the chair and drew his legs up. I nestled up close, using his shins as a backrest. My toes dug into the luxuriant carpet pile.

The remainder of the family joined us. Bagger happily trotted over, circled and clawed at the carpet before flopping beside me, his tail swishing back and forth across my leg. Kow the cat sized up the situation and used me as a springboard to bound up past Jeff's head to the seat of the chair. There she licked the back of Jeff's neck twice before curling up on the cushion.

"You haven't answered me," I said.

Jeff's smile of contentment disappeared and his face grew serious. "Tough question."

"But we need to tell them soon. Like tomorrow."

"Not yet, sweetheart. Give me a couple more days. I have an idea in the back of my mind. Just don't know if we can pull it off."

"Pull what off?" I was immediately curious and eager to grasp at any straw that might save our little cable show.

"Oh, no." He shook his head. "If I tell you now, you'll think of a thousand different reasons why it can't be done."

I turned and rested my arms on his knees, trying to look as imploring as I could with the clock about to toll midnight and me about to turn into a very tired pumpkin. It had been a long, exhausting day. "You're supposed to share everything with your wife."

He aimed the remote at the player and pressed the play button. I wrestled it back and turned it off again.

Reaching around and giving my ponytail a yank, he relented. "What if we buy *Zoofari* from the zoo?"

He paused for my reaction as he took a slug of coffee.

"Buy it?"

"Yeah. We buy the rights, take control of production and get ourselves some sponsors—hopefully the zoo will be one of them—"

"That sounds expensive. Can we afford that?" I sized up our tiny living room and the water stains we kept ignoring in the corner of the ceiling, one of several repairs our old farmhouse needed.

"It won't be cheap," Jeff admitted. "We'd have to keep our jobs at the zoo, keep on as we have been with *Zoofari* being a part-time gig. At least until we can get some top-notch sponsors."

"Or one of the big cable companies picks up our option, like

Animal Planet or Discovery Channel."

"Exactly. What do you think?"

My pragmatic side wanted to say it was too big a financial risk. Our roof leaked. You couldn't run the microwave and the toaster oven at the same time without throwing a circuit breaker. We both drove vehicles well past their prime. Zookeeping was a labor of love. It wasn't glamorous, and the pay was average at best. As curator, Jeff made decent money but not enough to support a film crew and all the production costs of a television show. Our current net worth was tied up in the hobby farm, which didn't leave much left over at the end of the month for risky business ventures.

"I don't know, Jeff."

He lowered the mug, his eyes brimming with his usual confidence. "It is a risk. But rewards only come to those who take risks. I risked all I knew to stay in America with you. And you risked the comfort of your old life hookin' up with a bloke you hardly knew from Down Under. And that's working out, right? And it's not like we're starting from nothing, Snake. The show's already a success. We're the highest-rated cable TV show in the Midwest. This show is one of our dreams, yes?"

I nodded back, feeling his irresistible optimism pulling me in like quicksand.

"If we want *Zoofari* to continue we have to make it happen," Jeff went on. "If we're going to do it why not now, while it's popular? That's when we have the most clout. It might not be that big a risk. Not if we work it right."

And working it right was the key. We'd be responsible not only for ourselves, but for our crew as well. If we didn't make money, they weren't getting paid. It was a big responsibility, one that up until now had been the zoo's burden, not ours. I'd never tackled anything so big in my life. It scared the hell out of me.

Yet if I was going to fail, at least I could find comfort in knowing I had tried to save our show. Ignoring the new knot in my stomach, I cuddled closer and nodded against his chin. It might have been the lateness of the hour, but I heard myself say to him softly, "At least if we fail, we fail together."

"That's me girl."

He gave my shoulder a squeeze. I smiled back then sat up a little at a realization.

"Jeff, how are we going to afford it?"

With the caution of a reptile hunter wading through a croc-infested lake, he said, "We could get a second mortgage on the farm."

"Would that be enough?"

"No. That's why I'm thinking of calling Jago."

I swiveled round. "To ask for money?" I couldn't believe my ears. Jago was Jeff's know-it-all older brother and prodigal son of the Jones clan, the only member of Jeff's immediate family I didn't like. He spared no moment to tease or put down his little brother. "You're going to ask Jago for money?"

"No, I'm thinking of selling him my interest in the Darwin Reptile Preserve."

Omigod. Jeff's father had started the Darwin Reptile Preserve two decades ago, had built it from nothing to one of the premier zoological gardens in Northern Australia, which was now run by Jago. For Jeff to give up his stake in the family business was a sacrifice I wasn't sure he should make and I told him so.

He pressed his lips together thoughtfully. "I'm still chewing it over, sweetheart. If my dad were still alive, I think he'd approve. This is a chance for me to do something on my own like he did. To make a name for myself, for ourselves."

He regarded me tenderly and played with a strand of my hair.

Whatever extra money we had should go into the house. So

said common sense. We'd bought our century-old hobby farm with the idea of fixing it up. The beautiful hardwood floors and paneling were intact, but previous owners had renovated the place to death. The built-in buffet had been painted over, owners in the 1950s had removed the stained-glass window and taken out the decorative walnut-scrolled posts to install curved archways between the dining room and living room. All things we wanted to restore.

And yet we had other dreams, some of which required more urgent attention, one of them being our TV show.

Jeff said nothing more and handed me the remote control.

I pondered him for a moment, then kissed him lightly on the mouth. It was enough for now. Time for us to focus on the task at hand. I took my position again, my back against his knees. I punched the play button in hopes we could finish our review of the tape in the next hour or two so we might yet steal a couple hours of sleep before heading off to work.

In this edited tape, Shaggy included only those scenes taken an hour before the Beastly Ball up to the murder of Anthony Wright. As the images unfolded before us, I muted the sound to remove the distraction of the surrounding noise, allowing us to concentrate on body language and the flow of people on and off the screen.

Having seen this footage once at the studio, I fast-forwarded through it, looking for the relevant parts. The whine of the accelerated video was the only sound in our cozy living room for a minute before I stopped the tape near, for me, a key moment.

Play.

The scene was at the crocodile billabong just before the ball was about to start. Jeff was repairing the plumbing with JR. Shaggy had caught the moment when Jeff leaned over too far and fell off the footbridge, a watery splash that showered droplets onto the camera's lens. Without sound, it was surreal.

There I was, rushing into the shot in my sequined gown and bare feet, looking frantic and pulling Jeff out of harm's way. A moment later, a sopping Jeff stood upright, safe, cutting loose a silent whoop of triumph. The flash of still cameras engulfed us as we kissed, me clinging to my husband for dear life. Images caught for posterity. One to show the grandkids some day.

My heart raced again when I saw how narrowly I had almost lost the man I loved.

I pressed my head against his legs and let out a small sigh of gratitude. He stroked my cheek then rested his chin on the top of my head.

"Did we really live through all that?" he asked, reading my thoughts as Shaggy's camera went in for a close-up of a much agitated but still living Anthony Wright thundering across the footbridge.

It was not a happy tableau. A furious Wright took out his ire on Jeff because the croc exhibit wasn't fully operational for the grand opening. Jeff, as always, retained his good humor despite the undeserved dressing down.

Behind me, the flesh-and-blood Jeff let out a troubled breath. "Hard to admit it, but Gary was dead on about him, wasn't he?"

"Looks that way. We still only have JR's word Wright was the one who framed him in Florida."

"I have to say, given the research Gary turned up, I believe it, particularly after hearing JR's story. Makes you wonder if Wright was doing the same thing here, doesn't it?"

That very thought had crossed my mind yesterday when I questioned Melanie about the young giraffe, the one loaned to the Lincoln Park Zoo in Chicago. But there had been other offspring born to our collection, other animals that had been loaned to zoos around the country. Had they all reached their destinations? Or were they now suffering at the hands of some ill-advised exotic pet owner or being killed for a hunter's gratification in a canned hunt? I couldn't believe that. There were too many safeguards in place. Too many good people involved in overseeing our collection for that to happen.

I ground my teeth together and shifted over to look at Jeff. "Do you think that was why he was so gung ho over the Australia Trail project? To have control of some new species coming to the zoo?" But it didn't quite fit together even as the words came out. "Wright was too high-profile a person here and the zoo too big and too well-run for him to be able to get away with it. You think?"

"There's no way Wright could have spirited out any of our lot without someone noticing—without me noticing."

I put the video on pause, annoyed at seeing Wright's flinty image dominate the screen.

"A record check would show if the zoo has been missing animals. It's easy enough to contact other zoos and see how our loaned animals are doing. I can't believe he would have done that here. Why would he have to? He had an important job with great standing and Mel's got money. God, she's swimming in it!"

"That's the point, darlin'. It's Mel's money, not his." Jeff shrugged. "He began as a poor boy from Backwater, Texas. Some bludgers never get over their roots. For some it's a challenge, the danger of being nicked. Others can't change their ways."

I sat up and faced Jeff, thinking aloud. "If Gary's right and this goes way back to the sixties, Wright would've been finishing high school, getting ready for college. Gary thinks that's how he put himself through school. How else does a poor boy from Texas afford a fancy Eastern college? Grants and scholarships don't cover everything."

"And look who his father was. Jungle Jack. Like father, like son?"

Jeff had certainly followed in his own father's footsteps, carrying on the family tradition of working with animals. His father had been a respected herpetologist, his older brother Jago a veterinarian until he took over the family animal park, while younger brother James became a marine biologist.

Jeff grew introspective. "Maybe he couldn't stop, it was so branded into him. Or maybe Wright was in too deep with his business partners and couldn't get out." Mulling the idea over, Jeff gave up, then gestured at the TV with the chipped mug.

I pressed the play button.

The camera was still on the confrontation between Jeff and Wright. Once done, Wright stepped back and the shot widened and panned. Curiously absent from the scene were JR and Gary who, it appeared, had discreetly faded from view once everyone's attention was fixed upon the other two men. In light of recent information, it was clear neither wanted to be around the zoo director.

The next clip showed the scene from a different angle, where an incredulous Senator McNealey and Butler Thomas joined the group. McNealey, grinning ear to ear, enjoyed Jeff's stab at defusing Wright's anger by suggesting he volunteer to help with the crocodiles. What a contrast to the McNealey I saw only forty minutes later giving his speech in front of the ball attendees. Interestingly, for the first time I noticed the tenseness in Butler Thomas's face in this moment: the forced smile, not a trace of the deep dimples that melted many a heart.

I looked at Jeff.

"If Wright was involved in the illegal animal trade at the zoo and Butler found out about it, it would explain his attitude when I talked to him the other day."

Jeff's face was a question.

"Maybe," I said, "that was the real reason he didn't want me poking around. He knew I'd actually find something."

"That might embarrass the zoo?"

"You can't blame him." I shifted my legs and crossed my ankles. "If the media got a whiff of any kind of scandal, the zoo would be ruined. Part of its budget still comes from the taxpayers. Imagine the hoo-ha this would cause at the legislature if it became publ—"

In my mind I was back in the zoo administration offices, where I had overheard Butler Thomas, Suzanne Terak, and Senator McNealey talking in private.

Had I really understood what those three had been talking about? Was there more going on than I saw? McNealey had said once Wright had gotten what he wanted, he didn't give a damn about keeping his promises. I assumed they were talking about construction contracts. Could it have been something more sinister? I explained my concerns to Jeff.

He let out a whistle.

"A cover-up?"

"I don't know. It's not hard to understand Butler avoiding bad publicity for the zoo. And Suzanne wasn't exactly forthcoming when I spoke to her that day. Maybe that's why McNealey was so worked up. Maybe he knew what Wright was involved in and wasn't happy at being associated with anything illegal."

Jeff didn't buy it. "I'd be more willing to believe it was the senator who was doing the shady stuff, covering up for Wright, but not Butler. He'd have had Wright dismissed in a tick."

"Yeah, I guess." I slumped back.

Bagger rolled over on his back, an obvious invitation to rub his belly. I slouched against Jeff's legs, one hand absently stroking the retriever's stomach.

The video continued to play, a panning shot of the crocodile exhibit that ended in a close-up of Sebastian undulating beneath the water like the neighborhood bully, his every movement saying, "I'm a tough guy. Leave me alone." Besides Jeff, Sebastian was the only other being in the sequence of images I'd just seen who I knew with absolute certainty could not have murdered Anthony Wright.

Then the locale abruptly switched to the Beastly Ball, where nearly everyone was dressed in formal attire.

When my face appeared on-screen again I cringed. My evening gown had not been designed for its wearer to run at full bore, and was slightly the worse for my wet embrace with Jeff after he'd left the water. This gala was one of the few events I gussied up for, and I had wanted to look my best. Compared to the ever-glamorous Suzanne Terak, I was a hopeless cause. "Now there's a beauty!" Jeff said, as if reading my mind. He leaned down and kissed the top of my head as his arms enveloped my shoulders.

More shots of mingling party-goers clustered in loose groups of three or four, with no concerns in the world at that point but having a good time. With a sharp eye, I could account for everyone involved with the zoo passing in and out of the frame; they were all there with the exception of JR, who had supposedly returned to the crocodile exhibit to keep an eye on his babies.

The scene switched to the dozens of round tables spread out in the plaza near the front of the entrance to the Walkabout and Tropics trails. The floral centerpieces were in terra-cotta planters hand-painted with little kangaroos, lizards, boomerangs and aboriginal touches. In the video, only a few people had taken their seats, others were rearranging the place cards more to their liking.

Gary Olson had stepped around a table to intercept Jeff, who did not see him. Gary was about to follow his hero when Shaggy touched his shoulder. The Shagster was explaining something at length to him, and he nodded back a few times, and then glanced at his watch before heading toward the ramp that led down to the gift shop and main zoo entrance. If I remembered right, there was a cute little blond volunteer he was eager to meet up with.

The next cut was the one Shaggy had told us about when we had our last meeting at Billie's condominium. He was filming along the Walkabout, getting some footage *sans* guests, when he came upon McNealey and Wright in a heated argument. Neither man was aware of the camera. McNealey's usually pale skin was crimson, his hands balled into fists at his side as he made no effort to hide his displeasure. Wright's eyes were narrowed, his mouth twisted in an ugly snarl as he argued with the other man. Then the scene blurred to the trail's path as Shaggy lowered his camera and ducked into the service tunnel.

This was the scene where I imagined Wright had told McNealey the construction company had lost their zoo contract and their option on building the next Hanley-Holm expansion. Or had McNealey just accused him of trafficking in exotic animals?

The following shot abruptly focused on the people seating themselves around the plaza, waitstaff bringing in plates of strawberry shortcake piled high with fresh whipped cream. An agitated Suzanne Terak stood in the back corner, discreetly casting her eye about in hopes, it is assumed, of locating her boss. At a table near the front of the room Senator McNealey stewed silently in his chair and when, a moment later, he was introduced as a speaker, you could see the annoyance in his demeanor as he strode up to the lectern.

All the good humor that had marked him at the beginning of the evening had been ripped away. He struggled to keep his calm, his eyes darted back and forth, a caged leopard having been poked once too often with a pole. And we knew who had handled that pole.

Jeff groaned behind me as his turn at the lectern came.

"Now there's a beauty!" I mocked his earlier comment about me.

In retaliation, Jeff confiscated the remote and began fast-forwarding through the tape, stopping as the crocodile enclosure came into focus and all hell broke loose. Jerky camera movements blurred into a hard focus of the body floating in the water. A swish of Sebastian's tail as he circled by, an eddy of current in the spreading murk of stirred-up soil and blood. Protecting his territory and his kill, the fifteen-footer was all too ready to use his quick speed and ripping jaws on the next interloper.

Thankfully, the camera turned from this grisly sight onto those who had stumbled upon it. From the safety of the sidewalk McNealey stared with a gray pallor at the bobbing corpse, one might wonder whether from shock or guilt.

Once more, I fast-forwarded the video a few minutes to the moment the security guards came rushing to the area with rifles ready to shoot poor Sebastian. I tried to talk them out of it and Jeff startled everyone as he dove headlong into the water with JR following almost immediately. The camera zoomed in on the feverish battle in the water as both men tried to subdue the angry reptile in an attempt to save his life. As they landed the croc onto the small beach, Gary rushed in, awkward as he moved through the pond, fell forward, and submerged himself in the murky water. His bare arms flailed as he struggled to right himself. The camera caught the back of Billie's head as she leaned over the fence and ordered Gary out of the water.

When the camera moved farther afield, Suzanne Terak came into focus, beautiful and stylish in her creamy white gown and dark flowing hair. She stood at the top of the exhibit, apart from everyone, her mouth gaping open, her fingers pressed against her temples in sheer disbelief.

Like a specter, Melanie moved into the frame and to the far railing, her expression blank. In the bewilderment of the moment, everyone hurried around or stood like a gaping idiot, unaware of her presence as she stood quietly, transfixed by the grisly sight below. It was a difficult moment to watch and I rewound it back to the after-dinner speeches. There was something I wanted to see.

I watched McNealey's body language as he approached the lectern again.

"What are you looking for?" Jeff asked, rubbing the tension out of my shoulders.

"I don't know. Some clue to what he was thinking, what had happened between him and Wright that evening."

I reversed the video even further, stopping at the argument Shaggy had caught between the two men. This time I saw something I hadn't noticed the first time through.

I rewound it again. "Look there. Just behind Wright."

Jeff squinted at the small TV screen. Behind Wright was the path that led across the billabong and into the tunnel that wrapped itself around the pool to give visitors a below–water level look at our crocodiles.

"Someone's coming out of the tunnel . . . no, someone's walking backward into the tunnel."

I played the scene once more, this time in slow motion. It wasn't distinct, the zoo uniform blending in with the sand-colored stone, but there was a man ducking back into the tunnel's entrance, a short, rather round man with a ponytail.

Jeff squinted. "Mitch Flanagan? What's he doing there?"

"Good question." I stopped the tape and looked at Jeff. "Mitch is our birdman. Last time I saw him that evening, he was in the Biodiversity Center showing the guests the bald eagle."

"He had no business being around the billabong and the crocs. He should have been in the aviary interpreting for our guests."

Mitch made it no secret he didn't care for Wright and his policies, one of which had landed Mitch on probation for three months. He was particularly bent out of shape during the Beastly Ball over the cancellation of his pet project, the raptor center. No surprise, then, that two days later, Mitch was thrilled that Wright was gone and Butler was in charge. Were Mitch's aspirations enough to kill a man over? I hoped not.

Jeff leaned forward and rubbed the side of his neck. "We could be reading too much into this. The police went over these tapes. They must have seen this clip and likewise questioned Mitch. If he's a suspect, I'm sure he would've let the whole staff know how displeased he was."

Jeff had that right. Mitch was the zoo hothead, a man with an opinion on every subject and everyone connected with the zoo. You might not like his opinions, but at least you knew where Mitch stood and that he wasn't talking about you behind your back. He'd tell you to your face. So why was he spying on McNealey and Wright that evening? It seemed like a very un-Mitch-like thing to do.

Chapter 23

The surgery track lights blazed overhead. They reflected off the white melamine cabinets and stainless-steel, washing brightly upon the unconscious patient on the table. For the second time in a week, the Komodo dragon was hooked up to the anesthesiology machine in the animal health center. Except for his shallow breathing, Rocky was immobile as four pairs of concerned eyes observed him. Most of that concern was for the welfare of the man-sized lizard, yet some of it was for us, too. If Rocky awakened suddenly and started thrashing or biting, he'd be a handful.

"I think we're ready," Dr. Steve said, checking the slackness of the animal's jaw. "He's had that thing inside his stomach for a week. I'd hoped the endoscope would've done the trick, but I just couldn't get a grip on that damned toy."

"He'll be fine," assured Jerry, his keeper, the man who knew Rocky best. The stocky African-American's experienced eye surveyed the limp body of the Komodo. "He won't be any trouble, Doc."

"Hope you're right, mate." Jeff eyed him with mock trepidation. "It's not you sticking your arm down his throat."

"True," Jerry conceded through a crooked smile and seemed awfully glad of it.

Dr. Steve turned to Carol, his assistant. She wore pale-green scrubs and closely monitored her patient's vital signs on the electronic readouts, ready to warn us of any sudden change. Dr.

Steve considered his patient from behind the lenses of oversized tortoiseshell glasses. "Surgery would work, but it's too invasive. This is our best shot, Jeff. Sure you're game for this?"

An urgent call from Dr. Steve sometime before the sun came up that morning had gathered us all to the zoo's health center. Rocky was doing poorly, and the veterinarian couldn't wait any longer to remove the small stuffed bunny the Komodo had swallowed last week.

I tried to stifle a yawn. Morning wasn't my peppiest part of the day, particularly after our late-night video session. It took two cups of go-juice to bring me around, a strong espresso with a shot of almond. What little sleep I'd had was tormented by my efforts to stitch together some coherence out of all the things I'd recently learned. What was I missing? There were too many unanswered questions. What was the deal with Senator McNealey and Anthony Wright? McNealey had really blown a fuse on the Walkabout Trail. Too much intensity for a simple business deal gone sour. And what did Mitch Flanagan want from Wright? Was he just being nosey, or did he have another purpose? Could I even be certain Mitch was after Wright? What if he was lurking on the trail for a chance to speak with McNealey?

Then there was the whole mess with Melanie and JR. Should I believe either of them? Was there really nothing between them now or was this story a smokescreen? JR could have gotten rid of Anthony Wright so he could finally be with Melanie. Was that the real reason he came to Minnesota? Or was it Melanie? What if she had pushed her husband through the temporary bridge railing so she could be with the man she couldn't have in Florida?

And now Suzanne Terak was part of the equation. I wasn't even aware she knew JR, let alone felt the need to visit him in jail and question him. She was up to something, but what?

What information did she have? It had to involve Wright's dealings with that old zoo in Texas, something in his old records. Great, my list of things to do had just gotten longer.

Too much. Just too much to sift through, like trying to grab a handful of sand. Most of it slips through your grasp. But this wasn't the time for distractions, so I forced myself to pay attention to where I was and what we were doing.

All eyes were on Dr. Steve, who carefully draped a hand towel across the back of our unconscious Komodo. A respectful distance away, Shaggy adjusted the lens of his camera to take in the entire scene for one of the last episodes of *Zoofari* this year—or forever, if things didn't change.

Shaggy was unfazed by his proximity to the Komodo dragon. I swear the man thought he was invisible behind a camera. Not so calm and collected was Billie Bradshaw, who stood near the far wall, clearly uncomfortable at being even that close to the large, unconscious lizard.

Wrapping his arm in plastic and duct tape, Jeff said pragmatically, "I've heard it done to dolphins. I'm willing to give it a go if it means not cutting the poor bloke open."

The veterinarian's nerves showed a little. "Yes." He glanced warily at Rocky. "That's commendable; however, shoving your arm down a dolphin's throat is one thing, putting it down a Komodo dragon's is another."

One of the world's largest lizards, the Indonesian native has long, sharp claws and serrated teeth that could rip apart an animal twice his size with little effort. And not just one row, but several rows of teeth. If one tooth falls out, another moves forward to take its place, much like the teeth of some sharks. But unlike a shark, their bite is deadly for another reason. In the wild their mouths are loaded with bacteria, enough to bring down a water buffalo. Once bitten, infection takes hold and the

Komodo simply tracks the dying animal and waits for the inevitable.

"That's why we have the PVC pipe, Doc." Jeff indicated the heavy-duty plastic cylinder which would prop open the Komodo's mouth. "That should be enough protection. Sure you don't want to have a go yourself?"

"Uh, only if you don't want to, Jeff."

The zoo's chief veterinarian wasn't squeamish by any means. Had it been necessary, he would have done the job himself. Yet, because Jeff was so eager to do this, and, given his druthers, Dr. Steve was quite ready to defer the task to someone else.

With one last check of his patient, the vet moistened his lips and nodded at the rest of us. "All right, let's do it. Everybody in their place."

We positioned ourselves along the seven-foot length of Rocky's dull-green body. Jerry, the reptile keeper, stood at the middle of the table. He placed his hands on Rocky's sides, ready to act at a moment's notice. Dr. Steve placed a gentle hand on the top of the Komodo's head while Carol stood beside him, opposite Jerry, monitoring the IV drip.

At the rear, I rested my hands near the base of the long powerful tail, the theory being if Rocky awoke or had a reaction, we'd all be able to feel it and could respond immediately.

Meanwhile, Jeff liberally applied mineral oil to his arm and waited for the vet to open the jaws of the animal. Dr. Steve unhinged the snake-like jaw and positioned the short section of PVC pipe in place, his forehead shiny with perspiration.

With the reptile's jaws opened as wide as possible, Jeff took a deep breath, then bent over and inserted his left arm into the animal's mouth and slowly, carefully, worked it down the esophagus until only his shoulder was visible.

It was a bizarre thing to see. Unsettling, too. Billie was in my direct line of sight and she looked away, perhaps trying not to think the unthinkable. Although Rocky was heavily sedated, Jeff was taking a big risk.

No one spoke for a minute, waiting for a sign from Jeff, whose face focused intently upon his task. Tension mounted in the room as the minutes passed. By all accounts the PVC pipe should easily protect Jeff's arm from being severed; but I was still anxious about it, an uneasy flutter in my stomach rising at the thought of something going horribly wrong. My heart quickened and I forced myself to take slow, calming breaths.

Shaggy squatted to film from a lower angle, his mouth agape at what he saw through his lens. I could only imagine how Jeff looked in close-up. Behind Shaggy stood Billie, her arms folded tightly across her chest, her careworn face distinctly ill at ease, enjoying none of this. Good video or not, I'm sure her anxiety for Jeff's well-being surpassed all other concerns.

Jeff broke the tension a second later. "Pretty messy in there," he said off-handedly, as if rummaging through the kitchen garbage. He bent lower and the muscles in his face tightened as he stretched farther. His sandy hair fell across his eyes and he shook his head to clear his vision.

There was a twitch.

I felt a movement in the Komodo's hindquarters. We all froze.

"Muscle spasm," said Dr. Steve as the moment passed.

Jeff went back to work, his hand exploring the insides of the big lizard. "I touched something . . . no . . . wait—almost . . . almost . . . ah! Got it." Slowly he withdrew his arm until it emerged intact from Rocky's mouth, in his hand a small slimy rabbit plush toy.

We all let out a muted cheer. Even the uptight Ms. Bradshaw seemed to deflate, her shoulders sagging as relief spread across her agitated face.

Carefully, Jeff removed the plastic pipe from Rocky's mouth as Dr. Steve kept a close watch.

"Carol, how's his heartbeat?" The vet turned to his assistant, who had a stethoscope against the Komodo's side.

"Good. He's good."

"Okay, then let's get our friend on the cart and move him to his holding pen. Great job, Jeff."

Wiping his arm clean with a towel, Jeff grinned openly and for the first time I saw a touch of nerves. He raised his left hand, which was trembling. "That's not something you want to do every day. Whew! I knew the little ripper wasn't going to stir—but you never know. He wouldn't be a happy camper to wake up and find me arm down his gullet."

As Jerry, the vet, and his assistant wheeled off their patient, Jeff slumped onto a nearby metal stool, weary and energized at once.

"Impressive, dude!" congratulated the Shagster, his camera dangling by his side. "That was righteous." He nodded significantly, as if bestowing his highest honor.

"Shaggy's right," agreed Billie, stepping forward, her approval contained. "That was a great moment to capture on film, but I swear you'll give me an ulcer yet."

"Then I must be doing something right," Jeff joked.

Chapter 24

There's no rest for the weary—or is that the wicked? Either way, I was hopping. The excitement of saving our Komodo dragon could not be savored, as there were too many chores to do before the gates opened. Exhibits needed to be cleaned and breakfast scattered and hidden, forcing the animals to forage as they would in the wild.

The Borneo sun bears had a bowling ball drilled with extra holes that I filled with peanut butter and rolled out into the exhibit. Children get the biggest kick out of watching the two bears tussle and tumble with this heavy ball, using their long pink tongues to dig the peanut butter out or pawing at it with their powerful claws. Later in the day I'd give them one of the fishsicles I had made up last week—fresh fish and chunks of melons and strawberries frozen in a large block of ice they could bat around their enclosure. After lunch, I was scheduled to take them into the back holding area, one at a time, and go through their target training, teaching them to present a paw on command and then rewarding them with a squirt of their favorite sports drink. While they might have considered it a game, this little trick made them willing participants in their own routine veterinarian exams and made administering minor medical treatments much easier and less traumatic for vet, keeper and animal.

Then there was my turn at feeding the baby gibbon and helping the Komodo's keeper, Jerry, transfer a now very awake and much healthier Komodo back to his sandy enclosure on the Tropics Trail. And I still managed to join Jeff in the zoo auditorium to teach and entertain four separate groups of grade-school children who all wanted to meet the star of *Zoofari,* Jeff Jones.

The fact that I was an afterthought didn't bother me in the least. I preferred the background. Jeff was the showman. He made learning about animals fun and exciting. After our presentation, we lined the children up and trotted them down to Crocodile Island to see Jeff toss some raw chicken to Sebastian and Babe, dangling it mere feet from their snouts, coaxing them to lunge at it as Jeff jumped away at the last second. Great theatrics. It also kept the crocs interested and in shape. I didn't doubt that half of the kids left the zoo determined to grow up and be a zookeeper just like Jeff Jones. Not a bad ambition in my humble opinion.

I just wished Butler Thomas and the board of directors could have seen the enthusiasm those kids greeted us with. Did they really want to cancel *Zoofari* and take this high-profile publicity away from the zoo? Did I really want to put the house in hock to save it? Jeff was willing to sell his interest in a family business—no, a family tradition—to keep *Zoofari* going. So what was I afraid of? Success? Rocking the comfy little world I had built around myself?

The questions nagged at me for the rest of the day. I cleaned and sanitized cages after lunch, inspected the newly repaired fencing along the bridge in the crocodile exhibit, and trained a couple of new volunteers—all while avoiding the issue of taking on a huge debt for a TV show.

By the end of the day the knot in my stomach tightened, heavy as a brick since last night. It gave me empathy for what poor Rocky, our Komodo, had gone through. Except in my case the sensation was imaginary—nervous tension about the future.

Work kept my mind off it, yet by the end of the day I was starting to run out of gas. Dragging myself along the Walkabout Trail near closing time, I found solace in the familiar and indescribable aroma of lush vegetation, damp straw, fermenting fruit and animal droppings, a richer bouquet to my discriminating nose than any mere floral arrangement could offer. For eight years I'd worked at the Minnesota Valley Zoo, longer than any other job. It was comfortable. It was safe. If *Zoofari* became the success Jeff predicted, I would have to leave all this to travel the world, to bring the message of conservation to more people than I ever could here. Perhaps to find greater fulfillment. And yet I hesitated to give it up.

The delighted squeal of a child snapped me out of my indulgences. The zoo had closed the doors ten minutes ago and all stragglers should have been on their way out. Up ahead, a tow-headed little boy wearing a bright blue zoo T-shirt that hung to his knees, stood on his tiptoes to look over the stone wall at the kangaroo exhibit. A rapidly melting ice-cream cone dripped down the hand he thrust out, teasing Boomer and the other roos while his mother took photos with a slick digital camera, blithely ignoring the *Do Not Feed the Animals* sign nearby. Past this little maternal scene I saw Mitch Flanagan bearing down on them like a charging rhino.

I quickened my step and sprinted past mother and son to intercept Mitch before he could inflict irreversible damage. Grabbing his arm, I pulled him a dozen yards up the path, hopefully out of earshot.

"Chastising the patrons isn't going to cut it with Butler any more than it did with Anthony Wright," I warned in a vicious whisper.

"People are idiots. Whether it's a kangaroo or a tiger. They think because they're in a zoo, the animals are cute, cuddly playthings," Mitch griped, pulling away from me. "These aren't domesticated animals. They don't like to be teased. Hell, my dog doesn't like to be teased. And one day one of them will get revenge. Just hope I'm around to see it when it happens."

"You know as well as I do, that scenario can only harm the animal."

Last year's tiger incident was a good example. Some teenager's idea of fun and bravado was to tease our Amur tigers. I have no idea what this yahoo did that particular day, but Sabu, our four-hundred-pound male tiger, took offense. Making a sprint at the fence, he climbed straight up the links and stopped just short of the electrified wiring at the top. If he had made it over, our security team would have been forced to shoot him. No negotiations or stall tactics here, as there had been the night Anthony Wright was murdered and Jeff had put himself between security's rifles and his beloved crocs.

Luckily, Sabu got a second chance. He was immediately put in holding and then loaned to another zoo before he figured out how to get over the fence and make one of our visitors into dinner. The offending human was banned from the zoo forever. He was lucky.

"Excuse me, ma'am." I thought it best to call out to the woman. "The zoo is now closed. We'd appreciate it if you'd make your way toward one of the exits."

She glared at me as if I were the Mother of All Wet Blankets, intent on ruining the fun of her offspring. I wanted to say more but Mitch's presence reminded me of a question that had been burning in my mind all day, so I steered him farther down the path. We pulled up in front of the dingoes' enclosure and I faced him. "I watched the *Zoofari* tapes we filmed the night Wright died."

"Any good?"

"I'd say so. Some really good stuff with the crocs, particularly around the time Wright was killed."

"Do they show who killed him?" Mitch fingered his moustache in an attempt at seriousness, which failed rather miserably. There was something of the smart-ass in Mitch, even when he wasn't trying—except when he was showing his birds; then he was the consummate professional.

"Well," I said, "that depends. You were in one of the shots."

"I imagine I was in a lot of them, kiddo. I was showing off my birds."

"In the Walkabout Trail tunnel? That wasn't your station."

Mitch didn't look at me, instead he focused on the dingoes lined up next to the half-hidden door, knowing dinner was about to be served.

"Why were you there, Mitch?"

His answer was interrupted by a loud scream on the trail behind us. A second later the woman at the roo exhibit came barreling toward us with her son tucked under her arm like a football.

"He's loose! He's loose!" she screeched.

Shit.

"Who's loose?" I tried to stop her, but she slipped easily between Mitch and me, only one thing on her mind: protecting her child.

"The kangaroo!" she shouted over her shoulder as her feet rumbled over the wooden planks of the footbridge.

"Shit." This time I said it aloud, loping back along the trail, Mitch at my heels.

At the next turn we stopped cold in our tracks.

There, standing calmly in the middle of the path, just outside his exhibit, was my old friend Boomer. Cocking his head to the side, he stood at full height, just over six feet, displaying why the red kangaroo is the largest of the macropods. He was taller than most men. Boomer's broad, intimidating shoulders reared back when he saw us.

Mitch's jaw dropped. "Good God." He had never been this close to a red roo before. "He's huge."

Ice cream dripped from Boomer's whiskers and a small clump of chocolate smudged his nose. He showed no aggressive behavior. Talking to him softly, I unhooked the radio from my belt and called security, then told Mitch to go get a handful of our homemade roo bars from the kitchen. Boomer couldn't resist the oats, soybean and molasses concoction I often treated him to.

"How the hell did he get out?"

Boomer was coolly assessing the situation and sniffing the air. I knew what he was looking for. "Not a priority just now, Mitch."

"422, Security." Static crackled from my radio as the security team answered my call.

I outlined the situation briefly, while nodding vigorously at Mitch to get his ass moving. Meanwhile, I kept my eyes glued to the kangaroo that had just taken a short hop closer. At full stride he could clear over thirty feet in one hop, so I wasn't about to take chances now that I was alone with him.

I clipped the radio back on my belt and spoke gently to Boomer, Mitch's question looming in my mind. I was amazed. The Walkabout Trail was state of the art. The exhibits were designed with their residents in mind: climbing ability, how high they could jump and how far. The back wall was steep and arched inward, effectively blocking a vertical leap. A ten-foot-wide trench separated the kangaroo exhibit from the four-foot wall that bordered the trail. The island grassland had low thorny plantings to discourage the animals from venturing close to the edge. It was enough to prevent the average alpha male from escaping but, apparently, Boomer was no average male.

I took a cautious step toward him, speaking in a pleasant singsong tone. Not interested in me, he sniffed the air, barked and bolted in the other direction, disappearing around the corner. Damn. These animals could speed across the grasslands of Australia at forty miles an hour. If he passed the koalas' enclosure, he'd be in the main plaza and have his choice of causing havoc along the Tropics Trail or heading for the main entrance to the zoo and the outside world.

The radio told me our security team had blocked off the head of the trail. Armed with sleep darts, they were prepared to sedate Boomer. There would be no standard rifles today. Kangaroos are not shoot-on-contact animals like our tigers. It could take a good fifteen minutes for a tranquilizer dart to affect an animal. And in fifteen minutes Boomer was capable of causing a lot of damage.

Rounding the corner, I came eye to eye with the giant macropod. He was leaning back on his great tail, legs up. A second later those powerful hind legs thrust out into the side of a trash bin, knocking it over and spilling its contents. Boomer sniffed through the rubbish, either deliberately ignoring me or laying a clever trap. I wasn't sure which. Trained to box, he had been pitted against anyone dumb enough to try to last three minutes in the boxing ring with him. I'm sure most of those tough guys learned the hard way. Fighting a roo wasn't as easy as it looked. And Boomer, in turn, learned to be as sneaky and premeditative as any human could be. Moreover, he packed a wallop with those feet. While you were busy dealing with his lethal forepaws, he could use his muscular tail as a third leg and bring up his feet to deliver the *coupe de grace*.

He had been neglected in those last years and was nowhere near what was considered a healthy weight for a kangaroo of his size. Months of rehabilitation in the barn of the Joneses' hobby farm had followed after Boomer was rescued, being pampered and nursed back to health. Hopefully, he had fond memories of those days and would treat me accordingly.

"Looks like we found our trashcan bandit," Mitch said, reappearing at my side with a bucket of treats. He was breathing heavily from his sprint to the kitchen and back.

The words struck me cold.

"That right, Boomer? You been helping yourself to some midnight snacks?"

It was as if I'd been shoved out of a closet into the sunlight, seeing things for the first time. It made sense. This explained all the overturned trashcans along the Walkabout Trail during the past week.

I swear, the kangaroo smiled at me, his velvety ears twitching. With a sharp bark, he closed the space between us in two short hops. I dropped the roo bar I was holding and backed up, Mitch right behind me. For a moment, Boomer hesitated, standing an arm's length away and weighing his options—terrified humans or scrumptious roo bar?

Creeping up the trail behind Boomer came Diane, our kangaroo keeper, along with Jerry and Sadie from the Tropics Trail. Diane held a tranquilizer gun in her hands.

"Shoot him!" Mitch hissed from behind me.

Boomer's ears went back and Diane hesitated. I shook my head vigorously, wishing she'd shoot Mitch instead. We didn't want to dart Boomer if we didn't have to. Being tranquilized was stressful on an animal, and there was no telling what position he'd be in when the sedative finally took hold. I've seen darted bears run up to the tops of trees, falling as they became too groggy to hold on to their precarious perches. I didn't want Boomer to try a half-dazed leap and end up breaking his neck in a fall. And if he were stung by a dart right now, there was no telling how he'd react. I didn't want to be the object of his ire at this range.

Rather than shout across Boomer and upset him, I backed up a step and carefully took out the radio again and called Diane.

Quietly advising her and the others to clear personnel out of the utility tunnel and tell security to keep out of Boomer's sight, I was going to try to lure him back into his holding pen.

Boomer crooked his head around to see what was behind him, but he didn't move. Diane's round face puckered with worry, but she did as I asked, she and the other two backing slowly down the path toward the nearest exit door on the far side of the koala exhibit.

"I'll go help," Mitch offered, trying to hand off the bucket of treats and back away.

"Oh, no, you don't." I seized his sleeve, my eyes watching Boomer. "You're going to stay put and answer some questions."

"Are you nuts?"

"Maybe. But you're going to answer me. Why were you in the tunnel spying on Wright the night he was killed?"

Bored with us, or certain of his power, Boomer shifted his attention to the roo bar at my feet.

"I wasn't spying on him. I wanted to talk." Mitch fell in step as I continued to inch backward toward the service exit, the knobby treads of my hiking boots scraping against the concrete path.

"And did you?"

"If you have me on tape, you know I didn't. Do those things bite?"

"It's not his teeth I'd worry about. See those claws? They could rip you apart." As if on cue, Boomer straightened, the nutritious bar held in his paws as he chewed eagerly at its contents. I looked askance at Mitch. "And those feet. He's got huge leg muscles. One well-placed kick could easily cause internal injuries."

Mitch blanched. He was a birdman. His eagles might have had wings that could span the length of Boomer, but a six-foot mammal was a whole different ballgame. Kangaroos were beyond his expertise and he was damned nervous. Maybe keeping him off guard would get me some honest answers.

"Did you talk to Wright?" I repeated with greater urgency. I broke a bar in half and tossed it to Boomer while moving us another step closer to the door of the service tunnel. The trick was not to give him too many treats before we got to the holding area, or he'd get bored and wander off to find something of more interest—like another trash bin.

"I left before he could see me."

"You realize you might have been the last person to see him alive?"

Mitch shrugged. Not his problem. "I didn't kill him, if that's what you're getting at."

"What were you going to talk about?"

"Cutting the raptor program. Thought I'd try one more time to make him reconsider, that's all."

"Only you didn't get your chance."

"No. He was way too upset with McNealey to listen to me. I saw that. So I gave up."

I latched onto that. "You saw Wright and McNealey arguing."

"Yeah, they were having a regular verbal donnybrook. It wasn't the first time I've seen them squawking at each other. But it was the worst."

"The worst, huh? Prop the door open."

Mitch ducked behind me and opened the door to the service tunnel, ready to use his bucket as a weapon.

I continued, "It looked pretty intense in the video. Did you overhear anything?"

"What difference does it make?"

"A big one for JR. Mitch, it could change everything for him."

The tunnel was cool and breezy compared to the Walkabout

Trail. The hum of machinery rumbled through the passageway—the equipment that filtered the water, heated the building and monitored the air quality.

Mitch kicked a wedge beneath the door. "I doubt it. Look, Snake, I don't want to get involved. Okay? I want to keep my job."

"What makes you think you'd lose it?" I moved slowly into the utility tunnel that circled behind the exhibits, leaving half a roo bar at the entrance. The tunnel houses our kitchens, keeper offices and holding pens for our animals. Boomer's holding pen was behind the kangaroo exhibit. Not that far if he cooperated.

Mitch wavered. "They were talking about the Australian House and the construction of the exhibits. Wright accused McNealey of bamboozling him. Said the construction was substandard. That we'd end up doing the entire thing over in ten years and Carruth Construction was going to pay."

So Wright had the same suspicions as Jeff and I. "Is that all he said?"

"Isn't that enough?"

Boomer poked his head around the corner, nose first, ears back. We were like Hansel and Gretel leaving a trail of breadcrumbs as we slowly made our way to the kangaroo's holding pen, leaving bits of roo bar behind us.

Diane and Jeff were standing at the door to the enclosure along with what looked like the entire zoo staff, Butler Thomas included. News got around fast. Diane chewed her bottom lip and held her breath as Boomer followed Mitch and me, inching forward on all fours now as he munched on the treats left in our wake.

The female members of Boomer's mob were in the holding pen, dining on a trough filled with grain pellets, lettuce, apples, carrots and alfalfa. Smelling the delicious meal ahead, Boomer raised his head and sniffed. The decision was instantaneous, and we all stepped back as Boomer hopped through the doorway and took his place at dinner. He didn't even flinch as the door was slammed shut behind him.

Disaster averted, Jeff draped an arm across my shoulders, grinning with pride. I tried not to relax under his touch, knowing if I did, I'd start to shake. The immensity of what had just happened and what could have gone wrong would hit me like a six-ton elephant.

Diane frowned. "This shouldn't have happened. He shouldn't have gotten out."

"Obviously, we've underestimated him," Jeff marveled. "He's capable of jumping a lot farther than we ever thought. We're gonna have to adjust the landscaping so our boy can't get a straight shot over that wall."

"At least we found our trashcan bandit." I told them about the waste containers he had tipped over.

Diane shook her head, clearly disappointed. "I should have figured. He's refused to come into the holding enclosure more than usual this past week. And each night he's been out, we've had an incident."

"We're just lucky he didn't get into more mischief," I said thinking of how easily he could have vandalized the trail further.

Butler stepped forward, his face drawn and tense. "Like toppling you into the billabong with the crocodiles?"

Chapter 25

"You can't be serious! Pushing over trash bins is one thing, but pushing me into the crocodile pool . . ."

Butler wore the slacks and vest of a navy-blue, three-piece suit without the jacket. The sleeves of his white shirt were rolled up to his elbows and the blue-striped tie was loosened at the throat, dangling askew. Normally fastidious about his appearance, for him he looked disheveled. Gone, too, was the easy charm and ready smile. His whole bearing was like a tightly wound spring.

The staff gathered round. He surveyed their expectant faces, rapt for the latest news, perhaps in hopes of fresh grist for the rumor mill. Instead he glanced at his watch. "Isn't it feeding time, people? I'm sure you all have some other place you should be right now. Thank you for your assistance."

The dismissal, however gentle, was clear and the staff grumbled out slowly to attend to their duties. There were animals to be taken in and fed, medications to be given, reports to be filled out and exhibits to be cleaned. Even Jeff took off, giving my hand a quick squeeze before running to catch up to one of his crew, asking about preparations for the soon-to-arrive sugar gliders.

That left Diane and me standing awkwardly in the passageway, while behind us came the sound of contented kangaroos munching their last meal of the day. I couldn't help but toss a glare in Boomer's direction.

"Was Boomer in holding quarters the evening Snake was attacked?" Butler asked Diane.

"No. He wanted none of it. That's one of the reasons—"

Butler waved her explanations off. "And trashcans were also turned over that evening?"

This time Diane and I both nodded. It was so obvious now. Not only was Boomer the trashcan bandit, he had also been my attacker. With chagrin I realized the hands I so vividly recalled shoving me in the back had been feet, feet driven by a pair of powerful legs.

I felt humiliated. All my ranting and raving. The fear after thinking someone had wanted me dead. I had even gone so far as to pin the guilt on Senator McNealey. I had jumped to all sorts of conclusions. All except the one right under my nose. Boomer had been my attacker. I had passed by his enclosure that night, apologizing for not having a treat, and he had clearly voiced his objection with a loud thump of that muscular tail. Had he also come after me?

"What about the evening Wright died? Was Boomer on exhibit?" Butler looked at Diane sternly.

"All the animals were on exhibit, sir. That's how Mr. Wright wanted it," she answered.

I took a step closer to Butler, my voice low, suspicious. "What are you getting at?"

"You're not the only one who can play detective, Snake. I can put two and two together as well. If Boomer kicked you in the water that evening, why couldn't he have done the same thing to Anthony a couple of days earlier?"

I scoffed. "Boomer killed Wright? I don't think so."

"Why not? A rogue kangaroo with the kicking power of a mule. If it happened to you, it could have happened to him."

Diane was shaking her head. "I was with the roos that evening, in or near the enclosure the whole time during the

Beastly Ball and dinner. That's when the police say Mr. Wright was killed. Boomer never left the exhibit, sir."

"You're positive?"

"Yes," she said with total conviction.

Butler's eyes narrowed and his jaw muscles tightened. "Tell me, Diane. If you were by the exhibit the whole time, then why the hell didn't you see who killed Wright? You're the only person who admits to being anywhere near Crocodile Island that evening."

"Butler!" I was shocked.

Butler never yelled at the staff. Never. He was red in the face, agitated. This was so unlike him. And poor Diane was on the verge of tears.

My comment must have caught him off guard, for he lapsed into silence, creasing his brow at some thought. "I'm sorry," he offered awkwardly and shook his head. "I gotta go."

He swung round on his heels and strode out of the tunnel as if on a mission.

Diane and I looked at each other blankly. Then I ran after him.

"Butler!"

He didn't slow down, didn't toss me a glance. I caught up and kept stride with him. "You were hoping to pin Wright's death on Boomer."

"It would have made things so much simpler, Snake."

"If Boomer had attacked Wright, there should've been some specific bruising or scratch marks. The coroner would've found those."

"Not if he didn't know what to look for."

I thought of the purple and crimson bruise across my lower back, thanks to Boomer's powerful kick. Yet that reminded me of the other evidence I had been privy to.

"It can't be Boomer. Detective Sorenson told me there was

bruising on Wright's throat. Kangaroos don't choke their victims. No, Butler, someone else shoved Anthony off that bridge."

"Then it looks like JR is still our man."

We pushed through the doors leading back onto the Walkabout and Butler headed purposefully toward the head of the trail.

"Melanie gave him an alibi for that night," I tossed at him, wishing he would slow down and talk to me.

"It only takes two liars to make an alibi."

That brought me up sharply, but Butler didn't stop.

"You think Melanie is lying for JR?" I asked in disbelief, his long legs forcing me to run to keep up.

He didn't answer.

"Why would she do that?"

Butler Thomas stopped and swung round with annoyance. "Look, I'm not about to speculate on that." He looked pointedly behind me at the keeper in the Tasmanian devil exhibit, who was raking out the soiled hay. He lowered his voice. "I'm only telling you what the police are going to think. They now have a real motive to hang that man with. If JR and Melanie had a relationship, it only stands to reason he'd want her husband out of the picture."

He turned away from me and continued his fast pace, lengthening his strides. I decided not to torment him and instead followed at a close distance up the walkway and through the Biodiversity Center. He hadn't told me anything I hadn't thought of myself. But I had to believe that JR and Melanie were telling me the truth when they said they had never let themselves be more than friends. Butler seemed satisfied to lay blame on JR or even Boomer, probably because either would wrap up things nicely for him. The idea Wright's killer could be someone else entirely didn't seem to be of any interest to him.

In fact, he had wanted to keep me out of the investigation and had discouraged me from doing anything that might clear JR. Did he have a personal reason for that? Did he know something about Wright's past or his dealings with Carruth Construction?

I cornered him again in the elevator that led upstairs to the administrative offices, slipping in just as the doors were closing.

"Would you please let this go?" He punched the button to the third floor.

"I can't. A man—a man you knew—is dead and another man may be convicted for a crime he didn't commit."

The elevator wheezed open.

"You said JR had an alibi for that night."

"That doesn't totally absolve him. This murder may be connected to the murder in Florida."

"Is that the cops' opinion or Detective Snake Jones's?"

I decided to ignore his snide comment. We walked along the empty hallway. The late afternoon sun streaked through a distant window. Butler fumbled with the keys to his office. I leaned against the wall, watching his face as the key finally hit its mark.

"What aren't you telling me about Wright?"

"Stay out of it."

The door unlocked and I charged in after him, shutting the door behind me. I was really sticking my neck out now, hounding our acting director this way. He was within his rights to order me out, even discipline me, if he wanted to. But I was as tenacious as a crab; I needed to know the truth. I was also gambling on my instincts about Butler. "Whether you like it or not, the police are going to be digging. If there's dirt to be found, they'll find it. The truth is going to come out. And when it does, the media is going to have a field day with it. It's not going to look good if they find out you were protecting him."

"Exactly what dirt are you talking about?" He plopped down in the chair behind his desk and leaned back, his annoyance rippling across his face.

He was calling my bluff. Only it wasn't a bluff. I drew in a deep breath and made the decision to fork over some information in the hopes he would reciprocate. "I think Wright framed JR for that murder in Florida—"

He slammed forward in his chair, hitting the desktop with his elbows, leaning forward. "And who imparted that little gem? Shari? That little bimbo would sell her soul if she thought it would free JR."

"It doesn't matter who told me. It matters what I've been told. And it isn't pretty. The police don't know any of it yet, Butler. They don't know about Wright's past and what he's done. But it won't be long before they do."

He ran both hands through his thick dark hair. For a wild moment I wondered if he was the murderer. He had objected to Wright's appointment as zoo director, having wanted the position himself. Does a person kill for a job? It seemed unlikely, at least in this case. Not Butler. He wouldn't do that. Then I remembered the look on Butler's face in the tapes. The tight-lipped concentration during Wright's confrontation with Jeff. Disgust? Jealousy? It didn't seem to fit.

With an air of capitulation, Butler closed his eyes and rested his head in his hands. "Can't you just keep out of this? You got want you wanted. JR will go free—"

"But he's still wanted in Florida." I sat in the chair next to his desk. "Was Wright doing anything illegal? Was he selling our surplus animals, Butler? Was he?"

I waited. If he was the man I thought he was, his conscience and sense of fairness would prevail over any momentary irritation with me.

His eyes flashed open and fixed upon me in an expression I couldn't read. For nearly a dozen seconds they bored into me, then, slowly, he sat back and with some deliberation pulled out the middle drawer of his desk. Reaching to the back of the drawer, he produced an envelope.

He handed it to me. “Read it.”

Puzzled, I turned the envelope over. Butler Thomas’s name was laser printed on the envelope in one of those comic fonts that suggested a child’s handwriting. The envelope had been neatly sliced open. The letter inside had not fared as well. The white bond paper I pulled out was crumbled, the folds worn, as if someone had read it over many times, folding it and refolding it, balling it up in his hands.

“Read it,” he said again, urging me to open up the sheet.

It was short and to the point.

I know what you’re doing. I know about the cover-up. Anthony Wright has taken advantage of his position in the world of conservation long enough. The animals under his care do not benefit. He is a card-carrying member of the illegal animal trade and will be exposed if he’s not removed. Justice must be served. Right will serve Wright.

“When did you get this?” Whoever wrote it knew Wright had been dealing illegally in the sale of endangered animals. It was melodramatic, but enough to strike fear in the heart of the guilty party, I’d wager.

“The afternoon of the Beastly Ball.”

“Did Wright know about this?”

Butler was reluctant to continue, visibly uncomfortable. “Anthony needed to know. He had to be ready for the attack when and if it came.”

That would explain Wright’s quick temper when the crocodile exhibit was having problems. “Did he deny it?”

“Emphatically.”

That didn’t surprise me. “What did he say?”

The elegant man with the winning smile was stone-faced

now. He took in a deep breath, stalling. "He said he knew who had written it and he was going to take care of it himself."

"And?"

"He stomped out of the office. He didn't identify the writer."

My mind flashed back to the *Zoofari* videos and the bitter argument between Wright and McNealey.

"Senator McNealey and Wright had an argument that night. Is it possible he wrote this? Blackmail to wheedle some more construction contracts out of the zoo?"

"Wright courted McNealey because he wanted support for the zoo. With all the state budget cuts and revenues flat, we're lucky we can pay our employees." Butler went on with heat. "Hell, we're lucky we can feed the animals. If things don't improve soon, we may have to loan some of our collection to a zoo that can afford them. McNealey was our biggest supporter."

"In exchange for some lucrative construction contracts for Carruth Construction, the family business. Isn't that a conflict of interest?"

"Technically, no. McNealey doesn't own the business. His mother-in-law does. But they were the lowest bidder in an open process. Wright saw to that."

His eyes looked away from me, drifting to the ceramic tiger pencil holder near his arm. "According to McNealey, Anthony 'guaranteed' him Carruth would be involved in Phase Two of our master expansion plan."

"Not exactly above board?"

Butler slowly shook his head. "No. But McNealey is a heavyweight in the senate. When he talks, people listen."

"And then Wright backed out? Why?"

"Substandard work." He told me the same story Mitch had overheard. "I don't know if Carruth did it intentionally, or if one of the subcontractors was at fault. But it's something we will get to the bottom of."

I held up the letter. It didn't look like something McNealey would write. But who then? "Why didn't you give this to the police? This is probably our killer."

"It doesn't exist." Butler leaned forward and plucked the note from my fingers. "Wright crumpled it up and tossed it in the wastebasket. By now it's in the city dump with tons of other bits of paper and refuse. It doesn't exist, Snake."

"You're withholding evidence, Butler. That's a crime."

"It would be a worse crime if the zoo was destroyed over this incident."

It was the last thing I wanted. Aside from Jeff, there was nothing as important to me as the conservation and the work accredited zoos around the world did to preserve the earth's wildlife. Yet a man had been murdered. And the pursuit of his killer had to count in the mix as well. That notion prompted me to think of Melanie Wright's directive to the zoo board—that the truth was more important than the reputation of her husband. It was a courageous stance to take, given the fact that the brush that smeared her husband's reputation would also splatter on her.

But this was about more than finding the person who had killed Anthony Wright. It was about clearing JR. He wasn't out of the woods yet. If the truth put the zoo's reputation at risk, it had to be risked. Even though the idea ripped at my insides, I could see no other way. And I was as guilty as Butler. I had my own pocket full of secrets I hadn't yet divulged to the police.

"Butler." It came out as a whisper. "It might be time to plan some major damage control. If Wright's illegal activities were the reason for his murder, there's no way they'll be kept from the public."

He nodded. His words sounded hopeful, but his voice was a defeated monotone. "We should be okay. Although there's no way to be sure. There'll be some fallout at first. The zoo will be under the microscope of every animal rights activist group in the country. And the government will get involved. We won't be the only zoo under scrutiny. But I've had time to follow up on some of the animals. The loans, the deaths. They're all legit. If Anthony was dealing in exotic animals, he wasn't doing it here. I'm almost sure of that. This letter is bogus. This zoo is not culpable."

I studied the scuffs on the toe of my new boots and noticed the dried sun bear poo stuck to the side of my sole. I wanted to feel relief at what he had said, but didn't. "Maybe we'll get lucky and his murder won't have anything to do with the zoo."

Butler's eyes met mine, fatalistically, with no trace of optimism. Could we get that lucky?

Chapter 26

"I thought you'd never get here."

Melanie Wright was out the door, pulled by her small dog, Lacey. At my bewilderment Melanie explained, "I just talked to Jeff. He said you were on your way."

Ratted out by my own husband.

During the drive into Minneapolis I'd worked on my spiel, steeled my resolve. Melanie owed me some honest answers. Twice before I'd backed off in deference to her grief, not pressing her. Not this time, Charlie. I hoped my sudden appearance would give me the element of surprise. Now that was blown away. Melanie and Lacey had emerged on to the front steps just as I shut the door to my Jeep.

Flustered, I joined them on the sidewalk, rethinking my game plan, as Lacey grew fascinated by my footwear, virtually inhaling the hiking boots and the innumerable zoo scents they had collected.

Melanie didn't seem to notice, her face wan and tired.

"Walk with us," she said. "Lacey's been driving me nuts to get outside. We can talk on the way."

We set a brisk pace westward along the well-landscaped boulevard. I wasted no time getting down to business. "Melanie, what's this about you giving JR an alibi?"

"Not important." She waved me off. "I've got something else to show you."

"It's important to me. You lied to me—and not for the first time."

She flashed me a look and said nothing, pressing her thin lips together tightly while the color rose in her cheeks. For an instant I thought she was going to snap back at me, but she struggled for her composure and lapsed into a thoughtful silence. It seemed smart to do likewise and give the moment a chance to pass.

We ambled through the pricey Kenwood neighborhood, surrounded by its grand old houses, manicured lawns and great old trees. Most cities had lost their majestic elms from disease decades ago, yet this area of Minneapolis had managed to keep most of its mature elms, which meant we had the pleasure of strolling among giants. As we neared the north end of Lake of the Isles, Melanie veered toward it.

"You deserve an answer to your question, Snake," she said, as we trod across freshly cut grass. Ahead was the asphalt trail that wended round the lake. She added with meaning, "Give me a minute."

I nodded back silently, moved by the heartache in her voice.

On the asphalt now, we walked parallel to the shoreline. The warm summer day ensured the paths were full. Minneapolis wasn't the City of Lakes for nothing; it boasted one of the best park systems in America, and people here loved their parks. Power walkers, young mothers with strollers, runners and bicyclists shared the walkways with us. In-line skaters were everywhere. No surprise in the city where they were invented.

I felt conspicuously out of place, still clad in my zoo uniform and boots while Melanie was the picture of casual stylishness in pressed denim twill jeans, a pink cotton top with banded stripes and white canvas shoes, none of which were marred by dried smears of bird droppings, paw prints or animal slobber, as was my charming ensemble. It was a good thing I didn't care much about fashion, otherwise I would have skulked away embarrassed by all the young twenty-somethings sashaying past us in their skimpy tank tops and shorts.

Fortunately, Lacey intervened. She scampered off the path, tugging at her leash, and we had to jog a few steps to keep up. For such a small dog, her little legs set a fast pace. She stopped to watch a young man play Frisbee with his cocker spaniel on the grass. As we continued, this became her pattern. Hurry and stop or hurry, sniff and squat to put her mark on the spot.

At last Melanie turned toward me, her tone apologetic. "Snake, I should have told you sooner about being with Jamie, only . . . I was afraid." She looked away. "Afraid I'd make it worse for him."

"Geez, Mel, what d'you think I've been doing the past week? I want to see him go free, too. I've made myself Public Nuisance Number One trying to help JR. Couldn't you have trusted me?"

"It wasn't that," she muttered.

"I thought we were friends."

"We are."

"Yeah, well you've done a poor imitation of it this week."

"Snake." She was stung by my words. "I wanted to tell you but the police were asking about my whereabouts that evening. They made me feel as if I was a suspect. They practically accused me of being involved. It—it shook me up." Confusion and latent anger washed across her lovely face. Her fingers tightened round the nylon leash. "I was thinking about Jamie, too, how the police would interpret our friendship."

"I still don't—"

"Don't you understand, Snake? Jamie was *my* alibi, too. All of a sudden I found I needed one. But I wasn't sure if I should tell anyone. My husband was dead and the police had their prime suspect. If I said I was with him during the murder, then the police would naturally assume there was a connection between us, a motive for him or me to kill Anthony!"

Melanie was right. Her assignation—meeting—whatever—could only prove there was a connection between her and JR. Enough to commit murder? Shari's reckless insinuations rushed back like the evening tide. Going to the police now with the alibi could simply be a gambit to clear herself and JR. To show she had nothing to hide. That was plausible enough.

Except for one thing: the Melanie Wright I knew wasn't capable of murder. And then I thought of the note Butler had shown me. Anthony Wright had known his killer. But would Melanie have written a note like that? What would have been the purpose? To discredit her husband? To force him to divorce her and give up his rights to the Hanley-Holm fortune?

Slow down, girl. I realized I was getting way ahead of myself. Taking a deep breath, I smoothed back my hair and secured my ponytail before my mouth got me in trouble. Nearby a flotilla of mallard ducks angled across the lake waters in the direction of one of the small islets.

"I guess I understand," I told her half-heartedly. "You were protecting JR."

"If I'd told the truth earlier, it could've made things worse for him."

"Or it might've helped him."

"I know—I know. I've been agonizing over this for days, Snake."

"What made you change your mind?"

"What Jamie told me about Florida kept pinging in my head. I didn't think it would matter if I gave him an alibi for Anthony's death. He'd still be extradited to Florida on another murder charge. And . . . well, part of me was confused. I mean, less than an hour after I spoke with him, my husband turns up dead and Jamie disappears. Just like before." She grunted fatalistically. "In the end, I realized the truth did matter."

Melanie Wright regarded me with the tranquility of one assured of her convictions. "The truth always matters," she added as an afterthought. "People will twist my story around, try to paint Jamie—or even me—with guilt, but coming forward with the alibi might help him. Lacey, leave that alone."

We stepped around a furry caterpillar inching its way across the asphalt.

"What did you and JR talk about?" I asked.

She offered a faint, pleasant smile. "Catching up on old times. We both managed to slip away before dinner was served, meeting out behind the administration building. Jamie had only a few minutes before he had to change out of his tuxedo and be at his station when the tours came, so we were a bit rushed. He was so afraid I'd condemn him. What he never knew was that I'd always believed in him. The idea he could have killed Al Beatty never made sense to me and it was good to hear his version of what had happened."

She repeated what he had told her. It was the same story JR had told Jeff and me the day we had visited him in jail. How he was under investigation by the U.S. Fish and Wildlife Service for illegally selling animals from his wildlife refuge and began to suspect Alexander Beatty; how they argued and that night JR found him dead in the cage of a Florida panther.

"The evidence was damning," she continued. "It looked like he was illegally selling exotic animals and profiteering. After he found Al's body, he panicked."

Melanie drew in a lengthy breath, her eyes sympathetic. "I was stunned. I'd been a zookeeper at Sweetwater, had taken care of those animals. The fact that he was able to sell any of our animals to the exotic black market trade without me knowing it—" Melanie tossed her hands in disbelief. "I never noticed! And I was there, Snake. I don't know how he did it under my nose."

Anger flashed in her eyes, then was replaced, slowly, by resignation. "Al had always lived high on the hog. He was a man with a family, a mortgage and a big boat he kept in the Miami marina. Some of us wondered how he could afford it, but his wife, Betsy, had a job. I don't think anyone thought any more about it. I guess we should have. Especially when the animals went missing."

"Sounds as if you liked the guy."

"We all did."

"Did you know him well?"

"Not well enough, it seems. He was something, though. A more gorgeous man you weren't likely to meet. Like Tyrone Power, the old-time movie star. Dark hair and eyes with the longest lashes I'd ever seen on a man."

"A heartbreaker?"

"Not really. Not a ladies' man, if that's what you mean. He was a decent, nice guy. At least I thought so at the time. I met his family once at Sweetwater. Al asked me to take a photo of the three of them with Al showing off a young alligator. I can't believe he was involved in this."

She lowered her head and grew quiet for a while. We scurried past the traffic on Lake Street and made our way to Lake Calhoun, the largest of the chain of lakes. Lacey's feet were finally starting to slow down, so we took a bench in front of the beach house, the smell of fried fish and hush puppies wafting from the seafood walk-up restaurant that now occupied the space that had only served ice-cream cones, pop and candy when I was a kid. With renewed energy Lacey ran to the end of her leash and started digging her way to China in the wet sand.

The sun was low in the sky and a cool breeze fed off the lake. Sailboats with colorful sails raced ahead of the wind, intermixed with a handful of wind surfers.

"I believe Jamie," Melanie said at last, her eyes avoiding mine.

"I believe he was framed. Running may have been a foolish choice, but who's to say I wouldn't have done the same thing under similar circumstances?" She shrugged. "All I know is that it took courage for him to tell me everything, not knowing if I'd turn him in to the police."

I thought of the note again. "And you're certain JR and Anthony didn't know each other? They had never met?"

"If they did, neither ever let on."

"Do the police know about your Florida connection with JR?"

"I don't think so. They haven't brought it up yet. I'm sure someone will realize it soon, which is why I want to give you these."

Melanie reached into her jeans pocket and handed me a clutch of folded papers.

"What's this?"

"Invoices and packing slips."

"For what?"

"From the Deaf Smith County Zoo in Texas. Anthony's zoo. Suzanne brought them over this morning."

I remembered the stack of cardboard boxes in Wright's office the night I went to talk to Suzanne Terak. Boxes Wright's sister had sent for Melanie to sort through.

"You asked her to search through all that stuff?"

"I did. Anthony's sister jumped at this chance to rid herself of the zoo and sent us all the records. She isn't much of a record keeper and I knew the stuff she sent would be in a mess. And that's Suzanne's forte—making order out of chaos.

"And there were other things." She kicked off her shoes and dug her feet into the sand. "When you suddenly find yourself alone in an empty house, your mind becomes prey to all sorts of random thoughts. I started remembering snatches of conversations we had in Florida, odd references about how some business deals weren't working out, stuff like that. Things that meant nothing at the time, but in retrospect seemed off. So I asked Suzanne to make those boxes a priority, and she came over with them. Afterward I called Jeff."

Listening to her with keen interest, I unfolded the tissue-like paper, pink faded to a dull umber in places, the blue ink smeared. The top sheet was from International Wildlife Supply regarding a shipment of three Florida panthers from SCWR.

"That's the Sweetwater Creek Wildlife Refuge," Melanie explained. "Look where they were being shipped to."

Deaf Smith County Zoo. From JR's wildlife park in Florida to Anthony Wright's zoo in Texas. This had to be the reason Suzanne Terak had visited JR in jail. She had wanted to substantiate the connection.

Melanie pointed to the bottom of the invoice. "And look who signed it."

I squinted at the faded and smeared signature. It looked like *A. Beatty.*

"Could JR have authorized this sale? I mean, without knowing where they were really heading?"

"I doubt it. He was trying to repopulate Florida with these animals, not other zoos."

"Then JR was right. After what you just told me about Beatty it makes sense. This, though, proves there's a link between Beatty and your husband."

I looked at her guardedly, uncertain how she would react.

Her reply was a simple, disappointed, "I know."

"Sorry, Mel—"

"Keep going, Snake, there's more."

The second sheet was a record of a payment to Deaf County Zoo from Wild Acres. That was the company Gary had connected to Wright, the one the smuggled macaws were traced to. Jeff and I were going to owe that boy a big apology. The sale was for three cougars. Cougars or Florida panthers? A smoke-screen? And where were they going? If we dug deeper would there also be an invoice for the hyacinth macaws that had gone missing while Wright was working for a bird sanctuary?

Big news.

But was it good news? That was the problem. I slumped against the bench backrest as ideas tumbled through my head. If Wright could be linked to the problems at Sweetwater Creek and with Alexander Beatty's murder, wasn't that just another nail in JR's coffin? Wasn't that a big, fat motive for murdering Wright, the man who had ruined JR's life in Florida?

My heart sank. Before registering my dismay, my better nature realized what this meant for Melanie. "Mel . . ." I fumbled for the right words. "I'm sorry, but it looks like Anthony was trafficking in the illegal exotic animal trade. At the very least, his zoo in Texas had dealings with Al Beatty."

Her eyes shuttered closed in silent acknowledgement. This was hard for her. You didn't live with a person for twenty-some years without thinking you knew him inside and out. A secret like this had to come as a shock.

"I wish I had listened when Anthony talked to me," Melanie said, her voice soft and searching. "I wish I had actually been hearing what he was saying."

"What do you mean?"

"The day I had come home from work—the same day Al was killed—Anthony had us all packed and ready to go. I was furious. He hadn't consulted me, just bought the plane tickets and was ready to go. Said the movers would take care of everything else, and I needn't worry about anything."

"Did he give you a reason?"

"He wanted to make a new start. Wanted a clean slate, to start over. At the time I thought he was talking about our marriage."

"He wasn't?"

Melanie looked down at the leash she held in her hands. "I can't be sure. We'd had a rough couple of years together, drifting apart. And I think—I hope—that was part of his reason, but now I think he was talking about the animals. About what he had done. There was something different about him. He looked really shaken."

Was it regret? Fear? Had Wright realized he had gotten in way over his head? Maybe he hadn't killed Beatty. Maybe the same people who had killed Beatty had threatened Wright. Was that why he had left Florida in such a rush? To protect himself and Melanie? Sadly, we'd probably never know.

I glanced at the papers still clutched in my hand.

"Melanie, what do you want me to do with these?"

"I don't know," she lamented. "They implicate my husband and give JR a reason to kill him. If the police get these records they'll tarnish two men at the same time. I was hoping these papers would help clear Jamie. But they only make the case for murder against him stronger." Her shoulders heaved in anguish. "The truth is tricky, Snake. Sometimes having only part of a truth is more damaging than having it all."

"Can I keep these?" I asked, treading lightly.

"You can't tell the police. Not yet."

"Mel, I've already kept way too much information from them." And the thought of another lecture from Ole Sorenson didn't exactly light my fire, let alone being charged for withholding evidence.

Her hands grabbed my forearm, her gaze locked onto mine. "Wait a couple of days before you decide. There could be more to come. Suzanne's still looking. She's only made it through half the boxes."

"Well . . ."

"Please. A little while ago you asked if I trusted you. Would I give you this if I didn't?"

"Even if I end up giving it to the police? Even if it ends up dragging your husband's name through the mud? If he was involved with illegal animal dealers, he could've been involved in Al Beatty's death."

We had skirted round the issue up until now. However, I'd gone and said it. I waited for her reaction.

She was cool. "I've thought of that. Anthony could twist the truth to suit his purpose. He could find a loophole where no one else could see one, and if he were still alive he would probably even be able to justify what he'd done. But—" Melanie said without equivocation—"he wasn't a killer."

She swept her hair back over an ear and regarded me with a tough exterior calm that had been forged over years of living with a dynamo like Anthony Wright.

"Besides," she continued, suddenly remembering, "Anthony was with me the night Al was murdered. We'd taken a late flight out of Miami and changed planes in St. Louis."

"He could have made a call from the airport." I was thinking out loud now.

"What are you talking about?"

"JR got a phone call that night. Someone called to tell him there was trouble in the panther house. He's convinced it was Anthony's voice. Your husband sent JR out to find Beatty's body."

It was evident JR had left this little piece of information out of his confession to Melanie. She brought her hand up to her mouth. "He did make a phone call. Said it was a client. I remember thinking it was odd he didn't just use his cell phone."

Probably because he didn't want his wife to hear what he was going to say. We sat in silence for a moment and Lacey came back, tired of digging, wanting to be petted. Melanie lifted her up into her lap, mindless of the wet sand the dog had all over her paws and legs. Melanie's eyes stared intensely into space, as if trying to zero in on the distant past.

"It's possible Anthony was warning Jamie. That he realized what his real priorities were and that's why he wanted to leave town so quickly. He was scared he had gotten in too deep. Or he just wasn't willing to pay the price anymore."

I gestured back noncommittally, not knowing what to say. I grabbed at straws. "Maybe Shari knows something," I suggested. "She was there the night Beatty was killed. She might have seen something."

"I wouldn't trust her to tell the truth about anything. She'd kill to save . . ."

Melanie's voice trailed off and I remembered what Butler had said. Shari would sell her soul to save JR.

I knew Melanie wasn't the most objective person to talk to about Shari, but I plunged ahead anyway. "We both know Shari told Anthony you were having an affair with JR. She admitted that herself."

"But we weren't!" Melanie protested.

"I believe you. But Shari might've thought you were and was afraid you'd steal JR from her."

"Or she just lied."

That thought had occurred to me as well. "Yeah, she might've just wanted to make trouble for you, both of you."

Melanie's hand stopped stroking Lacey's head and the dog pawed at her. But I had her owner's undivided attention.

I wondered, "Shari's life in Florida was rough, with a physically abusive husband. She needed to get out. If JR was also threatened in some way, he'd be looking for a way out, too. Could she have forced the issue?"

"Wouldn't surprise me in the least. You saw how she was that day on the Africa Trail when she ambushed us. The things she said."

I had to agree. "I saw an entirely different side of her that day. Collected, manipulative and vindictive. She doesn't seem to have a life outside of JR. If that life was threatened, how far would she go?"

"Women have killed for less."

"I always thought it was strange she didn't provide an alibi for JR after the murder." I drew my feet up to the bench and hugged my knees. "She said it was to keep the police from looking into her past. She was afraid they'd somehow contact her husband and he'd find out where she was. It seemed plausible when she told me. Now I'm not so sure."

Melanie sat up straighter. "You mean she didn't have an alibi the evening Anthony died?"

"I don't know. She wouldn't dare lie and say she was with JR, because she didn't know where he was or what he would say."

"And Jamie couldn't say he was with her, because he was actually with me."

"It had to have been a shock for her to find out Wright was here in the Twin Cities, director of the Minnesota Valley Zoo, no less. If she thought there was any chance Wright might expose JR to the police, she might have tried to stop him."

Could she have also written that note? An attempt at blackmail? Her silence in exchange for his?

Melanie tilted her head to the side, digesting what I had just said.

"We think of Shari as this blubbering mass of neediness. To be honest, after the venom she hurled at me the other day, I wouldn't put murder past that woman."

Chapter 27

Jeff and I waited outside the large double doors like bandits ready to pounce, our flatbed carts loaded with cages, crates and plastic containers. There was always a certain amount of pre-show jitters before each personal appearance. While Jeff was excited and raring to go on, I was nervous, not quite comfortable in front of a crowd.

This morning it was worse. It wasn't just the impending performance. It was the information Mel had told me the evening before, information that Jeff and I agreed should be turned over to the police. There were things I couldn't keep to myself anymore: Melanie's past relationship with JR both as employee and "special friend," the animal invoices Suzanne had uncovered, the note Butler had been hiding and the stuff Gary had found out about Anthony Wright. For the zoo's sake, I hoped Ole would be discreet. Not a word of this could leak to the press, particularly if it had absolutely nothing to do with Wright's murder. The zoo couldn't afford more bad publicity. Just the idea made me heartsick. A fat lot of good I was, too, which only made me feel worse. I still had no idea who murdered Anthony Wright and everything I had found out seemed to support the case against JR, both in Minnesota and Florida. Something about Alexander Beatty's death still bothered me. I realized I needed more details about what had happened the night he died, and that meant squaring off with Shari Jensen.

But first things first. On the other side of the closed doors came the high-energy buzz of children's voices—lots of them—laughing, giggling and screaming in nervous anticipation. While adult voices shushed them, we turned at the sound of a moving freight train.

Except it wasn't a train. It was Magdalene Marpell, public outreach director for the Science Museum of Minnesota, whose lower-level auditorium had been prepared that morning for our visit. She strode purposely toward us, the hem of her blue gingham dress skimming the tops of her white anklets and sneakers. Slightly out of breath and looking harried, she attempted to tame the wisps of blond hair fluttering errantly from a bun twisted on the top of her head before halting in front of us. Vigor in the form of a brilliant neon grin emanated from her face as she greeted us.

"They're so excited to see you," twinkled Miss Marpell. "So is the staff. We've been playing your videos. And, of course, the children all watch your show. We're all fans." Impossibly, her grin widened and brightened by several watts. "Thank you so much for coming!"

We loved coming to the Science Museum, which occupied sixteen acres on the bluffs overlooking the Mississippi River in downtown St. Paul. Today classrooms from several different area grade schools had come to see us.

This appearance had been on the calendar for a month, and though we were up to our necks in work and could have rescheduled, this commitment was an important one to keep. These children were the future stewards of the planet, future patrons of the zoo and future leaders in conservation, so sharing our message with them at this early age could make a difference with their view of the world in later life. We were also hoping to get a few more children interested in the wonderful summer school program the Minnesota Valley Zoo offered. It was good publicity for the zoo and it was good publicity for *Zoofari*. A win-win, as Butler Thomas would say. At least it would have been if *Zoofari* hadn't been cancelled. I knew technically we were on hiatus, but I found little comfort in that. If funding wasn't found soon, our little show was all but history.

Miss Marpell sucked in a preparatory breath and murmured, "Show time," flashed another sparkle of teeth, opened the door a crack and slipped through. Order was restored as she entered the small auditorium.

"Children, today we have a special treat for you, as you know. We have animals from the Minnesota Valley Zoo."

"Yay!"

"And you know who brought them, don't you?"

"Yes!"

Jeff and I exchanged smiles behind the concealment of the door. That was one enthusiastic crowd of kids.

A cheer went up as Jeff bounded in, no introduction needed. I held back at the doorway, along with Miss Marpell, who had come to help maneuver the carts containing our educational cargo. With his uniform shorts, safari shirt and ear-to-ear grin, the kids knew Jeff instantly. And he loved the limelight. Loved talking to children and seeing the spark of interest light in their eyes when the right chord was struck. Moreover, people responded to Jeff.

Surveying their excited, upturned faces, Jeff was like a kid himself, brimming with enthusiasm and giving Miss Marpell a run for her money. I never thought I'd meet anyone who could radiate as much energy as my dear husband, but Magdalene Marpell ran a close second. Still, when it came to sheer unadulterated gusto, my money was on Jeff Jones.

"Hello boys and girls! How're you today?"

"Fine! Yeah!" returned one hundred voices along with a round of applause and a few whistles.

"You talk funny," giggled a little girl in a pink flowered dress in the front row.

"That's 'cause I'm from another country far away, on the other side of the world! Down Under, as we like to say. It's called Australia. Now in my country we don't say hello like I just did. We say G'day, which means good day, like in 'have a good day.' You want to try it?"

"Yeah!" said the throng and Jeff proceeded to coach them in a proper Australian greeting.

"And over there is my beautiful wife. Her name is Snake."

This got the usual titters from the underage audience as I waved back.

Jeff moved closer to the first row of children, and leaned in a little, as if sharing some amazing secret. "We've brought some exceptional animals for you today, boys and girls. How many of you've been here before?" Jeff crossed the stage, scanning the crowd.

More than half of the youngsters raised their hands.

"This is a great place, isn't it? Did you see all the dinosaurs they've got here? That big old triceratops outside. Did you know it's one of only four complete mounted triceratops in the whole world? And they even have some dinosaur crocodiles, too, my favorite animal. And I can tell you they haven't changed much in sixty million years."

Jeff strode to the first container whose lid I popped open.

"Our first friend here is a reptile."

He reached in and removed one of the nervous inhabitants. "This is a leopard gecko. Check it out!" He held the lizard gingerly in front of him. "It's probably the most popular pet lizard next to the iguana. You see the spots on this little beauty? It's how he got his name. His skin feels like bumpy velvet."

Jeff was now in the audience, moving up and down the informal aisles of grade-schoolers, his hands cradled low, so each child could stroke the back of the gecko. I took the second gecko out of the container and did likewise, trying to give as many kids as possible a chance to touch the animal.

"You have to be careful handling these blokes 'cause their tails can break off. That's how they get away when a predator catches them from behind. It doesn't hurt the gecko. They'll grow a new one. But it comes as a surprise to the critter left holding just a tail." Jeff's eyes grew wide for emphasis.

Geckos lost tails to escape, people told lies. And like the predator left with only a tail in his mouth, the person who was lied to was also left with a tale. Usually a long, convoluted one. How was I going to get to the truth? Had our own zoo director possessed such little conscience that he could knowingly sell endangered animals to the highest bidder, knowing they were going to be used in canned hunts or sold to a collector who couldn't care properly for his own dog, let alone a wild animal?

I tried to put the morbid thought out of my head and concentrate on the children. "Can anyone tell me why this little guy is like a camel?" I asked.

Hands shot up all over. "Because he lives in the desert?"

"And how does he survive in that desert? Like every living creature, he needs water. And you don't find a lot of that where he comes from."

The room grew quiet, so Jeff explained. "This little gecko stores fat and water cells in his tail, just like a camel stores it in its hump. This enables him to go a long while between drinks."

With the grade-schoolers warmed up with something small and cute, Jeff brought out Billy, a yellow-crested cockatoo, to the delight of the gathering. Talking birds were always a hit and Billy could imitate police sirens and fire engines.

Next came Jeff's favorite creepy crawly, an orange-kneed tarantula. Little mouths turned into perfect capital O's as eight hairy legs slowly moved the spider up Jeff's bare arms. There was a chorus of disgusted "Eeew!'s" from a row of small girls near the front row.

"Eeew?" Jeff repeated. "Now what's not to like about our little hairy beastie here?"

"They're ugly," an older boy in the back replied with a down-turned mouth.

"Maybe to you, mate. But to a female tarantula, he's the bee's knees."

As if on cue, the spider slowly moved to face his audience, his front limbs, the pedipalps, reaching forward, feeling the vibrations in the air to detect predators or prey.

A nervous-looking teacher was concerned. "Aren't those things poisonous?"

"True enough. However, the poison's harmless to humans. A bite from one of these blighters wouldn't hurt any more than a bee sting."

At this point a chorus rose from the audience to touch or hold the creature. Unfortunately, we had to disappoint them.

Jeff explained, "These little beauties may look tough, but they're really very delicate. They extend their legs by changing blood pressure inside different parts of their bodies. It creates a lot of internal stress, so if they fell it could break a leg. And you know what would happen then, don't you?"

"They die!"

"Spiders may not be as cute as other animals but they're just as important. Every animal has a job."

Judging by the looks he was getting from some parts of the crowd they weren't entirely convinced.

"Not very sympathetic, I see. Well, there must be someone here who likes spiders." Jeff's eyes raked the group before calling on a small boy in the middle of the auditorium, an energetic youth who had been waving his hand for quite some time. The youngster couldn't have been much taller than three-and-a-half feet as he unwound his crossed legs to bravely hoist himself up in front of his classmates.

"I think spiders are cool!"

"Good for you, son. What's your name?"

"Jamal."

"What do you like about spiders, Jamal?"

"Well, um, I like the way they can spin webs and—crawl up walls! I know a lot about spiders. I've even got a Spider-Man watch!" He proudly displayed the red-and-black watch with the distinctive Spider-Man logo, whose band was too big for his wrist and slipped down two inches when he held up his skinny arm. A red blinking LED that would drive any parent crazy after five minutes flashed from the center.

"By Crikey, that's some watch!" Jeff was impressed. "Why don't you come up here and help me with this guy?"

Jamal hesitated at first, scratching his fingers through his already messy hair, his clear brown eyes electric in a dark face. With a little coaxing from Jeff, he was soon weaving his way through the seated kids, beaming proudly as he stood up front and was allowed the dubious pleasure of letting the spider crawl onto his shoulder. The blinking of the boy's watch seemed to match the rapid beating of his heart.

"Know what spiders eat, Jamal?"

"Little boys!" An older kid shouted from the back and was promptly dismissed from the room by a teacher who looked like a burly bar bouncer.

"They eat other bugs," Jamal said quietly, as the spider began slowly making its way down his skinny arm.

Jeff held on to the boy's arm to steady him, and no doubt keep him from swatting the poor thing should he begin to panic. The spider seemed attracted to the blinking light, as the oversized timepiece slipped farther down the scrawny forearm.

A clammy chill rose up my spine. An elusive, nagging thought weaved itself into the shadows of my mind. What it was, I wasn't sure, except that it was a clue. A clue to JR's innocence. Something I was missing. But it didn't make any sense.

"Snake?" Jeff snapped his fingers in front of my face.

I blinked back to attention as Jeff draped a ten-foot boa constrictor round my neck. I had to put my suspicions on hold until our Science Museum appearance was finished. I needed to pay attention. Ten feet of raw, powerful muscle was insinuating itself around me, capable of constricting around my neck and squeezing the life out of me. No need to show the children that kind of graphic detail.

So it wasn't until after the children had filed out and we were outside stacking the crates into the Zoomobile that I had the time to sort out my thoughts.

"Let's get these animals back to the zoo," Jeff said, shutting the door to the van. "Then we're going to pay your old boyfriend a long overdue visit."

I put my hand on Jeff's arm. "We've got something we have to do first."

"Snake, we agreed last night that this was the best way—"

"I know, I know, but there's something else. At least I think there is."

"What?"

"I'm not sure, but you need to do one thing for me. I think there's still some crucial evidence in the crocodile exhibit."

"The police went over that pretty thoroughly, luv."

I thought of the Komodo and the toy he had swallowed. "Not thoroughly enough. You may have to do a little doo-doo diving."

One corner of his mouth turned up in distaste. "I am, am I? And where will you be when I'm up to my elbows in croc shit?"

"I'll be paying Shari Jensen a long overdue social call."

Chapter 28

Shari Jensen was packing.

"I'm going back to Mexico."

And with haste, judging by the flurry of action. I followed her into the bedroom, stepping over clothes she had tossed carelessly to the floor. I had raced over after unloading the animals from the Zoomobile, in hopes of catching Shari at home. Good thing I got there when I did. An hour later and I would have been too late.

The entire first floor of her townhouse looked like it had been ransacked. Not a great housekeeper at the best of times, she had slacked off even more after JR was arrested. The sickly sour smell of week-old garbage assaulted my nose from the kitchen, where I had glimpsed dishes piled high in the sink, begging to be washed. A pillow and crumpled blanket on the couch suggested she was sleeping there instead of her bed.

"What's in Mexico?"

She snatched up a sequined sweater from the floor and flung it in the suitcase open on the bed. "Safety."

"From what?"

A shoe thumped into her luggage with unnecessary force. "I guess it wasn't important enough for you to listen to me the first time." She turned her back on me and rummaged through a dresser drawer. "Don't matter."

My shoulders sagged. Okay, this was going to be like pulling teeth from an ant, if an ant had teeth. I didn't have the time or the inclination to play a thousand questions with her again. I needed my own answers. Answers that might free JR.

"What's going on, Shari? And please, let's skip the histrionics, and get to the meat of it."

She tossed a waterfall of hair behind her shoulder. The dirty-blond curls bounced with defiance. "It's all over the news. Sooner or later he's going to find out. And I'd rather not be here when he puts two and two together."

Her foot tapped against the gold carpet as she shot me a derisive look, as if somehow I was part of the problem.

"Who's going to find out what?" I finally asked when no explanation was forthcoming.

"Cradus."

Cradus? Oh yeah. Cradus Moseley. The abusive husband. The one JR said had hands like anvils.

I sank down on the edge of the bed. "He hasn't seen you in what, five years? Don't you think he'd give up by now?"

"They never give up. I stayed at one of them battered women shelters once. I saw them women. I heard their stories. Just like mine. Them boys never give up. Not till you're dead."

"When was the last time you saw your husband?"

She looked at me sharply. "Johnny Ray told you all that."

"As much as he knows." I leaned toward her. "Which didn't sound like much. Either that or he's protecting you. I want to hear the story from you. I want to hear about the night Alexander Beatty was murdered."

Smoldering silence was all that came back.

"Shari, you want help? You want my understanding? Then talk. That's the night this all started. Your husband attacked you that night, didn't he?"

"Attacked? That's a good word for it. More like bait and tackle. He came home all juiced up. I could see he'd already been in a fight with someone. Blood was on his shirt; his knuckles were scraped and bleeding." She shuddered at the memory and I didn't rush her. "Blood was oozin' out these big ol' scratches across his face and arm. I kinda wondered if it was some woman who got him."

My heart jumped a beat as the fog lifted. I was willing to bet those scratches weren't from a woman. "What kind of scratches? Like from an animal?"

"Yeah, coulda been."

"You're not sure, though."

"They weren't from no knife, I can tell you that. His sleeve and shirt was ripped in little tatters."

A picture flashed in my mind of Alexander Beatty being found in the panther cage, beaten and left for dead. It didn't take a leap of imagination to realize whose fists had pulverized him. Shari's brutish husband must have had a little run-in with the panther while he was trying to move Beatty into the cage.

I looked hopefully into Shari's face. "Cradus didn't tell you how he got those scratches?"

"No, just said he took care of some shithead troublemaker."

"But no names."

"Cradus liked to fight. Made him feel good that he could whup most men. Usually when he won he barely had a mark on him. That night he was marked up and angry. I knew something was wrong."

"How's that?"

"If he'd won, he wouldn't have been home so early. When I asked him what had happened, he jumped to his feet and knocked me down. 'You shut up!' he said."

Shari slumped against the bedroom wall, her shoulders sagging, as the memory returned. Fright and misery colored her voice a moment later. "Cradus hit me a couple more times, accusing me of cheating on him. He said he should teach that lover-boy a lesson, too, while he was at it. He meant Johnny

Ray," she clarified a moment later in a voice barely above a whisper.

" 'Lover-boy'?" I looked at her askance.

"Don't go putting any meaning into that, Snake. I wasn't foolin' around on Cradus. I wouldn't have dared. He was ready to spit fire if he as much as saw me having a good time talking to another man. Cradus didn't like Johnny Ray because he was nice to me and made me laugh."

"So he threatened to kill JR."

She nodded, regarding me warily. "He was always making threats of one kind or another."

"What happened after he hit you?"

She remained silent.

"Shari, please, this could be important."

"If'n it's so important the police can ask me."

"Fine." I stood up, annoyed. "Things aren't looking all that good for JR, y'know. The police still think he did it."

"Don't try to con me, honey. Johnny Ray's got it made now. I know about the alibi Miss Goody Two-shoes give him. I knew they was together that night her husband died."

"You knew? How?"

Shari hesitated, as if she had already said too much. Finally, with an air of superiority, she blurted out, "I saw them."

She gave a smile of satisfaction at my look of surprise.

"Johnny Ray thought he got away from me," she snorted. "Almost did. I went to the croc exhibit with some dinner for him and he wasn't there. I kept lookin' and just happened to see him and Melanie behind some buildings. I was too far away to hear 'em but I could tell they were being sweet to each other."

She made "sweet" sound like some kind of perversion.

"They were just catching up on old times, Shari. He was telling Melanie how he was framed, how you and he ran off together. He wasn't cheating on you."

She didn't seem to hear. Or if she did, she didn't care.

"After all I've done for him." She was muttering now, resuming her packing, clothes flying out the drawer, some on the bed, some on the floor. The little tally sheet in her head didn't have a column for the love and support other people had given her. "I protected him. If I hadn't warned him, he'd be dead by now. Cradus would've killed Johnny Ray sure enough."

"So you went to the park to warn him about Cradus?"

She ignored me, viciously stuffing more clothes into a second suitcase, mumbling to herself, dramatically suffering the injustice of her situation.

"Shari?"

"Okay!" She wheeled round at last, eyes ablaze. "I'll tell you. Cradus started talking about going to the wildlife park to finish off Johnny Ray. I got scared. More scared than I'd been in a long time. Cradus would do it. There was no doubt. He was drunk and angry enough to go 'n kill Johnny Ray without a second thought. I panicked. He started swearing and lurched into the kitchen for a beer. When he reached into the fridge for a can I hit him over the head with a skillet. He dropped like a sack of potatoes."

She smiled and squared her shoulders as if gaining some small satisfaction from the memory of what she had done. "I raced to the phone to call Johnny Ray but he didn't answer. He was probably still at the park, probably didn't know what Cradus had done to poor Al. I—I had to go there'n tell him to watch out. So I grabbed the keys to the car and drove." Her sorrowful eyes glistened while her voice filled with despair. "When I got to the park Johnny Ray had found Beatty. I knew he'd get blamed and I knew Cradus wouldn't let up till he got him. He had messed me up pretty good. Johnny Ray could see what he had done. He knew I was serious. With the U.S. Fish and Wildlife people talking to him about illegal animal sales from his business, and with Beatty dead, he just lost all hope of clearing himself. That's when he decided to run away. I went along 'cause he knew I'd never be able to go back to Cradus, not after what I'd done . . ."

Shari had risked a beating—or worse—by warning JR, such was her devotion to him. Yet that devotion had evolved into something clingy and unhealthy. One had to wonder how far she would go to protect JR. Could it include murder? If she thought his safety and, by association, her safety, was in jeopardy, would she have had it in her to remove the threat—permanently?

"You worked at JR's wildlife park, didn't you?" I tossed out the statement like a grenade, waiting for it to burst.

Shari turned away, hauling out a canvas bag from the bedroom closet, into which she proceeded to dump more clothes. "What of it?" she huffed.

"And you knew about the animals being illegally sold?"

She looked over her shoulder and eyed me with suspicion. "Not until after the Feds came. I knew they were accusing him of some illegal stuff like that."

"And you knew nothing before? Had no suspicions of your husband's comings and goings? Never wondered why he took so much interest in the park?"

Her eyes flashed with anger. "What're you accusing me of?"

Off the bed, I closed in toward her, ignoring her display of indignation. I'd reached my limit and wasn't going away without answers. "I think you know more than you're admitting, Shari."

"I don't know what you're talking about." She tried to dodge past me, but I blocked the way with my arm across the doorway.

"A guy like that. He likes to brag, doesn't he? A big score, thousands of dollars for pinching a couple animals."

"I knew nothin'. He didn't talk about his work. And if'n I asked him he'd only yell back. Or hit."

"You guessed, though. You're not stupid, Shari. You must have wondered why he was hanging around the wildlife park when he didn't work there. Or did you think he was keeping an eye on you? How else would he have known about you and JR? You're not dumb enough to tell him you were attracted to JR, were you?"

This time she shoved me aside and ducked into the bathroom. I positioned myself in the doorframe, watching as she picked noisily through her considerable collection of makeup strewn across the vanity, huffing out a breath every once in a while.

And then something else clicked into place while I was watching her. Shari had tripped herself up this time. At last I had some proof of what I suspected. And I said it aloud. "Cradus killed Al Beatty."

She looked up, surprised, then confused. "I don't know—"

"Oh, yes you do. You just said you called to warn JR because he probably didn't know what Cradus had done to poor Al. But you did. You knew who killed Alexander Beatty and you said nothing. You could have cleared JR, and instead you convinced him to run away with you."

"I didn't know. I swear I didn't. Not until that day. Not until I found JR with Al's body and saw how he'd been beaten. I'd seen him do that to men before." Tears welled up in her eyes, though I doubted their authenticity. Unless they were tears for her, that is.

"Why didn't you go to the police?"

"What for? So they could let the bastard go? Cradus got picked up for minor charges a couple times a year. None of 'em ever stuck. Last time he was so mad he almost killed me when he got out. And if'n I had turned him in and he found out about it, he woulda made me pay for it." Her voice shook with emotion. "All I wanted was to get as far away from him as I could."

She lowered her head, a pouty lower lip protruding. For a moment she looked like she was going to say something, but instead, she looked away as one well-manicured finger traced an outline in the porcelain sink.

"So you forced JR into exile. To save your neck, you ruined a man's life. You convinced him to run. How does that feel, Shari?"

The words stung her. She sank down to her knees on the bathroom tile and buried her face in her hands. "I tried to make him happy. I tried to make him forget her—"

"Stop it!" I grabbed her by the shoulders and gave her a hard shake, which prompted a look of shock. "Stop feeling sorry for yourself! This isn't about you. Why did Cradus kill Beatty?"

"I . . . don't know," she half whispered, pulling away from me. I just dug my fingers deeper into her arms.

"Shari! If you really want to help yourself and JR, talk to me!"

For half a dozen seconds her eyes smoldered silently. With a sharp intake of breath she appeared to size me up, as though deciding whether to cooperate or to shut me out. In the end the fight went out of her. "I made a mess of it, Snake. I didn't mean to," she said, her voice anguished.

"You knew, though," I coaxed. "You knew your husband was up to no good."

She nodded back. "Cradus liked to brag. He liked to talk about how smart he was and how he'd hooked up with an outfit that was gonna make him some good money. All he had to do was take a couple of trips. Truck some merchandise out of the state. He'd be gone a week or more. And every time he came back, he had a big wad of cash. Nobody pays in cash anymore, not for doin' anything legal. So I knew something was up. But I wasn't going to press. If I did, I'd just get a hand up the side of the head."

"Was he working with Beatty?"

"Might have been. He started asking me all kinds of questions about the animals and the people I worked with. He might have hooked up with Al somehow, got him to help with the paperwork."

"Do you think they had a falling out?"

She swallowed. "It didn't take much to rile that man. It's possible."

Her small hand gestured with a sense of finality.

An errant thought began to percolate in my mind. Was it possible that Anthony Wright could have been involved with Cradus, Beatty and their tawdry business? Melanie's evidence showed a definite connection. Or had Wright been just another player slated to die at Cradus's hands? Is that why he had packed up and whisked Melanie away in such a hurry that night? Was he running scared? Or did he need an alibi? Had he sent Cradus looking for Beatty that night? Had Wright been the mastermind?

"What are you doing?" Shari's face went pale as I whipped out my cell phone.

"I'm calling the police. You're going to tell them everything you just told me."

Chapter 29

It took more persuasion on my part to get Shari Jensen to accompany me to see Detective Sorenson. She broke down in tears twice during the drive, and I thought I had lost her when I made a quick stop at the zoo. By the time we pulled into the Apple Valley government center's parking lot she was a bundle of raw nerves, making me swear she was doing the right thing.

"That was some story," Ole Sorenson said after Shari stomped out of his office, puffy-eyed and annoyed.

"You don't believe her?"

"Shari is a loose cannon," he commented with a shake of his head. "She doesn't have a great track record for truth in this investigation, as I remember from that first visit to your home right after the murder. Am I supposed to believe her?" He shrugged, unimpressed.

"So that's it? You're not going to do a thing? Geez, it's pretty clear her husband attacked and probably killed Alexander Beatty."

"You have proof?"

"The claw marks on his face and arms, Bubba. Those weren't made by an alley cat—or a person, from what Shari said. The panther probably attacked him when he dragged Beatty's body into her enclosure."

I was about to say more, but he held up his hand. "Don't get all pissy at me, Lavender. I'll call out to Dade County, Florida, in the morning. It's after eight there now. See what they say. At the very least, I'm sure they'll want to question her husband. Have a seat, please."

I had been standing since I came into his office, hands on hips, irritated at his casual dismissal of what I saw as very damning evidence. He indicated the chair across from his desk, whose surface had been tidied up since my last visit, although it appeared most of the paper mess had been piled into his "In" basket.

With one last gulp of coffee, he set his mug down on his much-abused blotter and looked at me with the same idiotic smirk he had used in high school, the kind he'd sprout whenever he thought he was playing it cagey. He puffed out his chest as if to illustrate he held all the cards and was being magnanimous in showing me his hand.

"Look, your accusation is plausible, I'll give you that. So it's worth checking out. Maybe this Cradus Moseley did kill Beatty . . ."

My hopes rose.

"Or maybe he was in on it with O'Malley," Ole added.

I shut my eyes in exasperation.

"Actually, I find something else more interesting." Ole sat forward in his chair and steepled his fingers on the desktop in front of him. "Shari said Melanie Wright worked with O'Malley back in Florida. Did you know that? She even said they were pretty chummy—close, if you know what I mean."

He raised an inquisitive eyebrow and waited. The jig was up. Was the truth written all over my face? He somehow knew I had been keeping information from him. "What else haven't you been telling me, Lavender?"

"About what?" I could play dumb, too. Trying not to look guilty was a little harder, but it was possible he still didn't have all the facts and didn't know everything I had been keeping from him.

His smile vanished. "About Wright. His wife. O'Malley. This guy your friend Shari is married to. What's the connection? You're Melanie Wright's friend. How much do you know about what happened in Florida?"

"All I had was hearsay and innuendo," I said in an even voice. "I didn't want to say anything until I had all the facts."

"And maybe you didn't tell me because you were afraid them facts would damn your friend?"

"Melanie and JR were not lovers, Ole. There was no plot to kill her husband."

His mouth soured as he shot me a critical look. "Says who?"

I didn't say anything, just gave him a cold stare. He wasn't going to make me turn on my friends and I wasn't going to let him punch holes in the last of my illusions.

"Okay, it's a free country. Everybody gets an opinion. But so do I, kiddo." He jabbed his chest with his thumb. "And mine happens to count more than yours. And you'll excuse me if I'm not a believer."

Or not as gullible is what he really meant. It was obvious by the self-serving smirk that had reappeared on his face. I wanted to chuck an ashtray at him. Only he didn't have one on his desk. I might have looked around for something else to lob at him, but I needed his cooperation and didn't dare antagonize the smug bastard.

"Neither is Shari," he added.

"God, Ole, if you don't believe her when she tells you about the kind of thug her husband was—and you see how terrified of him she is—then why should you turn around and believe her story about an affair between Melanie and JR? You seem awfully selective about what you want to accept as the truth. Is that so you can wrap this whole thing up nice and neatly?"

"It is nice and neat, Lavender, though not for the reasons you think. Why else would O'Malley, a wanted man, risk everything to come to Minnesota? Because Melanie Wright was here, that's why. He knew that. He wanted to see her again. To pick up the relationship where they had left off."

"He came here to clear his name."

"Really? Couldn't he have just as easily gone back to Florida to do that?"

Okay, Bubba, you got me on that one.

Rather than answer him, I decided to deflect the question. For the last five minutes Ole had seemed to be needling me, as if he could make me blurt out some juicy detail in anger. Well I could play that game, too.

"What do you make of Shari's involvement in this murder?" I said, changing the subject.

Ole smiled back. "Ah, Shari Jensen, killer of Anthony Wright. Yes, that possibility had crossed my mind. I remembered how we had to pry her off O'Malley the night we arrested him at your place. She'd do anything to protect him."

"Yes, she would," I answered unequivocally.

Ole angled his head toward me, his lips pressed into a thin line. "Now that scares me a little, you agreeing so quickly." A callused hand rubbed the side of his jaw. "Yeah, she's a tempting target to dump the blame on. Not too credible, though."

"How's that?"

"Like I said earlier, she's too much of a loose cannon. Too wound up. Not the sort I see capable of planning something as crafty as a murder."

"Don't bet the farm on that," I scoffed. "Shari manipulated JR into running away with her. In Florida, she telephoned Anthony Wright to tell him his wife was having an affair with JR—an outright lie. If nothing else, it put Wright on the alert about Melanie, maybe even put a wedge between her and JR. With that little fib she gets rid of her competition with JR, and makes it so he can't go to Melanie when he's in trouble. Who can he turn to? Who's in the same danger as he? Who needs to get away as much as he? Guess who?" I snorted. "Sounds pretty cagey to me, Bubba. She's made JR the center of her life. Would she hesitate to act if she felt her way of life threatened? I don't think so."

"Let me get this straight. You're suggesting she killed Wright because he knew JR was a wanted man and threatened to turn him over to the law? But if Shari's so afraid of Melanie Wright stealing her boyfriend from her, then getting rid of her rival's husband would seem to have done away with the one obstacle keeping them apart. Not too savvy a move."

"I didn't say Shari was logical."

"Lavender, Lavender . . ." Ole shook his head with bemusement. He sat up, sporting that stupid, dumb-ass I've-got-you-now grin as he hitched his sleeves up his forearms. "I can't tell when you're serious or just pulling my leg. Either way, it's entertaining. Anyway, Shari couldn't have killed Anthony Wright."

"Why's that?"

"She's too short."

"Too short?"

"Wright was struggling with his attacker on the footbridge, remember. Then he got pushed through the temporary barrier into the water. He had bruises on his throat where he was throttled by his murderer. Wright was a big man and Shari is a petite little thing. She'd have to have been on a step stool to get her hands at his throat. Even then she'd never get those tiny hands around his neck. And I can't see her pushing him hard enough to send him reeling backwards. Unless, that is, she got help from that kangaroo of yours." Ole winked at me.

There were some things you just can't keep quiet, my encounter with Boomer being one of them. I only hoped my face wasn't turning red. Once again, I opted not to deal with the question head-on. Instead, I decided to divert his attention elsewhere.

"I thought you might want this." From my pocket I produced the plastic bag I had stopped at the zoo to pick up and set it on the desk before him.

Curious, Ole opened the bag and pulled out the contents with a pencil. A nicked but still running analog watch with a twisted and mangled gold metallic band lay before him.

"A watch. Big deal."

"Jeff found it in a pile of crocodile dung. We think old Sebastian might have eaten it."

Ole drew back as if the watch were contaminated. "And what the hell am I supposed to do with this?"

"It's evidence, Ole. You're looking at Anthony Wright's watch."

He was unimpressed.

I nudged the watch closer to him. "Take a closer look, Detective. It's a Longine, not the sort of thing you pick up at the neighborhood Wal-Mart. In fact it's a Longine Grande Classique. These puppies have a retail list price of over eight hundred dollars."

He smirked ruefully. "Since when did you become an expert on expensive watches?"

"I dated a guy who liked jewelry," was all I volunteered. No need to elaborate. "Your average guy doesn't wear a timepiece worth three or four car payments. That's Wright's watch, Ole. Melanie will confirm it and in the *Zoofari* tapes you'll see Wright wearing a gold-banded watch." I gestured toward the artifact before him. "Remember, Sebastian bit off Wright's left hand. His watch came off with it."

"Wait a minute." He reached into his desk drawer and pulled out the plastic bag that still held Anthony Wright's personal effects. He jabbed at the Timex inside. "Who does this watch belong to then?"

"The murderer."

Silence.

Then he started up. "But anybody could've lost a watch in the exhibit—"

"Ole," I cut him off, "nobody reported losing a watch. None of our staff can afford a pricey timepiece like that. And the exhibit only just opened the night of the Beastly Ball. Wright was in the water before all those well-to-do patrons got there."

"Okay, okay, you've convinced me! But that doesn't mean this other watch belongs to his killer. Yeah, our guys found the watch in the croc pool near the body. But that doesn't prove it belongs to the murderer."

"No, it doesn't. But there's one way to find out."

More silence. This time with suspicion.

Off his dubious look, I explained, "We're having a wrap party for *Zoofari* tomorrow night. With your help, we might be able to catch a killer."

"I see."

I doubted that. Did I tell him the rest of it? Did I tell him about the invoices? Melanie had asked me not to, that it would look bad for JR. And what about the zoo? If Ole found out about Wright's alleged illegal dealings, could I trust him to keep his mouth shut?

No, he didn't see. Not yet.

Chapter 30

We invited everyone to what was to be the final episode of *Zoofari*. Whether for the season or forever, we didn't know, which lent the moment a certain bittersweetness. Despite the uncertainty of our situation, we had decided to make the event celebratory, gracefully bowing out on a positive note.

Word of *Zoofari*'s cancellation had hit the rumor mill and opinions were highly in our favor. How could a show that popular, a show that gave the zoo so much positive publicity, get cancelled? Such was the buzz. The final shoot was in the evening. Some of the staff had stayed around to watch and to share in the free food and drinks that our acting director, Butler Thomas, had cheerfully donated to thank the entire staff for their hard work over the difficult days since Anthony Wright's death.

The lights were low on the Walkabout Trail. Those animals that hadn't gone into holding for the evening were settling down for the night. Animals that had little chance of causing damage, escaping or hurting themselves during the night, or that were just too much trouble to catch, were allowed to stay on exhibit. A pair of cockatiels cuddled together on a tree branch above a tortoise that had found an added degree of comfort on a heated rock. Even Boomer was safely tucked in evening quarters with his girls. Except for the soft murmur of human voices, the trail was quiet.

Staff and *Zoofari* crew were subdued, knowing this could be our last shoot. Our *Zoofari* regulars, Billie, Shaggy and Gary were all on hand. It wasn't much of a wrap party, as they go: just a few pick-up shots of Jeff with the platypus and close-ups of a few of the more unique Australian animals the zoo had collected. But the one shot everyone anticipated would come when Jeff fed the crocodiles in their enclosure.

Jeff and I had met with the *Zoofari* troop earlier in private to explain the zoo's position on the show, and how we hoped to keep it going on our own. Rather than being angry or upset over our cancellation, they were supportive of our ambitions. Billie immediately volunteered to use her contacts to help us get some much-needed financial backing. But nothing was certain yet. We still needed to talk to the powers-that-be at the zoo, and until a new director was in place, no major decisions would be made.

Gary was the only member of our group who seemed visibly upset. The others were disappointed, even dumbfounded, but only Gary silently glowered, as if some great social injustice had been committed against him. Only much later, when he got me alone at the buffet table, did he vent his anger. He railed at the state legislature for not passing the bonding bills and at Butler Thomas for not seeing the value in our program. He vowed to post a scathing editorial on his website and launch a web-based write-in campaign on our behalf, until I put on the brakes.

"No, you don't, Gary," I snapped. "You've written quite enough."

"We could get great publicity for you! Thomas would look like a chump and would have to change his mind."

"Negative publicity—particularly coming from someone on our crew—is not going to look good. Keep out of it."

"But it could really turn things around—"

"Gary." I leveled my harshest look at our headstrong intern.

Gary's dreadlocks rained around as he drooped his head. His

cheeks burned a little as he looked pathetic and contrite, but I wasn't through.

"Do you ever stop to think through anything you do, Gary? Who knows how many people saw your website and your wild accusations against Anthony Wright? You have no idea what kind of damage you may already have caused the zoo."

"What I wrote was true. I had every right—"

I squashed his spark of defiance. "What? To ruin what so many people have worked so hard to protect? The zoo could lose its AZA accreditation if those rumors were spread. Not to mention driving away our funding, donations and sponsors." I waved my hand at the array of exhibits that comprised Australia House. "This is only a small part of what we work for, Gary. What about the programs the zoo supports? The wildlife refuge in Malaysia? The golden tamarin reintroduction in Brazil?"

He blinked back at me, deflated.

Just then Jeff loped noisily over to interrupt my dissertation. His broad, big-hearted smile bulldozed away the tension as he came up to join us. Standing behind me, he began to massage away the stress with his muscular hands, working my neck and shoulders.

"Ready for the big event?" he said. "It's past their feeding time, so I'm sure Sebastian and Babe are ready for some hearty tucker!" A small group of people gathered at the crocodile exhibit, waiting for the final shot. Zoo staffers and invited guests pressed against the wall and fencing of the upper level of the exhibit, while Billie and Shaggy, his camera hoisted on his shoulder, ready to film, stood on the footbridge. Moments later, Jeff burst out of the holding area inside the exhibit, holding a stainless-steel bucket. A wireless microphone hung round his neck. He waved to the crowd and spoke to them briefly, as a couple of other keepers emerged just outside the fence. He then turned to the camera, waited for a signal from Billie, and addressed the lens as he spoke.

For the benefit of the camera, Jeff told his audience that in order to give the crocodiles some physical activity, plus to keep up their interest, the animals were fed to coincide with their hunting instincts. With a raw eight-pound chicken, Jeff cautiously approached Sebastian, who was floating near the edge of the water, his eyes fixed on the intruder. Jeff dangled the raw meat scant feet away from the reptile, who immediately launched himself up at frightening speed, his jaws snapping at the prize as Jeff jumped back, withdrawing it. Half on the grass now, the large crocodile watched the human cautiously as Jeff stepped closer . . . closer . . . dangling the meal ever closer.

Several gasps escaped the small crowd as Sebastian surged several feet in the air toward Jeff, who only just barely got away as he let go of the chicken, this time in order to let the reptile make the kill.

Sebastian chomped once or twice on the raw meat before letting it drop out of his mouth. Disinterested, he slithered back into the water.

"What's the matter, boy," Jeff asked with concern. "Aren't you hungry?"

Looking bewildered, Jeff went to the fence and let himself out, conferring with the other keepers. A buzz started in the crowd. Clearly something was wrong. After a minute, Jeff walked up the footbridge, said a word to Billie and Shaggy, then continued up to the main path where the onlookers were. His face was somber.

"I'm sorry, everybody, but we're going to have to cancel. It looks like we have a sick crocodile. I've never seen Sebastian refuse a meal like that. He has been a little off his feed these last few days."

"What're you gonna do, Jeff?" shouted a voice from the spectators lined up on the upper level.

"Put these blighters in their holding pen and have them checked out tomorrow. In the meantime we'll drain the pond tonight so we can check the filtering systems."

Some of the rubberneckers had already started to go, while a few others lingered, engaged in private conversations or, perhaps, waiting to watch our crew remove the crocodiles to their holding pens behind the exhibit.

Shaggy, at the behest of Billie Bradshaw, kept filming, zooming in on Jeff's taciturn face as he gave a few of the keepers instructions and took charge of the situation. Gary Olson, holding a clipboard and stopwatch, edged closer to Jeff, waiting for instructions.

Before I had a chance to think of what I was going to do next, two familiar shapes maneuvered through the dispersing visitors. Suzanne Terak was escorting Senator Ted McNealey in my direction. We had lured the senator here with the promise of some free on-camera time to illustrate his backing of the zoo and its conservation projects. The green vote mattered and free publicity was never to be scoffed at, something a shrewd politician like McNealey could understand.

Still, I felt awkward as he neared, remembering my harsh words to him in Butler's office a week earlier. Inwardly I braced for the impending storm.

"Hello, Mrs. Jones," Ted McNealey greeted with surprising cordiality, taking the wind out of my sails. He offered a faint smile then peered over the fence railing and down into the water at the activity. "What's wrong with the little beasties?"

By this time Jeff had made it to the top of the footbridge. "Not quite sure, mate. We'll have to put them both off exhibit so we can do a complete medical on 'em."

"That includes sifting through their excrement for other clues to their health," I offered, watching McNealey's mouth turn down at the prospect. Suzanne took it in stride with a pleasant smile, as though I'd just proposed working our hands through cookie dough.

"Will that be tonight?" one of the keepers asked, having overheard Jeff. "Do you need us to stick around?"

"Let's move the animals now, drain the water and call it a night," Jeff said back loudly. "Senator, Suzanne, if you'll excuse me." And he hurried down the footbridge, his boots reverberating against the wooden planks, calling out to Gary to open the holding pen door, with Shaggy and Billie close behind filming every move. I heard Billie's voice in my head saying this might not have been what was originally planned, but it still made good theater.

Suzanne excused herself to speak with Butler Thomas, who stood near the Aussie Trail, watching the proceedings with displeasure.

Left alone with McNealey, I decided it was a golden opportunity to mend some fences. "I think I owe you an apology, Senator."

"Why is that, Mrs. Jones?"

"Because of the other day in Butler's office. I shouldn't have—"

"Please don't give it a second thought." He waved me off. "I admit you gave it to me pretty good, but I get hammered like that nearly once a month at the legislature." He managed a thin, amused smile. "I think we both said things we didn't mean. Let's just forget it. I have."

Spoken like a true politician. I almost liked him for that—almost.

Recalling his much-publicized promise to get to the bottom of Anthony Wright's death, I quietly asked, "Has your investigation into Wright's murder turned up anything, Senator?"

McNealey shook his head. "Nothing more than the police have found, if that much. The committee really didn't have much to go on."

Then I said something stupid. "I understand they've turned their attention toward Carruth Construction."

You dope! I couldn't believe my own ears. Why did I say that?

Although his expression hardened and the cords in his neck tightened, McNealey was restrained. Like an errant spark, the senator's eyes flared then faded. Slowly and with quiet deliberation, Ted McNealey smoothed back a silvery lock of hair. "Yes, Carruth is under investigation." He leaned his elbows on the metal fence rail and shifted his eyes toward me. "Turns out my esteemed mother-in-law has been cutting corners, using second-rate materials and, sometimes, not following codes. Actually, it was her oldest daughter who was mainly responsible."

"You knew nothing about this?"

"No. I work in business development, not Carruth's day-to-day operations. Still, it makes me look culpable."

Or worse. But this time I held my tongue.

McNealey said, "Elaine—that's Mrs. Carruth—says she didn't know what Lenore was doing. She trusted the wrong person." The senator shrugged philosophically. "We both know what that's like, don't we?" He passed me a knowing smile and rejoined Butler Thomas and Suzanne.

He was right. The people I thought I could trust had let me down, shown me a side of themselves I never would have suspected. JR. Melanie. Gary. McNealey had made the mistake of trusting Anthony Wright, but in the long run it was really his family who had let him down.

As I watched Jeff and the other keepers maneuver the crocodiles out of their enclosure, I looked around at the dispersing crowd. Most I knew by sight or name; some were invited guests. Mitch, our birdman, waved as he strolled by, a red-tailed hawk perched on his arm. He'd given a lively and entertaining Hawk Talk on predator birds earlier for our cameras. I'd rarely seen Mitch better—animated, patient, and, as Jeff would say, chock-a-block full of bird lore.

I waved back to Mitch, who had somehow managed to rope Shari Jensen into helping him with the hawk. She tagged along with a half-hearted smile. She could never be completely happy for longer than twenty minutes without finding fault with something. I wasn't in the mood to deal with her but didn't want her to feel snubbed, so I nodded enthusiastically back.

And so thinned out the Australia Trail. Eventually the cameras were turned off, the overhead exhibit lights were dimmed and Jeff returned to collect me. He glanced over his shoulder down into the large hole in the ground where there used to be a small pond, now drained.

"Let's call it a night," he said, gesturing Billie, Shaggy, and Gary up the footbridge as he made his way along the Walkabout Trail. "We're all dead tired and need a good night's sleep before we start checking out our reptilian friends."

Under the dim lights of the parking lot we stood by our cars and bade each other good night. It was well after ten p.m. Jeff thanked the crew for their hard work. "It's been a long day for all of us. Let's go home and get some rest. It'll be an even longer day tomorrow."

We drove off in little groups.

Except Jeff and I didn't go home. Instead, we cruised the neighborhood for twenty minutes before driving around to the back of the zoo and letting ourselves in at a service gate. Just in case, we kept the truck out of view and walked the half mile to the nearest staff entrance.

Detective Sorenson and several officers were already waiting for us.

"I hope your hunch pays off, Lavender," he said as we let them into the closed grounds. "I feel like a moron."

Even in the dim light I could see his unease at being off the main paths, tucked away along a wooded service trail where there were no nearby streetlights and the darkness seemed extra dense.

One of the officers turned anxiously at the distant sound of a tiger. “It’s safe to be here, isn’t it?”

“Yes,” I said. “All the animals are secure. At least all the dangerous ones.”

“That’s right,” Jeff piped back in a loud stage whisper. “Nothing’s bound to get you except your standard-size Minnesota coyote. There may be one or two wandering around the outer perimeter.”

Several pairs of apprehensive eyes trained on Jeff, whom I elbowed in the ribs. “Stop that. He’s joking,” I assured the officers, who did not seem entirely convinced.

It had all been planned. The entire feeding incident with Sebastian had been staged in order to spread the idea that we had to temporarily shut down the crocodile exhibit, when, in fact, Sebastian was quite healthy. He wasn’t off his feed. The reason he hadn’t showed much enthusiasm for the raw chicken Jeff had dangled before him was that the crocs had been generously fed thirty minutes earlier in private. Also, the chicken everyone had seen Jeff feed the big croc had been soaked in vinegar to make it taste bad. For the benefit of the crowd, though, Jeff had fretted and explained Sebastian and Babe would have to be put into their holding pens and the pool drained until morning.

The person who had lost the wristwatch during the struggle with Anthony Wright didn’t know the timepiece was in police custody. If he or she was brazen enough, they knew this would be their only chance to retrieve the evidence without being attacked by crocodiles.

If the watch was going to be reclaimed, it had to be tonight.

Or so we hoped.

We led the band of police through the zoo service tunnels, avoiding the open areas and main paths, to prevent being seen. At this time of night, the doors would be locked and required the use of our passkeys. Zoo security had been tipped off as to our plans in order to make things work smoothly.

I led our team underground to a service tunnel that came up under the Australia House. Once in the building, we quietly made our way to the back of Crocodile Island. Sebastian and Babe lay quietly in the small, fenced-in pool behind their exhibit. Nighttime was their element, and they shifted warily as we walked softly by.

We entered the back door of the exhibit, built of cinderblock walls, a staging area and storehouse facility some ten-by-twenty feet in size. It contained ropes, poles, buckets and other equipment used to maintain the exhibit. Slowly Jeff pulled open the door leading into the outer exhibit area. It, like the outer wall, was painted brown and green to blend in with the surrounding landscaping.

Squatting just outside the doorway in the dim light, Jeff indicated the top of the bridge. "The best view of the billabong is from the upper level. The trees and shrubs at the top of the trail should give you ample cover. Detective Sorenson, if you put a couple of your men up there, they should be able to see when someone approaches."

Ole nodded. "Baker, Vang, you take positions up there. And keep your radios turned low. We don't want to warn our visitor."

"We'll stay here," Jeff said, closing the door after the two officers had gone. "We can look out the window slats."

Our eyes had adjusted to the dimness by now, and the rising moon's light filtered through the glass roof and trees. Jeff retrieved several plastic buckets and offered one to Ole. He had upended one for himself and sat. The other he offered to me.

"Make yourself comfortable, Detective, it could be a long night."

Three hours later we still sat, the half-moon rising high in the sky and slowly moving out of sight. It was the only thing to watch. Hardly a tree branch swayed in the artificial habitat, except when the ventilation fans kicked in every once in a while, and a nearly silent rush of air swirled among the treetops. This was the hard part, the waiting.

As the night wore on, I reminded myself that if I wanted to return to the scene of the crime to retrieve evidence, I'd want to do it in the dead of night. And it didn't come much deader than this. By two o'clock I was starting to fade, the long tendrils of night insinuating into my consciousness and dragging me slowly, lightly into the dark realm of sleep.

I jerked my head up and stifled a yawn.

Ole smiled back encouragingly. "Stakeouts are about the most boring thing there is. And the tough hours are coming up. One of my first cases as detective involved a five-day stakeout of a suspect's house. It's not too bad if you're inside, like we are. But we were in a van parked half a block away. Let me tell you how much fun that is! Bathroom breaks were really a prob—"

Ole's radio squawked.

We all sat up and stared at it.

"Yeah," Ole said into the radio.

"This is Baker," came back a hushed voice. "Someone's coming."

"I copy. Wait for the signal."

With grim anticipation, Ole Sorenson's eyes held my gaze before turning to the window slats. "It's show time."

Raising my radio to my lips, I pressed the transmit button. "Marco, are you there?"

I waited for the security officer to reply, hoping to God he hadn't fallen into a deep sleep as I almost had. But Marco was one of the zoo's best security people; he had helped Jeff and me several times with crowd control when we were filming. He was excited for this little chance at adventure. I trusted him.

Two seconds later his mellow voice returned, "I'm here, Snake."

"Get ready. We have an unauthorized visitor."

Marco was near the main entrance to the Walkabout Trail, ready to spring into action.

A minute passed, then another. Still nothing. Jeff moved. "At the top of trail," he breathed.

I still couldn't see it. But I didn't have the jungle sense possessed by this man, who had lived for weeks at a time in remote areas tracking and relocating animals in his native land.

Then, at last, I saw movement. A dark silhouette worked its way slowly down the footbridge, faint steps barely resonating against the wooden planks. The figure approached with caution, producing a small flashlight and shining it into the exhibit. The yellow wedge of light swept furtively across the scrub grass, poking into corners near shrubs and trees before settling on the empty cement basin.

That's right, no crocodiles here. It's safe. You can come down.

As the figure stepped off the bridge to the bottom of the exhibit and I had a good look in decent light, my heart sank with recognition. I wasn't happy to see my suspicions confirmed.

It was quiet agony to watch as our prey opened the gate, entered the exhibit and then walked to the empty pond, shining the light in a jerky pattern, bending low and searching, eventually letting out a barely audible cry of success. A hand reached down and pulled up something from the damp, scummy pool bottom.

Ole turned to me. "Now, Lavender."

Into my radio I said, "Marco. Lights!"

Like a cataclysmic sunrise, the entire exhibit came ablaze to full daylight in an instant, temporarily blinding us and making our startled marauder stand out like a black bear in a field of snow.

Chapter 31

Like a terrified deer cornered by wolves, Gary Olson edged back in the empty pool basin, looking wildly around for a way out as we stepped into view. Panic rippled through his body like an electric shock. Then he bolted. His oversized sneakers slipped in the mud and green algae before they made purchase. He scrambled up the wet, grassy bank and made a mad dash toward the footbridge. Jeff quickly stepped over to block the way, glaring back at Gary with a look of mixed anger and disappointment. Wheeling about at a new sound, Gary saw the two police officers hurrying down the wooden bridge.

With a swing of his dreadlocks, our young intern jerked away, stumbled and crashed backward into the empty billabong. Surging to his feet, he spun around, hunting for a way out as we converged upon him.

But there was no escape. It was over.

In that moment of cruel acceptance, his shoulders slumped and his face slackened with the realization he was caught. A slimy hand wiped across the torn fabric of his T-shirt, already stained with grass, while globs of mud smeared his knees and well-worn Nikes.

"Mr. Olson," ventured Detective Sorenson, pushing his baseball cap back on his head to reveal patchy wisps of red hair. "Whatever are you doing here at this time of night?"

Gary was silent, swallowing hard. You could almost hear the wheels turning behind his puckered forehead.

"We're waiting."

"I-I can explain," Gary said.

"I hope you can." Jeff folded his arms across his chest, angling his broad shoulders at the young man, disapproval radiating out of every pore. I knew how deeply disillusioned Jeff was with Gary now. Jeff had genuinely liked the young student, had enjoyed his enthusiasm for nature and conservation, and with the open heart with which he undertook all things, had gone out of his way to help our intern succeed both on the job and in life. For me Gary was an okay kid, at times more of an annoyance than a help, but I could appreciate the raw material Jeff saw in him. I could only imagine the sense of betrayal behind Jeff's look of accusation.

Vang and Baker, Ole's two uniformed officers, made their way to the bridge that crossed over the crocodile exhibit. Vang, who looked no older than Gary, read him his rights. Baker, an older officer, kept a tight grip on his arm.

But it was under Jeff's uncompromising gaze that I watched Gary wilt in shame, though he tried to cover it up. "I was looking for something."

"We know that," Ole chortled humorlessly. "Isn't this an odd time to be looking for anything here?"

"I didn't want to bother anyone."

"Don't give me that! You came here 'cause you didn't want to get caught looking for whatever it is you found."

"No, no! You got it wrong. I didn't do anything!" Gary's voice was thin and brittle.

Jeff was having none of this. "What were you looking for, Gary?"

I interrupted him. "Gary, you're going to need a lawyer. Don't say anything you're going to regret."

Gary tried to wrestle away from the police officer who held him fast, ignoring my advice. He pressed his lips together into a crooked line, trying to summon up what to say next. Stealthily he moved his hand behind his back, hiding from view what he had plucked from the cement.

"How about it, Gary?" Ole taunted. "What's in your hand? A Timex watch?"

The other shook his head.

"Are you sure? I think you just picked up something from the mud. But it's the wrong one, kid. It's not yours."

Confusion came back.

I stepped forward. "Could this be what you were looking for?" I held up the Timex that had been in police custody as part of Wright's personal effects. "This is what you came for, isn't it?"

Gary's eyes seared into the timepiece I dangled before him, then examined the muddied watch clutched in his hand. He threw it to the ground in disgust.

"Wrong watch," I explained. "We planted that one for you."

"That's crazy!" He flexed his shoulders nervously, stroking his left forearm. "Snake, why are you doing this?"

"You came back looking for the watch you lost the night you killed Anthony Wright."

"No!"

"Don't deny it. You've been twisting and turning this metal band since I've known you. And since you've lost it you've been rubbing your wrist and arm—like you just did. And to top it off, we just caught you red-handed sneaking in here in search of a watch at the bottom of the crocodile pool."

"But—"

"Gary," I insisted, "you pulled a watch out of the mud. Give it up!"

He started to protest, but cut himself off. With a violent shake of his head, he stomped a foot angrily to the ground. "Okay! It's my damn watch! Are you happy? But it's not what you think! I lost it after Wright was killed. It came off when I jumped in the croc pool to help Jeff when he was trying to subdue Sebastian. I slipped on the bank over there. Remember how Billie kept yelling at me to get out of the water?"

Jeff glared at him. "If that's true, why didn't you say something about the watch earlier?"

"I-I didn't realize I'd lost it until I got home. I was embarrassed to say anything."

"Enough, Gary." My voice was harsh. "Stop lying. We know better. We have videos of you that night. Earlier in the evening, you're clearly wearing a watch—this watch. At the moment you jumped into the pool to supposedly help Jeff, there was no watch on your wrist. This Timex was found at the bottom of the croc pool when the police found Wright's severed hand. They assumed it was his watch. But it was yours." I shoved the timepiece toward his face. "For this to get in the water at that moment, you must have been in the area. You must have been struggling with Wright on the footbridge. During that struggle he grabbed your wrist and the cheap, battered links of the band gave way."

Gary Olson tried to choke out a reply but couldn't, his face a contortion of stifled rage. The watch. It had finally come down to the battered old Timex. Something had been bothering me for several days. Nothing I could put my finger on, just something I knew wasn't quite right. It wasn't until later at the Science Museum that the little boy with the oversized Spider-Man wristwatch jarred my memory.

That evening another look at the videos showed the truth. In slow motion it was so obvious. There was Gary jumping into the water trying to help Jeff and JR subdue the crocodiles so the trigger-happy security people wouldn't shoot them. Gary clumsily falling into the water—or so it seemed. Looking at it more closely, it was obvious he had intentionally submerged himself. So clear now. Submerged himself to look for the watch he knew would incriminate him if it were found.

Jeff walked over until he was nearly shoulder to shoulder with the younger man. "That's why you came to see me the next night, not to get background information for an article, but to get yourself out of a jam." I couldn't miss the hurt in Jeff's voice. The young conservationist he thought he was mentoring had turned out to have a hidden agenda. "You asked me what crocodiles eat and what comes out the other end because you suspected Sebastian had eaten your bloody watch."

Gary shook his head violently. "I didn't murder Wright. I swear! Sebastian did it. You saw how he attacks anything that comes into his territory."

"I'll take that as a confession of sorts," Ole put in opportunistically, unimpressed with Gary's denial. "The crocs aren't to blame. You strangled Wright—or tried to. There were bruises on his throat. You struggled with him. Sometime during the struggle you shoved him, he shoved you—I dunno—but you must have pushed him hard enough that he stumbled back through them makeshift boards along the fence. You couldn't have done it if he wasn't already half dead from being choked. Then to be dumped into the water like that, submerged, the water suddenly rushing up his nose. It can cause severe shock. Poor bastard passed out and he was gone." He snapped his fingers. "And that's on the record. It wasn't Sebastian, son."

"What?" the other gulped. "That can't be!" Gary swung round to me, a streak of mud across the lens of his glasses. "It was an accident! I didn't mean to hurt him. It wasn't supposed to go off like that. But I'm not sorry. The bastard murdered my stepda—Mom's boyfriend." He spat the last words out with disgust.

"Murder, Gary?" I started quietly, not wanting to tip my hand. This was it. The validation I had been expecting. "Your mother told me your stepfather was killed by a panther."

"Yeah, that's what Wright wanted it to look like. He arranged the killing, which was what he was good at. Not the physical stuff. For that he could hire goons. The son of a bitch had Al beaten to death. And like that wasn't enough, they threw him in with that big cat so he could get ripped to shreds!"

And there it was!

I drew in a slow, calming breath, while in my mind I heard the loud clank of a metallic door unlocking, opening into a room of dark secrets.

"Alexander Beatty was your stepfather," I said with total confidence. I smiled at a surprised Jeff.

A puzzled Ole swung round. "Beatty is this kid's stepdad?"

It was the photograph in Gary's living room that had slowly crystallized through my brain fog. A photo of a young Gary Olson with his mother, Betsy, standing next to a good-looking man in a zoo uniform struggling with a young alligator that was clamped onto his watchband. The same Timex watch Gary had worn. The same battered metal band, nicked and dented from gator teeth. The same Timex now clutched in my fist. The photographer was none other than Melanie Wright. Beatty had asked her to take a picture of his family. Such a charming family photo it was, too.

Slumped on the grass, Gary sat dejected. A faint cry of frustration escaped him. When he raised his head, his eyes looked out from behind rimless spectacles with anguish. "I didn't mean to kill Wright, honest. I just wanted to talk to him, wanted him to know how he had ruined my life."

I squatted down beside him and said softly, "Tell us."

The young man glared defiantly at me. "You don't know what it was like. Everything was great before."

I offered a sympathetic smile in return.

The venom faded from his voice, replaced by something more

thoughtful and melancholy. "After Dad died—my real dad—my mother struggled for years to keep us afloat. She worked herself ragged. Then she met Al Beatty and he started taking care of her, of us. She was able to take it easy after she hooked up with him. He could support us. Bought us a nice house. And more. After he was killed it all changed. I didn't exist anymore. All Mom talked about was Al this and Al that, and what a horrible thing had happened to her Al. She turned him into some kind of saint. Well, he wasn't a saint."

"Because he was involved in the illegal animal trade?"

"He was a dealer and a blackmailer. Stole endangered animals and sold them on the black market. That's how he could afford all those nice things he got for us."

My heart was racing. If Beatty was dealing in exotic animals and Gary had proof of his link to Anthony Wright, the scandal for the Minnesota Valley Zoo would be disastrous. "Keep going," I urged him, my voice barely a whisper. "What makes you think Al Beatty was connected with Anthony Wright?"

"Wright was definitely part of it. Maybe the ringleader."

"Why are you so sure?"

Gary smiled grimly. "I saw him." He darted his eyes from me, to Ole, then back to me. "Mom was working and Al decided to take me to the county fair, a spur-of-the-moment thing. While we were at the shooting gallery this guy comes over and starts talking, slips Al a brown paper bag and leaves. It was weird. Didn't last more than a minute and wasn't all that friendly. That's why I remember it. Looking back now, I can see it was a prearranged meeting, a payoff. Later, at home, I saw Al sneak a wad of cash out of the bag. The only other time I'd seen money like that was in the movies or on TV. No doubt in my mind it was a payoff."

"You're sure it was Wright, though," I cautioned.

"Positive. It was, like, three months later, there was this

picture of some charity event in the newspaper. And there he was. Third guy from the left. The same guy I'd seen with Al. Anthony Wright."

So money had changed hands and Gary had seen it.

"Money for what?" Ole scratched his head, not connecting the dots. "What payoff?"

"For keeping quiet. That's what I think." Gary raised his head and the overhead lights glared from his glasses, making it impossible to see his eyes.

Ole held up his hand. "Whoa, whoa! Not so fast. I can see Lavender knows what you're talking about. Wind it up a bit. Let's start from the beginning. What's this have to do with what happened here last week?"

"That's what I'm trying to tell you!" Gary complained, then grew pensive. I could see him physically struggle to tame the rage that had erupted earlier and having mixed success. When he spoke again, it was in a more subdued tone. "Finding out Al was involved in some illegal stuff took me by surprise. I used to make up stories. Pretend he was some kind of undercover agent. He wasn't a total bad guy—not to us, anyway.

"It was tough when he died, especially the way it happened, being murdered. Beaten up like that and almost mauled by a wild animal. But there was the money, too. He left us nothing. He was in debt up to his eyeballs. He and Mom weren't married and there was no insurance. Nothing. Just a lot of bills. Everything was sold, including the house. In the end the only thing we had left of him was some personal stuff—papers and clothes. It was like starting over again. Mom decided to move to Minnesota because she had a sister here."

Gary took in a heavy breath, scrunching his nose up in a vain attempt to adjust his glasses. "The older I got, the angrier I got. It wasn't right. We could have had a good life if he hadn't been murdered." Regret and annoyance tinged his voice. "Yeah, Al was into some dirty things, but he didn't deserve that.

"It was my last year in high school, I started thinking about it, doing some research. Who were these guys Al was involved with? Who killed him? At first the police blamed Al's boss, James O'Malley. They said he was involved in the illegal animal sales, too, and had run away. He'd disappeared."

Jeff angled his head. "Did you know JR was O'Malley?"

"No!" Gary snorted. "No idea. It was only after he was arrested that I learned who he was. It floored me."

Easy to believe. We were all startled by the news of JR's alleged nefarious past.

"So you did research," Ole prompted, trying to get back on topic.

"Yeah, I searched the Net, publications, contacted organizations and agencies. In an old shoebox I found some of Al's papers. Most of it was nothing, but there were some scraps with notes, an address book with some names and numbers. Some invoices, too, invoices copied from the wildlife park Al worked at, JR's park."

Ole leaned closer. "What kind of invoices?"

"Invoices that linked Anthony Wright to all sorts of dirty trades, mostly to that zoo of his in Texas. All sorts of exotic animals probably never made it there. It wasn't easy tracking it down. The invoices aren't directly incriminating. Digging into the names of shipping companies, tracking down the owners of obscure, illicit companies, that took months with lots of dead ends. In the end I found enough connections between the outfit Al was selling animals to and Anthony Wright. That, along with the payoff I remember seeing, was enough for me."

I wondered if these invoices were similar to the ones Melanie had shown me yesterday. If so, there could be more boxes of them sitting at the zoo. "The payoff," I inserted, with a new thought. "Could it have been blackmail? You think Wright got tired of paying and killed Beatty to silence him?"

"Kind of obvious, isn't it?" Gary fired back in that tone young people reserve for adults they believe are slow on the uptake. I opted not to volunteer the information about Cradus Moseley I had learned from my conversation with Shari.

Jeff listened to all this with a thoughtful scowl. "Gary, is that why you wanted a job at the Minnesota Valley Zoo, to get closer to Anthony Wright?"

The young man nodded, strands of dreadlocks rubbing against his shoulder. "I spent a year building up a file on Wright. My goal was to make him accountable. When I discovered he was in Minnesota and running the zoo, I couldn't believe my luck. I tried to get a job at the zoo so I could get near him."

"And I hired you as our intern." Jeff shook his head with self-criticism. The poor lug.

"Sorry, Jeff," Gary said with noticeable chagrin. "Working with you was a dream come true. You're one of the good guys, a great role model. I didn't want to upset you." His eyes were downcast.

"Go on with your story," Ole prodded.

Gary wet his lips. "After I had enough information to confront Wright, I went to interview him. I started with the usual questions. Then I asked him about his time in Florida. He grew pretty uncomfortable and started getting evasive. I pressed him about his connections to Wild Acres, one of the companies connected with the black market." Gary's voice turned acidic. "He really didn't like that."

I'm sure he didn't. Here was Anthony Wright, running from his old life, trying to start anew, at least according to Melanie, and he's confronted with the specter of his past by some kid not even out of college. "And he tossed you out of his office," I said.

Gary grunted. "I ran for my life. He went ballistic and

ordered me out. Said he'd get the cops on me if I harassed him with any more lies."

Ole shook his head in disbelief. "Why didn't you go to the police if you had hard evidence?"

"The police had done nothing in Florida. Neither had the U.S. Fish and Wildlife Service. They assumed everything stopped with O'Malley—JR. Why should it be any different now?"

Annoyed, Ole came back. "Because tipsters tell them where to look. The Feds have the power of the courts behind them. They act so boneheads like you don't get hurt or muck things up."

"I sent Butler Thomas a note about it. He didn't do anything," Gary pointed out. "And you saw my website. What good did that do me?"

"A note—" Ole stopped at the look on my face. "You knew about this note?"

I ignored him and urged Gary to continue.

Gary's eyes shifted between us, wary, but he went on. "Well, I had to do something. Nobody else would. I needed to confront Wright. Not that it did me much good. I blew it. Wright was a pretty intimidating guy and I got nervous. I vowed next time I wouldn't let him get to me, that I'd say my piece. I got my chance the night of the Beastly Ball.

"Just before dinner, I spied him heading for the Walkabout Trail with Senator McNealey. That was my chance. I knew it. I slipped away and followed them, hiding behind the curves and bends of the trail so they wouldn't see me, keeping behind kiosks and plantings.

"Then they reached Crocodile Island."

Gary looked at us momentarily. "They were pretty deep into it."

"Where were they standing?" Ole asked.

"At the top of the exhibit, looking down. I hid up the trail and watched through the branches of a low tree. Wright was upset, waving his hands, really chewing McNealey's ass about plumbing and construction mistakes. Wright was really worked up. I knew when he saw me again he was going to go ape shit. I should have left then. But I had to stick to my plan. I wouldn't let Wright get to me. Maybe I couldn't bring the guy to justice, but I could make him squirm. He wasn't going to get off scot-free." Gary was nodding to himself as he spoke, almost unaware of the audience hanging on his every word.

"So I waited. Eventually McNealey, burning mad, stormed off and Wright was by himself. I would have barged in and embarrassed him right in front of McNealey if I had had to. But this was better. I had him alone. I watched him pace. He went to the footbridge and walked halfway down it, standing at the railing and looking at the crocodiles.

"That was my chance." Gary swallowed, a glint of fire in his eye. "I hurried from my hiding place and walked down the footbridge after him."

CHAPTER 32

Gary drew up his knees and wrapped his arms around them, quietly gathering his strength. I glanced at the others. All eyes were locked on him. Gary cleared his throat and continued with new purpose.

"When Wright saw me coming, he swore, said something about calling security if I didn't leave. But I wasn't letting him off this time. 'Alexander Beatty' was all I needed to say. I hurled it at him like an insult. Man, was he shocked. Exactly what I'd wanted.

"I told him Beatty was my stepfather, that I used to live in Florida and knew all about his dirty dealings, that Al had told us. That was a lie, but Wright didn't know from shit. You should have seen the look on his face when I said that. I wish I'd had a camera. But that did something to him, knowing—or thinking, anyway—I was Al Beatty's stepson."

Ole said, "How's that?"

"Guilt. I think he felt guilty about Al. He sure seemed eager to explain. I confronted him about paying off Al and having him killed. Wright threw up his hands and denied he'd had him killed. A horrible accident, he called it, a horrible misunderstanding. He told me some redneck goon had attacked Beatty after flipping out."

And I knew who that redneck goon was. Without my having to say a word, Gary Olson had just corroborated Shari's account of the night Beatty was killed. Exciting as that was, it was painful to hear Gary confirm the worst about the former director of our zoo.

I looked our intern squarely in the eye. "Wright didn't deny responsibility in Al Beatty's death? So he did know about it?"

"Yeah. He said killing Al was never what he wanted. He tried to tell me how they had him under their thumb, how he had wanted to get out. And then Al decided he was a good mark for a blackmail scheme. Wright and his wife had left town the day Al was killed. In fact, he said he was worried something bad was going to happen. He couldn't reach Al, but he did try to warn JR."

"Warn him how?"

"Phoned him. But he was upset and said he wasn't sure if he came across the way he wanted."

Just as Melanie had told me the day before. "Then what, Gary? You're hashing it out with Wright on the bridge. What next?"

Gary became more agitated. "Wright's yelling this stuff at me and I'm yelling back. I didn't care how he felt. He was responsible. Al was killed and my mother was devastated. As far as I'm concerned, I blamed Wright. It was his fault." Gary's gaze intensified. "That set him off. He pushed me out of the way and started walking. Now I'm pissed. I tried to block his way. He swore and shoved me. I shoved back, calling him a thug, an eco-terrorist, a murderer. He tried to knock me down. He pushed me so hard against the boards you put there, that I heard them crack. I thought I was going in with the crocs. I grabbed him."

"You tried to choke him," Ole prompted.

Gary shrugged. "Guess my hands got around his throat. He grabbed me back. Like you said . . ." Gary looked up at me. ". . . by the wrist. We're shoving each other. This time we both stumbled forward and crashed into the boards. Only this time they didn't hold. And Wright dropped into the water like a sack of cement. I barely hung on to the fence rail, dangling out over the water."

Gary closed his eyes and dropped his chin. "His body didn't move." He swallowed. "My first instinct was to pull him out. But . . . but then I heard the second splash. Sebastian was moving in like a torpedo. Before I could think of what to do, he attacked Wright and I saw blood. I jumped back, panicking. It was too late to help Wright. And I was afraid someone would walk by and see me on the bridge. I got scared and ran off."

Gary gazed blankly into the distance, lost in his own thoughts. Ole nodded to the uniformed officers. There was no protest from our young intern as each officer hooked an arm and guided him down the Walkabout Trail. He hung his head and shuffled along between them, disappearing into the tunnel.

"That Cradus character was picked up in Florida and he sang like a canary," Ole Sorenson said a couple of days later. We had invited him to our farmhouse after work. He sat ensconced in a beat-up but comfortable armchair, his necktie loosened, enjoying a cup of freshly brewed coffee. "Seems he drove trucks for a company called International Wildlife Supply. Picked up a few animals at that park your friend O'Malley operated. Said he had no idea they were illegal."

"I bet."

"He changed his tune when they asked him about Beatty's murder. Seems Anthony Wright wanted to put the fear of God into the man. Scare Beatty a bit. But the good old boy got too much into it. Went overboard and killed him. Then he got scared and thought he'd cover it up. Dragged the body into the panther cage to make it look like an accident. The cat had other ideas. That's how Cradus got them scratches Shari described. Mmm, good coffee." Ole sat back in the chair and crossed his legs.

"Will they convict him?" I asked, thinking of Shari's fear of her husband and what he would do if he got his hands on her again.

"I reckon they will. With Gary's confession and what you got from Shari, Cradus just about peed in his pants when the Feds showed up to collar him. He talked in hopes of getting a lighter sentence. Even so, he'll do some serious jail time, believe me. Not only is there the manslaughter charge, but also the illegal selling of endangered animals and bigamy."

"Bigamy?" Jeff and I exchanged looks from either side of the sofa.

Ole grinned with perverse pleasure, happy to surprise me with some tidbit of the case. "Yep, seems the lughead went and married some other poor gal without the benefit of divorcing Shari. Oh yeah, his 'other' wife is royally pissed, too."

Poor Shari. I felt sorry for her. Although there were limits to my compassion, she often seemed the agent of her own misery, and it was difficult for me to ignore the way she had manipulated JR.

"She's in Florida, now, you know," Ole announced as an afterthought. "Shari, I mean. The Feds wanted her to give a formal deposition and with her husband in the slammer, she was more than willing to." Ole scratched a reddish eyebrow and chuckled to himself. He looked down at his shoe. A cat's paw reached out from beneath his chair and ferociously swatted at his shoelace. Kow the cat was after big prey. Her furry head popped out with a crazed look.

It was a light moment I let linger before asking my next question. I brought up my legs to sit cross-legged on the sofa cushion. "How's Gary doing?"

Ole dipped his head. "Fair. Finding himself in jail is a shock. He's kinda gone quiet. Passive. Some depression. A good lawyer might get him off, if he can convince a jury about what happened with Wright. Self-defense," he added when Jeff looked at him without understanding. "Gary could say he was being attacked by Wright. His mother, though. Whew!" Ole shook his head. "There's a handful."

Betsy Olson was the one I felt sorriest for. After the death of her husband she lost another love, Al Beatty, to a brutal attack. Now her son was arrested for murder. I couldn't imagine what she was going through. And how much had she known about the illegal activities of her boyfriend? But love can be blind. Mother love, especially, so Betsy might be more than ready to blame her son's woes on Anthony Wright.

A moment of silent reflection descended on us. Ole sipped his coffee and closed his eyes, savoring the moment. "This is the most relaxed I've been in four weeks. Got three other cases I'm working on." He uncrossed his legs but had difficulty in the maneuver when fourteen pounds of cat glommed on to his other foot. Reaching down gingerly, Ole disengaged Kow from his shoelaces. "Things okay at the zoo?" he said to us when he was done.

Jeff explained, "There's been one big, collective sigh of relief."

"That we nabbed the killer?"

"No, mate, that he wasn't a zoo staffer."

"Ah."

"That's for sure," I put in. "It's bad enough Gary was an intern with *Zoofari,* so that means the killer was connected with the zoo, which isn't a good thing. However, I think that'll be overshadowed by the news about Anthony Wright's past dealings. That's a whole lot juicier story."

"I see." Ole furrowed his brow. "That's big trouble for the zoo, I take it."

"Yeah, although I'm not so sure."

"Why's that?"

"Anthony Wright is dead. It's not like he's still in his job and will be an embarrassment to the zoo until he resigns. No, he's gone. And Melanie was adamant about not covering up the truth. I've heard she's prepared to back that up. She'll go public if she has to. She'll say her husband had cleaned up his act, that everything he did in Minnesota was on the up and up."

My admiration for her only grew, knowing she was still coping with new discoveries about her late husband. I'm sure it was hard for her to reconcile the man she knew with the profile the police had presented her. A man who had been involved with the sale of endangered animals since his college days. Melanie had blamed Anthony's father, Jungle Jack, for his lack of conscience. It was how he had been raised. As the father goes, so often goes the son. And yet people can change. When I had spoken to her after Gary's arrest, she had seized upon her husband's last comments on the footbridge about what had happened in Florida—how Wright told Gary he had tried to warn JR that trouble was coming. That fitted with her recollection of the telephone call from the Miami airport the night they left Florida. Wright might have sent Cradus Moseley to intimidate Alexander Beatty, to convince him to take the money he had been given and be content with it, but once Beatty had been killed, he realized things had gone too far. Whether it was true or not, I could see how Melanie wanted to believe that gesture, small as it was, had been the beginning of redemption for her husband.

"Melanie is willing to go the distance on this," I went on, touched by the level of her commitment, as well as her inner strength. "The zoo is blameless. Whatever her husband's misdeeds, they were in the past. Scandals don't intimidate her. She isn't going to let the zoo suffer because of them."

"Oh?" Ole shifted with interest. "How's she gonna do that?"

It was Jeff who answered. "Ka-ching!" He rubbed his fingers

together with an impish smile. "Money, Detective. Mel's got pots of it."

Wisps of thinning red hair wavered as Ole nodded with understanding. "I suppose it also helps that you officially have a new zoo director."

"Yes," I agreed. Butler Thomas was the right man for the job. Politically, it was the perfect move. He was an insider who knew how to get things done, the highly photogenic and charming new face of the Minnesota Valley Zoo. What better way to demonstrate to the press, and a legislature hell bent on chopping zoo funding for any reason, that a new regime was in charge?

The three of us sat quietly for a moment when a rumble came from the kitchen. The clicking of toenails on linoleum and the crashing of furniture. In ran Bagger, our golden retriever. He scampered in and jumped onto the overstuffed easy chair with Ole.

"Bagger. Down!" Jeff ordered.

With the shame only a dog can show, Bagger huddled by the floor, thumping his tail, then sniffed Ole's trouser legs, his nose rising up into the detective's crotch.

"Whoa!" Ole was half out of the chair.

"Bagger," I called, barely able to stifle a laugh. "Here." I snapped my fingers and he trotted over obediently. Then his ears pricked up. I heard a car door close outside, and Bagger bounded into the kitchen. A moment later the kitchen doorbell rang.

Bagger barked.

I got up to answer the door. Ole reached out and touched my arm. "That's a surprise for you, Lavender," he said with affection.

Intrigued, I entered the kitchen and unceremoniously opened the old wooden door. I squealed with delight. Standing in the doorway was a uniformed policeman and James O'Malley—JR.

"Get in here!" I said with a one-hundred-watt grin.

JR stepped in tentatively, looking as relaxed as I had ever seen him. He waved to Jeff and Ole. I threw my arms around him. "You're free?"

"For the moment," he said after I took a step back. "Detective Sorenson arranged it."

On his feet, Ole motioned to the officer. "That'll be all, Vang. Thanks for bringing him." After I closed the door, Ole explained, "Mr. O'Malley is a free man. The charges against him here have been dropped. There's still the matter of the Florida warrant. But those charges are being reconsidered."

Bagger gamboled in front of JR, who was on his knees, stroking the happy dog's head. "Hi, boy! Good to see you again. Yeah." JR faced us. "My attorney's trying to work out a deal for my testimony. Melanie knows a high-buck lawyer who works on this kind of stuff. I'll have to go back to Florida for a while, may even have to do a few months of jail time, but the murder charge is going to be dropped there, too."

Jeff beamed at him. "Fabulous news, mate! Woo-hoo!" He pumped the air with a fist.

JR rose to his feet, looking like a new man. He walked over to Jeff with a timid expression. "Jeff." JR swallowed. "You trusted me before. If you say you can never trust me again, I'll understand. But thanks for everything." He held out a grateful hand. Jeff pumped it vigorously.

"When are you leaving for Florida?"

"Not until next week."

"Then you can work a few shifts at the zoo."

JR was taken aback. "Y-you still want me to work for you?"

"If you want the job, mate. There's plenty to do. And the missus and I would love a little more time off."

JR broke into a wide smile. When he saw me again, he approached, looking like the JR of old. "They tell me I have you to thank for clearing my name. Snake . . ." He started to choke up then laughed, turning to Jeff. "Excuse me, boss, but I'm going to kiss your wife."

Jeff waved him on.

This time the embrace from JR lingered and after a light kiss on the mouth, he whispered in my ear, "Thanks for not giving up on me."

My eyes moistened and I felt I could fly. I smiled at Ole. "This was a nice surprise, Bubba. You did good."

"You stuck to your guns, Lavender. You told me O'Malley was innocent. You were right."

The look of approval from him was gratifying. I went to the kitchen feeling on top of the world. I retrieved the coffee pot and brought back a cup for JR.

"Help yourself to a cookie." I indicated the tray on the coffee table before turning to Ole. "Top off your cup, Detective?"

"Yes, thank you . . . Snake."

I stared at him. All through high school, during the year we had dated and beyond, Ole Sorenson had never called me anything other than my given name. It was a matter of principle for him.

And now he was making a gesture.

I laughed. "Nice try, Bubba, but it sounds weird when you call me Snake. You can call me Lavender."

ABOUT THE AUTHORS

An animal lover since she could walk, **Marilyn Victor** is a volunteer at the Minnesota Zoo and fosters small pets for a local animal rescue group. At the moment she shares her home with an overindulged bichon frise, and an ornery cockatiel. She enjoys reading all elements of the mystery genre and is the current president of the Twin Cities chapter of Sisters in Crime.

Michael Allan Mallory works with computers in the Information Technology field, which allows him to support his cats in the lavish lifestyle to which they have grown accustomed. Writing exercises the other part of his brain and allows him to make use of his degree in English Literature. An avid animal lover, he is interested in the welfare of wildlife and the conservation of nature. Michael is a member of Mystery Writers of America, and the American Association of Zoo Keepers.